This and Every Life

Emmy Sanders

Beta Reading by Christie, Jen & Maxie of Smut Readers Society, and Willow

Editing by M.A. Hinkle

Proofreading by Lori Parks and Charity VanHuss

Cover Design by Natasha Snow Designs

A special thank you to Gabs, Isaac Sutherland-Cash, and Milo Knorr for your help with Charlie

ISBN: 9798989542093

Content Warning: This book contains brief mention of religion that does not support same-sex love, a mythos that includes violence and suicide, a hospital visit for a character with a congenital heart defect, and a trans character who is lacking gender affirming care but whose story is overall positive and healing.

For the hearts that dream,
that love,
that know no bounds.

CONTENTS

PART I

Jasper and Abraham

CHAPTER 1

Jasper

It's a Tuesday morning when my life changes irrevocably.

"Jasper."

My mother's clipped tone has me setting down my spoon, abandoning my morning meal in favor of giving her the full attention she's demanding. "Yes, ma'am?"

"You're to visit the stables today. We need a carriage."

The instruction gives me pause. I glance my father's way, but his nose is in his workbook, one hand idly lifting a piece of warm bread to his mouth. The top is slathered in rich blackberry jam, but he chews as if tasting nothing at all.

"Why not send Catherine?" I ask my mother.

Her face pinches, mouth set in a moue of displeasure. "The maid is ill."

My inhale is sharp, but I keep the surprise from showing on my face, knowing my mother would not like it. She's never appreciated my fondness for our housekeeper, despite the fact that she tasked Catherine with the brunt of raising me.

"May I see her before I go?" I ask.

After a long pause in which I'm sure my mother will deny me, she inclines her head. "Fine. We'll need the carriage the week after next. We're to visit my sister in the countryside."

"Yes, ma'am," I mutter, struggling to stay in the present, my worry over Catherine at the forefront of my mind.

"See that you don't dawdle," my father puts in, not even lifting his head to look at me from across the table. Dust floats in the early morning light coming through the window, the motes swirling when he turns a page in his book. "You're to join me at the printer when you're done."

"Yes, sir."

My mother leaves the room with a swish of her skirts, and I hastily finish my hot wheat, the porridge having gone cold.

Once my father closes his workbook and stands, I collect our dishes and bring them to the sink basin. With Catherine ill, I take over the task of cleaning, idly wondering if it was her or my mother who prepared our meal this morning. Most likely Catherine.

Hands dried, I walk down the hall to her room and knock gently.

"Enter."

The curtains are drawn in the small space, the bed Catherine is lying on pressed against one wall, her dresser along the other. She makes to sit up, but I close the door behind me and approach swiftly, setting a hand on her shoulder to stall her.

"Please," I urge. "No need to trouble yourself on my account. I only wished to check on you."

"Sweet boy," Catherine says around a sigh, the wrinkles on her face looking more pronounced than usual. Her gray hair is escaping its bun, and although covered by blankets, it's clear Catherine isn't dressed for company.

"Is it bad?" I ask her, crouching on the floor beside her bed.

She shakes her head, further disrupting her bun. "No, of course not. I'll be on my feet again in no time."

The cough she lets out, leading into a series of painful-sounding hacks, has me doubting the validity of her statement. My mother would not allow her to rest, after all, unless it was serious.

"Can I get you anything?"

Catherine looks as if she's going to once again reassure me she's well enough, but then she asks, softly, "A glass of water?"

I nod and make my way out of the room. My father is leaving for the day as I pass, my mother nowhere in sight. I fill a glass from the carafe and then pause, eyeing the leftover piece of bread on the table. Heart beating fast, I rush over and slather jam on top, knowing I'll incur my mother's wrath if she catches me treating Catherine so.

Meal and water in hand, I hurry back down the hall. Our housekeeper is sitting up in bed when I arrive, her hair neatly tidied and a strained smile on her face. Her eyes dart to the door and then back to me when she sees the jam-covered bread I'm carrying.

"Oh, Jasper," she chides.

"You'll need your strength," I defend, handing it over, along with the water.

"You are too good for this world, my sweet boy."

Despite her words, Catherine doesn't seem upset with me. Her eyes close as she takes a bite of the bread, the jam a luxury she's not often afforded.

"This world needs more good," I point out, settling the blankets around her hips. "Will you be able to manage until I return? Father is having me join him at the printing press today."

"More lessons," she says evenly, an eyebrow raised.

I let out a sigh, the apprenticeship not of my own choosing. But what is?

Catherine pats my hand. "I'll manage fine. Go on, my boy."

Giving the back of Catherine's hand a quick kiss, I nod and take my leave. My own bedchamber is on the opposite end of the house, the room nearly four times the size of Catherine's. I'm already dressed for the day, but I pull on a coat from my wardrobe before setting off to complete my tasks.

The stables are on the outskirts of the town center, between a tavern and a saddler. Luckily, the weather is fair today, affording me a comfortable walk. I pass others on my way, nodding politely, avoiding looking too long at the clusters of women in their colorful dresses. Ribbons adorn the wealthiest of the bunch. Other men and women are dressed more modestly, their attire simple like Catherine's.

The smell of the horses reaches me first, manure a potent scent not easily masked. I relish the baseness of it. The musky undertones that speak of earth and nature. I prefer it over the burnt oil of the printer, the chemicals used for the process not pleasant to my nose.

I pull in a deep breath before rounding the corner of the stables, seeking out the stable master to reserve a carriage on my family's behalf. All I see, however, are the horses.

"Good morrow?" I call gently.

A head pops out from around a wooden partition separating two horse stalls, its owner quickly following. My breath this time is involuntary. A quick snap of my lungs I do my very best to conceal under a hastily pasted-on smile. The man who walks my way is young. Not much older than my twenty years, if I had to guess. And certainly not the elder stable master I was expecting.

The stranger sets his rake to the side as he stops in front of me. "Good morrow. May I help you?"

"You're not Victor," I say, although I'm sure he knows as much.

He smiles at that, and I twine my fingers together in front of myself, suddenly needing a task for my hands. "No. I am not. Abraham Morris."

I stare at the man's outstretched hand for a moment too long before taking his palm in my own. His skin is callused and warm, even a little dirty. Yet I don't mind it one bit.

"Jasper Sinclair," I offer. "Pleasure."

He smiles again, letting my hand go. Abraham's shirt is a simple white, laced in front, although not pristine considering the work he does. His breeches are brown, a complement to his lifestyle. He's not wearing a waistcoat, nor a coat at all, for that matter. He's dressed as commonly as any stable hand I've ever met, and yet my pulse quickens at the sight of him. I forget, for a moment, what I'm even here for.

Abraham's voice cuts through my daze, bringing me squarely back to the business at hand. "Is there something I can help you with?"

"Oh, yes. A carriage."

"Ah." His eyes skip to the large leather book sitting atop a table nearby. "Then you will need Victor. He should return tomorrow or the day after."

I deflate, knowing my mother will not be pleased to hear of the delay. "I understand," I tell him, not begrudging his being unallowed or unable to assist me. "Why is it I've never met you before?"

Abraham seems surprised by the question but not displeased. "I only started working under Victor earlier this year.

I assume our paths have not had the chance to cross before now. It is a large town."

That it is. And our social circumstances, different as they are, would have kept us naturally apart.

I nod idly, my eyes mapping Abraham's strong jaw and full lips.

"Jasper?"

My pulse hastens at Abraham's curious tone. Straightening, I take a step back. "I must go. I... I'll return again. Please let Victor know if you see him?"

Abraham nods, a furrow in his brow that speaks of concern, but I'm already turning away. Whether I can feel the heat of his stare on my back or am only imagining the sensation, I'm unsure, but it stays with me until the stables are out of sight. Only once I reach the center of town where the brick-building printer resides does my pulse slow to normal.

I stop in front of the building, knowing my father is waiting for me inside. Waiting to teach me how to print the newspapers and pamphlets men like Abraham aren't given the chance to read. I have a duty. A life spread out in front of me, waiting for me to live it.

I don't want to. I want none of it.

My feet carry me in the opposite direction before I have the conscious thought to move. My pulse is a steady drum now. Fear. Defiance. Exhilaration.

Abraham has a pile of bridles in his arms when I step back inside the stables. His eyebrows rise, a tentative smile on his face. "Jasper?"

"Yes. Me again. Would you be in trouble if I stayed?"

"Stayed here?"

"Yes."

He sets the bridles down carefully beside a tin of leather oil. "I don't believe so. Is something the matter?"

"No," I say, nearly laughing in delight. "Nothing is the matter at all. I would like to stay. If I could."

Abraham glances downward, his lip pulled between his teeth, his expression turning almost...pleased. My heart patters, although I cannot, for the life of me, say why.

"That would be fine." He sets into motion, grabbing a stool from nearby and placing it in a spot not easily visible from the front of the stables. When he waves me forward, I take a seat, the small act of rebellion like the finest port coursing through my veins.

"Thank you," I tell him softly.

His smile is sincere. I think it would be rather easy to be friends with Abraham Morris.

"What are you doing?" I ask him, watching as he opens the tin of oil.

"Caring for the leather." He deposits some of the oil on a rag, brushing it over the straps of the bridle quickly, his movements efficient and practiced. "This will help keep the material from cracking."

"Which means replacing it less often," I deduce.

"Correct." Abraham sends me another swift smile. "Do you like horses?"

"I do. I haven't much chance to ride unless we visit my aunt in the country. That's where we're going. Why we need the carriage."

"Is it far?"

"A couple days' ride."

He nods, setting aside one bridle and grabbing another. His eyes flit over me as he applies more oil to the rag, a quick up and down I assume is meant to take me in. I have no doubt he's aware of our differences, as inconsequential to me as they are.

"Please do not judge me before you know me," I say, voice quiet.

His motions still, brown eyes meeting my own. "How would I judge you?"

"By my birth," I answer. "I will not judge you for yours. Please give me the same courtesy."

He holds my gaze for the longest moment. "You are unexpected, Jasper Sinclair. But not unwelcome."

I pull in a breath, my chest expanding. "Does that make us friends?"

"It may. But I suppose that depends."

"On what?" I ask, my gaze slipping unintentionally to the pull of Abraham's shirt as he resumes oiling the bridle.

He lets out a soft hum that sounds playful, matching the boyish quality of his grin. "On whether or not you enjoy the creek."

For a moment, I flounder. "Our friendship hinges on whether or not I can swim?"

He barks a laugh from deep within his chest, the sound so arresting I nearly wobble off my stool. "If you cannot get your feet wet, I fear we won't get along."

"You're jesting, aren't you?" I realize.

Abraham's smile is warm, hitting me like a sunbeam. "Perhaps. Would you swim with me this Sunday?"

A million thoughts flit through my head. My obligations. My family, who would not understand nor approve of my association with Abraham. The simple prospect, even, of adventuring in the creek, a place I haven't been since my early childhood when such indulgences were still allowed.

How will I get away for a few hours? Can I manage it?

"Yes," I tell Abraham, knowing I'll find a way. "We'll go to the creek."

He smiles in answer, and I ask him more about the horses. About how he came to work here. About his life.

I don't leave the stables until nearly midday, when I know I can't put it off any longer without facing severe consequences. Walking away is harder than it has any right to be.

My one consolation, as I return to the only life I've ever known, is the promise of a few more stolen hours with Abraham.

Chapter 2

Abraham

It's a challenge to keep my pace steady as I head toward the creek.

My feet want to run. Fly.

Jasper returned to the stables the day before last, as he said he would. But there were no long conversations to be had between us. There was barely even the chance to exchange a smile. Victor had returned to his post, and Jasper had no reason—or excuse—to linger.

I pray he's able to meet me today. If not, well... I suppose I may get another opportunity to hear his voice when he comes to collect the carriage.

The sun shines brightly as I walk along the edge of the woods, the gurgle of water finally reaching my ears. I strain to hear any other accompanying sounds, but all is quiet. Peaceful.

I expect the bend of creek to be empty when I round the tree line, so seeing a shock of light hair has my pace stuttering to nearly a stop. Jasper turns quickly, having caught me from the corner of his eye. His wariness immediately settles. And then he smiles.

Oh, but he's beautiful.

I'm well aware men are not meant to think such things about each other, but I can't help it. I've never set eyes on someone as absolutely lovely as him.

His hair is golden in the sun. His skin pale and near flawless. He's fine-featured and fine-boned. And his eyes...the deepest, most fathomless blue.

If he knew what I thought of him, would he still smile at me so?

"Abraham." The relief is evident in his voice.

"Did you think me someone else?" I ask, continuing my walk to where Jasper is standing, my heart beating heavily beneath my rib cage.

He tugs at the sleeve of his coat. He must be sweltering in it. "For a moment, yes. I'm grateful it is you."

I blow out a small breath, the pressure beneath my ribs too great.

"Have you been waiting long?" I ask, reaching him at last.

"No, not at all. I... I hope you don't mind, but I brought a small loaf of bread to share." He indicates the wrapped bundle on the ground beside him with a nervous flick of his hand.

"Jasper..." I manage, more appreciative than he could possibly know. "That's incredibly kind of you. Thank you."

He smiles shyly, and my heart aches at the sight. "Would you...like some now?"

"Please."

Jasper lowers to the ground, carefully flattening his coattails under him. I seat myself with far less fanfare, and Jasper's eyes skip down my legs, throat bobbing as he takes in my lack of stockings.

"Does it scandalize you? To see me dressed so?"

"No." He says it on a breath, grabbing the cloth-wrapped bread and beginning to unwrap it. "I'm unused to it, is all. My family would not allow for such."

The admission by no means surprises me. Jasper's station demands a certain decorum. From the buckles on his shoes to the fine stitching on his clothing, it's clear to me—and was from the moment I first saw him—that Jasper and I are from different worlds.

Him sitting beside me now is nothing short of a miracle.

"You could remove your stockings here," I offer, watching Jasper's stillness closely. "And your coat. If you'd like."

His chest rises and falls, the bread in his hands temporarily forgotten. His eyes dart to me, and I can see him weighing his options. Deciding on what would be right.

Slowly, he sets the bread down, keeping the cloth beneath the underside of the loaf. With trembling fingers, he removes one shoe and then the other. Ever so carefully, he lifts the hem of his breeches and rolls his stocking down and off his foot. He repeats the process on the other side, leaving his feet as bare as mine. His eyes dart to me once more before he shrugs his heavy coat off his shoulders, placing it on the grass beside him.

He looks pounds lighter, even with his waistcoat in place over his fine linen shirt.

"Feel better?"

His exhale sounds almost like a laugh. "Yes."

With a smile aimed my way, he continues unwrapping the bread, revealing with it a small jar of honey. I nearly groan, only managing to keep the sound within myself by the skin of my teeth. Jasper breaks the bread into two pieces, offering me one before uncapping the honey pot.

We take turns pouring the sweet liquid on our bread and biting off mouthfuls. It's divine. I can't remember the last time I tasted honey.

Jasper chews his bite fully before speaking. "You live close?"

I nod, letting my toes stretch down toward the edge of the creek, the gentle breeze today welcome. "The walk here is short. Is it far for you?"

"Yes, it is. But I'm glad for it." He laughs once, the sound light. "I'm grateful to get away. Is that terrible? It feels terrible to admit."

"No," I say softly. "I understand."

His face falls. "Oh, Abraham. I'm sorry. You must think me horribly ungrateful. I don't mean to sound unappreciative of what I've been afforded in life, I truly don't. It's only..."

Jasper breaks off, looking surprised by my hand on his bare ankle, his skin warm beneath my fingers and palm. I give him a gentle squeeze. "Think nothing of it," I tell him before letting go, loath to do so. "I only meant because of my mother's condition. It's a guilty pleasure, taking a few moments for myself when I know I should be home, caring for her. Do you think that terrible of me?"

Jasper seems to consider this, which I find fascinating. I think I would rather enjoy trying to unravel the way this man's mind works and find myself desperate to succeed in doing so. "What is wrong with her?"

"She's lost the use of her legs," I say, pouring a few drops of honey on my last piece of bread. "She cannot work. Can scarcely get around."

"Abe." Jasper's tone is soft, the sound of that single syllable spoken so casually yet with such familiarity nearly stealing my breath away. "I'm so sorry. She relies on you."

It's not a question, but I answer nonetheless. "Yes, she does. I love her dearly. Please don't mistake me on that. And I don't fault her in any way. But sometimes... I wish for the impossible."

"And what's that?"

I hum lightly, dusting flour off my fingertips. "Freedom, I suppose. Choice."

Jasper gives a slow nod, his hand twitching as if his impulse is to reach for me. I wish he would. "I don't think you terrible, Abraham. I think you human."

A small smile lifts my lips. "So you see now why I couldn't think you terrible, either?"

He lets out a quiet laugh, licking a drop of honey off his thumb before closing the glass pot. "Except that my circumstances are not your own."

"And what are yours?"

He leans back onto the flats of his hands, his lithe body stretched out, his head dropping back as he looks up at the sky. "My father expects me to step into his shoes at the printer. My mother expects me to start courting. And soon. And the only one who ever asks what I want is the one person who can't give it to me."

"Who's that?"

"Our housekeeper." He winces as his gaze settles on me, wariness there.

I shake my head before he can utter another apology for something he has no control over. "You love her."

"I do. So very much. If I could, I would live with Catherine in the country and be content to simply...be."

His melancholic smile is both sad and lovely. It plucks at my heartstrings, making me long to give him that very thing. To be a part of it. Even as the notion is utter insanity.

"Could I join you there?" I jest, regardless of the impossibility. "Me and my mother both."

Jasper turns to me, gaze serious, his cupid lips a bright contrast against his fair skin. "Yes. You would be most welcome, Abraham."

I pull in a breath, facing the water flowing gently past our feet. It sparkles blue in the sunlight, the color muddied over the shallow, stony bed. "Would you like to swim now?" I ask before other words can escape my mouth.

His smile is soft and sweet. "I would."

I stand, and Jasper does the same. His eyes go wide in a way he can't quite conceal when I pull my shirt from beneath the band of my breeches and tug it over my head. His mouth parts, and I take my time, folding the material before setting it on the ground. With Jasper's eyes on me, I walk into the creek.

The water is cool as it runs over my toes, mud seeping upwards with each step I take. Stones press against the soles of my feet, but they're small enough not to hurt. Jasper has yet to move an inch when I stop at the deepest part of the creek, the water flowing over my knees.

"Are you joining me?" I ask.

He swallows, the motion visible in his slender neck. His eyes dart back and forth quickly, likely checking to make sure we're alone, before he reaches for the buttons on his waistcoat. I try not to watch him undress, but it's a hard-fought battle I lose in the end. Jasper removes his waistcoat, revealing the whole of his shirt, more finely tailored than my own. He toys with the material at his waist before tugging it free as I did. I do my best not to think of the single layer of clothing now covering his prick. Jasper is slow to lift his shirt over his head, and I force my eyes away before he can notice the sharpness of my gaze. Even still, the sight of that slim stomach and flat chest is a vision now seared into my mind.

I let myself drop into the water, floating along the surface, the burbling creek moving gently beneath me. In my periphery, I can see Jasper taking a moment to set his clothes flat. He approaches, a small whoosh of air leaving his lungs as he steps into the water.

There's nothing remotely untoward about two men taking a dip together. But the direction of my own private thoughts is forbidden. I know as much. If anyone were to find out...

I don't want to consider it.

The only opinion that truly matters to me is Jasper's. What would he think? Would he hate me? Condemn me for my nature?

"Feel good?" I ask, my head turning lazily to track my companion, water filling my ear.

Jasper smiles, his hair brilliant in the sun, his skin calling to me in a way I'm unsure if I'll ever be able to act on. "Yes. I haven't done this in a very long time."

"You've come to this spot before?"

He gives a quick shake of his head. "Not here, no. Although I prefer this spot over the creek I played in when I was young. It's far more...secluded."

I hum, sitting up as Jasper closes the distance between us. He lowers himself carefully, a stuttered exhalation leaving his lips as the water rushes up to his belly button.

"Whoo."

I laugh at his bark of surprise, and Jasper's smile widens. In a show of supreme playfulness, he splashes water my way. I feign offense, waiting for him to lower his guard before returning the favor. He sputters a laugh, water dripping down his face that he wipes away. Slowly, he flattens onto his front, head above the surface as he lets the shallow water run over his body.

There's a fierce tug in my chest as I watch him. An ache to run my hand along the soft swell of his back. To curl my arm around him and hold him to me, keeping him afloat, keeping him close.

It makes no rational sense to long for this man when I know my cravings can be satiated much closer to home. Safely. And discreetly.

But I've never wanted another as fiercely as I want Jasper. I desire to *know* him. To see a lifetime of his smiles. How wonderfully light would my world be?

It's foolish, utter nonsense, to consider testing his trust. But I can feel it approaching, like a compulsion, a knowledge deep in my core. I won't be able to resist forever.

He's the sweetest forbidden fruit. And I yearn to know his taste on my tongue.

We swim for quite some time. Jasper tells me more about Catherine. About her goodness and how he wishes this life were different for her. For all of us. He tells me about his father and the subtle edge of control that's a constant threat, a sharpened knife at the edge of Jasper's throat he has no choice but to obey. He tells me about his mother. How he knows she loves him, but she isn't kind. Not like she could be.

And I tell him more about my own mother, the only family I have left. How her days are spent at home, alternating between her bed and the chair that overlooks the only window to outside. How I'm trying my best to keep us fed. Keep her alive. He doesn't say it, but I can see the guilt in Jasper's eyes when I share this, and I wish I could clear it away.

We end up on the grassy shore after our swim, baking in the sun. Jasper's hair curls against his forehead, the strands blowing in the breeze as they dry. His breeches sit tight against his form, and more than once, I have to draw my gaze away.

"Have you ever wondered what happens when we die?"

Jasper's question is so unexpected on the heels of his tale about a stray tabby cat he used to sneak scraps to when he was young that it takes me a moment to answer. "The church would have us believe Heaven or Hell."

His head shifts my way, blue eyes seemingly trying to read me. "You don't think so?"

"No," I say, shaking my head slowly. "I do not."

"What do you believe?"

I ease out a breath. "There is so much in this world that is unknown to me. Places I will never see. Concepts I will never understand. But I cannot bring myself to believe there's one governing body who decides the fate of all mortal men on this earth. The will of man is great. And no matter the circumstances under which we are born and die, if I didn't believe us capable of commandeering our own fate, I would have nothing to fight for."

Jasper watches me for the longest time. He doesn't shy away, and I relish every heartbeat in which his eyes hold mine. "I want to believe what you do."

"You can."

"You make me think that's true."

No, I will not be able to resist Jasper Sinclair for long.

Jasper turns his gaze up toward the clouds, letting out a resigned sigh. "I must go. Will we do this again?"

"If you wish it."

"Do you?"

"I do."

Jasper's smile is warm. "Then we will. Next Sunday?"

I nod, and he reaches for his shirt before standing. We dress beside one another, Jasper in his fancy shoes, my toes digging into the dirt.

In a world of my making, I would clasp Jasper behind his neck and offer my lips to his.

In this world, we bid each other goodbye. And I watch as he walks slowly toward his home, dreaming of a time when his footsteps might draw near instead.

CHAPTER 3

Jasper

My mother is determined to thwart my plans, not that she knows it. She keeps me busy for hours, preparing trunks for our trip in less than a week's time. Catherine seems to be the only one who notices my desire to get away.

"What are you up to?" she asks the moment my mother is out of sight.

Catherine's condition has improved steadily over the past many days, much to my relief. Her ailment has eased to the point where she's back at her tasks, although her cough remains.

I debate lying to her for all of a second, not wanting to draw attention to my mission to sneak off. But if anyone would understand my newfound friendship with Abraham, it would be Catherine. She wouldn't judge me for it. That much I know.

"I wish to see a friend," I tell her, checking the doorway for my mother.

"Someone I know?"

I shake my head.

"Is it safe?" Catherine asks.

I nod slowly, even though the question is a complicated one. "We're merely swimming. But he's...a stable hand."

Understanding lights her eyes. Fellowship between men of our classes is not commonplace. Abraham would be more likely to be my servant than my friend, a fact that makes me unduly angry to contemplate. No one should be forced to work so much harder than another for something as simple as living.

My mother walks into the room before Catherine can respond, and we go back to packing up her scarves.

"Perhaps Jasper should fetch some salted pork from town," Catherine says, causing me to look at her sharply. Is she trying to help me escape?

The scrutiny on my mother's face is an obstacle Catherine deftly evades.

"I'm still recovering," she says, an excuse. Under normal circumstances, there would be no reason for me to do the duties of our housekeeper. "The reserve of dried meat is dwindling, ma'am."

"No," my mother says with a quick shake of her head. "We have plenty for our trip."

"I don't disagree," Catherine says carefully. "However, after packing what's needed, there will be scarcely any left upon our return."

My mother's expression is hard. She doesn't like Catherine attempting to run the household, as Catherine very well knows. The simple fact that she's willing to test my mother's patience on my behalf has me finding some confidence within myself. Or perhaps it's recklessness.

"I wouldn't mind," I tell my mother, shifting her regard my way. "I can visit the butcher."

After only a moment's consideration, she shakes her head once more. "No. Catherine will do it when we return."

I try not to let my disappointment show, but I can feel Catherine's sympathetic eye watching me.

I've all but resigned myself to missing my stolen hours with Abraham when there's a soft knock at my door. The hour is late, dark creeping over the sky and my stomach full with stewed beef, carrots, and corn from our meal. I ease off my bed, half-convinced the noise was only the wind. As it turns out, it's Catherine.

"Come," she says quickly.

I stare after her for a heartbeat before following.

Catherine leads me down the darkened hall and into the kitchen. My mother and father are nowhere to be seen, but I have no doubt they're near. Catherine swiftly shoves a loaf of still-warm bread into my hands, a hunk of dried meat, three carrots, and a jar of fine apricot jam.

"Catherine," I whisper, nearly overcome.

"Is it Abraham?" she asks, her hands gripping the outsides of my own. "The Morris boy?"

I can only nod. I'm astounded she guessed as much, but Catherine runs in circles outside of my own. She knows people in this town, inner workings, I never have nor will.

She nudges me decisively. "Then take it. Abigail is a good friend. I hate to see her and her boy suffer, but I haven't dared..."

She doesn't finish her sentence, but I understand. She hasn't dared bring them food herself. If she was found stealing from my family, the consequences would be dire.

But for me?

"Do we have any butter?" I ask.

Catherine's smile is bright, and she turns, fetching a small jar. She adds it onto the pile in my hands. "Go. I'll leave your window unlocked for when you return."

"Thank you," I tell her fervently.

A single candle flickers at the table as I turn and rush down the hall. My bedchamber is dark, but I reach under my mattress, feeling for the spare haversack I used to collect pine cones and sticks in as a child. Finding the strap, I tug it free, carefully loading the food inside. I stop for a moment, glancing at the outline of my wardrobe.

In the end, I leave my coat behind and crawl through the window.

The barest hint of light remains outside, the sky a dusky blue soon to turn black. I thank the moon and stars for their light as I jog swiftly in the direction of Abraham's creek. There's little chance he's still there, but he said he lives close. Perhaps I could find him? Or leave the sack for him to discover another day?

I feel almost giddy as I run, the haversack knocking against my hip with each stride. Hope flourishes inside my chest, even as my more rational mind tries to temper my excitement.

I've run away. For only a few hours, true. But I have never in my life run off to follow my whims.

Yet now, I have Abraham.

My lungs protest as I reach the hill that stands between me and my destination. Sweat beads along my brow, my breaths harsh. I ignore the burn in my calves and crest the hill without slowing. There, not far off, water glimmers under the light of the moon. I don't see Abraham, nor anyone for that matter. And for the briefest of moments, the weight of defeat crushes down.

But then I hear a noise.

I stop, working to corral my breathing, and listen. There it is again. A soft, questioning call.

"Abraham?" I shout.

I hear his responding laugh, and then there he is, a darkened form stepping out from the shadow of a tree. Exhaling a mighty breath, I tromp his way.

"I expected you to be gone," I call out, not worried about the volume of my voice here. We're alone save the earth and the starlight.

"I was for a while. I came back. Just in case." He sounds happy despite the trouble I surely caused him.

"I'm glad you returned," I tell him truthfully. "I apologize that it took me so long to get here. I was...waylaid."

The outline of him comes into clearer focus the closer I get, although the details of his face are lost to me in the dark. "I understand. You're here now. Although swimming may have to wait for another day."

I let out a soft laugh, swinging the sack off my shoulder. "I... Well, I brought you something."

Abraham accepts the haversack, his fingers brushing mine. "What is it?"

Voicing it aloud now that I'm here is harder than I expected. Will he find offense? Storm off?

No. He won't do that. Somehow, I'm certain.

"It's food," I admit, my voice not cooperating enough for more than a whisper. I clear my throat before going on. "For you and your mother. If you want it."

"Jasper." My name is spoken quietly, the moon affording me just enough light to see Abraham twisting the cloth strap in his hands. "This is a kindness I can't repay."

"You shouldn't have to," I choke out. "Food should be available to all. You shouldn't need to..."

I trail off, not wanting to insult Abraham's livelihood. There's nothing shameful about being a stable hand. But the fact that he earns such meager coin for a life so hard lived... It's not right.

"I don't understand why it has to be this way," I tell him.

Abraham steps close, his shirt stark against his tan skin, the fabric meeting near the middle of his chest, leaving his throat open to the air. His eyes, so dark, are difficult to see, and I wish it wasn't so.

"You have a tender heart." Abraham's words don't sound in the least like an insult, the way they would have had they come from my father. "I won't ever ask this of you, Jasper. But thank you for the gift. I will not refuse it, either."

My breath puffs out of me, and my hands itch with the desire to move, to show Abraham, somehow, how grateful I am for his easy acceptance. But how would I explain it's my own mind eased, knowing he'll have food on his table tomorrow and the day after? In the end, I give him the only words I can. "Thank you."

The noise that rumbles from his chest sounds like gentle laughter. "I hardly know what to do with you."

"You could sit with me," I find myself requesting. "Tell me more of your life?"

Abraham takes a seat on the grass, and I quickly follow. He sets the haversack aside, resting on his back with a sigh that has my chest squeezing tight. I lie down beside him, my heart thumping beneath its cage as I stare up at the stars, my breath coming short again for no reason I can detect. I force my breathing to slow. Let my pulse even.

Abraham hums before speaking. "When I was young, I imagined myself a fierce warrior. Do you know the constellation of the sword?"

"The one to the north?"

He nods, hands beneath his head. "I'd imagine plucking it from the sky and using it to defeat my foes. Maybe even hunt a boar for me and my mother. It was folly, but I remember thinking if only I had my sword, surely I could conquer all."

Abraham's story pulls at a place unseen, the unexpected melancholy of it nearly stealing my breath away. I swallow down the tightness in my throat, seeking out the stars that make up the constellation. The sword hangs suspended in the sky above, the tip of the blade the brightest, seeming as if it's staring directly at us.

"I think you're braver than me," I tell him. "I've never had grand dreams of defeating my foes. All I've ever wished for is to be happy. Happier than I am."

"What would make you happy?"

I look over at Abraham, his face close, a hint of brightness reflecting off his eyes. "I'm not sure. A simple life."

"With Catherine. In the countryside."

"Perhaps," I admit, voice hoarse.

"Where you aren't expected to court a wife."

My breath catches, my heart leaping into my throat. "I..."

"Do you know you have stars in your eyes?" Abraham's words are soft. Spoken low. "I can see them clearly. Your wishes."

I feel as if I can't breathe. The world hangs suspended, for just a moment, the same as that sword in the sky.

Abraham breaks the stillness. "Do you wish to kiss me, Jasper Sinclair?"

My exhale is one of surprise. Fear. Many things I have not the time to put a name to. "That... That isn't allowed. It's illegal."

Abraham watches me, not voicing a response. I'm desperate to understand what's going through his head.

Has he kissed men before? Is that why he's asking? Does he desire to kiss *me*? He wouldn't pose the question otherwise, would he?

Unless it's a ruse.

But no. I refuse to believe such. He wouldn't be that cruel.

Is kissing Abraham something I want? It's absurd, and yet... Women have never called to me. Not when my body was changing, turning me into a man. And not now, when I know I should appreciate their feminine allure. I should be looking for a wife, yet I've never wanted one.

Maybe there's a reason for that.

It's hard to make out Abraham under the darkness of night, but I feel as if I know him already. His dark brows and straight, patrician nose befitting the warrior he fancies himself to be. The brown eyes, like honeyed lacquer, that smiled at me upon our first meeting. The cadence of his voice, even, and the laugh I admire. The strength of spirit he possesses. The fortitude.

Abraham eases onto his side, bringing us closer. He seems to loom over me, and yet, I'm not afraid. Not of him. "Jasper?"

I bring my shaking hand to Abraham's jaw, feeling a hint of coarse hair he must shave away. He covers my hand with his own, holding me to him, shifting his lips to my palm and placing the smallest of kisses there.

It rattles me to my very core. Shifts the foundation of all I know. It snaps into place the certainty that I have answers for those questions never before solved.

Would I have ever found the truth without Abraham? Without his lips pressed to my skin?

"Yes," I say at a hush. "I wish to kiss you."

Abraham pulls my palm from his lips, a sigh of aching relief leaving his lungs. He holds my hand to his heart as the world around me goes dark. As Abraham leans in, blocking out the stars. There's the whisper of his breath. The pulse beneath my fingertips. And then Abraham's lips on mine.

My world explodes in a shower of white.

Abraham kisses me again and again, each press of his lips a greeting, as if he's loath to say goodbye. I would gladly linger in an infinite state of introduction with this man given the chance. In fact, my heart races at the very idea of this ever coming to an end. Perhaps he senses it. Because Abraham shifts his hand to my face, grip settling beside my ear, his fingers carding through my hair and making my very skin feel as if it's alive. His heart beats under my palm, the lifeblood of this man calling to me, reminding me of how very alive we are indeed.

When his mouth parts from my own, I nearly shake him. Because no. That isn't right.

"Abe," I plead.

"My heart." His voice trembles, and I can only pray he feels the same desperation as me inside his chest. "Do you wish for me to kiss you again?"

Surely he must know?

"I wish for you never to stop."

CHAPTER 4

Abraham

I fear I did not weigh the full effect of kissing Jasper Sinclair. He's far more potent than I imagined. A luxury so indulgent I know not how I will ever quit his taste.

If this is ruin, let me be a man in shambles.

"Abe." The whisper of Jasper's lips against mine is full of an awe I understand in my marrow. "Is it always like this?"

"No," I tell him truthfully, passing my fingers through his silky hair, the heat of him beneath me assuring me this isn't a dream I've conjured only in my head.

His hands shake against my shirt, one still resting over my heart, the other at my side. I feather my lips over his. His lips, the corner of his mouth, his jaw, and then back again.

His voice is breathless. "Will it pass?"

"No," I say again, sure of it. "Does that scare you?"

The light of the stars looks back at me from within his eyes. "Yes. This is impossible. How will we..."

I quiet his concern with a press of my lips to his. "Carefully." Another press. "Cautiously."

"If we're caught…"

"We won't be."

He lets out a soft laugh, his hand sliding against my chest in a way that makes me long to feel the touch of his fingertips on my skin. His tone turns playful, needing, I suspect, to make light of the danger we're in. "If we are, will you fight for me, my warrior?"

"With my every breath," I promise, the certainty of it startling me.

Jasper sobers, his drifting fingers coming to a stop. "My family leaves soon. Can I see you again before I go?"

"Every day if you please," I answer, capturing his hand to bring his fingertips to my lips. I kiss each slowly. Revel in each intake of breath. Five in total. "How long will you be away?"

"A month, perhaps?"

Such a long time when I've only just found him.

I offer a smile, hoping Jasper can see it. "A month to miss you, then."

"Abraham…"

"Will you think of me while you're away?"

His response nearly sets my heart on fire. "How could I not? Forgetting you must mean I am dead, for I cannot see how it would be possible otherwise."

I find the bow of Jasper's lips in the dark, memorizing the shape of him with my thumb as my voice rattles from my lungs. "If you expect me to leave you tonight, you can't speak so."

"It's the truth." His words come winded, as if the kiss of my thumb is as exhilarating to him as my mouth. He doesn't sound pleased to add, "But I must go."

"I know," I exhale, letting my hand drop away.

Leaning back, I offer my palm to Jasper, helping him to sit. He straightens his waistcoat before sifting his fingers through his hair. There's a soft plop in the creek, like a frog in motion.

When Jasper stands, the moonlight casts a silver glow atop his head. "If this is a dream, I hope I can return."

Without another word, Jasper sets off toward the hill that will take him out of sight. I watch him until he's gone, his silhouette disappearing amongst the dark. Picking up the sack he left for me, I head toward home.

My mother is awake when I arrive, a candle at her bedside as she darns a sock. I close the door behind me, setting the sack on the table.

"What do you have?" my mother asks.

I let out a soft breath. "Food," I tell her, pulling the items free. My stomach nearly drops to my feet when I see the jar half-full of what must be butter. *Oh, Jasper.*

"Abraham," my mother says, fear in her voice. "Did you steal it?"

"No, Mama," I answer quickly, setting down a loaf of bread and finding a salted meat of some kind. Pork, I believe. "It was a gift. From a friend."

She looks unconvinced, but she doesn't press for more information. Perhaps she doesn't believe me and wishes not to know.

I set to work cutting one end of the bread into pieces. Atop two, I spread a fine layer of butter. It clumps, cool as it is, but I don't concern myself with warming it. My mother won't mind, and neither will I. Atop that, I add small hunks of the dried meat. On the other two pieces of bread, I lather the fruit spread. Orange, perhaps? Apricot?

"Here," I tell my mother, passing her a plate as I take a seat at the edge of her mat. "An extra meal will do us good."

She doesn't object. Not after two days of eating only corn-bread and our last ration of beef. We're quiet as we chew, but I have no doubt my mother is savoring the experience as I am.

"Your friend," she says slowly once done. "Did he steal this?"

I laugh softly, my spirits high with my stomach so pleasantly sated. "No, he did not."

"He is wealthy, then."

"Yes. Here. Let me take your plate."

She hands it to me, empty of even crumbs, and I stand, wiping each with a cloth before storing the rest of the food. I set the sack near the door to return to Jasper.

"Do you need to use the pot?" I ask.

My mother nods, and I go to her side, helping maneuver her so she can relieve herself before bed. After emptying the pot and taking care of my own needs, I return indoors. The candle continues to flicker, although I know my mother will extinguish the flame soon enough.

"Abraham," she says gently.

I pause, standing in front of my own bed mat, my shirt set aside for tomorrow. My mother seems to weigh her words, her exhaustion evident on her face, even in the limited light. I can't help my worry that, despite my best efforts, this life is pressing down on her more forcefully than I can counteract.

"I feel that I am nothing but a burden to you," she finally says.

"Mama."

"Please," she goes on, her hair spread darkly across her pillow as she looks my way. "This isn't what I wanted for you. I can scarcely help. Scarcely contribute—"

"Hush," I say more forcefully, returning to her side and kneeling beside her. "You do the best you can. And I wouldn't ever ask more of you. Who raised me, hm?"

She lets out a soft sigh.

"You've worked hard your whole life," I remind her. "Now it's my turn. Let me carry the weight. I am strong enough to do so thanks to you."

She nods, tears in her eyes. After making sure her legs are in a comfortable position, I blow out the candle and return to bed.

The morning brings with it sunshine, a soft breeze, and a contented stomach as I rake horse stalls. Victor does his own tasks within the stables, checking on me rarely. I take pride in his trust, and, like always, I work hard to ensure I keep it.

Jasper is on my mind near constantly. His voice. His lips. The prospect of seeing him again. My stomach flips at the mere thought, a smile on my face as I lug a wheelbarrow full of manure out back.

As I'm feeding the horses their morning grain, I sense him. He's standing outside the doorway to the stables, his waistcoat and breeches a light tan, his coat dark green. He lingers only for a moment, but the sight of him has me wishing for Victor's absence once more so that we might steal the day away in one another's company. As is, we're only afforded a quick, shared smile.

It's enough. Even when my night passes without a single sighting of Jasper.

The following day is much the same. A morning meal of bread, meat, and butter. Clearing the stables and preparing the horses for labor. A brief glimpse of Jasper as he slows on his way to the printer.

Bright, golden hair. Blue, blue eyes. His soft smile and blushing cheeks.

Have any other seen those cheeks light so?

It's a proprietorial notion, desiring that hue to belong to me and me alone. But Jasper is meant to be mine. I know it the same way I know the sun will rise every day and the stars will return at night. He was made for me. Or me for him. I'm meant to cherish him. I'm sure of it.

He leaves in only two days. It's a temporary absence, I know. But I ache with it all the same.

I return to the creek once it's dark, waiting, hoping. My heart lifts when a shadow moves over the top of the hill to the east.

Jasper wastes no time in rushing toward me. His teeth gleam in the starlight as he grins, a bundle in his hands that he quickly drops to the earth. He all but leaps forward, his mouth pressing to mine without a word spoken between us. We go stumbling, my arms around him helping to steady us. Jasper utters a quick apology against my lips, but the smile in his kiss never wavers.

Shifting my hands to his hair, I grasp the short strands, my soul settling at his proximity even as my body burns. Jasper allows me to tilt his head, a gasp leaving his lips as I drop my mouth to the pale skin of his throat. His grip on me tightens, body swaying, his voice but a whisper.

"Abraham."

"Yes?"

"You make me dizzy."

With a soft groan, I map a path up Jasper's throat to his lips. I kiss him once, twice, before stepping back. "Then let us sit."

Jasper settles in front of me on the grass, his knees close enough to brush mine. He clears his throat before reaching for the bundle he dropped and handing it over. "For you."

By the shape of it, I can tell it's more food. "Thank you," I tell him earnestly, feeling spoiled by Jasper's care. I set the bundle at my side and grab the empty sack I brought with me. "Yours."

He laughs quietly, accepting it, placing the sack beside himself. His hand finds my knee, but he retracts it quickly, as if startled by his own boldness or perhaps the feel of my skin. I reach for him slowly, giving him time to pull away. He never does.

Taking hold of his hand, I draw it between us, keeping it tangled with my own as a small animal rustles in the brush somewhere off to our right.

"I no longer wish to go." Jasper's voice is soft, but it holds an edge of panic.

"To the countryside?"

He nods. "I always enjoy visiting my aunt. But this time... This time, I am leaving you behind. And I hate it."

I bring his hand up, kissing his knuckles. "Only for a while. I'll be here when you return."

"Abraham..." Whatever it is he has to say, he seems to hesitate over it. "Are you able to read?"

Ah.

"No," I admit. "I was never taught."

He doesn't seem surprised by this. "I could teach you. If you'd like."

"I would like that very much," I say, my throat tight. "Thank you."

He nods, his fingers brushing against my own. Playing, almost. "If I write to you...while I'm away... Would you let me read you my letters?"

"You don't need to go through the hassle," I tell him, not wanting him to worry over me when he should be enjoying his trip.

His fingers tighten on mine. "You don't understand. I must. Because when I see you again, I will surely forget everything I thought of you in my absence, and I don't want to let a single recollection go missing. I want to write them all down, and I want to share them with you."

My breath aches in my lungs.

I have no doubt Jasper Sinclair will bring about my destruction.

"I would be honored, Jasper. To hear your letters."

He lets out a short sigh. "Yes. Good. I feel as if I must be going mad, Abraham. To want you so."

I twist his hand in mine, letting the sting in my throat settle before speaking. "Then we will be mad together."

Jasper stays with me at the creek for what must be an hour or more. We talk as the crickets chirp and the night owls sing their songs. The weight of duty pulls at us both, but we resist. For at least a little while.

When we can no longer delay the inevitable, Jasper leans close, his eyes a flicker of brightness in an otherwise dark night. "If I don't have another chance to say it, fare thee well, Abraham Morris. Until I can return to you."

"Be it swiftly, I hope."

Jasper kisses me, his hand on my cheek shaking. I do my best to soothe his worry, distracting him with soft nips and teasing caresses of my mouth. He's calmer when we part.

I see Jasper off, walking with him up the hill. I could almost imagine I'm on top of the world, even though I know I'm but a small speck underneath the blanket of stars. Jasper is but a speck, too, when he walks out of sight.

I glimpse Jasper the next day, a smile on his lips as he passes. The fresh bread, hard cheese, and mustard seed paste he gifted me the prior evening sit comfortably within my belly. I wish I could tell him of my mother's sigh as she ate her own meal. But I don't have a chance. Jasper is gone almost as quickly as he arrived.

The following day, Jasper returns to the stables. The carriage is prepared, and I check the connections to the horses as the man I presume to be Jasper's father converses with Victor. I keep one eye on Jasper, careful to temper my smile. Jasper seems less inclined to hide himself away, but I find I can't chastise him for it, not even inside my own head.

Once payment has been made, Mr. Sinclair steps into the carriage, waving for Jasper to join him. The hired coachman settles in his seat, and I have only a moment to lock eyes with the man I won't see for likely a month or more. There's a sadness in his gaze, but he musters up a smile to send me. I give a short nod, and Jasper steps up and out of sight.

Be it swiftly.

I hope, I hope, I hope.

Chapter 5

Jasper

My fingers drum against the sill as I watch our trunks return to the carriage waiting outside my aunt and uncle's house in the country. Their dog races around the butler's feet, yapping excitedly.

Five and a half weeks. It's been five and a half weeks since I last set eyes on Abraham. It will be six by the time I arrive home.

Has he forgotten me? Does he still want me as I want him?

The letters I wrote are tucked safely away inside my trunk, bundled within the pockets of a coat so no one will find them. Even so, I watch the butler lift the trunk into the carriage, my heart in my throat. He moves on, and I breathe a sigh of relief.

Voices come from the hall behind me.

"Yes, well, you should try your best to return before next summer," my aunt is saying, talking, I assume, to my mother. "You know how much I adore your company. It can get so quiet here."

"Traveling in the winter would be difficult," my mother says, although she sounds as if she's considering it. Sometimes I think my mother would have preferred to stay in the countryside instead of moving to town when she married my father. But she's never said as much.

"It would be near impossible," my father cuts in. "Besides, I can't afford to be away from the printer for so long."

"Perhaps my sister could come alone before the snow arrives," my aunt proposes, the five of them, my uncle and Catherine included, in the parlor now. She looks at my mother. "You and Jasper both. Surely Catherine could stay and tend to the home?"

My mother looks wistful, but my father shakes his head. "We'll talk about this another time. Is the carriage packed?"

It takes me a second to realize my father is asking me.

I nod quickly, glancing once more outside the window. The butler is approaching the house now. "Yes, sir."

"Good. Let's be on our way."

My father says a quick goodbye to my uncle, a rather quiet but kind man. Father nods my aunt's way before beckoning me out the door. I watch my mother and aunt for a moment, their parting words to one another far more heartfelt and lingering than my father's. I've never seen my mother as soft as she is here with her sister.

When I get out to the carriage, I push the small window covering aside so that I may watch the countryside as we travel. Catherine settles beside me.

She saw me, one day, writing to Abraham. She didn't ask, but I've seen her curious gaze aimed my way often. Perhaps she thinks I'm courting.

It's almost absurd to realize I am, in a way.

What would she think if she knew it was a man my affections lie with, not a woman? Would she—*could* she—understand that, too?

It's not accepted. But a small corner of my mind recognizes the fact that it must happen. Men lying with one another. Maybe women, too. If no one ever felt this way, there wouldn't be laws prohibiting it.

Surely, I should care about that more than I do. But I can't see how it's wrong. Not when, for the first time ever, looking at another, touching them, feels right.

My mother waves to my aunt as our carriage sets into motion. We rock with it, and I offer my mother a small smile when she wipes discreetly below her eye. She looks away quickly, and I wish, not for the first time, she didn't feel the need to hide herself so.

I let my mind drift as we begin the steady journey toward home. Toward Abraham.

Five and a half weeks has been far too long.

I wash myself with quick movements, despite the water being pleasantly warmed from the hearth. As soon as I'm certain I'm clean, I step from the tub and dry off. My clothes have been returned to my wardrobe thanks to Catherine, a few articles set aside for laundering. I nearly trip over my own feet in my haste to dress.

I pass Catherine in the hall. She's unpacking the last of our trunks from our arrival yesterday evening.

"Eager to get to the printer this morning?" she asks, amusement in her tone.

My heart thumps painfully. I don't care for secrecy between me and Catherine, but what could I possibly say to explain Abraham?

"Yes," I lie. "I didn't realize I'd miss it so."

I wait for her to catch me out, but she only hums. "Then be off with you."

With a nod, I head out the door.

My walk feels as if it lasts hours instead of mere minutes. I pass familiar faces, buildings and houses I've gone by hundreds of times, even a gaggle of children being led to school. I see almost none of it.

The scent hits me first. The horses. The sound of a gentle whinny. I can scarcely breathe.

I slow at the front of the stables, grateful there's no one close enough to be paying attention to me. Victor and a single patron are standing inside, but neither notices my presence. My pulse races as I search for him.

What if he's gone? What if he doesn't wish to see me? What if—

Abraham steps through a wide door at the back of the stables, and it's as if all the air leaves my lungs. There's sweat along his brow, his hair disheveled from his work. His shirt is streaked with dirt, the laces along the top open enough for me to glimpse his chest. He's broad and young, yes, but not youthful in appearance. His physique is that of a laborer. He's not soft. Not feminine.

Yet I ache for him in a way I never have for another, expectations be damned.

When Abraham spots me at long last, the world simply...stops. His throat catches, his entire body going still and everything around us seeming to quiet. I wait with breath held, sure his dismissal now would crush me. But his lips tip into a smile, and my very being soars and expands, as if I'm a bird taking its first flight of spring.

I can't temper my own smile. It bursts from me big and wild, and I swear Abraham nearly comes to me. Nearly strides my way to wrap his hands in my hair and press his lips to mine.

But, of course, he doesn't. He can't.

Victor says something to Abraham, and he nods quickly, his attention diverted for a moment before coming back to me. I see the apology in the eyes. The absolute longing. I nod in return, taking a step away, knowing I've already risked far too much in my transparency.

Catherine's question from so many weeks ago returns to me. When she asked about my friendship with Abraham.

Is it safe?

No, I daresay it's not. Not anymore.

It isn't easy walking away, but I force my feet through the motions. I meet my father at the printer, my fingers smudged with dark ink before long. I nod along as one of the older men discusses the importance of the newspaper, not disagreeing with him yet angry, all the same, that so few are allowed the opportunity to read.

Should knowledge and wealth not be shared equally? What benefit is it to have extra food on the table when others have not enough to get by? Should not all men and women learn the alphabet? Are we not stronger if we gain wisdom from all?

It's a relief when my father and I leave for home. He looks over at me proudly, not knowing the thoughts inside my head. Not knowing how much I've surely failed him already.

Our meal is quiet, my father's nose in his workbook, my mother seemingly preoccupied with missing her sister. Catherine, of course, is absent, not allowed to share food with the rest of us. Is she not family? Does she not deserve to eat at the table considering all she does for us?

By the time the sky is dark, I feel nearly ill. It's in my head; I know it is. But I don't understand the motives of men. Greed and pride and malice, even, to stand atop the weak in order to feel strong.

What would happen if those at the bottom stood up? The thought nearly has me laughing. Surely, the men up high would topple.

I wait until the house has drawn quiet before slipping out the window. My letters are tucked safely within my waistcoat, a sack of food in one hand and a lit oil lamp in the other. It's a risk bringing it with me, but I chance it this once. The trek feels infinitely long tonight, my desire to see Abraham seeming to put me further and further away from him. But finally, finally, I crest the hill.

He's there, as I knew he would be, standing beside the creek. I don't realize at first that there are tears tracking down my cheeks. I feel them once I start to move swiftly down the hill, the wind cool against the moisture on my skin. I couldn't care less. Abraham meets me at the bottom, and I don't stop or think. I set down the oil lamp, drop my other possessions to the ground, and the moment warm palms bracket my neck, all the noise, all the worry and anger and unease...it melts away.

Abraham's lips meet mine, and it feels like falling. We *are* falling, I realize a second too late. He lands on top of me, the both of us grunting at the impact before laughing. His mouth presses to mine again, his body blanketing me, warm and strong and secure.

"Jasper." His voice is but a whisper, his thumb rolling over my cheek. He does it again, wiping away my tears as the curves of his lips brush mine.

"Don't stop," I beg of him, pulling him into another kiss, wondering if I could tie us together, never to be parted again.

The world makes sense when Abraham is near.

A soft rumble leaves his mouth, his body rubbing against mine in a way I'm not expecting. I gasp, hardening in my breeches at the touch. He does it again.

"A-Abe," I manage.

He rocks against me once more, his lips on my jaw and then my neck. "Do you wish for me to stop?"

Do I?

"No," I say at once, my head going dizzy, my breath coming short as I feel his hardened prick pressing insistently against my hip.

His mouth finds mine again, full of passion and reassurance both. It seems to pain him to pull back, and I don't care for it either. Not when I told him to stay. His absence leaves me cold, but his voice is gentle.

"Come. I know of somewhere private we can go."

Abraham offers his hand, and I don't know where he intends to bring me, but I trust him implicitly. So I accept his help in standing, pick up my things, and follow him through the dark.

The babble of the creek quiets as we walk for only a minute or so along the edge of the woods. Abraham passes between two trees, waiting to make sure I'm at his heel before guiding me a handful of steps further. The light from my lamp illuminates the edges of a manmade structure. My shoe thunks against a lone wooden board as I follow Abraham through the open doorway. Shadows darken the small hovel, the roof long since having fallen away. I look up at the stars before Abraham's voice beckons me.

"Here."

I set the oil lamp down in the corner of the room before joining him. There's a roughly woven blanket spread out on the dirt floor, as if waiting for us.

Did Abraham put it here?

His fingers trace my cheek lightly as I settle beside him, the touch like sparks. "Jasper. How I've missed you."

"Have you really?" I ask, relief making me nearly weak. I tug him closer, wanting his body over mine again. He comes easily, settling against me, just as it should be. "I missed you terribly. I don't want to be away from you again, Abraham."

He lets out a breath, his face tucked to the side of mine before he lifts his head, his lips finding my own. His kiss is both sweet and ragged, hard edges tempered by the fondness I know he must feel for me. He must. Otherwise he wouldn't kiss me so.

I don't know how to ask Abraham to continue what he started before, but I must not need to with words. He spreads my legs wider with his hips, pressing me to the ground, the weight and friction of him bringing me to life quicker than my own hand has ever managed. I hardly know what to do with it, not having ever been aroused in close proximity to another person before.

Abraham kisses me as he rolls against my prick, stealing the breath from my lungs. His fingers thread through my hair, his voice quiet. "Jasper. Have you lain with men?"

My pulse is thready as I answer him. "I have not lain with anyone."

He's quiet for only a moment, half of his face illuminated in flickering light. "Would you allow me to touch you?"

"Yes, but I... I don't know how..."

He shushes me gently, his lips on mine. "Allow me."

I nod, and Abraham leans back on his heels. He unbuttons my waistcoat as my heart thrashes about wildly inside my chest. I help him finish the task, setting the garment aside with the bundle of letters tucked safely within. His hands go to my breeches next, slipping button after button free. He pulls my shirt up gently, the fabric brushing against the length of my arousal in a way that has a gasp falling from my lips. I'm almost mortified by my state of being until I remember Abraham is similarly affected, his breeches straining with his own need. It's a balm on my nerves.

Abraham pushes my shirt up only slightly before stopping, leaving it in place in deference to the cool night air, if I had to guess. He leans down to press a kiss to the skin of my lower stomach before eyeing me again, his hand going to my open breeches. When his fingers wrap around the length of me, I nearly sob. "*Abe*."

"Does it feel good?"

"Yes. *Please*."

He strokes his hand up and down, and I twist reflexively, reaching for something. Anything. Abraham gives me his hand, his other pulling on me in a way I've only done to myself. It's far better with Abraham's grip, and I don't know that I'll be able to last. I don't know if he needs me to.

His voice is hoarse, as if he too is affected. "Can I kiss you?"

Somehow, I know what he's insinuating, even though I don't understand it. I know, and I nod. "Yes, I..."

Abraham lowers his head, and the moment his lips wrap around me, I find my completion. I empty into his mouth, my own voice rough with my shout, Abraham's hand wringing me until I slump flat. I'm breathing hard, the stars twinkling overhead, my thoughts pinging around in a million different directions.

There's a gravity tethering me to this moment. One I don't have the capacity to comprehend.

Abraham swiftly unbuttons his own breeches, drawing my attention his way. With one hand on my thigh, he pulls himself free, his eyes locked with mine as he works himself over. I can only watch, rapt, as his chest heaves and he bows, his spend landing on the blanket between my legs.

He drops his forehead to my stomach, hunched over as his breaths saw through the air. I bring my hands to his hair, running my fingers through the strands, the sight of him so undone making me want to comfort him the way he so easily comforts me.

"Abe," I whisper.

He lifts his head.

"We won't give this up, will we?" I ask, desperation bleeding into my tone. "We'll find a way to keep it?"

Abraham's response is solid and sure. "Yes, my heart. No one will ever take this away. I won't allow it."

CHAPTER 6

Abraham

Jasper settles on the blanket, his shirt tucked into his breeches once more, the lamplight casting a soft glow over his features. I find my place beside him, the mess I left now beneath us, tucked away against the dirt.

He reaches for the sack of food he brought, passing it over. "Would you like something to eat?"

I accept the offering, pulling a small hunk of bread free. Water would also be welcome, but we don't have any.

"How was your time away?" I ask, setting the rest of the food aside.

He hums, waiting for me to lie back down before finding a home against my shoulder. "Pleasant enough, but... I kept wanting to be back here. With you."

It warms me to hear it, if only to have proof that Jasper thought of me as I thought of him.

His voice turns almost shy. "Could I read you a letter now?"

I nod, and he hurries to collect his waistcoat. From inside, he pulls out a bundle of papers, so many of them it takes my breath away. He unfurls the stack, picking one off the top before pulling the oil lamp closer and resettling against me. He clears his throat, face downcast, my only view of him the top of his head as he begins to read, his words nearly piercing my heart with their sweetness.

"My warrior. It hasn't been long that we've been apart, but I fear any length of time is too long for me. I don't understand how I could have passed from day to day without knowing you. It feels like another life, one not my own. Because now, all I see is you. Do you think it's possible to know someone before you've met? That's how I feel. As if I've known you far longer than mere weeks. I imagine a world where our being together would be as easy as breathing. But it's not, and that truth aches in my lungs. I pray it is not only me falling down this rabbit's warren. Please tell me you are with me? That you'll walk by my side through these dark and dampened trails? I won't be afraid if I have you. I couldn't be. The stars were out last night, my warrior, and I smiled at the sight of them. Did you look at them the same? The sword in the north called to me, and I felt close to you, as if I could reach up and touch your skin. Soon. I'll return to you soon. With every promise, J."

My throat is tight as I swallow. Jasper sets the letter onto his leg. He doesn't look up, is quiet for a long moment.

"It's not only you," I tell him, a rasp and nothing more.

"What?"

"Jasper, it's not only you. Would you look at me?"

He does, finally lifting his head. I pluck his chin higher into the air, a position of pride he should always feel worthy of carrying. He sighs against my mouth as I kiss him, as I make my feelings perfectly clear. His eyes shine darkly when we part.

"Would you read me another?" I ask.

With his lips in a small smile, he nods, clearing his throat before picking up a new page.

"My warrior..."

Jasper reads letter after letter, each signed inconspicuously with the letter J, until the oil lamp goes out and he's forced to stop. Even then, we stay wrapped up in one another for a long while.

It's easy to believe—when the rest of the world is out of sight—that we could exist just like this. Without worry. Without repercussion.

Without end.

The days and weeks pass quickly. With Jasper home, my time feels less monotonous than it once did. Interspersed with my days at the stables are glimpses of Jasper and his smile on the way to the printer. And at night, whenever he's able, Jasper comes to the creek. We touch. Kiss. Lie together under the stars.

Until it's once again time to part.

One Sunday while we're basking with our toes in the creek, Jasper says, "Why do they say it's wrong? The two of us."

The sun overhead feels far too bright for this conversation. "Because their god said so."

Jasper's retort is full of fire. "But he didn't. His teachings were written by men. And men are fallible."

I hum, loving the way Jasper's mind works.

"I don't understand how it could be wrong," he goes on, his pale skin having tanned some in the summer months we've spent together. His breeches are still wet from our swim, and my gaze drifts lazily along the outline of his soft prick before I refocus on Jasper's words and his brightly lit cheeks. "It does not feel wrong to me. It feels like the most perfect thing. Why do people fear what they cannot control?"

"I think you may have answered your question," I say, shifting to run my fingers along his arm. "Powerful men seek to command. Even when it comes to love."

Jasper's head rolls my way. "It's not right."

He shivers when I trace my finger up the inside of his elbow. "I seem to recall you telling me you never dared to fight your foes. Yet you sound ready to take up arms, my starry-eyed boy."

He snorts indelicately. "If I were as brave as you, maybe I would. But I don't know how to fight something so...vast."

"We do it in our own way," I tell him, covering Jasper's body with my own. He welcomes me, his arms wrapping around my neck, his smile sweet and hopeful.

"And what way is that?"

I kiss his neck, the soft spot that makes him moan for me. "I can think of many, many ways. Allow me to show you?"

His voice comes out breathless. "If you make me spend, we'll need to take another dip in the creek."

"Perish the thought," I murmur, rolling against his hips.

Jasper's eyes close, his parted lips a temptation I can't ignore. We rut and kiss, blunt nails raking down my back as Jasper swells beneath me, his cry one I swallow down. I follow him mere seconds later, my very heart pressed to me from outside my chest.

Jasper is boneless when I drag him into the creek. His smile is languid, his eyes catching mine as he washes out his breeches. "That was careless of us. To be in the open like that."

I don't disagree with him, but we were quick. "Next time, I'll carry you inside."

"To our crumbling home?"

I laugh softly, but I like the sound of that more than he knows. A home for us, crumbling or not.

"I should be getting back shortly," I tell him. "My mother wasn't her best this morning, and I want to check after her."

Jasper is quiet for a moment. "Could I... Could I meet her, do you think?"

My head whips his way. "Jasper... I don't know if that would be wise."

His voice comes out almost pleading. "She wouldn't have to know about us. But we're friends, are we not?"

"You know that's complicated for men like us."

Jasper looks down at the water, and I hate to see him turning his face from me so. I reach for his hand, relief loosening my chest when he squeezes me back.

"I won't ever be able to bring you home, Abraham. But if we can trust your mother, I'd really like to see yours."

My heart aches. It's not my mother I'm worried about. She already knows of Jasper, at least in part. She may not know him by name or even the true nature of our relationship, but she's aware of our family's benefactor. She's never pried for more details than I've given her, and I don't expect she'd do so now.

But everyone else? Those who live near us who might see Jasper walking by so out of place?

"We'll need to be careful," I tell him.

He brightens immediately. "Of course. I'll follow your lead."

"And my home... It won't be what you're accustomed to."

"I don't care." The words are as forceful as the look in his eyes. "It's yours, which will make it perfect."

I let out a slow, slow breath. "I wasn't made to resist you, Jasper Sinclair."

"I do not wish for you to try."

I laugh at his candidness, swooping forward to steal a kiss from his lips. By his answering grin, it wasn't so much stolen as a gift freely given.

Jasper and I dry the best we can before re-dressing and starting off toward my house. His hand tangles with mine until we're too close to the inhabitants of town to chance such proximity. Jasper follows me at a steady pace inside the tree line, the path keeping us out of sight for a long while. We pass the small, wooden houses along the stretch where I live, their roofs thatched, many in need of repair.

Once my home is in sight, I ask Jasper to wait so I can prepare my mother. She won't want to be caught unawares by company.

I'm quick to head inside, finding her sitting near the open window. She's working on a blanket for the winter, but she stops when I walk in.

"Mama," I say, not mincing words with Jasper waiting so near outside. "I have a friend who'd like to visit. May he come in?"

"I... Yes, of course," she says, smoothing her hair back. She leaves the blanket on her lap and gives me a nod.

I head back outside, finding Jasper peeking at me through the trees. I smile and wave him forward, and he walks my way as if lacking a single care in the world, when I know that's not the case. With his stockings off and his waistcoat held in his hand, he could almost pass as belonging here at the quickest of glances.

Almost.

I open the door for him to pass through, and once inside, I shut us in. My mother is quick to appraise Jasper. From his fine clothing to his posture and the filled-to-bursting haversack slung over his shoulder, I have no doubt she realizes exactly who he is.

"Mama, this is Jasper Sinclair," I introduce. "Jasper, my mother, Abigail Morris."

Jasper steps forward, tugging the sack off his arm. He opens it, rifling through the contents until he pulls a small container forth. "Ma'am. I brought blackberry jam. Catherine says it's your favorite, and she made up this batch fresh. I hope you like it."

My mother accepts the glass jar, looking somewhat shocked. "Catherine," she says slowly, understanding dawning in her eyes. "Catherine Turner. She's your family's maid."

Pain flashes across Jasper's face before he hides it away, offering my mother the smallest of smiles. He takes a seat across from her in one of our wooden chairs. "She is a kind woman who has always been good to me, even as she never needed to be. It's a pleasure to meet you, Ms. Morris. Thank you for having me in your home."

My mother looks from Jasper to me, holding my gaze for a long moment. My stomach twists, but finally she hands me the jar of jam. "I'm certain I will love this, Jasper. Thank you for bringing it."

He looks relieved, a wide smile gracing his face as he passes me the sack of food. I unload the rest of the items, my ear on the conversation as I work to steady my breaths. Jasper is speaking now.

"You knit? Catherine does as well. I never learned it."

"No, I don't suspect you would have," my mother says, not unkindly. "I do. More now than I used to."

"That's a lovely blanket. Do you need more wool? I'm sure I could procure some."

"Jasper," I say, turning from the table, the empty sack in my hands. "You don't need to do that."

He looks from me to my mother. "I wouldn't mind."

"Why is it you are helping us?" my mother asks slowly.

Ah, heavens.

Jasper's brow creases for only a moment. "Because Abraham has become a dear friend. He's a good man, and by extension, I know you must be good, too, by virtue of how he speaks of you. I don't pretend to be a savior. But, ma'am, surely you must know I have more than I need. I do not mind parting with it. Not if it eases even a little of that tension beside Abraham's eyes."

I close my eyes tight, stars dancing in my vision.

"And if your mother finds out? Your father?"

Jasper answers my mother steadily. "Then they will chastise me for my excess. Nothing more. I will not tell them the truth of it."

I open my eyes to find my mother regarding Jasper. He's far too transparent. Innocent. I should not have brought him here.

"A red, perhaps, or yellow would make a fine border for this blanket," my mother says at last.

Jasper looks thrilled. "I will see to it."

My heart squeezes as he turns his grin my way, so very pleased. I offer a smile, not able to deny him such.

Jasper stays for near an hour before he must go. I check outside first, and then we walk to the edge of the trees, my pulse calming only once we're within their protection. We move in silence for some time, until Jasper breaks the quiet.

"Thank you, Abraham. I'm glad to have met your family."

I pull Jasper's hand into mine and kiss his soft skin, my chest so very tight.

When we reach the creek, Jasper stands on tiptoe to brush his lips against mine. "Be it swiftly."

It's our most treasured farewell, as it's not a farewell at all. Only a promise of meeting again.

"Swiftly," I agree, hoping for it with everything I am.

Once Jasper disappears over the hill, I turn for home, a rock beside my heart. My mother hasn't moved in the time I've been gone, although her knitting is set aside.

"Abraham," she says, voice low.

I pull in a breath, waiting. She knows. I'm sure of it.

"You must be careful. Promise me you'll be careful."

"Mama..."

"I can't lose you," she says, her voice cracking over the words. "I cannot lose you, Abraham. My heart couldn't take it."

I reach her side quickly, curling my hand around hers. She squeezes me tight, fear in her eyes. Fear and acceptance of what she knows to be true.

"I will, Mama. I promise. I'll be careful."

CHAPTER 7

Jasper

I waffle between the yellow and red wool before deciding on a hefty dose of the red. It's such a nice shade.

I pay with my own coin before leaving the shop, the dyed yarn inside the haversack that has become a constant go-between for Abraham and me. It would make the most sense to return home and pass the wool off later, and yet I can't quite resist the chance to see him now.

Knowing he'll be at the stables, I walk in that direction. The day is sunny yet mild. Cooler weather will be upon us shortly, and, after that, snow. The thought has worry taking hold inside my chest. It will be far more difficult to meet with Abraham once winter hits.

Surely, we'll manage. Somehow, some way.

The stables are busy today, a carriage setting off and another gentleman leaving on horseback. I slow near the entrance, watching as Victor walks away before glancing inside. My excitement ratchets when I see no one but Abraham.

I slink inside the wide doorway, walking quickly out of sight to the corner where Abraham stowed me the day we first met. Hopefully, Victor's business will keep him for a minute.

"Abe," I whisper.

He comes around the corner, head cocked, his eyes going wide when he sees me. He darts a look around. "Jasper? Are you well?"

"Yes, certainly. I have your mother's wool."

He lets out a breath, sounding both relieved and worried. "Jasper, you shouldn't keep coming like this. We need to be more careful."

I frown. "It hasn't been a problem before."

"No, but if you keep returning here without business, someone is bound to notice."

He's right. I know he is. But it's difficult to stay away.

"Well, then, be quick," I say, holding out the haversack. "Give me a kiss, and I'll be off."

Abraham's expression is one of chastisement, but there's a glint in his eye that assures me he's not truly upset. He walks my way, backing me against a wooden stall, his presence all-encompassing, the brown of his eyes a comfort I never knew I was missing before I met him.

The kiss isn't hurried, even as it's short. Abraham stretches a single second into many, and I swear I can see it. The life we could have together.

If only things were different.

All too soon, his lips leave mine, and he steps back, loosing the haversack from my fingers. "A debt paid."

I let out a quiet laugh, moving from the shadows as Abraham tosses the sack over his shoulder. "Until we meet again, my warrior."

This time, it's Abraham chuckling, the soft sound accompanying me through the doors. I pass Victor not far from the stables, and I say a quiet prayer of thanks our paths didn't cross sooner.

The walk home is pleasant enough, but the moment I step inside, I come to a halt. There are voices I don't recognize.

Catherine must have heard me arrive because she appears quickly, ushering me down the hall to my bedchamber. "I've set out a basin for you," she says, pushing me inside the room. "Wash up. Quick. You've company."

"Who?" I ask, bewildered.

Catherine sets her jaw. "A young woman your mother and father wish for you to court."

My chest falls away from me. "Catherine..."

"I know you're not ready," she says at a hush. "But you have no choice in this. Wash quickly and meet them in the parlor."

I nod, and Catherine closes my door, leaving me alone. My hands shake as I loosen my waistcoat, setting it aside before removing my shirt. I feel chilled to the bone, my heart racing.

I wash my face and neck in the basin, the water cool. My reflection wavers on the surface, the Jasper I see looking at me with pity in his eyes.

After drying myself, I re-dress, check that my clothes are in fine shape, and exit the room. Voices drift lightly from the parlor as I walk closer, dread trying to weigh my feet to the floor. Despite every instinct screaming at me to stay away, to *run*, I step into the room.

"Jasper," my mother says, spotting me and standing. "There you are at last. Come. Have a seat."

I approach the empty chair beside my mother. My father watches on with a stern expression, the room deathly quiet apart from the soft scuff of my shoes on the rug. No one says a word until I'm seated, and then my father clears his throat.

"You may recognize the Bealls," he says, indicating our guests sitting opposite us. "This is their daughter, Ellener."

I incline my head stiffly. "Pleasure."

"Our son, Jasper," my father finishes.

"Good day to you," Mrs. Beall says. She's seated on one side of Ellener, Mr. Beall on the other.

I want to scream with all the power I carry in my lungs.

"Jasper," Mr. Beall says in greeting. "We hear you have a promising position at the printer?"

"Yes, sir," I say, my eyes briefly turning to Ellener. She looks vaguely familiar, flaxen-haired and slight, someone I've likely crossed paths with in town, although we've never spoken. I refocus my attention on Mr. Beall. "I've an apprenticeship with my father. I appreciate greatly the opportunity to learn under his guidance."

The words taste ashen on my tongue, but Mr. Beall offers a pleased smile and a nod.

"If I may," Catherine says, standing in the doorway. "Dinner is prepared."

My mother pushes out of her seat, skirts swooshing, and waves a hand for our guests. "This way."

The table is set with our finest dishware. I'm placed opposite Ellener, like a prop in a play. Laughter bubbles up in my throat, but I quickly swallow it down, my eyes burning.

I wish I were with Abraham a thousand miles from here.

The lamb Catherine prepared is delicious. I pick at it as pleasantries are discussed. Ellener sits as quietly as me, and I can't help but wonder if she wants to be here.

How am I supposed to wed? How can I possibly make a home with someone soft and pretty like Ellener when all I want is Abraham, with his sturdy arms and deeply spoken words? *Stars above.* How will I ever bed a woman?

The mere thought makes me feel ill, and I have to forcibly quell my stomach, lest I lose Catherine's lamb.

Will Abraham still want me? If I must court and marry and carry out my duties, will he still accept me into his arms?

That gravity I felt before—that inevitable, unstoppable pull—tears at me anew.

I'm forced to make polite conversation when we retreat back to the parlor. The afternoon sun streams into the room, the angle such that I imagine scampering under it and slipping away. If only I could.

The Bealls take their leave before long, not daring to over-stay their welcome. Ellener gives me her hand at the door, and I hold it as she curtsies. If pressed at a later time to describe a single detail of her face, I wouldn't be able to do it.

The hall is quiet once the door shuts, my mother turning my way. "Will you see her again?"

I don't know how to answer her.

She speaks at my hesitation. "If not her, it will be someone else, Jasper. It is time."

I give a short nod, and, blessedly, she lets me be. Heart in my throat, I make my way to my bedchamber. The door shuts with a quiet click, and I barely resist dropping to my knees.

It's not even dark when I make my escape out the window.

I arrive at the creek before Abraham. As soon as I reach the water's edge, I tear off my waistcoat, toss my shoes, and pull down my stockings. One snags, and I breathe a quiet apology to Catherine as I throw it aside. Raking my fingers through my hair, I walk along the side of the creek, pacing back and forth. My pulse won't settle. My mind won't quiet.

I can do nothing but let out a scream as I drop to the earth.

"Jasper?"

I nearly collapse at the familiar, worried voice. Abraham is running my way, concern etched into every line of his face and body. He drops down beside me, hands cradling my face, callused thumbs swiping at my tears.

"My heart, what is wrong?"

I cry harder at the question, and Abraham pulls me onto his lap. I cling to him, my face tucked against his shoulder, his hands on my back like a shield.

"I don't want to touch another," I finally manage between breaths. "I cannot *love* another. Not as I love you. Why can't they let me simply love you?"

Abraham's chest hitches against me, his grip tightening on my back. "Oh, Jasper."

"Will you leave me if I wed?" I ask, not wanting the answer, even as I need it. "Will you hate me?"

"No." The word is quick. Soft. "Never could I hate you."

"And the rest?" I ask, pulling back enough to see Abraham's face.

"They would have to tear us apart." His fingers brush through my hair as he holds my gaze, his touch so gentle it's as if I'm glass he doesn't wish to break. As if I'm a treasure.

"Would you take me, Abe?"

His breath is sudden and harsh. "Is that what you want?"

"More than anything," I admit. "I want to be as close to you as possible. If I can feel you inside of me—" My throat catches, and I have to clear it before going on. "Then maybe they will never be able to take you away."

Abraham kisses my cheek, one and then the other. He stands with me in his arms, my finery lying on the grass as Abraham brings me to our small and crumbling sanctuary. He sets me down on the blanket, the last of the sun affording me a view I haven't oft witnessed as Abraham strips to the nude. He holds my eye before turning, and I nearly lose my breath at the sight of his backside, his muscles flexing as he crouches to the ground.

He comes back with a small tin in hand.

"What is that?" I ask, recognizing the object as soon as the question leaves my mouth. "Leather oil?"

He nods as he kneels on the blanket in front of me. "I brought it here last time we came. Just in case."

"In case of what?"

Abraham smiles, and my pulse hitches. "In case you might want me in this way."

"Oh."

He begins unbuttoning my breeches, and I have neither the wherewithal nor desire to stop him, even as my head spins. Abraham seems to sense my confusion, or perhaps he sees it plainly on my face, because he bends down, kissing me gently before meeting my eye.

"I do not wish to hurt you. And it may hurt some. This will help."

"Will it keep me from cracking?" I ask, mostly in jest.

Abraham barks a laugh, his grin causing me to smile. "You will not crack like leather. But this will make it more pleasant for you. Trust me."

"I absolutely do."

His expression softens, and he tugs my breeches the rest of the way off. His eyes turn molten as they trace over me, my prick stiff beneath the bottom of my shirt. He lifts the fabric slowly, bending to lay a kiss upon my skin. This time, it's not my mouth he shows his affection to. A sound escapes my lips, and Abraham kisses me again, licking over the top of my prick and rumbling his approval at my answering whine. He moves upwards to tug off my shirt, and with the both of us bared before one another, Abraham lies over me and captures my mouth.

My hands shake as I hold him close, the rightness of this bringing me nearly to tears. This—him and me—isn't wrong. I refuse to believe it.

His lips dance with mine, each swipe enticing me, each parry a lure designed to draw me in. He can have the whole of me. I'd gladly lay myself at his feet if it meant even a minute more with Abraham.

He kisses down my neck. Over my clavicle. His lips press to my chest and my stomach and my hip. Deft fingers guide my knees to bend, my feet pressed flat to either side of Abraham as he settles back on his haunches.

My heart beats swiftly as he grabs the oil. He doesn't coat his prick as I expect him to. He rubs it over his fingers.

"Abe?" I question, his name a gasp as those fingers touch me lightly.

His voice comes smooth and gentle. "I must stretch you, Jasper. If I do not, this won't be a pleasurable experience for you."

"You've done it before?" I ask, the answer seeming obvious.

"Does that bother you?"

"No," I say, even as my chest aches at thinking of Abraham with another. "I suppose I should be grateful for it if I'm to benefit."

He lets out a quiet hum, lips pressing to my knee as his fingers rub over me. I try not to tense, but it's entirely foreign, what he's doing, and when he pushes, there's no stopping my surprise.

Abraham's voice is hoarse, his words distracting me away from the fingers pressing inside my body. "There won't ever be another for me, Jasper. Not now that I've found you."

"You mean that?" I ask, choking over the words.

"I do."

"I can't promise..."

"I know." He leans down to feather kisses along my waning prick. "I won't harbor upset over it, my love. I will not judge you by your birth."

I nearly sob at the affirmation of the request I gave Abraham when we first met. By all accounts, we shouldn't be here. We never should have become friends. Never should have become lovers. If not for Catherine falling ill, I wouldn't know Abraham's name. His eyes. His smile. The kiss of his lips.

I wouldn't know *him*, and that is not a world I wish to live in.

"Please take me, Abraham. I cannot bear another second apart."

His eyes meet mine, both tender and fierce.

I have no doubt Abraham Morris would grant me my heart's every desire. If only he were able.

CHAPTER 8

Abraham

Resisting Jasper has never been a strength of mine. With him all but pleading for me to mount him? I haven't the will to stay away.

I run my tongue up the length of his shaft, listening to his inhale, taking him into my mouth until he's fully hard once more. He watches me with trusting eyes, his cheeks rosy in the last of the evening sun.

I'd capture him like this if I could. Draw him for my own so that I'd never forget a single second.

But I am no artist. Nor keeper of time.

So like many things in life, I let myself appreciate the fleeting beauty in front of me before it's gone.

"Turn over," I request. "It will be easier for you. This first time."

Jasper nods, twisting onto his stomach atop the blanket, the sight of his bare cheeks before me nearly as arresting as his smile. I press a kiss to each side of his bottom.

"On your knees," I whisper.

Jasper hastens to comply, and it's near impossible to stop myself from touching. So I don't even try. I map my hands over his backside, down his thighs, brush my fingers up along the insides of his legs as they shake. His prick is hard, his body bared to me.

"Are you ready for my cock, Jasper?"

He inhales a shuddering breath, his audible shock at the improper word causing me to let loose a soft laugh. "*Abe.*"

"Have I scandalized you at last?"

Jasper looks back at me as I coat myself in oil. He licks his lips. "No. I'm ready for you. Please."

It's a true miracle I'm able to hold myself still as I press against him. His body doesn't yet know what to do to make this easier, so I ease forward slowly, whispering sweet words I hope will help him to relax.

"You are beautiful, my star. If I could, I would spend eternity here with you, and I wouldn't want for anything. I would look into your eyes and have everything I need."

"Abraham." The hitch in his voice has me running a hand over him soothingly.

"I know, tender heart. Is it manageable?"

He nods quickly, reaching back, searching. I twine my fingers with his, falling over his back, halfway inside of him now. I kiss his hair, his ear, his neck as I work myself further.

"You feel lovely. My cock is in Heaven, if such a place exists. There has never been a home as perfect for me as you."

Jasper's breath stutters out of him. "Abe."

My hips meet his skin, and I press a kiss to his cheek, his jaw, down to the top of his shoulder. "That is all of me."

"It is a lot."

"I know," I say, our joined hands braced together on the ground, my other closing over his prick. He's softened some, and I stroke him slowly, hoping I can bring his focus back to pleasure. "What does it feel like for you?"

His back rises and falls against my chest, sweat forming between us, the still night air making it all too easy to believe we're in a world of our own.

"I feel as if I have met your sword at last." His words stun me into silence and then scattered laughter. Jasper laughs with me, starting to swell in my grip as I rub my thumb along his sensitive skin. He moans lowly, a single syllable breathed into the air before his voice turns serious. "I feel as if we are one, Abraham. That we are meant to be so."

"We are," I agree wholeheartedly, shifting my hips slightly. Jasper makes a sound deep in his throat, stoking fire to life within my chest. "Again?"

"Yes."

I press into him again, over and over, a slow rolling of my hips that seems to suit Jasper. His fingers dig into the blanket around mine, and I move my other hand up to his chest, holding tight as I fit my lips to his neck, the salt of his sweat on my tongue. I kiss up and down the side of his throat, his shoulder, Jasper's small exclamations as I rut into him making me wish I were a poet, if only so I could do justice to the way he sets my soul alight.

"If I could wed you, my heart, I would do so in an instant."

Jasper pulls in a breath, his answer a whimper.

"I would hold you in our bed at night. Take you like this whenever you pleased. I would kiss every inch of you, swallow down the spend from your cock. I would belong to you happily, Jasper Sinclair. I already do. No matter our fortune in life, I will love you for all of our days and long after."

"Abraham." The hoarseness of his voice matches my own.

"I know, my love. Do you need to finish?"

"*Please.*"

I return my hand to Jasper's cock, tugging in time to my thrusts. His head is bowed, breath leaving him in ragged pants. He says my name—"*Abe*"—again and again, a note of fear there I understand all too well.

"Shh. I'm not going anywhere," I assure him.

Jasper cries out as he swells in my grip. It sounds anguished. Lovely and tortured. I squeeze his hand tight as his body ripples around me, and I let go of all I've been holding back. I flood Jasper as my desire for him consumes me. As it coalesces into a point so tight in my sternum, I lose my breath.

I remain wrapped around him for long minutes, our skin flushed, our breaths almost as one. When Jasper finally stirs, I slip carefully back, letting myself fall from his body, my hand guiding him to lie down. He edges to the side of the blanket, his form more difficult now to make out in the dark. But the outline of him shines, his eyes glittering as I lie beside him.

I sift my fingers through his hair, untangling the strands without hurry.

Jasper's voice is soft. "We're a mess."

"We'll wash in the creek before we go."

He nods, his fingertips trailing along my side, gentle points of contact. "I'm scared, Abraham."

My chest aches, a fierce thing. I pull Jasper's head around with my fingers at his cheek, and he meets my kiss eagerly, his grip on me tight. "What can I do to soothe you?"

"Would you tell me more? About the life we'd live?"

I swallow roughly, giving a single nod before continuing the slow passage of my fingers through his hair. "Our home would be small. Enough for the two of us. There would be a hearth, of course, to keep us warm. We'd cook our meals there, bread topped with honey."

He turns to rest more fully against my side, wrapped still in my arms. "Where would we get the honey?"

"Our bees, of course."

"Is that so?" A touch of amusement laces his tone.

"Mm. There would be a bed, made soft by layers and layers of straw and blankets. A chair in the corner where you'd write."

"Letters?"

"Yes," I tell him. "And you'd teach me to do the same. We'd have gardens out back. Pigs, perhaps. And not another soul in sight. Except for maybe Catherine and my mother, if they wished to join us."

Jasper sighs against my chest, his breath a whisper over my skin. "It sounds like a wonderful life."

I bite the inside of my cheek hard enough to cull back the sound that wants to escape my throat. "Yes," I say at last. "It does, doesn't it?"

Jasper lays his head on my arm, looking at me in the dark. Is he picturing it as I am? The future that will never come to pass?

"Are you sore?" I ask quietly.

"Only a little. I would weather it a million times over to be close to you again. Will you do that to me often?"

A smile pulls at my lips. "As often as you'd like."

He hums, a contented cat with his cream. "I wrote you a letter the other day."

"Did you?"

"I was missing you."

He offers himself so readily I have the sudden urge to craft a suit of armor for Jasper so that no one could touch him save for me.

"Will you tell me what you wrote?" I ask.

He makes an almost frustrated sound. "I can't remember all of it, but... The stars were out, and I could see them from my window. It was a comfort because when I look at the stars, I'm reminded of you. I was imagining you with your sword and how handsome you'd be."

My chest warms. "Do you find me handsome, Jasper?"

His voice is full of nothing but earnestness. "Very. You make my breath come short and my heart leap. I never felt that for another before you. I didn't know, at first, what to make of it."

I run my fingers along his jaw, the skin smooth and warm. "I think you're the most beautiful man I've ever set eyes on," I tell him seriously. "But even if I didn't have eyes, I would want you just the same."

Jasper captures my wandering hand, pulling it over his heart. "What are we to do?"

"Continue as we are," I answer, the hitch of his breath causing my chest to constrict. "It's all we *can* do."

Jasper nods, his forehead brushing mine before his mouth seeks my own, urgent in its demand. He pulls me on top of him, and I go easily, settling between his legs, taking from his mouth at a pace matched only by what he's willing to give me. He reaches for my cock, coaxing me to hardness, tugging me toward him as if desperate to have me within his body once more. I slow only long enough to grab the oil, and then I'm sinking inside Jasper a second time.

Our coupling is frantic, Jasper leaving the evidence of his arousal smeared along my stomach as I punch soft grunts and whispered moans from his lips. His hands tug at me, and I plant my palms on the ground, seeking to imprint myself inside his very being so that he'll never again be without the memory of my touch.

Jasper throws his head back when I wrap my hand around his prick, his cry of ecstasy one I tuck away inside my heart. He heaves against me, his spend on our stomachs as I empty inside the tight clasp of his body, grateful to be leaving myself there. To be giving Jasper evidence of our time together, however brief.

He doesn't unwind his arms from around me, and I leave soft kisses over his cheeks and chin as he trembles.

"Don't lose hope," I beg of him quietly. "Never that. When you feel lost, look at the stars and know I am looking at them with you."

A tear slips down his cheek, cold against my nose. "My warrior."

"Forevermore," I vow.

It's late when Jasper and I finally move off the cold, blanketed ground. I'll need to clean the wool again before long, but I leave it for another day, walking half-clothed with Jasper to the creek. We wash under the light of the stars, the moon but a sliver tonight.

Jasper looks like a dream, bare skin glinting, soft laughter leaving his lips as he splashes cold water over himself. "If we must do this in the winter, I'll freeze."

"We can use cloths instead," I assure him. "It will be enough until you can return home and wash properly."

He hums his agreement, climbing out onto the grass and shaking out his limbs.

"Here," I say, handing over my shirt. "To dry off."

"You'll need it."

"I'll be fine."

He sighs softly, but he accepts the garment, drying perfunctorily before slipping on his clothes. I pull the damp shirt over my head, not minding the chill. Jasper finds his stockings in the grass, pulling them on, followed by his shoes. He stalls once he has his waistcoat buttoned, as if he doesn't want to go.

"Thank you, Abraham."

His words are quiet, but I hear them nonetheless.

"What for?"

He lets out a slow breath. "For freeing me."

I pull Jasper's hand to my mouth, kissing the back of it lightly. His fingers twist with mine for a moment before he steps away. He's nearly halfway up the hill when he stops, turning around abruptly.

With a single stutter-step, Jasper runs back my way, not stopping until he's within the clasp of my arms. He kisses me soundly, a lingering smile on his lips, the shape of him so familiar I'm more than certain I could pick him out in the darkest of nights.

When Jasper finally steps back, the smile on his face never wavers. He turns once more. And then he walks off.

Maybe ruin isn't the right word for what Jasper has wrought by coming into my life. There's another that feels far more appropriate.

Rebirth.

CHAPTER 9

Jasper

It seems cruelly fitting that it's once again a Tuesday, nearly a year after I met Abraham, when everything breaks apart.

My feet drag tiredly as I walk the distance back home after my evening spent in Abraham's company. I'm in my own head, remembering the sweetness of his lips and the softness of his touch, not paying attention to my surroundings, when I notice candlelight coming from within my house. My pulse stutters before beginning to race.

I hurry the remaining steps home, ready to climb through my open window when Catherine comes racing out the back door.

"Catherine, what—"

She clamps her hand over my mouth before I can utter another word, pulling me off to the side of the house where we're hidden.

"They know," she says at a whisper.

My stomach plummets toward the ground. "That I've gone?"

She shakes her head quickly, dressed in her nightclothes, her hair in disarray. "About *him*."

A lance of fear hits me square on. "No."

"Yes," she says urgently. "You were spotted, Jasper. By one of the men from the printer. He saw your face but not the Morris boy's."

Relief fills my lungs, allowing me to speak. "So Abraham is safe."

Even in the dark, I can see Catherine's agonized expression. "But you are not, sweet boy. Don't you see? Word will spread. You can't stay. It's a death sentence."

My breath is promptly knocked from my lungs, and I curl in on myself, grabbing my knees to remain upright. "Catherine."

"I know, my boy. Your father is securing a horse. Your mother is packing clothes."

I shake my head, feeling faint, her words not making any sense. "I don't understand."

Catherine's hands pluck my face up, her touch grounding. "Despite their hard countenances, neither your mother nor your father want to see you dead, Jasper. Your father will say you ran and he went on horseback after you. Your mother will deny knowing a thing. You will leave, and you will never return."

I inhale deeply, my body starting to shake. "I can't..."

"You must."

"But Abraham..."

"Will watch you die if you do not run."

Ah.

Catherine squeezes my shoulders as I work to steady myself. She's right. Of course she's right.

But *oh mercy*, how will I go?

"Do you... love me less... now that you know?" I ask around my labored breaths, my throat constricting tightly.

"Oh, my sweet boy," Catherine says, a waver in her voice. "Never."

I nod again and again, trying to get my wits about me, looking around frantically as if I'll find answers somewhere out here in the dark. "How long do I have?"

"Your father will return within the hour. No more than that. Be quick."

"I have to say goodbye," I choke out.

"I know. Go, Jasper. Do not be seen."

Catherine tugs me in close, placing a trembling kiss on my cheek. I wrap her in my arms, realizing this is the last time I'll be able to do this. If I never return...

The pain nearly causes me to crumple.

I kiss Catherine's forehead before spinning and running back the way I came.

My feet take me toward Abraham faster than they ever have before. I ignore the pain in my side and the way my shirt has lifted from my breeches and run. A branch scrapes my cheek as I move through the woods toward his home, so I hold my arm out in front of me, stumbling over roots, my breathing much too loud.

When I see his house through the trees, I stop, pulling in air and watching for anyone who might be passing at this late hour. The seconds tick painfully by, but, finally, I step out into the clearing and approach the small home. The window is covered, but I pray Abraham hears me through the thin barrier.

"Abraham," I call at a hiss.

I wait before attempting it again, raising my voice only slightly. Seconds later, the door opens, and Abraham's wide eyes meet mine. "Jasper?"

"Come," I say quickly, racing back toward the trees. I don't check to confirm he's following, knowing he will.

I stop only once I reach the safety of the creek, and then I work to catch my breath.

"Jasper." Worry is heavy on Abraham's face as he comes to a stop in front of me, his hands bracketing my cheeks, callused thumbs stroking over my skin. "What is it?"

I can't find the words. I wrap my arms around him, my face pressed against his chest, and cry. Abraham shushes me gently, his hands rubbing soothing paths along my back. It feels like a lifetime before I'm able to speak, even though I know it's only minutes. Minutes neither of us have.

"I came to say goodbye," I manage.

Abraham stills, pulling me back from his chest to look at me in the dark. "Goodbye?"

"Abe," I croak. "I've been found out."

He stiffens further, his voice a harsh whisper. "Jasper."

"I'm leaving. I must."

"I'll go with you."

Another sob wracks my throat. "You can't. Your mother."

"I..."

This time, it's me soothing Abraham. I run my palms along his neck, anchoring there, his skin warm and his pulse feathering against me. His mother would not survive without him; we both know it to be true. She hasn't the means to do so. Nor can she travel. I would never—could never—ask Abraham to choose me instead.

"You cannot leave your mother," I voice softly. "And I cannot stay. If they learn who you are, you'll be killed. If I don't go, I suffer the same. If we run together, we condemn your mother to death. There is but one choice here."

Abraham looks as if he's been gutted. "Oh, my heart."

"You know I am right."

He lays his forehead to mine, his whole body shaking. "There must be a way."

"This is not a battle we win, my warrior."

The sound he makes tears at me viciously. Tears run down my cheeks. Down Abraham's. His voice is no more than a rasp. "I cannot watch you go."

"Then you will not watch."

Abraham rubs his jaw along my cheek, his breath stuttering, his tears hot on my skin. "Please don't ask this of me, Jasper. How am I to let you walk away from me? How am I to live with it?"

"Abe," I say roughly. "You *must*. You must live and live well. It will be my only consolation, my only salve, to know you are here, healthy and strong. I will not survive it otherwise. I do not wish to know a world that does not have you in it. Please. *Please*, live as happily as you can. For me."

His lips find my temple, and my eyes slip shut. If I could prolong this moment, I would. I'd live in it forever. But I know I must go. I must run. And soon.

I could not bear it if Abraham had to watch me be put to death.

"Where are you to go?" The question seems to pain him, hoarsely spoken as it is.

"I do not know. Far away, I suspect."

He pulls in a reedy breath, his chest shuddering against me. "Will... Will I ever see you again?"

My swallow is harsh. "In this life? I am not certain. If there is a way for me to safely return to you, I will find it, Abraham. I promise you that."

"Jasper." He rocks me, his face buried in my hair. "My heart. My star. My love. Whoever it was that wove the fabric of my being did it with you in mind. I was made to love you. And I will do so no matter where on this earth you are. My love for you will never, ever flicker out."

"Then I will look at the stars," I say, voice catching, "and be reminded of it every day."

Abraham holds me as the moon reflects gently off the surface of the creek. The stars fill the sky with their twinkling light, the sword high to the north, blade aimed as if ready to pierce a heart.

It feels as if it's piercing mine.

"I must go," I say at last.

Abraham doesn't loosen his hold.

"Abe," I say softly, pulling his face around. I kiss him in a gentle press, lips meeting, a greeting, a farewell, beauty and sorrow. I offer him my own promise. The only reassurance I can give. "I will love you no matter where. No matter when."

He nods, even as a terrible sound leaves his throat.

"Turn around now," I whisper. "And don't look back. The next time you see me, it will be upon my return to you."

His inhale is broken, but he doesn't move. Perhaps he can't. I pull his hands off of me slowly, one by one, squeezing each before letting them drop to his sides. With a small nudge on my part, Abraham turns stiltedly in place. Tears slip down my cheeks as I hear him crying.

His voice, when he speaks, is a fragment of itself. "Be it swiftly."

I take in a small, steadying breath, even as I break apart. Every piece of me. Every atom. "Be it swiftly."

When I reach the top of the hill, I look over my shoulder. Abraham is standing beside our creek, his back to me, his arms around his stomach. He shimmers in place until I wipe the tears from my eyes.

I turn back around, keep walking, and don't look back.

My house is a flurry of activity when I arrive. Catherine spares me a quick glance as I come through the door, packing a hunk of hard cheese into a sack already full. My mother spots me and hurries over, her eyes fluttering over me before her hands come to rest on my shoulders.

"You know," I say before she can utter a word. I need not tell her of the conversation I had with Catherine. It would be clear in any case that something is greatly amiss.

"Jasper," my mother says thickly. "*Others* know. We must get you out."

My breath shakes once more. "You do not hate me for it?"

She doesn't answer, but her face falls.

"I'm sorry," I tell her, my tears back in full force. "I'm so sorry."

"Hush now," she says, leading me toward the front of the house. "There isn't time for it. Your father is waiting."

I let out a sudden gasp. "A moment," I say, racing to my bedchamber. I find the bundle of letters I wrote for Abraham and tuck them into my waistcoat, unwilling to leave them behind.

Catherine hands me the sack at the front door. I swing it over my shoulder, feeling as if I'm floating along in a dream, none of this real. How is it real? Yet deep down, I know there's no waking from this. This is it. I'm going, and I know not if I'll ever return.

My mother urges me out the door. Catherine says a soft goodbye. I find my father a ways down from our house, out of sight, preparing the horse. With no words spoken between us, he helps me atop its back and follows.

We race out of town in the middle of the night, my memories of Abraham tucked against my heart, my chest so tight it feels as if I'm dying.

Heartbreak, that's what they call this.

I only wish the last I saw of my beloved Abraham wasn't his own heart broken to pieces because of me.

PART II
Charlie and Arthur

CHAPTER 10

Charlotte

"On behalf of God and his church, I now pronounce you husband and wife. You may kiss the bride."

There's a collective sigh as Arthur leans forward, pressing a chaste kiss to my lips. His hand squeezes mine, a silent show of support, before the organ starts up again. I inhale sharply at the sound, and Arthur chuckles, the light in his eyes making me feel as if we're the only two people standing within the expansive church.

The resonant music encourages us down the aisle, and I'm fortunate Arthur is there to lend a hand, as my head is feeling light. We pass our gathered family and acquaintances seated in the pews. I don't look directly at them, knowing my mother would chastise me for forgetting etiquette, but I have no doubt there are many glassy eyes watching us.

I wonder, briefly, if I should feel poorly for not crying myself. It is, after all, one of the happiest moments of my life, truly.

But a single glance at Arthur and those still-teasing eyes sets me at immediate ease. My husband does not judge me for my lack of tears. He understands me more than I could have ever known to hope for.

My husband.

Arthur gives the hand I have resting on his forearm a squeeze, as if sensing I may be in need of it. I smile at him softly before refocusing on the exit in front of us, not wanting to trip in my heels so close to escape. I might never get up again, considering the heft of my skirts.

We're collected outside of the church, a buggy waiting to take us to a home I won't return to again after today, not unless I'm a guest. Arthur helps me to board the buggy, and then he follows, both of us seated on the plush bench facing forward. With a whip of the reins, our coachman sets us into motion.

"How do you fare, my love?" Arthur's voice is quiet but carries over the clomp of hooves.

"I can't breathe," I tell him truthfully.

He lets out a gentle laugh, his hand clasping mine tight. "I'll see if I can help with that once we're inside."

"Will you really?"

Those clever brown eyes smile at me in that way I'm so used to. "Really, truly. No wife of mine shall be forced to lose her breath for the enjoyment of others."

My throat feels tight, and I bring my hand to our joined ones, squeezing Arthur with both. It's not the easiest position to manage considering the bulk of my dress, but Arthur looks pleased at the gesture. And like he very much would like to kiss me again.

Arthur keeps his voice low, mindful of our company, even as his thumb strokes over my gloved palm. "You look lovely, my dear Charlotte. I've never in my life been graced by a more beautiful sight."

"I look like a powder puff."

Arthur laughs, a loud boom that causes the coachman to clear his throat. My husband quiets quickly, but my lips twitch as his shoulders continue to shake.

He leans close to whisper at my ear. "The loveliest powder puff."

I hold my tongue, knowing the extravagance of my wedding gown is a luxury I should be grateful for. Not only is it bleached starkly white, a fortune in and of itself, but the fabric is hand-stitched with light blue flowers along the hemlines and veil. Even my pristine white gloves have a blue flower each near my elbows. No expense was spared, and I'm honored by that.

But it doesn't change the fact that all I want is to get out of this corset and to throw the stiff crinoline under my skirts into the river so that I never have to wear the uncomfortable garment again.

A woman—especially a bride—is supposed to want to look beautiful. Delicate and proper.

All I want is to breathe.

Arthur holds my hand all the way to my parents' manor. We're the first to arrive, of course, everyone else following us from the church. The butler opens the door before we've even departed the buggy, his arm held behind his back, the epitome of poise. Arthur assists me to the ground, and I wobble on my heel before righting myself and walking with him to the door.

"Good morning, Mr. and Mrs. Kane," the butler says, bowing low.

My heart stutters. *Kane.* No longer Valentine.

"How do you do, Clarence." Arthur's greeting is casual. He's never been one to stick to formalities, not even those expected from one of his station.

"More than fine, sir," Clarence answers, waving us inside. "Please. The drawing room is ready for you."

Arthur thanks the butler as we pass, his arm held aloft as a guide. Instead of leading me into the drawing room, Arthur walks down the hall into the downstairs bath not generally used by guests of the house. He closes the door, the two of us barely fitting inside, my skirts pressed to both the wall and the small sink.

"Arthur?"

"Turn around. We don't have much time before our reception guests are to arrive."

With a skip in my chest, I spin, wondering if it's possible to fall more in love with this man with every passing day. I knew early in our courtship that Arthur was special. That I could have a marriage based on what my heart desired, the kind you only hear about in romantic tales. It's rare to find that, I know. I'm lucky Arthur met my father when he did.

And yet, no matter how many hours we share, no matter how many days, my affection for Arthur Kane only seems to flourish more wildly. Will that ever come to an end? I can't bear to think of a time where I might not love him so.

Arthur's fingers slide lightly over my shoulder blades before he begins unbuttoning the top of my gown. It takes time, but his movements are deft and practiced. It's certainly not the first occasion in which he's undressed me, not that my parents are aware of such.

Once through the fabric of my dress, he tackles my corset. At the first loosen of the laces holding it tight, I draw in a breath, my lungs stinging in both relief and aching pain.

"Better?"

"So much," I say, sucking in gentle breaths as Arthur reties the laces, ensuring my corset is looser than before. He begins the arduous task of relooping the small fabric hooks over the delicate buttons on my bodice next, not once complaining. If anything, he seems happy simply because I am.

He tugs me back around once done, eyes roaming over me from top to bottom. "If we had time for it, my love, I would gladly climb under your skirts."

"Arthur," I admonish, even as my cheeks heat. "Please don't make me feel so when I must stand in front of everyone we've ever known and pretend as if my newlywed husband doesn't already know precisely what's under my skirts."

His eyes dance, his handsome face the picture of devotion and joy. Plus no small amount of mischief.

I would capture it for all of eternity if I could.

Arthur's voice is gentle as he opens the door, his hand holding mine. "Come, my dear. Let us receive our guests so that we may be alone once more."

I surely won't argue against that.

Arthur and I find a place to stand in the drawing room, and for the next many hours, we accept well wishes, congratulations on our union being given to Arthur only. To speak the words to me would be considered rude, as a bride is meant to be a prize. My mother looks proud to have a daughter married into such a respected, highborn family, whereas my father wears a small smile I suspect is equal parts pride for having found me such a good match and happiness at knowing my marriage is one I so heartily approve of.

It will be strange not to come back to this house except to visit. My home will be with Arthur now. I will live in his manor with his staff and a bed we call our own. I've never had that: the chance to simply sleep by this man's side. To love him openly, instead of under the watchful eye of others. There will be no more sneaking around simply because we couldn't wait to see one another again. No more trysts in the most uncomfortable of locations.

This man is tied to me. For the rest of our lives. He is my husband, and I... I am his wife.

Arthur catches my eye, a tiny smile on his face as he mouths, "Breathe."

The reminder is welcome. I pull in a breath as Arthur's hand discreetly smooths down my spine. It's a quick and subtle caress, but my tension abates nonetheless, and I return my focus to talk of the university where both Arthur and my father teach.

After breakfast is served, of which I barely eat any courtesy of my corset not allowing for such, my mother collects me from Arthur's side under the guise of helping me to freshen up before we're to travel. She leads me to the bath upstairs, which has a large, standing tub, and then closes the door.

I've barely sat on the toilet, my mother helping to hold my skirts out of the way, when she says, "Are you aware of what's expected of you tonight, Charlotte?"

My pulse skitters before I force a calming breath through my body. "Yes, Mother."

"You're to be at the disposal of your husband. Whenever he pleases. It is not your place to express disapproval at any time. Do you understand?"

"Yes," I say quietly.

"We have our duties," she continues, dropping my skirts as I stand. "It's best to remember that. Your husband will not appreciate your...flights of fancy. You're a wed woman now, and you'll need to behave as such."

I keep my eyes on the sink basin as I wash my hands, the urge to correct my mother that Arthur is different, that he loves me for me, bit back like so many other words I don't dare speak aloud. My mother wouldn't understand. No one would.

"Charlotte," she says, voice firm. "Did you hear me?"

"Yes, Mother," I respond, my eyes catching my reflection in the mirror. Fair skin. Pink cheeks. Chestnut hair pulled up in curls and blue eyes that hold my own for only a second before skittering away. I turn for the door, swallowing heavily. "I heard you."

I seek out Arthur as soon as we return to the drawing room. As if sensing my silent plea for rescue, his eyes find mine and he weaves his way through the crowd.

Upon reaching me, he loops his arm with mine. "Are you refreshed?"

"Quite," I say, glad my mother seems to have missed his saucy tone based on her pleasant smile.

"Then we can be off."

Our guests see us out the door, throwing rice as we approach the waiting buggy. Arthur once again helps me to board, and I catch my father's eyes as I take my seat. He inclines his head, an almost wistful smile on his face that reminds me of years past. Of sitting with him in his study, hearing tales of the stars and looking through his telescope before he deemed me too old for such things. A lady, officially.

I offer a scant smile in return, and Arthur takes his seat beside me. As the buggy brings us away from the home I grew up in, I say a quiet farewell to Charlotte Valentine.

I wait until we're a good ways away to give Arthur's hand a squeeze. "Will you tell me now where we are spending our newlywed solitude?"

His lips twist, a teasing smirk. "Home."

I suck in a gasp, and Arthur goes on.

"Two full weeks hidden away where not a soul will think to look for us."

"Oh, Arthur."

"Does that suit?" Nerves enter his voice that weren't there before. "If you'd rather travel away, I can certainly make that happen, my love. But I thought—"

"You thought right," I assure him, letting my shoulder rest against his. "There's nothing I'd love more than to go home with you."

He lets out a happy hum, his hand curling over the top of mine. I wish I could feel the heat of him without the glove in the way. Soon enough.

The buggy pulls up in front of a beautiful manor a mere half an hour later. The façade is light tan, windows placed in every direction, the home made of more rooms than the two of us could ever need.

"Arthur," I say, astounded. "This is where you live?"

He brings my hand to his mouth to place a gentle kiss over my glove. "Where we live. May I show you?"

I nod, allowing Arthur to help me from the buggy. He leads me to the front door, opening it himself, walking me from room to room as I take everything in. It's opulent, furnished in the finest trappings, and yet still, every detail is warm and inviting, reminding me of Arthur himself.

"Where is everyone?" I ask, the two of us ascending the stairs.

"I asked the staff to give us privacy while we settled in. Is that all right?"

"Yes," I say, throat happily tight. "It's quite perfect, actually."

His smile is softly pleased.

Arthur leads me to the master bedroom, opening the door and standing just inside as I walk the space. The bed is covered in red linens, the coverlet red and gold. Plush chairs sit to either side of the bed, wardrobes next to each. Past windows that overlook the front lawn is a vanity made of fine mahogany wood with a soft tufted stool in front. A large mirror is attached, the piece not something Arthur would have needed for himself. Which means he placed it here for me. In anticipation of my arrival.

A soft rug passes underfoot as I recross the room, Arthur watching me carefully.

He accepts my hand as I near. "You can change anything you like."

I shake my head. Our possessions are of no matter. Not truly. "It's lovely," I tell him, knowing the thought Arthur put into it is unmatched.

The worry in his expression eases, the barest hint of early silver beside his temples the only indication of Arthur's age. I've never minded the ten years that separate us. If anything, I'm glad for Arthur's wisdom and patience, even if he doesn't care for the gray hairs I find so charming.

I run my fingers through those hairs lightly. "Would you kiss me, husband? The one time I met your lips today was not nearly enough."

Arthur's mouth curves into a smile before he cups my face, leans close, and kisses me softly. He's always so soft. So sweetly affectionate. I've never felt anything but loved in his arms. Even in the times where his mischief comes out to play.

He breaks from my lips but doesn't go far. "Would you like to get rid of this corset now?"

I whine in relief, and Arthur chuckles.

"Turn around then."

I go gladly, Arthur's lips meeting my neck as he unbuttons my gown for the second time today. Warm fingers trail inside the fabric, teasing my skin. He loosens the corset, and I nearly sag. Arthur goes for the band of my crinoline next.

"Oh, please," I encourage.

Another chuckle passes over my skin, and then the band is opened around my waist, even as the structured petticoat doesn't move an inch.

"Here."

Arthur directs me to the edge of the bed. I lean my weight there as he drops to the floor, lifting my skirts. My pulse skips, the sight of him disappearing under the fabric devilish in the best of ways. He tugs the crinoline loose, helping my legs and feet from it before tossing the entire thing behind him. I laugh as it rolls a ways before coming to a stop.

"That's better." Arthur's words are murmured as his head pops back into view, his hands sliding over my legs. His eyes meet mine as he places a soft kiss atop my knee. "What would you like, my wife?"

My heart skips again for an entirely different reason, my mother's words returning to me. It's not hard to see how aroused Arthur is beneath his elegant trousers. "Whatever you desire," I answer, even as my pulse races. "Do you wish to bed me, husband?"

Arthur stills, his hands warm on my thighs. Perhaps he could hear the tremor in my voice because his own tone is gentle. "Charlotte. We've discussed this."

I nod, swallowing. "Yes, but it's your wedding night. Surely you'd like to experience all that entails."

Arthur lets out a soft breath, hitching my skirts higher as his hands climb, the fabric yielding now without the crinoline in the way. He kisses my inner thigh once, a second time even higher. "It is *our* wedding night. And the times we've tried intercourse, you have not liked it. It's all right if you don't want that, my love. I'm more than happy to use my mouth."

My breath stutters, and Arthur smiles, a glint entering his eye.

"That's it, isn't it?" He shifts the fabric higher, until I'm exposed. "Let me love you, Charlotte Kane. It's the only thing in this world I desire."

Helpless to argue against what I want most, I nod, tears pooling unshed in my eyes as Arthur holds my gaze. He drops a kiss to my skin, and I help hold up my skirts, allowing myself to experience the pleasure I've only ever known with him.

The day Arthur Kane came into my world was the most fortuitous of my life.

I think, quite possibly, that good fortune is here to stay.

CHAPTER 11

Arthur

Charlotte is asleep when I wake, her dark hair spread atop her pillow. Her face is soft in slumber, and my chest eases at the sight.

She's here at last.

The sun is streaming through the window, but for once, I don't rush to start my day. I have the next two weeks off from the university, my time reserved for far more important matters than geometry.

Charlotte stirs when I run my fingers along her bare shoulder. I'm about to apologize for waking her when her eyes flutter open and she offers me a soft smile.

"Good morning," I say, keeping my voice quiet.

"It is, isn't it?"

She rolls toward me, the move causing the sheet to drag lower on her body. I can't quite help but follow its path, yet the moment my fingertips draw close to Charlotte's breast, she tenses.

I quickly redirect my hand, running the backs of my fingers along her arm. "Would you like something to eat?"

"Please. Is your staff here to prepare a meal?"

My lips twitch into a smile. "They are. But even if they weren't, I'm sure I could manage to cook an egg or two."

Charlotte's eyes widen in obvious surprise. "Truly?"

"Indeed," I answer. "Would you like tea with your meal? Coffee?"

"Tea, please."

After pecking a quick kiss to Charlotte's nose, which has her wrinkling her face in feigned offense and me chuckling in response, I roll out of bed. She watches me dress, a sort of appraisal in her eyes I've always found curious considering how shy she is with her own body. But I do not mind it, neither her shyness nor her bold eye, so I let her have her fill as I ready myself to walk downstairs.

"I'll return shortly," I tell her, earning a smile.

The hall is quiet as I head to the bath to wash my face and hands and take care of necessities. It's quiet still when I reemerge.

I find my staff in the kitchen downstairs, conversing over their own morning coffee and tea. They jump up nearly as one, but I quickly raise a hand.

"Please, no need to fuss," I assure them all. "I only came down to procure breakfast for Charlotte and myself."

Ella, my head cook, gives me a stern roll of her eyes. "As if we wouldn't fuss," she says, going to the counter, where an apple tart sits. She begins to cut slices from it. "We're absolutely beside ourselves to have the girl here, and you're hiding her from us."

Ruby, the new kitchen maid, looks at Ella, aghast.

"It's all right, Ruby," I say, knowing what she must think of Ella's seemingly insolent tone. "Ella is free to speak her mind here, as are you. And I am not hiding her." I raise a challenging brow at Ella. "I only wish to give her time to acclimate."

She waves a hand over her shoulder as my longtime butler, Willard, clears his throat. "I've brought her trunks into the parlor, sir. But I didn't think it wise to attempt unpacking them last evening."

"Certainly not," I agree, attempting to hold back my smile as I remember my evening with Charlotte. "Whenever we are free from the room today will suit."

Willard nods, and Ella cracks an egg into a pan while Ruby prepares a kettle for tea. I quickly realize one member of the staff is missing.

"Where's Bess?"

Willard is the one to answer me. "Already up and about the house, sir."

"I hope she stopped for breakfast first?"

Ella nods. "She did. But you know Bess. Everything must be pristine for our new arrival."

In other words, Bess is nervous and taking out her energy on the house. Not that I mind, as her position as housemaid is to keep the manor clean and orderly. But I don't want her overexerting herself.

When Ella finishes with the eggs, she sets them on plates beside the apple tart and a couple spoonfuls each of baked beans. The kettle is added, as well as two cups, and Ruby reaches for the tray.

"Allow me," I say, picking it up.

Ruby, once again, looks aghast.

I can hear Ella chuckling as I exit the kitchen, using my shoulder to push open the swing door into the pantry and then another out into the dining room. I pass by the table and find Bess on my way upstairs. She's in the drawing room, dusting the same furniture she tackled the day before last.

"Bess," I say gently.

She wheels around, hand at her chest. The young woman has been at the manor for over four years, but she still startles easily. "Goodness. Can I help you, sir?"

"Arthur is fine," I remind her, although Ella is the only one who seems comfortable enough to forgo the title when addressing me. I do understand. "Only a reminder that the day is fine and the sun is already shining. Perhaps a stroll in the gardens is in order."

She blinks at me before some of her tension eases. "Are you requesting I stop to smell the roses?"

"Oh, well, that does sound nice. Don't you think?"

Bess smiles as I continue on my way toward the stairs. It takes some finagling to open the door into my chamber with my hands overfull, but I manage it at last. Charlotte sits up in bed, holding the sheet high to cover herself. She looks relieved once she sees no one is with me.

"Look at that," I say lightly, shutting the door behind me. "I stumbled across some breakfast."

She lets out a soft laugh. "Arthur. Please tell me you didn't make that tart yourself? If you have, I shall demand you tell me immediately what else I've failed to learn about my husband."

There's no concealing my grin as I set the tray on the bed, sitting bent-legged beside it. "The tart was not my creation," I admit. "Nor did I cook the eggs this time. I can, however, whip up a fairly tasty fricassee."

"You've been hiding yourself." Charlotte's words are said in good humor, her eyes watching appreciatively as I pour our tea.

"The only surprises will be pleasant ones," I assure her. Although her comment about hiding does remind me... "Would you like to meet the staff today? There's no rush, of course. Or we could go for a walk around the gardens. They're quite plentiful out back."

"Both, I think. I'd very much like to learn everything about this place."

I nod, and Charlotte accepts a plate from the tray, tucking the sheet under her arm to hold it in place. It looks difficult for her, the way she's balancing both tasks in order to eat.

"Charlotte, dear. Would you like a shirt?"

She looks surprised by the offer, but I recognize the hope in her eyes and hop up to grab one in haste. I take her plate once I'm seated back on the bed and hold the opening of the simple cotton shirt in her direction. She slips her arms inside, letting the sheet fall as the garment covers her breasts and stomach. She tucks it around herself with a soft smile, looking immediately comforted.

I breathe a sigh of relief, offering her the plate once more. As Charlotte cuts into her tart, I sip my tea.

She hums before long. "This is lovely. Your cook is very talented."

"That she is," I agree, breaking the yolk in my egg before piling a small piece of it with beans onto my fork. "I'm certainly lucky to have her. She's keen to know your preferences, by the by. I think she'd rather appreciate the chance to try cooking a new dish or two."

"Then I'll gladly think on what I may like." Charlotte's eyes return to her plate as she asks, "Will I...have a lady's maid?"

"I have interviews lined up at the end of the week," I tell her, noticing the pinch in her brow. "Unless... Do you not want one? It's entirely up to you."

"It's proper, is it not?"

"I don't much care about proper," I readily admit. "If you prefer to bathe and dress yourself, I haven't a problem with it. I do not have a valet, Charlotte."

"You don't?"

Her relief is palpable, and not for the first time, I try to puzzle out what, exactly, I have yet to pinpoint when it comes to Charlotte's every comfort being met.

"I do not," I confirm. "You'd like for me to cancel the interviews, wouldn't you?"

"Please." The answer is soft but decisive.

I tuck an errant strand of Charlotte's hair behind her ear. "Consider it done, my dear."

Charlotte and I finish our meal with talk of the manor. I give her more details about the library, which is filled with books from generations past, as well as go over our extensive indoor plumbing, which I know Charlotte herself is used to. I explain the gardens out back and tell her of the roses planted using cuttings of those I grew up with. She seems especially interested in seeing the third floor and the spiraling staircase that leads there.

Once our stomachs are satisfied, I set the tray aside. Since the only clothing of Charlotte's we have access to is her wedding gown and the corset she surely doesn't wish to wear, I jog downstairs to grab an outfit befitting the day.

Charlotte looks stunned as I come through the doorway with a full trunk in my hands, since I wasn't sure what she'd prefer.

"Arthur." There's laughter in her tone as she steps off the bed as if to help me. In the end, she simply watches me place the trunk near the foot of the bed, my shirt covering her hips but not her bare legs. I quickly double back to shut the door, although the staff is nowhere near.

Catching my breath, I wave to the trunk. "Voila."

With a chuckle, Charlotte opens the top. I give her privacy to dress, closing the drapes and making myself busy with straightening the various items on her vanity. When I finally turn around, Charlotte is pulling the tie at the back of her dress tight.

"If you ever can't reach, I'm happy to help," I tell her, knowing her more formal attire may be difficult to navigate on her own. But if Charlotte doesn't want a lady's maid for such, I certainly won't force her.

She nods, giving me a soft, grateful smile. But the moment she finishes her tie and runs her hands over the fabric, smoothing it at her waist, I see it. The dimming of her eyes. Like a candle blown out.

"Do you need a different trunk, my love?"

"No." Charlotte's reply is quick, another smile offered my way. "This is perfect. Now let me tidy my hair, and you can show me the gardens."

Putting away my frown, I collect our breakfast tray and bring it back to the kitchen while Charlotte pins her hair. By the time I return, she's ready, her locks in a gentle twist at the back of her head. I offer my arm, and she accepts it easily, the two of us walking to the back lawn.

Charlotte's gaze roams over the hollyhocks that are in bloom as we stroll leisurely through the gardens. "What time do you regularly leave?"

"For the university? After breakfast. My lecture ends by midafternoon, and I'll return shortly thereafter."

"May I use your library while you're gone?"

"*Our* library," I say, giving her hand a squeeze on my arm. "And of course. You're welcome anywhere within your home. And...if there's anything you need to be happy, please do tell me, Charlotte. I will get it for you."

She aims a gentle smile my way before stopping in front of a wall of roses, the blooms here a mix of red and white. "I've always liked roses."

"Is that so?"

"They have a bite." She flashes a grin before tapping, ever so gently, the thorn at one stem. It doesn't pierce her, but she rubs her thumb over her fingertip nonetheless.

"Then they are like you," I say, understanding now why she likes them.

Charlotte looks at me in surprise. "How so?"

"Charlotte, love, you are so much more than your finery and the fairness of your features. Surely you must know it's the very reason you stole my affection?"

A second passes. And then two. "Do you not fear me drawing blood?"

"I would gladly shed it for you," I tell her, lifting her fingertip to my mouth and kissing it. "If it would bring you closer to me, I would shed it all."

Charlotte's voice shakes, although her expression gives little away. "That's not how it's supposed to be, Arthur. A man is to own his wife. Not bleed for her."

"And when have I ever expressed interest in controlling you, Charlotte Kane? It is you who holds my very heart in your palm. You own me with every flex of your hand. And I am your willing captive."

"So if I demand for you to kiss me?"

"I would ask where."

Charlotte tugs me in by my cravat, her request clear. I meet her lips with my own, the softness of her mouth a temptation I have no desire to resist getting lost in. Her beauty has drawn me in since the moment I met her; that's true. But it's the person she is at her core that had me scheduling a second visit. And then a third. And a fourth.

Like these roses, Charlotte is soft. Fragile, even. Yet with the smallest encouragement and room to grow, she flourishes beyond the bounds of what most gardens could ever hope to accomplish. I've often thought Charlotte wasn't born for this time. Or perhaps, she was made to change it.

But she is here, in the now. And all I can do is ensure she knows these gardens have no walls. That I won't ever tame her. Won't even try.

Charlotte melts in my arms as the kiss goes on, as if she's able to forget the outside world for a while. I do my best to keep her there, but soon enough, she pulls back, a shy smile on her face as she brushes a piece of hair off her cheek.

"Well." She clears her throat lightly, a lovely blush on her skin. "Keep kissing me like that, Arthur, and I might forget the staff."

"The staff will turn a blind eye," I assure her. "Are you ready to meet them?"

"Yes, I think so." She sets her shoulders back, a little of her pluck returning. "I'm a Kane, after all. Am I not?"

"For the rest of our days," I promise.

And surely far beyond that.

Chapter 12

Charlotte

The staff line up in the dining room when Arthur and I turn in for our midday lunch. I do my best to hold a smile on my face, hoping they do not secretly mind me joining Arthur in his home.

Our home.

I take a breath and stand taller.

Arthur leads the introductions. "Charlotte, my dear, this is Ella, Ruby, Willard, and Bess. I also employ a coachman for my travels. You'll meet him when he returns in a couple weeks' time."

"Pleasure," I say, inclining my head.

The women each curtsey, and Arthur's butler Willard bows low, answering for all of them. "The pleasure is entirely ours."

Willard and Ella are older, near my parents' age if not more. Whereas Ruby and Bess must be close to my twenty-four years.

Arthur lets out a soft hum. "Before I forget, we'll be cancelling the call for a lady's maid. Charlotte doesn't wish to employ one."

Ruby looks visibly surprised by this, but Ella appraises me anew. I remain standing tall in her gaze, wondering what judgements she's formed of my character. If she finds me lacking as a lady, well, she wouldn't be the first.

Bess bows her head my way. "If there is anything I can assist you with, please do not hesitate to ask."

I glance at Arthur, who doesn't seem the least bit perturbed by this offer, and my admiration for my husband grows. It's certainly above a housemaid's station to tend to the lady of the house. For Bess to offer so openly speaks volumes about how Arthur treats his staff. She had no worry of reprimand.

"Thank you, Bess," I say sincerely. "If you wouldn't mind showing me later where the pot is to warm the bath, I would be grateful."

She bows her head again, and Arthur graces me with a smile.

As the staff disperses, Arthur pulls a chair out from the table. Instead of sitting opposite me, he chooses a seat beside my own, his expression warm in a way that causes my stomach to flutter. Ruby returns to set small bowls down in front of us before quickly taking her leave. A soup to start our meal.

Arthur holds up his drink. "To the next many years by your side."

As far as toasts go, it's perfection.

When our lunch is finished, Bess materializes to take me into the kitchen. Arthur watches me go with fondness in his gaze, never once trying to intervene. I appreciate the freedom more than I could possibly say.

Ella and Ruby are inside the kitchen, cleaning up after our meal. There's a large table used for preparing food as well as for the meals the staff shares here, and along one wall is the stove. Ella comes over, explaining which side of the flat surface is kept hottest, while Bess fills a pot with water. I watch both, so that I may replicate the process myself without assistance.

As the water heats, I head upstairs to fill the tub. It's beautiful, plenty big enough to fit me fully inside. There's a sink and toilet, as well, and a freestanding mirror framed by more mahogany wood. I run my finger along the edge of it, avoiding my reflection as much as I can. There's a pinch in my gut I do my level best to ignore, used to such discomfort.

Back downstairs in the kitchen, I find the pot of water ready to boil. Bess grabs a large towel with which to hold it.

"Please," I say, realizing she's about to do it herself. "May I?"

Bess and Ella exchange a quick look.

"Please," I repeat, gentler, as I meet each of their eyes in turn. "There is very little in life I've been allowed to do. And there are surely ways in which I'll need your help. I cannot cook. I'll likely get lost a time or two inside these walls before I learn the manor. I may have questions. About Arthur and how I may make him happier as his wife. But it's obvious to me this is no ordinary home."

I pause, allowing the truth of that to sit in the air. Neither woman offers argument.

"And I do not wish it to be," I say honestly. "I'm capable of carrying a pot. Please allow me."

Without a word, Bess hands over the towel. I give her a grateful smile before wrapping the fabric around the handles. Filled with water, the pot isn't light. But I heft it easily enough, the linen providing protection, and go to exit the room. Bess and Ella watch me, and it isn't until I'm to the pantry door that I realize Arthur is there, watching me, too.

I pass through the small pantry and walk slowly up the stairs, careful with the scalding water. By the time I reach the bath, my arms are shaking slightly. I rest the pot on the lip of the tub before dumping the contents inside. With the water warmed, I set the pot aside and remove my clothes.

There are items set along a tray beside the tub, soaps and perfumes likely picked out by Arthur. It brings a smile to my face. Towels are resting there, as well. Fluffy and pristine white. Such indulgence.

As I slip into the tub, I let out a sigh. I pull my hair down once I'm seated, setting the pins on the sill of the window. The afternoon sun shines inside, lighting the space I realize is now my own. All of this is mine. For the rest of my life.

It's a thought that has butterflies taking flight inside my chest, even as I begin the unwelcome task of running my hands over my body to wash. I've just submerged my hair when I hear a soft knock.

"Arthur?" I call, sure it must be him.

"Yes. May I come in?"

Unease swells, but I push it quickly aside. This is Arthur. Baring myself to him is nothing new.

"You may," I answer, sitting upright, my hair wet down my back.

The door opens only enough for Arthur to slip inside, and then he shuts it again. His eyes stay on my face as he approaches. "Is it warm enough?"

"Yes," I assure him, even as he kneels beside the tub, dipping his fingers into the water to check. "Quite pleasant."

He hums, looking me over at last. My breath stutters when his gaze reaches my breasts. I glance away on instinct, not realizing he's noticed until his voice beckons me.

"Charlotte. You do not like when I look at your breasts."

I inhale as shallowly as I can, trying frantically to think up a lie, but Arthur catches my gaze, his gentle eyes imploring me.

"You don't like when I touch them, either." It's a simple observation devoid of judgement. "Nor do you like my cock inside your body."

"I'm sorry," I say quickly, my eyes burning.

"No." The word is whisper-soft, Arthur's hand finding mine beneath the water. "Don't apologize. I only wish to understand. You are lovely, Charlotte. Every inch of you, inside and out. It pains me to know I may make you feel otherwise."

"You don't, Arthur," I tell him, not knowing how to make him understand. "It's what I feel inside, not how you've made me to feel."

"Oh, love." He brings my hand out of the water to kiss my knuckles. "Have I not told you enough how beautiful you are? I would erase every doubt if I could."

I press my lips tightly together, the words I've been told my whole life doing nothing to change what I know to be true.

Arthur notices my silence, perceptive as ever. "What is it? Please tell me, Charlotte. Please don't keep yourself from me."

"I do not *want* to be beautiful," I say at last, the truth escaping before I can pull it back again. I gasp at it, the inhale shuddering in my chest.

Arthur's voice is quiet, barely there. "What?"

"This body is not mine, Arthur. It feels wrong on every level. I look at myself in the mirror, and I see a person I'm not meant to be. I don't know how to explain it rationally, for it makes no sense. But I'm stuck. I'm stuck, and I cannot get out."

He's quiet for a long moment, and I don't dare meet his eye. I stare at where the water is pooling around my knees, sure these are my final moments with my husband. Arthur will demand our marriage be dissolved so he can find a proper wife. And it's my own fault. It's my own doing for not keeping my mouth closed as I should have.

I've tried so very hard to accept my lot in life. And finding Arthur has been a bright point. But I'm tired. I'm tired of fighting with myself every single day. Tired of being alone while I do it. I'd hoped marrying this man would settle me at last, for I love him as I have no other. The thought of losing him, of being apart, is a fierce ache in my chest I fear will never abate.

Yet my love doesn't make me the woman Arthur deserves.

He said he does not fear my thorns. But surely, *surely*, this cut is a betrayal neither of us will come back from.

I hold myself still as Arthur reaches for me. His touch on my chin is gentle, his pull a request I cannot deny. I meet the amber-brown of his eyes, waiting for a blow that never comes.

"Who do you wish to be? If not beautiful, how is it you see yourself?"

My breath hitches. "Arthur..."

"Charlotte, I cannot judge you for what you've told me. I can't tell you that you must be wrong. I do not know how you feel, but I want to understand it. I would give the world to see you happy. Truly happy. Will you let me try?"

His words are impossible, yet his eyes hold nothing but sincerity in their depths.

"Why?" I ask, my throat so tight it's hard to speak.

"Because, Charlotte Valentine, you are my heart. If you are hurting, then so am I."

"I thought..." My voice comes out so watery I have to try again. "I thought I'm a Kane now."

Arthur's lips tip into a gentle smile. "So you are. And I have vowed to love you through all of our trials and tribulations. I don't plan on breaking that promise now."

"Art... I don't deserve you."

"Oh, I think we are very much deserving of each other, my love. Now, the water is cooling. Are you finished?"

I shake my head, sinking down to submerge my hair once more. Arthur watches me as I soap the strands, the scent of rosemary floating on the air. Once I'm done, he stands and holds out his hand. He helps me from the tub, wrapping a towel around me but affording me the courtesy of drying myself. I re-dress once done, and with a small, almost sad smile, Arthur opens the door.

I follow my husband into our chamber and sit in front of the vanity, my thoughts swirling. Without a word, Arthur steps up behind me and picks up my comb.

"May I?"

I nod, and, with gentle hands, Arthur proceeds to brush my hair.

"When you say this body is not your own..." He pauses, meeting my gaze in the glass. "What would you change to make it fit?"

I let out a slow breath, having contemplated that very thing innumerable times over my life. Putting it into words, however, acknowledging it when I never thought I'd be given that chance, is both frightening and exhilarating. Perhaps Arthur can see it in my eyes because he offers his own observation.

"Your breasts?"

I give a small nod, and he continues brushing my hair.

"Would you be rid of them?"

"Yes," I admit at a whisper.

He simply nods, and it feels as if I've cracked apart. As if something painful and tight is spilling from my chest, the release of it nearly bringing me to tears.

He goes on, voice soft. "Your genitalia. Do they suit you?"

I can't form the word. I can only shake my head, my breath caught in my lungs as I hold Arthur's gaze.

"Charlotte." My name comes out pained, and Arthur steadies himself with an inhale. "Is it a man you wish to see in the mirror?"

I can't bring myself to answer him. I can't. I'm afraid if I confirm it aloud, this moment will shatter, taking me with it. Yet the way Arthur so effortlessly puzzled me out is proof he knows me like no other. He's watching me still, and he must see the answer in my eyes because, suddenly, he closes his own.

With the comb still in his hand, Arthur bends low, his arms wrapping around my stomach and his face sinking against my hair. The tear I see running down his cheek has me trembling in response.

"Do you find me loathsome?" I ask, my voice scarcely cooperating.

"No." He says it immediately, and then again, louder. "No, Charlotte. I could never."

"But it's anathema."

"Not to me." Arthur's eyes open to meet mine, his chin on my shoulder and his voice firm. "Not. To. Me. We'll sort this out."

"How?" I ask, not seeing a way.

"I don't know." The admission is quiet, Arthur turning his head to press a kiss to my hair. "But we will. I promise it."

I want so desperately to believe him. But how can I possibly? This is the life I was born into. And though Arthur is a better husband than I ever hoped to find, I'll always be his wife. His Charlotte.

No amount of wishing or hoping will change the person I see reflected back at me in the mirror.

Arthur presses another kiss to the side of my head before brushing the last of my hair. He takes his time, clearly lost in his own thoughts, and I don't attempt to interrupt him. He has every right to think this through. To decide if this is what he wants after all.

If *I'm* what he wants.

I wouldn't fault him for finding me lacking.

We eat our supper in our chamber, like we did our breakfast. And when the sky turns dark, Arthur lights the oil lamps. We lie across from one another on the bed, quiet, although neither of us sleeps. Arthur's hand drifts through my hair, twisting and twining, twisting and twining.

My mouth opens of its own volition, the words no longer able to rest. "Do you think you could love me again after what you've learned?"

Arthur's eyes snap to mine, clarity returning. His voice comes out on a breath. "My love. I've never stopped."

CHAPTER 13

Arthur

I watch Charlotte through the window, her hands clasped behind her back as she wanders the gardens. Her skirt brushes the ground as she moves, the picture of eloquence and mindful rearing.

To know she's felt a disconnect her entire life with who she...*she?*...is and who she was raised to be is an agony inside I cannot quell. No amount of tea or critical thinking these past many days has brought me a solution.

Charlotte believes herself to be a man. A man stuck inside a woman's body.

How do I help her?

"Oh," I breathe aloud, the absolute simplicity of it walloping me upside the head.

Him.

How do I help him?

"Sir?" Willard says, stumbling upon me standing in front of the window near the staff halls at the back of the house. "Is there something you need?"

I let out a slow breath before turning his way. "Yes, in fact. Could you please tell the others that the upstairs of the house is to be reserved for only myself and Charlotte until I say otherwise."

Willard nods a tad jerkily. "Sir."

"Thank you, Willard."

Walking to the door, I step outside, the sun shining in a way that feels disingenuous. As if it has the gall to be so merry when others are not. Charlotte turns my way, a small, forced smile on...his face I wish I could erase into something honest and true. I stop before him, my fingers brushing the softness of his cheek, waiting for any indication I'm not welcome. There is none, so I replace my fingers with my lips.

My love's smile is a little brighter when I lean back.

"I had a thought," I say.

"Oh my." Charlotte's retort is quick, his humor, apparently, still in good repair. "Thinking can be quite dangerous, I hear."

My laughter is soft but relieved. I hold out my arm, and Charlotte takes it. "Would you join me in our chamber?"

"Arthur Kane, what could you possibly want with me there?"

"It's not what you think," I tell him, although that clearly would not have been ill received. "Trust me?"

His blue eyes are soft yet curious. "I do."

I lead Charlotte...my love through the house and up the stairs, closing the door behind us. I have no doubt Willard will spread my request for the staff to stay on the first level until I give the go-ahead to resume normal duties, so our privacy is already ensured. But I'm more than certain my love would appreciate the peace of mind a closed door allows.

"First," I say, leading him to sit in the chair at the corner of the room and standing before him. "There's a matter I must ask you, for it is weighing on my mind. Your name."

He nods slowly, brows drawn.

"Would you prefer another?"

Those eyebrows rise, his surprise evident. "Another name?"

"Yes. Does Charlotte suit you? It is quite feminine."

He blinks at me, looking so very lost I drop to my knees, my hands resting on his own.

"You are a man," I say softly. "Inside your heart. Are you not?"

He licks his lips before nodding ever so slowly.

I ease out a breath, immensely glad I'm still on the right track. "Then perhaps you would prefer another name? If not, say the word, and Charlotte you will be."

His words come slowly. "You would call me by another?"

"Forevermore," I promise.

He swallows several times, his gaze not on me but unseeing within the room. Finally, he says, "Could I be Charlie?"

I pick up his hand, kissing the back side once and then again. "Charlie," I repeat. "My Charlie."

He looks close to tears, but they don't fall. Never have I seen him cry, in all the years we've known one another.

"How is this so easy for you?" His voice trembles, words hoarsely spoken. "You do not ridicule me. Do not look at me with disgust. I don't understand how you can possibly accept it."

I close my eyes for a moment, Charlie's hand warm in my own. He's shaking, but he hasn't pulled away. "Have you heard of René Descartes?"

"The philosopher?"

I hum and open my eyes. "There's a principle by which he's most known. 'I think, therefore I am.'"

Charlie watches me curiously, so I go on.

"I know I exist because I think. Because I think, I exist. I have no real proof that anything else is real, but I know my conscious thoughts to be. Correct?"

He nods slowly.

"The same is true for you," I say, squeezing his hand. "Which brings me to two conclusions I came to earlier that are, in fact, one and the same. Either you think you are a man, therefore you are one. Or my own brain has produced all of this, in which case I am to decide what's real. And you're real to me, Charlie."

His chin wobbles. "So you accept me? As I am?"

"Exactly as you are."

"Arthur." My name on his lips is the same as it's ever been. Lovely and warm. "I thought you were a mathematician. Not a philosopher."

I expel a soft laugh. "Scientific thought belongs to us all, my dear."

Charlie's eyes twinkle with a lightness I'm beyond grateful to see, but then he sobers quickly. "And what of religion? What of our vows to the church?"

My sigh is small. It's a complication I considered, of course. No one—not in the church, not elsewhere—would understand Charlie's predicament. It's unheard of, as far as I'm aware. But I've never been devout, and my conviction in my love far outweighs the teachings of faith.

"Despite what they would have us believe," I say slowly, "the church does not reside within these walls. I will not have you feeling ill at ease in your own home, my love. The rest of the world may not understand nor condone it, but they do not need to, as far as I'm concerned. Here, at home, you will be who you were always meant to be. As long as that is your wish."

His inhale is broken, his hand squeezing mine to the point of pain. "And the staff?"

"I will talk with them. If there are problems, we will find new staff."

"Arthur, I don't know how to take this all in. You have to understand—I feel as if I'm dreaming."

"If it's a good dream, let's not wake, hm?"

Charlie lets out a laugh, a lopsided smile transforming his face into near radiance. I give his hand another squeeze before standing.

"May I try something?" I ask.

He nods, brushing his hair back as I walk around the bed to my wardrobe. I pull out a pair of trousers that haven't fit me in some time, as well as a simple white shirt with a cravat tie. Charlie watches me with curiosity as I walk back his way.

"Would you stand for me, Charlie dear?"

His breath stutters again, at the name perhaps? But he does as I request, smoothing the fabric of his ill-fitted dress down, the reminder of its presence seeming to sour his mood. I backtrack to the vanity, returning with a pair of scissors in hand. Charlie's eyes widen when I tug the fabric away from his skin and cut it straight down the middle.

"Arthur, good grief!" His hands move to cover his chest before he laughs and lets them fall at his sides. I pull the ruined fabric off his arms one at a time before tossing it aside, meeting Charlie's eye as I pinch his petticoat between my fingers. He throws his hands into the air. "Oh, why not?"

With a grin, I cut the petticoat away. It falls at Charlie's feet, leaving him nude in front of me apart from his stockings and heels. There's a heavy pinch in my gut knowing this body is not one he feels safe in. It's lovely to me, always has been. But it doesn't define the person I fell almost instantly in love with.

I crouch down, helping Charlie from his heels, my eyes meeting his as I pull his stockings away. He swallows, cheeks pink, and I kiss one bare knee before standing.

Charlie's expression is serious as I pull my spare shirt over his head. With his arms through and the cotton covering his modesty, I slowly tie the fabric around his neck into a standard cravat. I grab the trousers next, holding them as Charlie steps one and then two legs inside. It's too wide around his waist, so I pluck a pin from his hair to keep the extra fabric together. A curl lies loose in front of Charlie's cheek as he watches me, and he doesn't protest when I walk around him to tuck it away. I do the same to the other loose pieces of hair framing his face, until every single one is hidden away behind his head.

Stepping in front of him, I hold out my hand. "Shall we have a look?"

Charlie remains unmoving for a long second before finally accepting my palm. I walk with him to the vanity mirror, realizing only once we're in front of it that Charlie's eyes are closed.

"My love," I say softly. "You can open your eyes."

It takes time. Time in which I don't rush him. He breathes in and out, preparing himself, I'd wager, for disappointment. Or perhaps precisely the opposite.

Finally, his eyes draw open, the blue flitting wildly from his shirt to his trousers, up to his hair, and then completing the circuit again. It's not perfect. I know that. His chest still swells the fabric of the shirt, and his hair is not how a man would wear it. But even so, the way his shoulders square at once and how his chin lifts at the sight of himself in the mirror has my happiness ballooning.

I give Charlie's shoulders a soft squeeze. "You are so handsome, my dear."

His hand finds mine, tightening, his eyes in the glass near frantic. "You cannot be real."

"I am to me," I assure him. "And if you believe it to be true, then, well... I suppose I am real to you, as well."

Charlie spins, kissing me swiftly, his nails biting into my skin. I do not mind it. I kiss him back, hitching him up into my arms, holding tight as his legs tighten around my waist. The move is far easier without the skirts.

"I love you." He peppers me with kisses amidst his words, the onslaught most welcome. "I love you. I love you so."

"My heart," I say, my insides light. "I pray you never stop."

Charlie frames my face, pulling back enough to look at me. "How do I repay you for this, Art? How could I ever?"

I let him drop slowly to the floor, although I don't let go completely. I can see the war in his eyes, the fear that this could be taken from him. I don't know how to soothe his worries other than through consistency and time.

"There is no debt here," I say in seriousness, turning Charlie once more so he can see himself in the mirror. The high neckline of his shirt is quite fetching. He'll need waistcoats, as well. A couple warm coats for when it's colder. And trousers in his size. Boots. More shirts. A full wardrobe. "Seeing you happy is a gift you need never repay. I don't quite think you understand, my dear. I would give all of myself, freely, if only to ensure your smile."

His expression flickers. "But then you would be left with nothing."

"No," I disagree, straightening his cravat. "I would have gained quite a lot."

Charlie's lips press together, the look in his eyes almost reproachful except for the good humor I can so clearly see: the enjoyment he gets from these word games we play. I quite think I've found my match in Charlie Kane.

I give his shoulders another squeeze, our reflections staring back at us. "What do you think?"

Charlie takes a moment to look himself over. Slowly this time. A measured appraisal. "I think I've never felt this free. Even if I look ridiculous."

"You do not," I promise, wrapping my arms around his shoulders. His hands come up to hold my wrists.

"What if we have company?"

I hum, quickly mulling. "Would it pain you to put on a dress for such an occasion?"

He takes a moment to consider it. "I think it would be bearable. If I know I can return to this after."

I kiss his cheek, pleased to hear so, even as I wish such a thing weren't a necessity. "No unexpected visitors will be allowed. Any company, we will plan for. It'll be a play, my love. A short one. And when they go, you and I will be free to be ourselves once more."

"You as well?"

His tone is curious, but my answer is easy.

"Yes. It will not bring me any measure of joy to pretend you're someone you're not, Charlie. But I won't risk your safety. To the outside world, nothing will have changed."

"Even though everything has."

I don't refute it, knowing, to Charlie, his world *has* changed. Drastically. And, I hope against hope, for the eternal better.

Yet I can't help but think this world is due for much bigger. Not just within these walls, but far and wide.

I suppose change only happens because of those who press for it.

"Where have you gone?" Charlie's question is gentle. Inquisitive.

"Not far," I assure him. "Shall I grab us some lunch? And then perhaps we could discuss how you'd like the staff to address you going forward?"

He nods, and I give his cheek another kiss before leaving him to settle into his new normal. All the while, my mind conjures ways I can make this world a better one for the only person I've ever wished to share it with.

Chapter 14

Charlie

I keep quiet inside the dim pantry, the voices from within the kitchen having caused me to come to a halt. Arthur and I finished our breakfast upstairs only minutes ago, and he was to return the tray. His tone of voice, however, tells me he's now engaged in a serious conversation with the staff.

The water for my bath will have to wait.

"The reason I asked for Ruby to step outside is because I'm unsure if this news will be welcome to her. Ella, once I reveal what it is I've come here to, I will ask your opinion on this."

I suspect Ella nods because Arthur continues. My pulse hammers as I take a step closer to the kitchen door.

"I've known the three of you for years. Willard, Ella, you've been with me for over a decade. I consider all of you closer to family than staff, so I ask for you to not react harshly to my words. From now forward, within the walls of this house, Charlotte is to be referred to as Charlie. Or sir."

There's a pause in which I imagine Arthur is gauging the shock of his audience. My own breaths shorten, my pulse a steady drum I can hear within my ears.

"Mr. Kane would also suit." Arthur's voice is calm but firm. "Not Charlotte. Not ma'am. And not Mrs. If that is not something you feel you can do, I will pay for your time as you find a position elsewhere."

There's another silence, and then Ella speaks, her voice a lower register than Bess's.

"Are you saying we're to pretend Charlotte is a man?"

I swallow heavily, my breakfast sitting ill within my stomach.

"He *is* a man." Arthur's words, so steadfast, nearly steal the breath from my lungs. "At the heart of him, it is who Charlie knows himself to be. And he's never had a chance to be seen as such. Not until now. I don't expect you to understand. Not fully. And mistakes may happen along the way. But so long as you are trying your best to treat him as he deserves, I will not chastise you for simply misspeaking. If you cannot accept him, that is another matter. So what say you? Will you try your best to make Charlie feel welcome in his home?"

I can't stay to listen. I simply can't. I pad quickly but quietly through the door into the dining room and then rush up the stairs to our chamber. My dress floats around my knees as I shut the door, sinking to the floor in front of it. Almost immediately, I stand again, pacing to the bed, over to the window, and then to the vanity stool. I sit, my back to the mirror, not wanting to see how I presented myself in order to go downstairs for hot water.

I'm up again in an instant, untying my dress with fumbling fingers. It feels too tight, my lungs battling for air, everything within me screaming to get out, get out, *get out.*

I nearly sob in relief when the fabric pools at my feet. I tug off my petticoat next and throw it as far as it will go. It hits Arthur's wardrobe before the fabric sinks in a slow cascade toward the rug.

Naked, I drop to the floor, my knees up in front of me, my arms around them tight. I can feel myself shaking, but there's nothing to be done for it.

The door clicks open before I've moved. The ache in my body tells me I've been in this position for quite some time.

"Charlie." There's alarm in Arthur's voice. He comes quickly my way, warm hands settling on my arms as he drops to a crouch in front of me. "What on earth is the matter?"

I can feel his gaze sweeping over me, but I don't know how to explain all I'm feeling.

He stills when he notices the dress on the floor nearby. "Did you put that on?"

I nod, my eyes stinging yet my cheeks dry.

He lets out the softest puff of air before reaching for the garment. "Should I fetch the scissors again?"

I let out an unexpected laugh, the sound like a pressure release. "I went downstairs."

"Ah." The single syllable is full of understanding. I have no doubt Arthur has already figured it out. He stands, bringing the dress to his wardrobe. He picks up the petticoat, as well, stuffing both inside.

"I may need those," I point out.

"Then we will free them from their prison when the time comes." Arthur returns to me with a shirt, holding it in front of me, a question, not a demand. I accept the cotton, tugging it on and drawing it over my knees as Arthur seats himself on the floor once more, inches in front of me. "Will you tell me?"

"I went for a pot of water for my bath," I say, my throat feeling raw, as if I've been crying, when I know I have not. "I could have waited for you, I know that. But I wanted to do it on my own. I wore the dress because..."

"I understand." Arthur doesn't need me to explain it. The staff seeing me in trousers and his shirt would have been alarming, at best. "You will not need to do so again, Charlie dear. You heard me talking to them, I gather?"

"In part," I admit, tugging the hem of the shirt at my ankle. "Did you discuss it with Ruby?"

"Yes."

"And?"

"And although each of them is bewildered by the request, they've agreed to honor it. You won't be made to feel shame here."

"Arthur," I say on a breath. "Surely it can't be that easy."

"And why not? I've employed good people I trust. My primary concern was with Ruby, as she is new, but I don't believe she will share our secret. And if she does, what of it? No proof will be found. Willard will not allow any unwelcome company past these doors. Ella and Bess will stand on our side because I've asked it of them. I'm choosing to trust Ruby will be on our side, as well. If nothing else, I trust Ella's judgement on the matter. No one will know Charlie Kane exists, my love. He is safe here. I will see to it with everything I have."

I pull in a shuddering inhale. "I'm frightened, Arthur."

The admission isn't easy, but Arthur has never once made me feel badly for shows of emotion. Nor has he ever tried to tell me I'm being foolish or dismissed me simply because I'm...because I appear to be a lady. He's the person I trust most in this world, and I trust him with all of me. I'll never doubt him again, not after this. Not for as long as I live.

"Why are you frightened, my dear?"

I abandon picking at the hem of my shirt to grab the fabric of Arthur's trouser leg. He takes the hint, scooting closer, his legs outside of my own. Speaking about this isn't easy, even as I know it must be done.

"I'm frightened that someone will find out. And of what that means for me. For us. I'm afraid I'll allow myself this luxury to live as I've always wished only to be forced back into my cage. It will hurt a hundred times worse, Arthur. To spread my wings only to have them clipped."

He lets out a slow breath, that mind of his considering all angles. It's something I love about Arthur. His big, open mind.

"Let's address this one at a time." His voice is calm, and it settles me in turn. "The first matter, that someone will find out. We'll be careful, all of us. You'll stay inside or in the back gardens when dressed for yourself. As I've said, no visitors will be allowed without notice, so no one will have the opportunity to see you as such. When we go out, it will be different, but we'll tackle those occasions as they come. I don't feel as if the staff will talk, but if they do, money can pave many roads. We have plenty of that, my love. It will work in our favor."

I nod, and Arthur rubs his hands up and down my legs.

"As for the second point." He frowns slightly. "It should not be a luxury to live as yourself, Charlie. I understand why you would consider it such, and I know all of this has to be overwhelming to a large degree. But I will never, not *ever*, force you back inside that cage. You're free from it already, don't you see? As archaic as it is, in the eyes of those around us, you belong to me. And I'm never handing you back. I'd rather perish than cause you injury, internal or otherwise. So if you wish to never wear a dress again, we will close our doors and become hermits."

I let out a laugh, and Arthur smiles, looking so very pleased. "But how then would you teach?"

He shrugs. "I would further my own knowledge. Or we could learn together, if that's an endeavor you're interested in."

Exhaling, I offer a small smile. "I would love to learn more of astronomy."

"Truly?"

"Yes. My father used to sit with me, teaching me what he knew, telling me stories of the stars. Until I was too old for it. Then, he stopped."

Arthur makes a soft, knowing sound. Ladies are not permitted to learn as gentlemen are. It's not their place.

Or so some say.

"I've often thought about how my life would be different if I were born a man," I say quietly. "I would likely be at the university right now, a telescope beneath my fingertips, pages and pages of notes spread out before me charting the position of celestial bodies moving within our sight. And to think of how much more there is out there... Stars we'll never see. Those that have already died."

There's a tiny smile on Arthur's face when I meet his eye. "May I show you something?"

I nod, and Arthur stands.

He only takes a step before stopping and looking back at me thoughtfully. "Trousers might suit."

I laugh, getting to my feet as Arthur returns to his wardrobe. I put on the trousers he hands me, and, once dressed, he opens the door, his hand held in invitation.

It takes me a moment to move forward. I straighten my shirt, my hands drifting over the loose fabric tucked into my trousers, the fit making me all too aware of the differences between my husband's chest and my own. Arthur seems to understand I need time because he never presses me. He simply waits as I gather my nerves and step with him into the hall.

I look down both sides of it, my heart galloping, but there's no one in sight. Even if there were, Arthur assured me I'm safe here. I believe him.

Arthur gives me a soft smile when I accept his hand, and then he leads me toward the end of the hall. He opens a door there, revealing the staircase to the third floor he told me about but we've yet to visit.

He makes a contemplative sound as we ascend the stairs. "I haven't used these rooms much. Haven't had a reason to. Although I suspect that's changed."

Arthur's twinkling eyes meet mine as we come to a stop at the end of the corridor. He opens another door, the hinges creaking, and waves me on. I step tentatively forward, the room in front of me flooded with sunlight, the floor bare and dust swirling around me. My gaze is drawn upwards, and I can't stop my gasp.

"Arthur. What is this?"

His voice is light as he follows me into the room. "A solarium. I was quite shocked to find it here, but the previous landowner had the room modified for his late wife, who had a passion for growing flowers. Quite beautiful, is it not?"

I walk the perimeter of the room, my gaze trailing from the large, wide windows on three walls to the pitched roof covered in glass. Though the windowpanes are dirty, I can clearly see the cloudless sky above. Beautiful doesn't begin to cover it.

Arthur hums gently. "I think this would make a fine observatory, don't you?"

There's a stutter in my chest as well as in my step. I turn back around to find my husband smiling.

He goes on almost offhandedly. "It could use a bit of cleaning. The outside glass will be tricky, but I'm sure we can find a way. We'll want furnishings, as well. A desk. A settee, perhaps, if I'm to lounge in here while you work. Likely an extra blanket or two, as the room does suffer an unfortunate draft. The telescope may take time, but I'll place an order as soon as I'm back in town. What do you think, my—"

Arthur's words cut off as I wrap my arms around him. He laughs, a joyous sound, his own arms coming around me tight as I press my face against the hollow of his throat. I breathe him in, my chest feeling tight, my love for this man too big for my body to contain.

And I realize, with a start...

"I never would have known you."

Arthur stills. "What's that?"

"If I had been born differently," I say, the revelation as shocking as it is comforting, in a strange sort of way. "If I were raised as a gentleman, I wouldn't know you as I do now. Our paths may have crossed, but we wouldn't be here. I wouldn't be standing with you in this home. You wouldn't be my husband. We could never be."

He's quiet for a moment, his hand soothing up and down my back. "I don't like the idea of you suffering to be with me, my love."

"No," I say quietly, bringing my face away from Arthur's throat. He's looking at me with a frown I wish I hadn't caused. "What I mean to say is... If I can find some comfort in the lot I've been given, it's this. I would choose you countless times over. I'd take a lifetime of being loved by you, Arthur Kane, over any life lived without. I'm more than certain there's not a storm I couldn't weather, so long as I have you at my side."

Arthur's eyes are wet, his inhale measured but shaky. "To hear you say so is a great joy. And it will be my honor to stand at your side through rain and thunder, my dear heart. Sunshine, too, for I hope we have plenty of it."

"I have no doubt," I say softly, looking around the room once more. It's all too easy to envision a desk sitting in the middle, a grand telescope pointed toward the sky. Arthur in his settee as he drinks an evening cup of tea, and me in front of my lens, the stars bright overhead. At night, the view in here will be impeccable.

Arthur chuckles lightly. "Are you already plotting?"

I smile ruefully in response, not even trying to deny it.

He holds out his hand. "Come. Let's sit down for lunch, and you can tell me what you need."

I accept Arthur's palm, giving the room one last glance before walking away. For now.

Perhaps there are some attributes about my person I would rather like to change given the chance.

But when it comes to Arthur, to us, I wouldn't alter a single thing.

Chapter 15

Arthur

Returning to the university is a necessity, not one I've ever minded before. I quite like my lectures, as well as my position as a professor.

But being away from Charlie for the first time since our wedding is proving far more difficult than I had imagined. And it's only partway through day one.

After our shared breakfast, I took my leave, as is custom. Yet with every passing minute the coachman brought me further away from the manor, I felt as if a string were being stretched taut between Charlie and myself. I only hoped he didn't feel it, too. Preparing my materials was an exercise in focus, one I felt I was failing as my thoughts continued to wander back home, time and time again. Even now, with my final lecture all but concluded, I can barely keep from running for the door, anxious to see for myself that all is well, even though I know, surely, it must be.

This unease will pass. I know it will.

But I do so wish Charlie could be here with me as he ought to be. Not back at home, confined to the walls that will keep him safe.

A few of my students come to me after I'm done lecturing with questions on the material. I do my best to be patient, taking the time to answer them fully. Even so, it's an immense relief when I finally exit the door of the lecture hall.

I'm nearly to my small office when I run into Mr. Valentine, Charlie's father. I come to a slow halt, smiling as pleasantly as I can.

"Mr. Valentine," I greet. "How do you do."

He inclines his head in a nod. "I was hoping to check after Charlotte." Seemingly remembering his manners, he quickly adds, "Although I trust you are well?"

"Quite," I assure him, though I have to bite back my discomfort at hearing him calling Charlie by his given name and knowing I must do the same. "Charlotte is well, settling in and quite happy with...her new home. I'm sure she'll be pleased to hear of your concern."

He seems to relax at that. "Please do not take my worry as criticism, Mr. Kane. You have to understand—I love my daughter dearly. It's why I was so grateful to know she approved of your match."

I consider his words. "Do you truly mean that?"

"Pardon?" he asks, his surprise evident.

"You care for your daughter's every happiness?"

"I... Yes, of course."

I watch Mr. Valentine for any sign of dishonesty but see none. "Charlotte has mentioned fondly that she enjoyed your lessons on the stars as a child. I admit, it's made me curious to know more. Would you have any books on the subject I could take home with me?"

Mr. Valentine blinks before nodding once. "I believe so, yes. Would you have time to come to my office?"

"Certainly. Let me grab my belongings, and I'll join you."

Charlie's father waits as I collect my coat and bag, and then I walk with him to his office far from mine. He appraises his small bookshelf for a moment before plucking one heavily weighted book out and then a second. After a quick glance my way, he moves around to his desk, retrieving something from inside one of the drawers.

He hands me the stack of books, a leather-bound journal set on top. His palm rests on the journal for a long beat before he finally lets go. "My personal accounts. Charlotte used to enjoy them."

I let loose a small breath and smile genuinely at Mr. Valentine, beyond pleased to realize I have an ally in the man. At least in regards to Charlie's personal pursuits. "Thank you. I'm sure I will enjoy them as well."

Charlie's father nods and leads me to the door.

"Is there anything you wish for me to pass along?" I ask before we part.

Mr. Valentine closes his eyes briefly, his voice almost wistful. "186,000 miles."

"186?" I check.

He nods once. "Good day to you, Mr. Kane."

I leave Charlie's father at his office door. The walk into town takes some time, though I keep my steps brisk. I already asked for Howard, my coachman, to collect me later than normal today, despite my desire to return home swiftly. There are a couple matters I must attend to first.

The small shop that produces telescopes is near the center of town, flourishing, I'm sure, because of the astronomy department at the university. They have several models of telescopes on display, ranging from small handheld units to those on large stands. I find the biggest one they have and place an order.

Next, I make a stop at the theatre. I garner a curious look or two from the head seamstress, but money truly does work wonders. I acquire what I came for and head off to catch my buggy home.

My knee bounces on the ride back to the manor, my hands returning to the books from Mr. Valentine, as well as Charlie's discreetly wrapped gift. I do so hope he likes it.

When I arrive home, it's already suppertime. I thank Howard before making my way inside. The front of the manor is quiet, and a quick check inside the dining room confirms Charlie is absent. I have my suspicions about where he'll be, but Bess appears before I have a chance to go check.

"Sir," she says politely, carrying a stack of freshly laundered towels.

"Bess," I say before she can get far. "Have you seen Charlie today?"

She hesitates before shaking her head. "I haven't. I don't believe he's come down."

My chest stutters at the simple usage of the masculine pronoun, and I give Bess a warm, appreciative smile. "I believe he may be in hiding."

Her lips quirk slightly at that. "Anything I can do?"

I nod slowly, considering. "If he doesn't come down tomorrow, perhaps a visit? Some subtle encouragement that he is welcome. I fear he may not believe it to be true until he hears it from someone other than myself."

Bess inclines her head. "Consider it done, sir. Should I have supper brought upstairs tonight?"

"Yes. Thank you, Bess. For everything."

She smiles warmly before continuing on into the dining room, carrying the towels toward the kitchen.

I take the stairs two at a time, my heart thumping as I near our chamber. I knock once to alert Charlie of my presence, and then I open the door.

He's sitting in his chair at the corner of the room, a book open on his lap that he must have found in the library. I pull in a breath at the sight of him lounging so comfortably in trousers and a shirt, his hair pulled back out of his face. His head lifts as I enter the room, a small smile lighting his lips. I set the items in my hands onto the bed and approach.

Charlie's welcoming words are teasing. "He returns."

"Did you miss me, my love?"

"Oh, perhaps a little."

Charlie lets out a startled gasp as I swoop down, hauling him into my arms. His book lands on the floor with a thud, my love laughing as he wraps his arms around my shoulders.

"I missed you greatly," I tell him, finding his lips with my own.

He softens, every muscle relaxing as I prove how very much I yearned for him these past many hours.

Charlie speaks around kisses. "Should I expect... a mauling... every time you're to return home?"

"Quite," I assure him, sinking my face to his neck and biting lightly.

He laughs once more, squirming until I stop.

"I have something for you," I say, letting Charlie lower to the floor. "Two somethings, more accurately."

He follows me to the bed, sitting on the edge of it. "Color me intrigued."

I pick up the books first, sliding them his way. "I had a brief encounter with your father today," I inform him, watching Charlie's reaction. There's curiosity on his face, but not surprise. "I told him I was interested in learning more about astronomy. And he offered me these."

Charlie turns his focus to the books, interest there. His fingers skate over the small leather journal before freezing. There's an intake of breath, and then he quickly plucks it up, opening it and flipping through the pages. "This is..."

"Your father's personal findings," I confirm. "And the textbooks he gave me are far above a novice's level."

His voice is hushed, shaken. "These aren't for you."

"No. I don't suspect they are."

Charlie looks up at me, his breath stuttering.

"He asked after you," I tell him softly. "And he told me to tell you... 186,000 miles."

A pained smile breaks over Charlie's face, as lovely as it is heartbreaking. He lets out a long sigh, holding the leather journal to his chest.

"What does it mean?" I ask him, running my fingers along Charlie's neck, over the smooth skin there.

He turns his head my way, his blue eyes covered in the slimmest sheen of moisture. He blinks, and it disappears. "Do you know how far the human eye can see?"

I shake my head. "I do not."

"Less than three miles on a clear day." He sets the journal on his lap, running his fingers over it once more before picking up the textbooks one at a time, examining each. "Three miles. That's the distance from our eye to the horizon when on flat ground. Do you know how far light travels in a single second?"

"186,000 miles?" I guess.

He nods, drawing in a breath through his nose. "186 *thousand*. The world we live in is so much more vast than we can see. Imagine what's out there, Arthur. In a time and place far from now."

Charlie's lips curve into a smile as he opens one of the textbooks, looking inside. It's all too easy to see the young child he once was, so full of wonder and a will to learn. An eagerness that was snuffed out, confined with no room to roam simply because of the shackles we put in place upon a person's gender assignment. Why shouldn't Charlie learn? Why shouldn't anyone?

Charlie flips a few more pages before closing the book. "It was our code. 186,000 miles. It meant it was time to look at the stars."

I give Charlie's leg a soft squeeze, the pain of loss evident in his voice. "I think your father wants you to look still."

He presses his lips tightly together, eyes meeting mine. "I think you're right. You said there was a second item?"

I nod, not surprised by Charlie's change of subject. He's never done well with emotion, not feeling nor showing it. Likely, I realize only now, because he's battled with far too many emotions his entire life. Hiding equated to survival.

I push the melancholic thought away and pick up the wrapped present, passing it over to Charlie as he sets the books aside. He spares me a curious glance before opening the bundle with deft fingers. He pauses once the paper falls loosely away, the construction of the item not entirely unfamiliar to him.

"It's not what you think," I say before he can come to the wrong conclusion.

He lifts the garment carefully. "A corset?"

"No. A corset falls under one's breasts in order to highlight them. This covers the chest fully."

His eyes spring to me. Shock. Hope.

"It will bind your chest, my dear. Women at the theatre use one if they are to play a man. The circumstances are different, of course, but I thought it might help you feel…more yourself."

Charlie examines the material, the laces at both sides meant to be pulled tight, shaping the upper body as smoothly as possible. "Can I try it on?"

"Of course."

Charlie stands, and I hold the material as he unties his cravat and pulls his shirt over his head. He stands before me seemingly unabashed, but he doesn't meet my eye. I help secure the binding fabric around his midsection, pulling the laces on one side tight and then the other. It takes a couple times to find the right fit so that it's even, but once done, I step back.

"Is it comfortable?"

Charlie's fingers drift over the edges lightly, voice soft. "More comfortable than a corset. My shirt?"

I hand it over quickly, and Charlie pulls the garment back on, tying his own cravat as I watch. My chest feels tight in a way I suspect is different than what Charlie is experiencing. He's come so far already. Taken immeasurable steps. I can see it in the way he stands and how he no longer tries to act the part of a lady, a role that never fit. For the first time in his life, he's being granted the opportunity to let his inner self shine through. And it's absolutely breathtaking.

I loved him before. From almost the very start.

But what I feel now seeing Charlie find the person he was always meant to be? It can't be categorized by four simple letters. It's so much grander than love. Far more vast and dangerous. I fear I would burn the world down just to watch Charlie walk free.

Maybe, one day, I'll be able to.

With his shirt in place, Charlie walks to the mirror. I follow behind him, watching his gaze in the glass. His chest does look flatter, and he runs a hand over himself, turning to see the effect from all angles.

"If you do not like it, you never need wear it," I tell him gently. "You're handsome with or without the bindings, my love. Your comfort comes first."

He turns to me without a word, his eyes meeting mine as his hands slip under the edges of the coat I've not yet removed since arriving home. He slides the heavy fabric off one arm and then the other, taking a moment to hang it in my wardrobe before returning.

Charlie unfastens my waistcoat next. "I love it, Arthur. I do. I wish I didn't have need for it, but I can't deny I like how it makes me feel."

"And how is that?" I ask, fairly certain, by Charlie's current intentions, I can hazard a guess.

He rids me of my waistcoat before guiding me over to the bed. The backs of my knees hit, and I sit down, welcoming Charlie into my lap.

"Bold." His hand finds my cock through my trousers, bringing me to hardness as his lips press wet kisses to my neck. "Confident and desired." He tugs my head back, a breath leaving me as he presses his weight down onto my lap. "Covetous."

"Is it your husband you covet, dear Charlie?"

His lips touch feather-soft to my own. "Always."

"Then take what you will from me, my heart. I am yours in every way."

Charlie kisses me fiercely in response, our lips locked as he unbuttons my trousers with a swift hand. He opens his own, too, sliding them down his hips and pulling me free before pressing my weight to the bed. With a roll of his hips, he slides himself along my cock, our breath stuttering in tandem. Charlie uses me to bring pleasure to himself, the friction along his sensitive bundle of nerves ratcheting him higher and higher until, minutes later, he cries out into my mouth, shaking and shuddering, his nails digging into the bedsheet and against my chest. It's all I need to find my own climax, Charlie's pleasure the tipping point that has my muscles locking tight and every fiber of my being vibrating like a plucked cord. My shirt catches the mess, Charlie continuing to roll against me as he lets out a panting sigh, not allowing a single moment of his gratification or my own to be lost.

When he finally speaks, it's on a breath. "Arthur."

The knock at the door has the both of us stilling.

"Your supper," comes a strained voice.

I clear my throat. "Thank you, Ruby. You may leave it at the door."

Charlie's wide eyes meet my own.

"Well," I say lightly, not wanting him to worry over what Ruby likely heard. "I think it best you feed me, my love. Being ravaged is quite hungry work, I'll have you know."

As I'd hoped, Charlie's lips spread into a smile, a shy yet satisfied glint there. He runs his fingers through the hair at my temple, his expression turning serious. "Art. I cannot imagine many people have the capability to love someone the way you love me. I will never take for granted the breadth of your heart. Please know it is always safe with me."

I lean up enough to pull Charlie in for a kiss, my pulse a quick beat within my veins. His cheeks remain flushed when we part, and I'm certain I've never seen a lovelier sight.

I don't speak it aloud, but what I've always known is that Charlie and my heart are one and the same. There's no splitting the two apart. I was made to love Charlie Valentine, now Kane.

No matter the form in which he came to me.

CHAPTER 16

Charlie

The sound at the door is quiet, almost tentative. A soft rap of knuckles against wood.

"Yes?" I call out, my heart tripping over itself at the unexpected company. It's far too early for Arthur to be home, which means someone else is at the chamber door.

Bess's voice filters through the wood. "I don't mean to intrude. A quick word, if I may?"

The silence weighs heavily as I drop my feet slowly to the floor, setting my father's astronomy journal aside. I contemplate, ever briefly, changing into my own clothes. Into a dress. But then Bess's voice comes again.

"Sir?"

I inhale a shuddering breath at the honorific and reach for the doorknob. Bess stands in the hallway, a polite smile on her face that never wavers, even as she sees me in Arthur's attire. If anything, she smiles brighter as she inclines her head.

"Yes?" I ask somewhat shakily.

"Would you prefer to come down to the dining room for your luncheon today? Ella has prepared an assortment of sandwiches and is keen to know which you prefer."

"Oh. I..."

"The front drapes have been drawn. The door is locked as always. You are quite welcome in all areas of your home, Mr. Kane."

It takes me a long moment to speak, my disbelief warring with immense gratitude. With fear and relief and an aching sort of desire to hear those words again and again and again.

Mr. Kane.

"All right," I say at last, glancing back at the room before following Bess into the hall. She gives me a wide smile.

The dining room table is already set. One place setting that reminds me of how lonely I've felt my entire life.

"Bess," I say before she can retreat. "May I sit in the kitchen?"

She looks surprised but nods quickly. We pass through the dim pantry, one door swinging shut before the other opens. Ella and Ruby are both inside the room, Ella putting the final touches on a tray of food as Ruby cleans the stovetop. They pause, curtsying quickly before standing with their hands clasped in front of themselves.

The younger woman speaks first. "Ma—sir."

Ruby looks mortified by her disjointed greeting. Ella simply appraises me.

I give them both a nod, my heart beating furiously in my chest. "Good day. Would it trouble you if I had my meal in here?"

Ruby looks to Ella for guidance. Ella is the one to answer me. "The dining room is more befitting your station. Surely you would be most comfortable there?"

Squaring my shoulders, I pluck up some of that nerve waiting inside of me. That voice I've squashed time and again since I was young. My *flight of fancy*, as my mother would call it. My confidence.

My wings.

"I've rarely been comfortable in my life, Ella," I tell the woman truthfully. "Sitting alone in the dining room while I wait for Arthur to return sounds quite boorish, if I'm to be honest. You must see I am no lady. It's an endeavor I've failed, no matter how hard I've tried. And perhaps I'll never be a lord, but what I would like, for once in my life, is to sit in a nice warm kitchen and not have to pretend like titles are the marker of a person. It's asinine, is it not? To be who we are simply because it's what someone else told us to be? I'm done standing on custom, and I hope that does not offend, but I don't need anyone here to stand on custom, either. This is a table, correct?" I pat the surface of the roughened wood beside me. "Surely I may eat on it?"

It's quiet for all of a beat before Ruby scrambles forward. She moves a tea towel off the table and then motions me toward the nearest seat, a smile on her face that takes me by surprise. I sit down, and Bess joins me, just as the door opens.

Willard steps through and stills, his eyes sweeping the room. He lingers, briefly, on me, but politely doesn't stare, his head dipping in a bow. "Has there been a problem?"

I don't have time to answer him before Ella does, speaking matter-of-factly while dusting her hands on her apron. "Charlie is joining us for lunch. Take a seat, Willard."

The butler, looking rather startled, sits down opposite me. I pull in a slow, steadying breath, my eyes stinging and my chest oh so tight beneath my bindings. Ella places a tray in the center of the table, laden with petite sandwiches. Ruby passes out plates.

So this, I think to myself, *is rebellion*.

I'm in the library when Arthur arrives home. There's a smile on my face before he even clears the doorway, the quick cadence of his heavy footsteps easy to identify. He stops at the door, locating me before striding forward. He's still wearing his coat, and I can only imagine Willard, flustered in the parlor as Arthur breezed by, not wanting to stop for a task as simple as removing the outerwear.

I expect the bodily upheaval of my person this time, so it's less of a surprise when Arthur lifts me into his arms. It's no less welcome, however.

"My love." He kisses my cheek and then my lips and my nose, of all places, smelling like the outdoors, his hair ruffled and his own cheeks carrying the slightest chill. "I'm glad to find you out of our chamber."

"You make me sound like a turtle hiding in his shell."

He snorts an indelicate laugh. "The loveliest turtle, perhaps."

Arthur lowers to the nearest settee with me still in his arms. I settle on the cushion beside him, Arthur crossing one leg over the other before he notices the small plate on the tea table in front of us.

Letting his leg drop, he leans forward, plucking a delicate cookie off the plate. "Are these my favorite honey cookies?"

"They are," I tell him, pleased to hear his happy moan as he takes a bite. "Ella taught me how to make them."

He stills, eyebrow high as he looks at me. "Truly? You've baked these yourself?"

"With help," I amend. "Does that bother you?"

"My dear, you could run naked through the gardens, and I wouldn't be bothered." At my dubious expression, he tosses his eyes about and says, "A bad example, perhaps. There is not a single endeavor I would ask you to abandon, not if it makes you happy."

A smile quirks my lips. "You're quite committed to my happiness, it would seem."

The bounce of Arthur's eyebrows is all mischief, yet his eyes remain warm. "You've caught me out, I fear."

A laugh bubbles up from my throat, and Arthur looks immensely gratified.

"Oh, I've good news." He reaches for a second cookie before leaning back against the couch, popping the buttons on his coat. "Your new wardrobe is here. Boxed up still. But Willard assured me he'd have everything steamed and hung by this evening."

"Arthur. You didn't have to go to such trouble."

"Charlie, my love, what's mine is yours. But you have to admit, my trousers do not fit you well."

No, I suppose I can't deny that.

He goes on, voice ever gentle. "If any of the fabrics or colors don't suit, let me know, and I'll exchange them for another. And if any pieces need adjustment, I'll have them brought to the tailor. It's no trouble at all."

I let out a breath that draws Arthur's concern. He relaxes at my smile. "I learned something today."

"Is that so?"

I nod and wave a hand toward the desk, where the book I was looking through still resides. "I found your family history. Kane. Do you know what the surname means?"

Arthur looks curious, but he shakes his head. "I'm afraid I don't."

"Descendant of the battle," I tell him, swinging my leg over his lap. Arthur's hands settle on my hips, broad and warm. "You've gone to battle for me, Arthur Kane. I wonder if it's in your blood."

He hums. "What would that make you then? My king?"

A shiver rolls through my body.

Arthur's hands glide up my sides as he leans closer, his lips near my ear. "Say the word, my darling king, and I'll vanquish any and all that stand between us."

"I daresay you're telling the truth," I whisper.

Arthur doesn't answer, but the fire in his eyes leaves little room for doubt. I bring my lips to his, a gentle press, a thank-you for more than I could ever hope to encompass with a single word or touch. Arthur tugs me closer still.

"Pardon." The voice comes from the doorway, Ruby standing in the opening with her eyes downcast. "Supper is ready."

Arthur's newly hired kitchen maid walks off, cheeks flushed. I turn my gaze back to my husband, who's biting his lip and looking rather unrepentant.

"We'll traumatize her at this rate," I say, stepping to the floor. "It'd be a shame. I rather like Ruby."

"Is that so?" Arthur follows after me, taking off his coat as he goes and settling it over his arm. His waistcoat today is gray, the fit accentuating the broadness of his shoulders and his tapered waist.

"Mm. So do try to be a little less alluring, would you?"

Arthur's laughter has me smiling as we walk together down the hall.

When we enter the dining room, two place settings are out on the table, an oil lamp near for the impending night. I grab Arthur's hand and lead him right past. He makes a small, befuddled sound but doesn't try to stop me. We walk through the pantry, the fine dishware to our right, and on into the kitchen.

Ella barely blinks at our arrival, continuing to ladle soup into bowls. "Did he like the cookies?"

"He did," I answer, pushing Arthur toward a seat before taking my own. "Although I'm certain, even if he hadn't, he would have finished every bite with a smile on his face."

She chuckles. "He's no fool, that one."

Arthur watches us with what looks like amusement, and Bess sweeps into the room.

"Ah, you're here." Bess inclines her head toward me and then Arthur. "Sir. Sir. Are you joining us for supper?"

"Are we?" Arthur sounds delighted by the prospect.

"It seems a shame to waste such good conversation," I say, noticing Ruby's smile as she brings over a stack of plates. "Of course there's plenty of room at the dining table if we'd rather eat there?"

Ella raises an eyebrow.

Arthur simply hums, settling back in his seat as he looks around the room. "I quite like it in here. But perhaps we should put it to a vote? Dining room or kitchen?"

Ella tsks, the sound light. "The two of you will see the order in this house brought to ruins."

Ruby and Bess exchange a look. I give Arthur a smile. Willard walks through the door, once again coming to a perplexed halt.

Arthur nods slowly, a gleam in his eye I recognize well. "I think it's about time. What say you, Willard? Kitchen or dining room?"

"Sir?"

Ruby covers her mouth as she begins to laugh.

We end up staying in the kitchen for our evening supper, and I feel, for maybe the first time in my life, settled in a way I haven't before. Arthur helps scrub the dishes. Bess shows me where the linens are laundered. And once the house has grown quiet, I draw myself a bath without any assistance whatsoever.

While lying in bed with Arthur, the oil lamps and candles extinguished, my mind turns over. Arthur seems to notice, although how in such dark quiet, I'm unsure.

"Charlie? Are you quite all right?"

"Yes," I tell him, knowing it to be the absolute truth.

His hand drifts up my arm to my shoulder before he brushes my hair back, the motion soothing. "Yet your mind is spinning."

"There is...so much, Arthur. So much I want to do."

"Ah." He understands, as always. "Where do you wish to start?"

The answer to that is easy. "The observatory."

"And then?"

"I don't quite know. That's the problem."

He chuckles softly. "You have time to figure it out."

I do, don't I? I have all the time in the world now that I'm with Arthur.

"Do you think I'll ever have the body I want?" I ask, an ache in my voice I can't quite disguise. "Without the bindings, I mean."

Arthur makes a soft, thoughtful sound. "I cannot say, my love. I hope for it. If there is a way, I will find it. I can promise you that."

I nod, my throat tight. Arthur's fingers threading through my hair help to keep me rooted in the present. In all the good I've found, my husband included.

There's a wistfulness in Arthur's tone when he speaks. "Perhaps we should wish upon the stars. One is never too old to wish, don't you think?"

Maybe not.

If I could wish for anything, it would be for Arthur's love to follow me into whatever is waiting next. Heaven. Hell. I don't much care, so long as we can be together.

But if I had a second wish... Then perhaps, yes. I would wish for the chance to be seen for exactly who I am.

Chapter 17

Arthur

The telescope arrives on a Friday afternoon. Willard helps me bring it into the observatory, the room no longer the barren, dusty space it was once. Over the past many months, we've brought it to life. Charlie and me, but also the staff.

Ruby, as it turns out, is an expert climber. The outside glass is sparkling thanks to her. Although poor Willard nearly had a heart attack the first time she scaled the roof.

Charlie shoos me away from the telescope as soon as it's unboxed. I watch raptly as he adjusts the focus and positioning of the device, looking through it occasionally despite it being daylight still.

I suppose the stars are always there, even if we can't see their light.

I leave Charlie to his machinations, checking in on him every so often. He doesn't stop to eat the snack cakes I bring in, simply takes a bite and keeps moving.

He only stills once it turns dark.

The window at the south end of the room is open, Charlie positioned in front of it, the telescope giving him a clear, unobstructed view of the sky. The breeze blows in gently, but he doesn't seem to notice nor mind.

Despite my own view being limited by the power of my sight, I lie on my back in the middle of the floor and take it all in. The star-littered sky above is beautiful. So much of it is visible from within this room, an endless swath of black filled with tiny bursts of light. I imagine how far away the stars must be, but it's hard to grasp.

"Arthur." It's the first word Charlie has spoken in hours. I wasn't even sure he realized I was here in the room with him.

I hop up immediately. "Yes?"

"Come look at this."

I walk over, the outline of him and the telescope only lightly illuminated by the moonlight. He grabs my arm once I'm near and pulls me in front of the telescope's eyepiece.

"Close one eye, and look through here."

I do as he instructs, blinking a few times to acclimate my eyesight. "Charlie," I breathe. "There are so many stars."

"Yes." He sounds nearly giddy.

"This is...this is stunning. What am I looking at?"

"It's our universe, Arthur. The Milky Way."

I back away from the telescope, blinking again and looking out through the open window. The band of stars is visible to the naked eye, a hazy streak of light in the dark, but it's nowhere near as defined as what I can see through Charlie's telescope.

I never knew so many stars made up our sky.

Charlie eases in front of the telescope again, his voice soft. "The Romans called it the *Via Galactica*. The 'road made of milk.' They didn't have a way to see it as we do now."

"Did they know of the stars?"

"Oh, yes. They associated many constellations with their myths."

"Such as Canis Major," I realize, thinking of the dog-shaped constellation that comes out in the winter.

Charlie's voice is excited in a way that doesn't happen often. "Precisely. There are so very many constellations."

"Do you have a favorite?"

He hums, backing away from the telescope. I join him in the center of the room, Charlie lying on the blanket I set out earlier. I lie down beside him such that our shoulders are pressed together.

Charlie takes my hand, guiding it upwards, aiming my pointer finger at the northern sky. He draws a shape with it, up and then down again. "There. The Sword of Leandros."

I find the sword in the sky, the star at the bottom of it brightest. It seems to flicker, the shape ever so slightly obscured in the glass. Charlie returns our hands to the floor, fingers intertwined.

"What's the myth?" I ask. "I haven't heard it."

Charlie lets out the softest of sighs. "It's not a happy story."

"No? Are any myths happy?"

He snorts at that. "Not many. But this... It's quite the tragedy."

"And yet it's your favorite?"

His answer is quiet. "Yes."

"Will you tell me?"

He nods, his head settling beside my own. "It's said Leandros was the fiercest warrior there was. He bested every foe he encountered. He never failed. Never fell. One day, a deity decided she wanted Leandros for her own. She went to him, asking for him to join her."

"I take it he wasn't keen."

Sadness is evident in Charlie's tone. "No, he wasn't. He was already in love."

His fingers play with my own as he collects his words.

"Leandros refused the deity. Time and time again. She was livid, so when she returned one day to discover Leandros's love with him at his home, she fell into a rage. They were killed, both of them."

I look over at Charlie, his face difficult to make out in the dark. His voice, however, is steeped in such strong melancholy that I bring his hand to my lips, kissing the back of it gently in hopes of soothing his distress.

He sucks in a small, shuddering breath. "Of all the battles he faced, all the adversaries and trials and monsters, not a single one could fell him. Not a one except for love."

"Charlie. My dear."

"I know it's sad. Terribly sad. But that sword reminds me of how powerful love can be. It's a weapon far greater than any steel. And no one, not even a vengeful god, can take it away."

The pain in my chest at Charlie's words is visceral, an ache that has me clutching his hand tight. "And what of our love, dear heart?"

Charlie's head turns my way, his eyes specks of light in the dark. "It will outlast all the stars, Arthur. Every last one of them."

When Charlie and I wake, we're in the observatory still. The window is open, sun streaming into the room but the air around us cool. Charlie lets out a groan before tucking his face against my chest.

"Oh Lord, Arthur. What have we done?"

I laugh quietly, even as my back twinges. "You, my love, have youth on your side. I fear I may be stiff all day."

Proving my point about his youthfulness, Charlie rolls swiftly to his knees and holds out his hands. His hair is disheveled, falling from its pins, but there's a soft smile on his face that has my heart tripping over itself as I accept his aid in standing.

I only wince some. "Why, thank you, kind sir."

Charlie rubs a hand over my lower back, trying to soothe the ache away. "Come. Let's set ourselves to rights."

After closing the window, Charlie and I make our way down to the second floor, taking our turns on both the toilet and at the sink. Charlie pins his hair in front of the vanity in our chamber as I re-dress, my clothes from yesterday wrinkled after their time on the floor.

"I wonder what Ella will have prepared for breakfast," I say, tucking my shirt beneath my trousers. "I would happily clean the dishes again in exchange for some apple tart."

Charlie remains quiet, not answering, so I turn his way.

"Charlie?"

"Arthur... What is this?"

The box I placed on the vanity yesterday is open now, the contents held in Charlie's hand. *Ah.* I'd forgotten about it in Charlie's excitement over his telescope arriving.

"That," I say slowly, heading his way, "is a fake cock."

His eyes swing to me, wide. The cock is made from ivory, surprisingly lifelike in its appearance yet smooth to the touch. At the base is a set of straps I had specially commissioned.

"These," I explain to Charlie, running my fingers over the straps, "would go around your hips. You'd wear it, my dear, if that is something you'd have interest in trying."

His chest rises and falls as he looks at the smooth ivory, his thumb close to the flared head. I can't yet gauge his opinion, but he hasn't tossed it away.

"It's...erect. Would that not draw attention?"

A smile tugs at my lips. "It's for intercourse, my love."

His eyes widen further, an aborted sound leaving his lips. "I would use it with you?"

"If you'd like," I tell him, running my finger along the ivory as Charlie swallows. "Do you wish to try it?"

His voice comes out at a whisper. "Will it not hurt?"

"I don't quite know," I tell him truthfully. "I have...oil...that was suggested for easing the way."

"Arthur..."

"If it's too much—"

"No." The word is quick. "I...I want to try. Desperately."

"Whenever you're ready," I assure him.

"Now."

"Now?" I repeat on a laugh. The look in Charlie's eye has my laughter dissolving, abandoning me as heat flares low in my belly. I take a deep breath, and then two. "Let me wash up."

Charlie nods in a quick jerk, and I retreat to the bathroom, my own cock starting to strain my trousers. I make quick use of the wash basin, cleaning as well as I can manage, before returning to Charlie. He's waiting on our bed, starkly naked, the ivory cock on the linens in front of him.

"I don't know what to do."

The urgency in Charlie's tone has me stepping forward quickly. I stop for the oil, stashed in my wardrobe, before removing my trousers. Charlie watches me approach the bed, his chest heaving, his hand moving slowly between his legs in a way that has me groaning. Seeing the man I love pleasure himself is second to very little. Perhaps it's why I have no qualms about what's to come. If Charlie enjoys it, little else matters.

I set the oil on the bed and remove my shirt. "The straps run around your hips and between your thighs. May I?"

Charlie nods, and I pick up the fake cock. I'm careful as I maneuver the straps into place, tightening them only as much as necessary. The fabric is soft to the touch, the straps between his legs thinner than those around his hips. I run a finger underneath each, making sure the fit is as directed.

"All right?" I check.

Charlie nods. "Yes, I believe so. You're hard."

The observation is given as a statement, yet there's surprise in his voice.

"Because you desire me, Charlie dear. I require little more than that."

He blows out a breath, shuffling closer on his knees. "Show me what to do."

I open the oil, handing it to Charlie before turning onto my hands and knees and dropping to my elbows. "Could you get me wet, my love?"

"Oh, Arthur." His hand slides slowly over my backside. "If you do not like it—"

"We'll deal with that possibility if it occurs," I assure him. "Now... You'll need to wet me and the cock both."

Charlie lets out a breath, his hand leaving me for only a moment before it returns, slick with oil. His touch is gentle, slow as he rubs against me, taking his time. The sensation is not one I'm used to, but I try my best not to be dissuaded from it. I've been assured this can be pleasurable. If the necessary steps are taken.

Charlie's voice comes breathless. "Arthur. How will this work? I'm afraid I will hurt you."

"My body should accept it," I tell him, breathing out as Charlie's hand slides down toward my cock. He encircles me, twisting his grip slowly, the glide smooth with the oil on his fingers. "As for the rest, well... I believe you're aware of the mechanics."

Charlie's hand returns to where he started, his thumb pressing against me until my body yields. He stills. "Art?"

"This part is as new to me as it is you," I say softly. "It doesn't feel bad, my love. Try the cock. Go slow."

His hand leaves me before returning, braced near my hip. The next second, the ivory is there. It must be. It's harder than Charlie's touch, an entirely different sensation. I keep myself as relaxed as I can manage, but even so, it's a lot to take in, both physically and mentally.

"Just a moment," I tell Charlie.

He stills, the end of the cock pressing against me the same way his thumb did, demanding me to yield.

"Arthur." Charlie's hand slides up my back and then down again before smoothing over my bottom. "You're lovely. Do you know that?"

"You think so?"

He hums, his hand journeying underneath me again. He strokes my cock, and I sink further onto my elbows. "So very lovely. I've never wanted another the way I want you. You're charming and handsome, and the sight of you right this instant, down on your knees for me, makes me desperate to see you unraveling at my touch."

I realize, as Charlie continues to stroke my cock, that he's edged further into me. Not far, but enough to feel distinctly...open for him. There's a stretch. A sting. The instinctual rebelling of my body that wars with what Charlie is doing to my cock. He focuses his attention there, the distraction a welcome reprieve that has my legs beginning to shake.

Charlie sounds awed. "You've taken an inch of me, Arthur. Did you realize?"

"No," I admit, the pressure intense but the sting accompanied by a restlessness I don't know whether I should lean into or away from. Charlie decides for me, pressing further inside, his soft moan stoking the fire within me, the burn inescapable. One way or another, I have no doubt it will consume me, body and soul.

"Arthur, please tell me if I am hurting you. I'm desperate to have you, but I hate the thought of causing you pain. I can slow. Or we can stop altogether."

The hoarseness in his voice is evidence of both his concern and his desire, but I don't need him to stop.

"My heart," I say softly, more than ready to offer every fiber of my being to the person most deserving of it. "Have me as you will. Have my body, my love, and my everlasting soul. For there is not a single other in this universe I wish to share eternity with."

Charlie hiccups a breath, his hand leaving my cock to brush against the pulse point at my neck. "Arthur Kane. I pray I can show you the stars."

I turn my head, pressing a kiss to the pad of his finger. "None will ever be as exquisite as you."

I'm certain of it.

CHAPTER 18

Charlie

I was told often in my life, once of age, that love was no different than a contract. That my love would be carefully cultivated over time, that I would find things to appreciate in the husband chosen for me, and I'd ignore the rest. That the decisions made in the pursuit of...*love* weren't mine to make. Marriage could be happy if I was able to keep my tongue.

Perhaps, for many, love is a business. For women, more often, a part of life.

But the love I've found with Arthur is as bountiful as the roses he keeps in the gardens. It's as vast and breathtaking as the galaxy we're spinning in. It's honest, and it's true, and there's not a single thing I wouldn't do for the man who shares it with me.

I pull back enough to slip from Arthur's body. He makes a soft, curious sound, but I guide him to turn onto his back, needing to see his eyes as forcefully as I need my next breath. He settles with his legs spread, and I ease over him, not knowing how to possibly explain all I feel.

The acceptance of my very being I've only ever had with him.

"I love you," I tell him, my hand on his face, my breath drawn tight. "I love you wildly."

His gaze softens, and he pulls me close, his lips meeting mine in a tender press. "Then love me as wildly as you dare."

I nod jerkily, sucking in a breath as Arthur encourages me inside his body once more. His legs are drawn upwards, the oil still glistening on his skin. I hold the ivory cock as I press against him, marveling at the sight of him opening for me. The way his body gives, wrapping the cock up tight, how it disappears piece by piece as Arthur lets out a sound that might be a groan.

I wrap my hand around his prick again, not wanting him to flag, not wanting this to be anything other than pleasurable for him in the end.

When he's accepted all of what I have to give, I stall, my heart pounding rapidly, my skin flushed.

Sweat gleams on Arthur's brow, his tone light. "Have I done it?"

"Yes," I say, awed.

"Then by all means, husband mine. Show me the stars."

With a stutter inside my chest and my eyes stinging, I pull back and thrust the gifted cock into Arthur's body. He grunts, a soft sound followed by another when I do it again. I can't feel the way the cock is entering him. Not in the same way he'd be able to. But I can feel the reverberation of it jolting against me with every snap of my hips.

I have never in my life felt as connected to another. As utterly at home as I find a rhythm that has Arthur's own cock bucking lightly in my fist. Ensuring his pleasure becomes my own. My bliss. My vow. My most prized possession.

"Charlie." Arthur's gaze is clouded, his cheeks red. I recognize the expression on his face.

"You enjoy it," I say, not a question.

He exhales breathily, his hand slipping beneath his knee. I move my fist firmly over his cock, trying to keep up the tempo that has his muscles clenching tight. I ignore the bounce of my chest as I roll my hips, my absolute focus on Arthur and the way he's swelling in my hand as the ivory strokes a place inside of him that's new to the both of us.

"Charlie." His tone this time is frantic, and he loses purchase on his knee, his entire body twisting before he erupts with a broken shout.

I have never seen anything more magnificent. Never felt as if my being was truly inside another. My own body throbs, desire heavy as Arthur unravels more beautifully than I've ever witnessed. I pull the cock from his body, scrambling over him, taking his face in my hands, the mess between us spreading from his skin to my own.

"Art?" I ask when he doesn't say a word.

He lets out a tiny laugh. And then another. My insides swell as his beaming grin finds me, his brown eyes so very bright.

"I quite think I like your new cock." He laughs once more, a joyous sound. "Will you use it on me again?"

I kiss him. As hard as I dare. Arthur works to loosen the straps around my hips. He spins me the moment the cock drops to the bed, his dark gaze sending a delighted shiver down my spine.

"May I suck you, my love?"

I nod rapidly at the request, and Arthur scoots down my body. I grab onto his hair as he settles between my legs, his mouth and tongue wet, the sensation divine as he drives me relentlessly toward orgasm. It hits me like a cascade of sparks, warm and all-encompassing, my back arching up off the bed as I see my own version of a constellation.

Arthur keeps at it lazily until I give his hair a tug. The ivory cock rests beside us, Arthur's head on my thigh now as we work to catch our breath. His fingers stroke over my hip, and I realize he's tracing the indentation from the straps.

"It wasn't uncomfortable," I assure him.

"Even when you were moving?"

"Even then. It felt quite...heavy. In a good way. I liked it, Arthur. It felt as if it were mine."

He kisses my thigh, turning his face up to look at me. "It is yours. It was remarkable."

"Truly?"

"Yes. It took some adjusting, and I won't lie and say there wasn't a hint of pain. But it was entirely worth the end result. Not to mention the look on your face while you were inside of me."

My cheeks heat as Arthur's fingers trail over my stomach. The man himself lifts after a moment, crawling over my body to give me a slow kiss that steals my breath. His expression is one of mischief as he leans back, his thumb running over my bottom lip.

"Did you enjoy fucking your husband, Mr. Kane?"

My breath catches anew, and Arthur grins.

"Mm. Thought so." He kisses me again. "Shall we clean up?"

With a nod, I let Arthur lead me from the bedchamber. We take care of our own cleanliness, as well as that of the fake cock, and then we head downstairs for a rather late breakfast.

Ella is the only one in the kitchen, preparing a dough for bread baking.

Arthur greets her warmly. "Morning, Ella. Don't worry yourself over us."

She smiles bemusedly as Arthur heads for a small tray of tarts and biscuits nearby. He grabs it, as well as a jar of jam and a knife, before meeting me at the table.

We eat our breakfast as the house staff moves about, tending to their duties. A blush returns to my cheeks every time I look at Arthur and remember our morning together. His broad body at my disposal. The sound of his delight. My name rolling off his lips as he spilled onto his stomach.

He catches me watching him and sends me a wink.

We take a walk around the gardens late morning. The roses are no longer blooming, the last having wilted over a week ago. A scattering of petals lie below the sprawling bushes, the color that of dried blood. I press one with the toe of my boot.

Arthur seems to sense my indrawn mood, his voice softly questioning. "Charlie?"

"Is a rose without petals still a rose? Or is it only a bush?"

He hums, his hand clasped with my own. "It's still a rose, surely. Otherwise we wouldn't wait for it to bloom every summer."

"And if it never blooms again?"

Gentle fingers lift my chin, Arthur's eyes finding mine. "If it never blooms, does it not still have its thorns? Is it not still a rose at its roots? What is it that's troubling you, Charlie dear?"

"I wish to cut my hair."

Arthur draws in a quiet breath, his lips lifting into a smile. "Then come. I know a perfectly good pair of scissors."

My heart paces rapidly as we return indoors. Arthur goes to locate Bess as I take a seat upstairs in our chamber. I roll the scissors over in my hand, the wig Arthur bought me a good month ago catching my eye. It's brown, like my own hair. A close match. No one should be able to detect the difference should I need to wear it.

Arthur knocks once before entering, Bess right behind him. She gives me a warm smile as Arthur approaches the stool I'm sitting on, the mirror at my back.

"Are you ready?"

I blow out a soft breath before answering my husband. "I've been ready all my life."

Arthur sits on the floor, his knees bent and his eyes on me, as Bess begins cutting my hair, having acquired the talent through a lifetime of cutting her brother's. I keep my gaze on Arthur as long strands of chestnut brown fall to the floor. Bess takes her time, removing most of my hair before slowly shaping what's left. The absence of weight is...startling. I never realized quite how heavy a shroud of hair could be.

Bess's hands run over my head a few times before she finally steps back. "All set, sir."

"Bess," I say quietly.

"Charlie." The amendment is quick, Bess's eyes wet with her smile.

I pull in a breath as Arthur stands, reaching for me. I accept his proffered palm, letting him guide me to my feet.

He gives my hand a gentle squeeze. "Stay here."

I wait as Arthur walks to my wardrobe, pulling a light green waistcoat from inside, followed by a dapper wool coat with long tails. He returns, the coat hanging off his arm as he buttons the waistcoat over my shirt, the bindings already in place underneath. The coat goes on last, Arthur walking around behind me to slip it up my arms. There's a smile on his face as he buttons the front, but his eyes look sad in a way I've rarely ever seen.

"Arthur?"

He shakes his head quickly, swallowing once. "It's nothing, my love."

"It is something," I counter, my chest feeling tight. "Does it displease you seeing me so?"

"Charlie."

His voice is soft, but I shake my own head.

"No, Arthur. Be honest with me. Always."

He puffs out a breath, smoothing the fabric of my coat before his eyes meet mine, his hands settling on my shoulders. "I am upset because you are breathtaking, and the world will never see it. They don't understand it. And I wish, more than anything, they could understand you, Charlie dear. I wish they could see what I see."

"What do you see?" I ask, my voice shaking.

"I see the person I fell in love with looking more comfortable than ever before. I see him standing tall, his thorns ready for battle. I see my husband, the man I married, looking so handsome it hurts my chest. But, my love, it doesn't matter what I see. What's important is how you feel. All I wish for is your happiness. I'm quite selfish that way."

I let out a laugh, my eyes stinging.

Arthur's hands slide up to my face. He cups me as if I'm precious to him. It's easy to believe it's true.

"Charlie, you will always be my heart, no matter how many times your name may change. No matter your body or age or the years we see pass. There is nothing in this universe that would stop me from loving you. Dare I say not even death."

He leans close, lips pressing to my temple as my hands shake against his wrists.

"I didn't fall in love with you for your petals, my dear heart. So let them fall. Summer is but a season, and I suspect it's long since passed."

My breath shudders as I look down at the floor between our feet. Strands of brown lay fallen, the last vestiges of the

Charlotte I was scattered like dried flowers that never fit my vine. I press the toe of my boot against a curl, imagining it crumbling to dust.

When I bring my gaze upwards again, Arthur is watching me, waiting. Bess, I realize, has left the room, giving Arthur and me privacy I appreciate.

It's not easy, turning toward the mirror. It feels like an immeasurable trek. Miles and miles of distance crossed over landscape both harsh and foreign. There's fear that the end of the journey won't be what I expect. That, for all the ways I've come to be accepted in this home I never expected to have, I won't be able to accept myself. That I won't see myself as I am. As who I'm supposed to be.

My gaze starts on the vanity. Mahogany wood, lovingly crafted and polished. A brush sits to the right. The scissors near it. In one drawer rests the ivory cock Arthur and I used just this morning.

How has it only been mere hours since then?

Further up is the frame of the mirror. My eyes stay there for a long moment, the vision of myself unfocused but waiting just up ahead. I close my eyes. Blackness. An inhale of breath. And finally, light once more.

There's a profound beat that passes in which I don't recognize myself. A man stands before me, his short hair not quite reaching his ears. His cheekbones are sharp, and his jaw soft. But there's steel in his gaze. A flattened chest. A slim figure covered impeccably in the height of men's fashion. A cravat expertly tied around his neck. A coat ending at his trousers, the tails of which nearly reach his boots.

It takes me a second to put a name to this man.

Charlie.

Arthur's thumb wipes away the tear that rolls down my cheek. That one and the next. He stands behind me, my sword and my shield, every ounce a Kane, whether by blood or sheer determination.

Arthur presses a kiss to my wet cheek, his hands on my shoulders squeezing once. There's a hitch in his voice he doesn't try to disguise. "My husband. Look at you."

I find Arthur's hand, holding tight, seeing in the mirror two men who fell in love.

Love.

The most powerful weapon there is.

For no one, not even a god, can take it away.

PART III

Grayson and Ezra

CHAPTER 19

Grayson

"Drop the weapon, Victor."

"You know I can't do that."

"You can, and you will," I say, keeping my gun level with Victor's own. I see the moment his eyes flick to the side. "Don't."

My best friend's arm swings to his right, toward the hostage bound in the corner of the room, and I pull the trigger. Red blooms over his chest as he falls in staggered steps to the floor. His knees, first, hitting the now red-tinged wood. His hand, catching his weight. His eyes, looking at me with betrayal.

"Why did you have to do that?" I ask, my voice coming out choked in a way I don't even have to force. "Why, Victor?"

His smile is pained, his hand at his chest ineffectually blocking the blood still pouring free. "I knew you'd be the end of me, McKayle. One way or another."

"Was it worth it?" I ask, lowering my gun to my side. His is several feet from him, lying uselessly on the floor.

He laughs almost bitterly. But there's amusement there. Even facing death, he relishes the fight between us. It's easy to see.

"I would do it all again." Victor slumps the moment the last word leaves his mouth, his hand out at his side, red streaked across the floor in a gory visual befitting the villain's end.

He really did play such a good villain.

"Cut," comes a voice, followed by a couple of cheers.

I let my smile show. "Please tell me we got it that time?"

"No kidding." Ezra groans, lifting from the pool of fake blood surrounding him. "This stuff is a mess."

"Pretty boy doesn't like the blood?" I tease.

Ezra, no longer Victor, shoots me a scowl that has Harper laughing from the corner of the set.

"Seriously," she says. "Did we get it? I want out of the rope."

"We got it," our director answers, his eyes reviewing the footage. He gives a big thumbs-up. "That's a wrap for now, folks. Check your schedules on Monday for a list of reshoots. And do *not* get hammered this weekend. Save it for after the premiere, all right?"

Harper snorts as one of the assistants frees her from her bindings. Ezra gets to his feet and heads my way.

"Ez," I caution, taking a step back, knowing full well what that glimmer in his eye means.

He grins sharply. Right before he tackles me to the floor.

The wind puffs out of me, and several people on the crew laugh as my very *worst* best friend proceeds to wipe fake blood all over my face and neck.

"Gonna get you back for this," I wheeze.

He pats my cheek twice. "Who's the pretty boy now?"

Ezra stands, holding out his hand to pull me to my feet. I accept it, only to tug him right back down. He grunts upon impact, rolling onto his back next to me to catch his breath. Harper shakes her head as she passes, a smile on her faux-bruised face.

I reach over to slap Ezra's chest. "All right?"

"You suck."

I keep my voice at a whisper. "Not as well as you, I've heard."

He flips me off.

"People are going to hate you for this," I point out. "The literal golden boy of Hollywood, turning rogue?"

"Nah." His head lolls my way, a rakish grin on his blood-smeared face. Even at forty-six and covered in blood, Ezra Gold is as handsome as ever. "Everyone loves a bad boy."

"If you say so."

With a mighty grunt, Ezra pushes to his feet. He holds out his hand again, willing to gamble I won't pull him to the floor a second time. Or just not caring. I clasp my hand with his, and Ezra hauls me up, the two of us heading off set.

There's a lightness to the air within the studio, smiles on people's faces now that the brunt of filming is done. We'll likely have a few reshoots to take care of, but we're in the final stretch now.

No matter how many times I do this, it never ceases to amaze me. If asked twenty-some years ago if I ever saw myself as a movie star, my answer would have been a resounding no. It wasn't even on my radar.

How quickly life can change.

Ezra and I split into our respective trailers, my friend grumbling about the fake blood as he goes. The man's prima donna act is purely a show, meant for others' amusement, even my own. It's how Ezra is hardwired. Wanting to make people smile and laugh. Wanting them not to take him too seriously, even.

Because if people expect one thing, they're not likely to look closer. Who would possibly think the flippant superstar Ezra Gold is actually one of the most genuinely thoughtful and caring individuals out there?

If you keep people at a distance, well, then they can't hurt you where it matters, can they?

Ezra may play it up for the crowd, but despite the fame and glory that follow him around like a gnat seeking light, he's humble beneath it all. A kind soul.

Assuming you don't piss him off.

Red dye circles down the drain as I shower, my clothes in a bag I'll take to Wardrobe later. I let out a sigh as I turn my face into the softly pelting water, the weight of this shoot so close to being behind me.

It's not that I dislike filming. I don't.

But each role I play consumes my life for however long it is I have to live it. It's different for Ezra. He can slip into anybody's skin in a moment's notice. Action star? Romantic lead? Villain? There's not a set of shoes out there he doesn't feel comfortable in.

Whereas for me, it doesn't come easy. It takes time to prepare for my part. To figure out who the person is I'm supposed to be embodying. To understand what makes them tick, their mannerisms, their patterns of speech.

Ezra often jokes I've lived a thousand lives because of how deeply I immerse myself into a role. And he may not be wrong. It feels that way sometimes.

But it's a relief when I can finally shed the mask and let myself settle back into my own skin and bones. Sometimes I wonder how much longer I'll keep doing this. Probably as long as Ezra.

Once I'm out of the shower and dressed, I go searching for my phone. There's an influx of messages waiting for me. The usual rabble, but also an email from my lawyer and a single text from my now ex-wife that catches my eye. *"It's done,"* is all it says.

Two words to signal the end of an era.

How...utterly anticlimactic.

The email is confirmation of what my ex sent. Our divorce has officially gone through. It was a long, long time coming.

I sit down on the small couch inside my trailer and call my daughter. It only takes a couple rings before she answers.

"Dad."

The evenness of her tone tells me her mom has already called with the news. I'm not surprised.

"Hey, Peaches. I take it you heard?"

"Yeah," she says quietly. "Are you okay?"

My heart clenches at her concern. "I'm fine," I tell her, meaning it. Camilla and I have been separated for quite some time. Years, now. The divorce was simply the final door being shut on a house long since gone dark. "How are you?"

"It's not really about me, is it?"

I'm not sure when my little girl went and grew up, but here we are. Me, in my mid-forties. Madison, twenty now and in her second year of college. *Christ*, I can remember her in diapers.

"It affects you, though," I say gently. "And your feelings matter."

She lets out a quiet huff. "It sucks, but it's fine. We're all adults."

My lips twitch. "Ah, yes. How could I have forgotten. And...how many more months before you're allowed to legally drink alcohol?"

"As if you'd ever forget my birthday," she counters. "Please, *please* don't do anything embarrassing this year."

"When have I ever?"

"*Every* year. You and Ezra get these elaborate ideas into your head, and I'm the one who suffers. Just...take it easy for once?"

"I'll try."

Her responding sigh is proof she doesn't believe me. "Moving on. Do me a favor?"

"Of course."

"Do something for yourself this weekend," she says, shocking me. "I don't know what. Have a nice glass of scotch or...buy a first edition of your favorite book or whatever. Just...you deserve to be happy, Dad. You don't have to pretend you're sad about the divorce."

"Peaches..."

"You don't," she repeats. "You don't owe me or anyone else a certain emotional response. I know you and Mom weren't happy together. Not for a long time. So just...be happy. Okay?"

"I'll do my best," I tell her, wishing I could give my daughter a hug. "I'll be back in town in a couple weeks. Dinner?"

"You bet. Love you."

"Love you, too."

When I hang up, I let my phone rest on my leg. The background is a picture of my daughter, her auburn hair lighter than my own, giving her the peaches-and-cream complexion that's responsible for her nickname. Next to her is Ezra, dark-haired and wide-grinned, looking proud of his honorary niece for moving into her first college dorm.

With a soft sigh of my own, I shut off the device and get up to find my friend.

A nice glass of scotch.

Yeah, that doesn't sound half bad.

The party at Harper's hotel room is loud, a good many of the cast and crew getting hammered, despite the warning we received. The scotch in my hand is nearly gone, but the woman hanging off my arm makes it difficult to finish the last dregs.

"What's it like?" she asks, her smile too big. "Being famous, I mean."

Lonely, I want to tell her. Even though it's not entirely the truth. I have plenty of people in my life who keep the loneliness at bay.

But when you're surrounded by people who don't see you? Well, it's more than a little isolating.

My eyes seek out Ezra in the crowd, but I can't find him. He disappeared not long ago.

"It's a dream come true," I tell the woman. "Excuse me."

"But—"

I politely remove her hand from my arm and walk off, my gaze swinging around. Harper gives me a grin from atop the lap of one of the crew members she's taken a liking to. She holds her drink up in a silent cheers, and I give her a nod before moving on.

I finish my scotch as I walk toward the wet bar stationed in the adjoining room. I get stopped along the way, another fan I don't recognize asking me questions and holding on to me. It takes a good few minutes to extract myself.

I've just reached the bar and am waiting on my second scotch when a new arm loops through my own. This time, it's Ezra. He gives me a beaming smile.

"What are you doing?" I ask in some amusement.

"Figured you might be tired of batting women off with a stick. I'll be your shield."

I snort at his cheekiness, accepting my scotch from the person manning the bar. "You think that'll stop them? Being married never did."

Ezra shrugs. "Well, sure. Because they'll be hitting on me instead."

"You're so full of it," I inform my friend.

His smile widens, and he winks. Ezra leads me away from the bar, conversation buzzing around us. He finds a door to the balcony, and for a brief moment in time, the two of us escape. It won't last forever, but I breathe in the cool evening air, the lights of the city stretched out in front of us.

Ezra lets me go to lean against the railing, picking up the thread of our conversation. "You're not married anymore."

"No," I say, taking a small sip of my drink.

He turns toward me, quiet in a way he only ever is around me. He doesn't have to fill the void with chatter. He's thinking, I can tell.

Finally, he opens his mouth. "Move in with me."

I nearly drop my drink off the balcony. "Ez. What?"

"Come on, Grayson. You're newly divorced. We both know I'm never getting married. For fuck's sake, we're well on our way to fifty goddamn years old. I'm never as happy as when I'm with you, so just...let's be together. What do we have to lose?"

My pulse is sprinting, but Ezra looks dead serious. "Every-thing," I answer, as obvious as it is. "No one will understand."

"Who gives a shit?"

I scrub a hand over my face, huffing out a breath. "Ezra...you're not even out."

"And you're not even queer."

"What's it going to look like to the outside world?" I go on. "Two high-profile celebrities living together? Two *men*. Do you really want to do that to your career?"

"Fuck my career." The words cause my mouth to snap shut. Ezra *loves* acting. "If you don't care about the optics, then neither do I. Goddamn it, Gray, if I can't live my life the way I want to, then what is it all even for?"

My heart hammers, my mind running through the implica-tions. No one *would* understand. Ezra and I have had a Hol-lywood "bromance" for nearly twenty years. Everyone knows we're best friends, and the media eats it up.

But to move in together?

"Gray." Ezra's voice is soft, his hand squeezing my arm, the touch like a tether. "I don't care what people think. We've talked about it for *years*. How nice it would be if it could just be...us. The two of us. Why can't it be?"

"They'll assume we're a couple."

He shrugs.

"It won't stay quiet," I continue. "This will blow the fuck up."

A smile begins to form on Ezra's face. If I didn't know him inside and out, I'd be alarmed by that smile.

But it's not the chaos Ezra craves. It's the fact that he knows he's already won.

I drop my head with a groan. "This is the stupidest thing we could possibly do," I tell him, knowing he's well aware of that fact.

Ezra simply holds out his hand, waiting for my answer, a wide grin on his face.

It feels inevitable as I clasp my palm with his. This will go supernova. All the media sites, all our fans, our agent, our family and friends. There won't be a way to come back from this.

Do I care?

Madison wanted me to do something for myself this weekend. Something that would make me happy.

Somehow, I doubt moving in with fellow movie star Ezra Gold was what she had in mind.

CHAPTER 20

Ezra

Grayson unpacks the last of his books as I make us a quick lunch in the kitchen overlooking the living room. He hums to himself every so often, stopping to read a line here or there or simply stroking over a spine.

My lips twitch, my chest ballooning as it's been doing ever since Grayson agreed to move in with me weeks ago. I figured he'd prefer it to the reverse. His old home... Well, it was full of memories I think he'd rather part with.

The front door opens without a knock, slamming shut a moment later. Our agent's voice rings out before he's even in view. "You're really going through with this?"

Shawn stops at the entrance to the living area, looking between me and Grayson. Grayson's head is out of his books now, and he stands with a resigned sigh.

"Well, hello, Shawn," I greet, grabbing an extra plate. "So nice of you to drop by."

His lips purse, and he struts forward, taking a seat at the island in front of me. "I asked you to wait."

"And I said no," I retort, giving him the ghost of a smile.

"We need to get ahead of this. Put out a statement. Plan an announcement on our end that you and Grayson are—"

"No," I repeat, sliding him a plate piled with buffalo wings and fries, blue cheese dressing on the side. At his look of abject horror, I say, "Filming is done. Enjoy the calories with me."

"I can *not* eat like you do and still fit in my clothes," he says, inching the plate away.

Grayson takes a seat beside him at the island, digging into his own meal. I shoot him a pleased smile.

Shawn lets out a big gust of a sigh. "If we don't control the narrative, rumors are going to fly rampant. You two need to announce that you're in a relationship—"

"Gray and I are not in a relationship," I tell the man for the umpteenth time. "Not the kind you're thinking."

Shawn's shoulders deflate. His eyes ping to Grayson, who's immersed in his food, before coming back to me. "Drop the act. It's the twenty-first goddamn century. Are you two going to get flak for this? Yes. Big time. You—" He points to me. "Are one of the biggest movie stars on the fucking planet. And Grayson is right there behind you. You'll have fans who won't like it, but you'll have plenty of people rooting for you. If I can't convince you to keep this hidden, which *apparently* I cannot..." He pauses, flourishing a hand around at our now commingling possessions. "Then let me set the fucking narrative from the start. You two are in a loving, committed relationship. You've always been friends but it wasn't anything more until recently. Grayson wasn't fucking around behind his wife's back, and you two are going to be the picture of a happy, gay, monogamous couple. Got it?"

Grayson speaks up, his voice calm. "We've never fucked."

Shawn's wide eyes shift to me.

I shrug. "We haven't. I told you—it's not like that."

Our agent shoots out of his seat, pacing around the kitchen. "Then what the ever-loving fuck are you two doing? How is this worth the shitstorm coming our way?"

I slam my hands down on the counter, and Shawn jolts. "It's worth it to us. *Him*. And *me*." I aim a finger between Grayson and myself. "It's *our* life, Shawn. Let us live it."

He breathes heavily for a moment. Grayson, for his part, is eating a buffalo wing.

"You expect people to believe you're two bachelor friends shacking up and nothing more?" Shawn asks, shaking his head. "They won't."

"I don't care," I tell him, taking my own plate over to the other side of the island. I plop down next to Grayson, Shawn at my back. "It doesn't matter what people think. It doesn't matter what they say."

"And your careers?" he asks, walking around to the front of us. "You'll lose opportunities because of this."

I open my hands wide. "There'll be others. Like you said, I'm the biggest movie star on the planet. If someone doesn't want to work with me because I'm queer, well...I can't say I want to work with them either."

"One of," Shawn says tiredly, scrubbing his eyes. "I said you're *one of* the biggest movie stars. Not *the* biggest."

I huff.

"And you?" Shawn asks Grayson. "You're willing to risk your career for him? Some guy you're not even fucking, apparently?"

Grayson lifts his gaze steadily, his blue eyes like the calmest ocean. "I'd risk everything for him."

Shawn throws his hands into the air once more, storming a step away before coming back. "You two are making a mistake. The biggest one of your careers. Of your *lives*."

"And yet, somehow, I'm still smiling," I point out, grinning Shawn's way.

He looks near murderous, although I know underneath it he has our best interests at heart. He's been a good agent to us both, and he didn't blink twice at the news that Grayson was moving in. He simply went into damage control mode. On top of trying to stop us a good dozen times.

But what he can't seem to understand is that I'm done playing to other people's expectations. I grew up in a time where being bi wasn't talked about or readily accepted. It was barely understood. It's different now, and the world needs more queer representation in mainstream media. So I'll lose the support of a bunch of homophobic or biphobic assholes. Big deal. Maybe I'll even lose my standing in cinema.

But I've been doing this for nearly thirty years. I think it's time I play myself for once.

"What if I release a statement that Grayson is staying temporarily on the heels of his divorce?" Shawn asks, a last-ditch effort to control the story.

"I'm not gonna lie," I tell him.

He groans. "You two are going to have to face the music at some point. Some paparazzi is going to catch Grayson coming or going, and the stories will start. People will speculate. You'll be hounded."

"We'll deal with it when it happens."

"Fine," Shawn says, voice clipped. "If you're determined to implode like dying goddamn stars, by all means. I'll be in touch."

Grayson waits until the front door slams to speak. "I don't think he likes us very much."

I snort. "He likes us fine. He doesn't like not being able to do his job. And this... Well. It'll cause problems."

Grayson chews his lip for a moment, his plate mostly clean. "Should we care more? About how this affects others?"

I scoff. "We're not harming anyone with our actions, so no. We damn well should not."

Grayson chuckles lightly. "You've got a bee in your bonnet about this."

"In my bonnet?" I question. "Really?"

"If you had one, there'd be a bee in there. You're on the warpath, Ez."

I shrug, putting the remnants of our meal in the fridge. "Yeah, well. Maybe I've realized there are some things worth fighting for."

He doesn't argue against that, but I can feel his gaze following me.

"Have you told Madison?" I ask. "Camilla?"

"Yeah. Madison wasn't shocked, exactly, but I can tell she has questions. Camilla is...angry."

I try to keep my thoughts about *that* to myself, but Grayson must see something on my face because he goes on.

"My ex will be fine once she's had time to think about it. Right now, she's reacting on instinct. She's hurt, and it's easier to assume I might have been unfaithful all these years than to accept the fact that we simply were never going to last."

"You shouldn't have started," I say under my breath, regretting the words immediately.

He doesn't disagree. "No, but it brought me Madison. And I'll never regret that."

I let out a sigh. "Me, neither."

Grayson is quiet for a moment. "She never hated you, you know. Camilla. She likes you, and I think that makes it harder."

"Because I stole so much of your time."

"Yeah."

I nod, putting Grayson's plate in the dishwasher before washing my hands. Leaning against the counter, I watch my friend. "People will assume you're bi. Or, hell, even gay. That you were closeted."

Grayson doesn't flinch. "We already talked about this."

"And we're going to talk about it more. I want to make sure you've considered every angle."

His lips curve into a bemused smile. "Really, Ez? You think I'm going to change my mind now, after I've already moved all my shit in?"

I roll my eyes, but he's not done.

"You've been full speed ahead since the moment you suggested this. What changed? Why are you doubting now?"

"I'm not doubting," I tell him truthfully. "It's just... This will impact you, Gray. Heavily. You didn't spend your life considering the implications of coming out as I have. And no matter the truth, people *will* assume. You'll be labeled and treated differently. And it won't always be kind."

Grayson lets out a slow breath, his large shoulders shifting as he sets his elbows on the countertop. Whereas I've always had to work to maintain my muscle, Grayson doesn't have to try. He's not heavily bulked. He's just...big. Combined with the dark auburn hair and freckles across his nose, he makes an impression.

"Ez, I've always been different. People just didn't know it. Let them think what they want."

"Like I said, they'll think you're queer."

"I'm nothing."

I make a displeased sound at that.

Grayson only chuckles. "Stop. You know what I mean."

I puff out a breath. "What will you say? If they ask?"

"The truth. That I've never had a preference for any specific gender."

"Then they'll probably go with pansexual."

He shrugs. "I suppose that's as accurate as it gets. My lack of preference is certainly equal opportunity."

I study my friend, his gaze watching me back closely.

Finally, he blinks. "Ez. If you don't care, neither do I. We've already covered this."

I nod slowly before holding out my hand. "To upsetting every major news agency, directors around the world, dissolving fan clubs, and destroying our images in the process."

He snorts, but he clasps my palm. "Destroying? That's a little harsh, isn't it?"

"What did Shawn say? Something about imploding?"

Grayson's lips pull up at the corner. "Like dying stars."

"Is that what they do?" I ask, knowing full well he'll have an answer. At Grayson's raised eyebrow, I urge him on. "C'mon, you know you want to tell me."

He lets out a sigh like he's summoning patience, but I know there's almost nothing he'd rather talk about. "When a star burns all its available fuel, it no longer has the energy to fight its own gravitational pull. It collapses in on itself, the result sometimes devastating. It can create a black hole. It can white out an entire galaxy for weeks on end. It can birth new life. New stars. It's...cataclysmic. Ruinous and miraculous."

The awe in Grayson's tone has goose bumps spreading up my arms. "In that case, if we're gonna go out with a bang one way or another, might as well make it a big one, yeah?"

Grayson shakes his head, but he's smiling, his hand still clasped with my own. I give it a swift kiss before letting go.

"Come on, Mr. Fox. We still need to set up your bedroom."

With a nod, Grayson follows me down the hall, most of the house on this floor. There's also a spacious basement with another living area, a gym, and an indoor sauna. His bedroom is across the hall from mine, nearly as large as my own, with a bathroom just next door. He's using the bedframe I had in here before, but we moved his mattress in, the old one now propped against the wall until someone can come take it away. The dresser was already here, but Grayson added his own chair in the corner for reading, and the rest of his possessions are sitting in boxes beside the bed.

We go through each box carefully, fitting the sheets to his mattress, putting away his clothes, hanging up a couple pictures. Madison features prominently in those.

When I pull a frame from a box I haven't seen in years, I go still. Grayson pauses as well, his gaze snagging on me and the picture.

I was with him when he found this. Grayson saw a sign for an estate sale, and, as fascinated as he is with old antiques and the like, we stopped and went in.

Grayson and I were upstairs looking through the bedrooms when he opened a chest and made a sound I'd never heard from him before. Like pain, almost. An exquisite kind. When he stood back up, it was with this picture in hand. He was crying. I'll never forget that.

Grayson's voice is quiet now. "I couldn't get rid of it."

I shake my head. Of course not.

The picture is old. *Very* old. There's no writing on the back or indication of when or where it came from, but our best estimate based on the clothes and style of furniture is the mid to late 1800s. There's one person standing in view, in front of an elaborate four-poster bed, a wooden vanity off to the side with a low stool in front. The picture is black-and-white. Faded. And the serene smile on the man's face...

I swallow hard, taking him in all over again. The stranger could certainly be called beautiful, but the pose is beyond bold for the times, I'm sure. He's wearing an open shirt, his hands in the pockets of his trousers. His hair is short, dark, and he's lithe, although not exactly young when this was taken. In fact, he's probably close to our age. Late forties or possibly early fifties. Along the bottom of his flat chest, in two slightly curving arcs, are a smattering of stars. Tattoos, as black as night.

I run my finger over the glass. "Your star-boy."

"Yeah." Grayson takes the picture gently from my hand, his breath stuttering as he looks at it. "I know it makes no sense, but I know him, Ez. I feel it when I look at this picture. I *know* him. I just wish... I wish I knew who he was."

My throat is tight as Grayson sets the frame in a place of honor atop his dresser. He stands there for a long moment, looking at it.

"Perfect," I tell him.

He gives me a small smile before grabbing a box of toiletries to bring to the bathroom. I stay for a minute longer, staring at Grayson's star-boy. I know my friend has always felt a connection to the man in the picture.

But me? I can't help but wonder who's standing out of frame. Who it was that put that smile on his face.

Maybe one day we'll figure it out. Or maybe some things are simply meant never to be known.

CHAPTER 21

Grayson

"I don't get it," Madison is saying to Ezra. The two are in the living room, Madison having come to visit. I stepped away a minute ago to take a call, but my daughter's tone has me stopping outside the room, listening despite the invasion of privacy.

Ezra's response is calm. "Which part?"

He's always been like an uncle to Madison. Or even a big brother. Their relationship has been close since the time Madison was a child, as that's when Ezra and I became close, too.

"I know you two have always had this weird, overly familiar connection," Madison says, to which Ezra snorts. "But he says you guys aren't...*you know*. That he's not gay."

"He doesn't consider himself to be. He's explained this to you?"

"Yeah, but... He has to be lying to himself, right? Is it internalized homophobia?"

My chest twinges, and I nearly step out from the hall, but Ezra's voice halts me.

"He's ace, Madison. And aro. He's not interested in anybody like that. Not sexually. Not romantically."

"But he married my mom."

"He did. When he was very young. When he felt like it was what he was supposed to do. How he was supposed to feel."

Ezra lets out a sigh that's loud enough for me to hear.

"Your dad doesn't consider himself to be straight, queer, bisexual, or anything. He doesn't identify with those labels because he doesn't feel attraction to people on that level. He never has. But that's not something most people understand. Even ace people can enjoy sex or want a romantic partnership. Gray...doesn't."

The two of them are quiet for a moment. The silence seems to last a lifetime.

"Do you love him?" Madison asks.

The hum Ezra lets out is so familiar my heart squeezes tight. "Yeah. Of course I do. I love him more than anyone."

"And you're bi," she says.

"I see where you're going with this, but don't, okay? It's not like that."

"Then explain it to me," my daughter pleads, almost frantic. "Because all I see are two grown men who've been in love with each other for decades and aren't doing anything about it."

"Peaches." Ezra's tone is steady, but my pulse hammers. "We are doing something about it. He moved in."

"Yet you both say you're not in a relationship."

"That's right."

Madison makes an incredulous sound. "But don't you want more from him? Doesn't this hurt you?"

"No." Ezra's answer is immediate and sure, a direct line to my chest, soothing and stilling the nervous beat of my heart. "What I have with Gray is perfect as it is. There's not a single thing more I need from him."

"But you're giving up so much," she practically whispers. "To be, what...roommates with my dad?"

I look up at the ceiling, blinking heavily as Ezra answers my daughter.

"Do you know what I felt when I first met Gray? It was like I'd found a piece of myself that had been living outside of my body. And I didn't even know it until he was close enough to bring it home. If soulmates are a thing, he's mine. It's not romantic. It doesn't have to be. He's part of me, and I would no sooner cut out my own lungs than be without that man in my life."

A tear slips down my cheek, and I hastily brush it away.

"So you're happy?" my daughter asks.

"So fucking happy. So be happy for us, okay? This is what we want."

I step into the room, and Madison straightens, ducking her face as she wipes below her eyes. Ezra's smile is warm. I have no doubt he knows I heard at least some of that.

"Are we ready for dinner?" I ask, cutting through the tension.

Madison nods.

The three of us head into the city for our meal. It won't be long before the media catches wind of my new living arrangement, so this might be our last chance for a while to enjoy a night out in relative peace. Relative because, no matter where we go or when, fans and paparazzi always show up if Ezra is there.

The man is like a flashing beacon. He can't even help it. He doesn't try to draw attention to himself, but draw it he does. It's always been this way, as long as I've known him.

I get my fair share of requests for autographs, as well, or people sneakily taking my picture. But it pales in comparison to the infamous Ezra Gold.

If charisma had a face, it'd be my best friend's.

We decide on a cozy restaurant that can seat us at a fairly secluded table. Ezra browses the wine selection as Madison removes her light jacket. She's seated opposite us. Less likely to be caught in a photograph that way.

"How are classes?" Ezra asks her.

She makes a quiet sound, glancing at the menu. "Fine. Are you scared?"

We both pause at the question, and Madison's gaze lifts, her blue eyes catching Ezra's first and then my own. She looks worried—for *us*—and I hate that we live in a time where being anything other than straight still comes with stigma and potential danger. Add onto that being high-profile like Ezra and I are, and I understand my daughter's concern.

"We'll be okay," I assure her.

"I know you will," she says, although her voice shakes. "But that's not what I asked. I asked if you're scared."

Ezra reaches for Madison's hand from across the table. "Peaches. I've been ready to come out for a very long time. This is just the push I needed. Our agent will be assigning us extra security until things die down. Our assistants will be checking our mail and email and filtering out any hate we don't need to see. It won't be easy. I know that. *We* know that. But I'm not scared. I'm...relieved."

She nods, swallowing.

"It'll be worth it," I put in, knowing it's the absolute truth. "It's hard to understand for you, I get that. But spending the rest of my life with this guy?" I tip my head in Ezra's direction. "Worth everything coming our way."

Ezra bumps my shoulder with his own, his smile so warm and familiar I ache with it. His eyes flick up the next second, and he leans back, letting Madison's hand go.

Our waiter takes our order as my mind turns over. No, none of this will be easy. We'll be bombarded with attention, questions, requests for interviews. The world will make assumptions, but Ezra and I already decided we'll let them think what they'd like. We won't lie by saying we're in a relationship. But we won't bother defending the truth, either. Shawn is right. No one would understand it. They certainly wouldn't believe it.

But every bit of the attention will be worth it at the end of the day. Because I'll have Ezra. Close, like I've always wanted, even before I understood it.

I notice a few gazes finding our table throughout dinner. It's no surprise, and I ignore it like usual. When the waiter comes with the bill, Madison takes a moment to use the restroom. I keep one eye on the back hall while she's gone, even though I know my daughter is perfectly capable of looking out for herself. The mace in her purse is a nice reassurance, too.

Ezra chuckles lightly, apparently having noticed my protective glances. "Life of a dad."

"Yeah? And what's your excuse?" I ask, knowing he's just as watchful of Madison as I am.

He snorts. "Loving said dad?"

"Ez," I say without heat, my gaze turning his way. "Maybe keep that to yourself until after all hell breaks loose? I'd rather not have someone overhear you and get swarmed on our way out the door."

He shakes his head, arm on the back of my seat as he finishes off his wine. "Gray, buddy. If people can't see how much I love you, they haven't been paying attention."

I let out a sigh. "You're going to have a field day with this, aren't you?"

He grins. "Honestly? I can't wait. Do you think Shawn would have a conniption if I tell the reporters I enjoy taking it up the ass just as much as dishing it?"

"Christ, Ez."

He laughs, the sound of his infectious enthusiasm catching the other diners' attention. Ezra Gold. Can't take him anywhere.

When Madison returns, we leave the restaurant. The moment we're out the door, there's the flash of a camera bulb.

"Everywhere we go," I mutter.

Ezra doesn't even blink, giving the paparazzi a winning smile. "More. Give me more. C'mon, you know I love it."

Madison snickers as the camera flashes again.

I merely shake my head at Ezra's antics, glad we're almost to the parking lot. "The only actor who's friendly with the paparazzi."

Ezra shrugs, unlocking his vehicle for the three of us to get in. "If I'm nice, they get my good side."

"You have a bad side?"

Ezra acts astonished, looking at Madison in the back seat. "Did you know your dad is such a charmer?"

"You two are ridiculous," she says, although she's smiling.

"Me, yes." Ezra checks both ways before pulling out onto the road. "Your dad, on the other hand, is an unfortunate passenger in my ridiculous life. I've kidnapped him, I'm afraid. And I'm loath to let him go."

"A poet," I tell him. "Such beautiful words."

He all but cackles before his voice falls soft and solemn, as if reciting verses. "'The strongest affection and utmost zeal should, I think, promote the studies concerned with the most beautiful objects. This is the discipline that deals with the universe's divine revolutions, the stars' motions, sizes, distances, risings and settings...for what is more beautiful than heaven?'"

I stare at Ezra, shocked. "Did you just quote Copernicus? He was an astronomer, you know. Not a poet."

Ezra's smirk is devastating. "And yet his words are poetry to you."

I can't deny it.

When I glance in the back seat, Madison's gaze is out the window. But her expression is pensive.

Once we get back to Ezra's house—*our* house—I give Madison a hug. "Be safe," I tell her. "I love you."

"You, too, Dad." She squeezes me tight before letting go. "Mom will come around."

I nod. "She will."

Not that Camilla's opinion of how I conduct my life has any bearing on my happiness. Not anymore. But I don't want our relationship to end up any more strained than it already is. For Madison's sake.

Ezra gives Madison an equally hearty hug. "Remember, I know boys are pretty, but if he won't wrap it, he's not worth it."

"Oh my God," Madison groans, shoving Ezra away as he laughs. "Gross. Bye. Don't call."

"Love you." Ezra's shout is followed by Madison shutting her car door. "Kids. They grow up so fast."

I shake my head, a pang in my chest as Madison drives toward the gated exit. "She's not going to appreciate the extra bodyguard we assigned her."

Ezra makes a thoughtful noise. "Maybe not. But it'll be temporary. Dying stars, remember? We can only shine for so long."

I hum, but I don't think there's a star out there with as strong a gravitational pull as Ezra. When he goes out...the blast will be felt worlds over.

Ezra hits the button to shut the garage door, and I follow him inside, looking around the house that's now my own. The spacious, open-concept living space, tall windows and ceilings, state-of-the-art appliances and tech, and a well-concealed backyard with a heated pool.

It's extravagant, yes. But it's also home. Every inch of this place was decorated by Ezra himself, with my help. There's the antique Hepplewhite sideboard the TV sits atop. The beautiful bronze oval mirror that hangs in the entryway just behind me. The blues and light grays of the furniture, drapes, and pillows that are both comfortable and comforting.

I've always felt at home at Ezra's. Now I really am.

"All right?"

The question comes from Ezra, the man himself vaulting over the back of the couch and landing in a sprawl. He grunts immediately afterwards, regretting, I'd bet, the move at his age.

"Fine," I tell him, walking toward the wall of windows at the back of the house. The pool glimmers darkly in the evening light. "It's just...odd. This is the point in the evening where we'd usually be on a video call. Assuming we weren't already hanging out."

Ezra shoots me a grin I can see in the glass. "Now you have me all to yourself any time you want, and you're wondering how you managed to get so lucky."

"Something like that," I mutter wryly, although my lips twitch. "I like it here, Ez. I always have."

"And you've always been welcome."

"I know."

"But it's just now hitting you."

"Yes," I agree.

Ezra rolls off the couch with a groan, the reflection of his silhouette getting closer in the window. He stops beside me, his presence warm. Big, too, even though he's not quite my height. He's always been...big.

"I would have had you here years ago, Grayson. If you were ready."

My swallow is a harsh thing.

Ezra opens the slider door in front of us. "Come on."

The air is cool outside, the lights surrounding the pool making it easy enough to see. Ezra plops onto one of the poolside loungers, his hands behind his head. I sit down beside him, looking up at the night sky. The stars are hard to spot here, both because of the glimmer of sunlight still spreading over the horizon and the city's light pollution.

I ache to visit somewhere I can see the sky in all its natural glory. It's been a long time.

Ezra's voice splits the quiet air. "Gray. There's never been anything wrong with you. I know you know that deep down. But Camilla made it hard for you to accept because she saw your lack of interest as a problem. It wasn't. You and her were just never meant to be."

He's not saying anything I don't already know, but having my friend speak aloud those thoughts that continue to plague me at times is a relief. Aloe on a healing, scratchy burn.

"And us?" I ask, turning my head to see his profile.

Ezra smiles, the corner of his lips drawing upwards. "We're inevitable, Grayson Fox. Bound by fate or luck or maybe even gravity. The moment I found you, I knew there was no escape."

"There's a name for that, you know," I tell him, my heart so full it's a wonder I can speak through it. "When two stars are drawn together. Their energy shared."

His head lolls my way. "Yeah? And what's that?"

I can picture the blast of light in my mind's eye clearly. A collapse of two stars and an explosion so great it can be seen across the universe, causing ripples in the very fabric of space-time.

Cataclysmic. Ruinous and miraculous.

No words better describe what Ezra is to me.

There's a smile on my face when I answer my friend, the world around us dark. "Supernova."

Chapter 22

Ezra

"It's starting."

At Grayson's words, I drop the dish I'd been rinsing in the sink and round the island, drying my hands on my pants as I go. "Let me see."

He shifts his phone screen in my direction. In bold letters is a headline from an online rag.

"Could Ezra Gold and Grayson Fox's bromance be a romance?"

"Oh, good grief," I mutter. "So unoriginal."

Grayson starts to read, paying me no mind. "'Movie star Grayson Fox has been spotted arriving at Gold's home at all hours of the day and staying through the night.'"

"Ooh la la," I intone, waggling my eyebrows. Grayson shoves my face away without even looking, and I laugh.

"'Although the stars' agent is currently unavailable for comment, the two have been reported not to be actively working together on roles now that filming for *A Worthy Deception* has wrapped. Which begs the question: what are they doing all hours of the night at Gold's home? Surely not sleeping.'"

My phone pings. Most likely a message from Shawn.

"How are you feeling?" I ask Grayson. He's my first priority. Always.

He sighs, scrolling down to see a picture of himself in his car right outside the front gate. It's slightly blurry but clearly him. "People are so fixated on sex."

"They are," I agree.

"They can't imagine it being anything else."

I place a kiss on Grayson's temple, and his shoulders lose some of their tension. "If they can't fathom love without sex, it's their loss."

He sets his phone on the counter, face down. "They don't know it's love. They just think we're boning. That's not even why I'm upset."

"Why are you upset?" I ask, sitting on the stool next to him.

Grayson's chest rises and then falls with his swooping breath. "It's like...everyone assumes the most important relationship they'll have in their life is a romantic one. They want *the one*. They want the person they'll share passion with and go on dates with. They want to settle down and maybe have a family. They want romance, and as soon as they have that, it eclipses everything else."

The light catches Grayson's eyes as he turns my way, the blue so light it's nearly clear. There's an urgency in his gaze, the same present in his voice.

"What about friendship? What about family? Why can't a person feel fulfilled if they never marry? Why can't the absolute love of my life be my best friend?"

The last question is asked so forcefully, I'm nearly brought to my knees, never mind the stool I'm sitting on.

"It can be," I say softly.

He flicks his hand toward his phone. "Yet they think it's about sex. As if there couldn't be a better reason."

I let out a slow breath. "I have an idea. What would you say to getting out of here for a couple days?"

Grayson looks intrigued. "Where would we go?"

My lips quirk. "Somewhere...quiet."

Grayson and I pack a bag each before getting in my Escalade and hitting the road. I've been wanting to bring him to this planetarium for years, knowing his love of the stars and all things cosmic. But there never seemed to be a good time where we both had breaks in our schedules or where life in general wasn't pressing against us from all sides.

Well, fuck that. We're making time.

Not only is the planetarium out of dodge, but it runs shows on the weekends. I bought tickets for tomorrow night before we left, which gives us a good day to fill in the meantime.

Not that we'll have a problem finding something to do.

Grayson glances over at me when I finally take the turn onto our exit several hours from home. "Just a break or are we stopping?"

"We're stopping," I confirm.

He's quiet, which means he's likely figured it out. I wouldn't be the least bit surprised. This venue is fairly notorious for its spectacular visual presentations.

Grayson and I drop our bags at our hotel first, and I take a few minutes to search my phone for a distraction.

"Oh, shit," I mutter, finding the perfect thing.

Grayson eyes me. "Do I want to know?"

"If Shawn calls, we were very, *very* good on our trip."

My friend tips his face toward the ceiling. "Christ. Someone save me from Ezra Gold."

I laugh, and Grayson shoots me a small smile. Before heading out the door, we don our baseball caps, doing what we can to hide who we are. More often than not, it's a losing battle, but it's also fun, seeing how long we can blend in and be inconspicuous. Like real-life versions of the undercover agents we sometimes play.

The dunes are only a twenty minute drive from our hotel. Grayson gives me a look once I park.

"It's safe," I assure him, tacking on a quiet, *"ish."*

He heaves out a breath, but he's the first to exit the vehicle. I follow quickly behind, loping to catch up to my long-legged friend.

The dune buggies are rentable by the hour. The attendant gives us an extended glance, probably wondering if the two guys who look like movie stars from some of the most popular action flicks of the day are, in fact, the real deal. But he doesn't ask, just hands over keys and gives us a spiel about safety as we sign the necessary waivers.

Once we're heading toward our buggy, I hear a curse. I'm guessing the attendant finally saw our signatures.

"He's onto us," I hiss.

Grayson's eyes are filled with amusement as he looks my way. "You know what that means."

"Go, go, go!" I shout, breaking into a sprint.

Grayson laughs as he chases after me. I catapult into the driver's seat of our buggy, going through the open window feet-first, ignoring the door altogether. Grayson opens his, but he's quick to rush inside. I turn the ignition, glance back one last time at the attendant who's gaping at us, and then I floor it.

Grayson's laughter is nearly as loud as the engine, and I can't help but grin in response. He needs this. Fun. An escape every once in a while. It's not that Grayson is a glum person, but he takes his responsibilities seriously. Being a dad. His career. Even the persona he shares with the world, a carefully controlled shell of who he really is.

And I understand that. You can't give the public all the pieces of yourself. They'd chew them up and spit them right back out. Some things are too important to let outside of your chest. They're safer there, tucked away and kept close.

But I also know this lifestyle weighs on Grayson more than it does me. He doesn't love being an actor in the same way I do. He enjoys it, sure. And he's good at it. But sometimes I wonder why he got into acting in the first place. Why he wasn't an astronomer or, perhaps, a librarian.

I chuckle at the visual of Grayson surrounded by books. Piles of them. Towers. A giant shield between him and the world.

The limelight... It's not for him.

Sand kicks up behind the buggy as I press on the gas. Grayson is holding on to the roll bar, a wide grin on his face as we bounce along, the sun beating down on us from overhead. It only takes a couple minutes before the attendant's station is out of sight, rolling hills of sand surrounding us on all sides.

It feels as if we're in our own desert oasis.

Reaching the bottom of a hill, I do a few donuts, the back end of the buggy skidding in a way that has Grayson letting loose a few choice swear words.

His voice carries above the noise of the engine. "You're not a stuntman."

"Semantics."

He braces a hand on the dash.

After a good twenty minutes, I pull the buggy to a stop, grinning at my friend. "So?"

"You're a menace."

Yeah, well, he doesn't sound too upset about that fact.

Grayson slaps my shoulder. "My turn, hotshot."

I unclip my seat belt, and the two of us trade places, an awkward feat in the confines of the small caged cab. Once Grayson is seated behind the wheel, he belts himself in and looks over at me, the brim of his ballcap shielding his face from the sun. The glimmer in his eye catches me off guard.

"What?" I ask slowly.

His lips pull into a smirk. "I think you forgot I once trained to play a racecar driver."

Oh, shit. I did.

With a sly grin that's entirely unbefitting my friend, Grayson straightens the brim of his cap, faces forward, and guns it.

I laugh wildly as we fishtail, the wind rushing past us once the wheels gain traction against the sand. Grayson drives like a bat out of hell, taking turns at a far higher speed than I dared, zigging and zagging and racing over hills quick enough for us to go airborne for a second or two before landing and continuing onward.

Shawn would never believe me if I told him Grayson is the daredevil he should have been worried about all along. Not that our agent will hear a word about this.

As our hour draws to a close, Grayson drives us back in the direction of the attendant. He barely slows, only slamming on the brakes in the last couple seconds, turning the wheel harshly such that we spin twice in a controlled slide before coming to a perfectly parked position beside the other vehicles.

"Good God," I say to Grayson, more than a little impressed. "If we ever need a getaway driver, you're up."

He chuckles, straightening his cap once more before un-clipping himself. The attendant's eyes are big as we walk his way. Grayson slaps the keys onto the counter in front of him. "Thanks. That was fun."

The guy's eyes stay on my friend as he walks off. "Is that...?"

"Yep," I answer.

His gaze pings my way next. "And you?"

I give him a wink. "Sure am."

I chuckle to myself as I follow Grayson through the nearly empty parking lot. We slip into my vehicle, Grayson smiling almost serenely as he gazes out the window.

"Hungry?" I ask, fairly sure I know the answer.

"As a horse."

We decide on takeout, bringing it back to the hotel so we can eat in privacy. Grayson wolfs down his burger at the tiny table inside our room, finishing it in four bites. I eat a little slower, my heels on the end of the bed, our drapes open to let in some light.

"We should do this more often," I tell him.

"What? Disregard the *no reckless behavior* part of our con-tracts?"

I huff a laugh. "No. Just...get out. Go somewhere. Madison is in college now, you're divorced, we can just...go."

"When we're not filming?"

I shrug. "Or film less."

Grayson looks at me carefully, chewing his fries before speaking. "You want to take a step back?"

"Maybe," I admit. "I've been thinking about it a lot. Shit's about to change for us anyway. It wouldn't be the worst thing to...slow down a little. It might be nice, actually."

Grayson considers that for a long moment. "What would we do?"

I lean toward him, my grin huge. "We could see all the places we've wanted to visit but haven't had a chance to. Go skydiving. Read more. Find the most obscure antiques shops in the tiniest towns across the world. Finally learn how to make meringue."

He looks amused. "That's quite the varied list."

"We could do whatever we want, Gray," I say more seriously. "We could even sit at home and do nothing at all. We could be so boring the world forgets about us."

Grayson's smile is rueful. "Somehow, I doubt that's possible."

"Then we ignore them." I drop my feet to the floor, my heart hammering. I'm not sure how to explain this frantic edge I'm feeling. Even so, I try my best. "In a few years, we'll be fifty. *Fifty*. We're not young anymore. Our lives could easily be half over, and I just... I want to make the most of what I have left. With you."

Grayson swallows heavily, his lips pressing together for a moment as if he's doing his best to stow his emotions. Pushing away from the table, he stands and motions for me to do the same. The second I'm out of my seat, Grayson's arms come around me tight. He's safe and warm, and my breath stutters with it.

My friend speaks softly. "We have time. What is it you said to me the other day? It's just now hitting you?"

I nod, my throat tight.

"I know what this is, Ez. I knew the moment you asked me to move in what you were really asking. I said yes, and I mean it. It's you and me. For the rest of our lives. Unless you get sick of me."

"Impossible," I croak.

He squeezes me a little tighter. "Then I'm not going any-where. We have time. You have *me*, okay? You won't lose me."

I exhale in a swift whoosh, wondering how it's possible for one person to understand me so completely. "I'd leave it all behind for you."

His breath puffs out. "I know. But I don't need you to."

God.

"I love you," I tell him, needing to say the words. "I love you madly. I know you know that, but I do, Gray. No matter what happens, no matter what they say, don't doubt that for a second. We were made for this. To be together. I'm sure of it."

Grayson turns his face, his lips pressing to the side of my head. "I have never in my life doubted you. I'm not about to start now."

CHAPTER 23

Grayson

"My phone won't stop blowing up," Camilla says in lieu of a greeting. "Everyone wants to know if I'm aware my ex is apparently off the market. And with a *man*, no less. As if I'd somehow missed the news."

"Cam," I say, my tone weary in a way that has nothing to do with the early morning hour.

"I'm not going to talk," she snaps. "I'm not out to hurt you, Grayson. But a little heads-up would have been nice."

"You're right," I reply, closing the bathroom door behind me so I don't wake Ezra. "I should have texted the moment I saw the article. I just...wasn't thinking about any of it."

She lets out a gust of air. "People want to know if I ever suspected. That you and he... *If* you and he were together all this time. Do you know what that's like? To be asked to my face if my husband was unfaithful?"

"No," I say quietly. "I don't. I'm sorry."

"What would I even say? If I could say anything to anyone other than my own mother, what would I tell them? That of course you loved him all this time? You always loved him more than me."

I close my eyes, resting my forehead against the wall. My heart thumps dully, the conversation one we've had so many times over the past couple years. It never seems to end. The apologies. The explanations. "Camilla... I love him as a friend."

"I don't believe you."

"I don't need you to."

There's a long beat of silence. "Is that how you loved me? As a friend?"

"Yes," I whisper.

"But not the same as him."

No.

I don't speak it aloud, but she knows it to be true. No one has ever been like Ezra.

"Be honest with me," she says, voice cracking. "You're sleeping with him?"

"No," I say evenly. There's a shuffle on the other side of the wall. Ezra moving. I don't open my eyes. "We've never even kissed, Camilla."

"I don't understand it," she says, frustration thick in her tone.

"I know."

"Fuck, Grayson. Why couldn't you have just been normal?"

My grunt is involuntary, and Camilla immediately starts to backtrack.

"I'm sorry. I am. That wasn't fair of me. But goddamn it, I'm pissed off."

"I know," I repeat. "And I could say I'm sorry for all the years I couldn't love you the way you needed. I could apologize for not understanding myself for so much of my life. For not knowing the way I felt wasn't...how did you put it? Normal? I could tell you again and again that our divorce had nothing whatsoever to do with Ezra. But you don't seem to want to believe me. So what else can I say? I just want to be happy, Cam. I just want to be allowed to be *me*."

It's quiet on the other end of the line. There's the softest of thumps on the outside of the bathroom door, and I reach over, twisting the knob. Ezra steps inside as Camilla lets out a small, shaky breath.

"I'm not going to talk," my ex says again. "Don't make me look a fool, Fox."

With that, Camilla clicks off the call.

Warm hands bracket my shoulders before circling around to my front. Ezra takes my phone, setting it aside before his chin hooks over my shoulder. "Normal is such a terrible word."

I heave out a breath, and he grips me tighter.

"Okay?"

"No," I answer. "And yes."

Ezra hums. "There's an antiques store in town. Should we visit?"

"Is that what we came here for?"

His laughter passes quietly near my ear. "No. But you know why we're here. You'll just keep pretending otherwise so it's a surprise."

I lift my head off the wall and open my eyes, but Ezra doesn't yet let go, his voice soft but lined with an edge of steel.

"I'm glad you're not normal. If you were, you'd probably be with Camilla or some other perfectly nice person in your midwestern two-story home with a white picket fence and another one-and-a-half kids."

I croak out a laugh, and Ezra squeezes me harder, his hand resting over my heart.

"Normal doesn't exist for guys like us, Gray. And I can't bear the thought of having missed out on all of this. If I'd never found you?" He shakes his head quickly, as if he can't even bring himself to contemplate it. "Camilla can keep her normal. You're extraordinary, and I wouldn't have it any other way."

I blink back tears, my eyes stinging and my chest tight.

"Antiques?"

I nod at the offer, and Ezra lets me go.

The antiques shop looks like nearly every other I've been in. Cramped aisles. Knickknacks of all varieties interspersed with furniture and tools and old magazines. The sections are split by seller, small tags on the items indicating their price.

Ezra stops in front of a rack of faux-fur coats. He pulls one free, slipping it on with a flourish, looking absolutely ridiculous with his ballcap and sunglasses in place. "Ooh. The perfect disguise."

"Yes, no one would possibly see you and think *Hollywood*."

Ezra snorts, not taking off the coat. There's a display of vintage watches he examines as I step into the next aisle. A small, handheld telescope catches my eye. It looks like brass, collapsed and nestled in a cushioned box.

Ezra speaks before I have a chance to pick it up. "You're getting that."

"I doubt I'd be able to see the stars with this," I point out, even as I take it out of the box. The metal is cool to the touch, matching the air in the room. "This was probably used at sea."

"You could bird-watch, then."

"Am I seventy now?"

He cackles, picking up the empty box and looking at the bottom. "It's forty bucks. You're getting it."

"It is neat," I admit, expanding the telescope. At its full length, it's maybe six inches long.

Ezra lets out a soft, thoughtful sound. "Would you ever want to move?"

The question takes me by surprise, but before I can answer him, my phone rings. I pull it from my pocket, seeing Shawn's name.

"One guess," I say to Ezra.

He groans.

The ringing stops, only to start up again. Ezra plucks the phone from my fingers and answers the call, putting it on speakerphone. Considering the only other person in the shop when we entered was an elderly employee, it seems like a safe bet.

Ezra greets our agent with his usual cheer. "Why hello, my good man."

There's a beat of silence on Shawn's end. "Why am I not surprised you're picking up Grayson's phone but not your own?"

Ezra looks nonplussed. "Mine's off. What can we do for you?"

Shawn huffs. "You can start by telling me where the hell you are. I'm getting inundated with requests for a statement about Grayson being at your home, people are starting to form opinions, as we knew they would, and the two of you are trending across almost every social media platform. There are reporters camped outside your house, for fuck's sake, but you're not here. Where *are* you?"

Ezra simply hums. "On vacation."

Shawn sputters into the phone. "On *vacation*? Do *not* tell me you're getting oiled up by some cabana boy while I'm standing inside your empty fucking house."

"No cabana boy." Ezra makes an almost contemplative noise. "Although I am holding a very nice telescope right now. Do you like bird-watching, Shawn?"

I stifle my laughter as our agent sounds as if he might actually explode. I swear I hear ticking. Most likely his molars grinding together. "Ezra, can you take this seriously for one goddamn minute?"

Ezra sighs, handing me back the telescope. "I don't see what the problem is. Like you said, we knew this wouldn't stay silent. Grayson and I are just spending a couple days out of dodge."

"And leaving me to pick up the shrapnel. Hold on, what's this..."

Ezra's eyebrows bounce up, barely visible above his sunglasses, but his expression is one I know all too well. Amusement.

I shake my head, silently telling him to behave, but then Shawn is back on the line, letting out a string of curses.

"Who the fuck is Naveen Arya? And why is he telling major news sources that you and he used to be a thing?"

My pulse drops before sprinting ahead, the mention of Ezra's longtime—and secret—hookup going public a possibility I hadn't even considered. My friend, however, doesn't look remotely surprised. He only smiles.

"Ah, good for Naveen. I wondered if he'd do it."

Shawn sounds as if he's gritting his teeth. "You're going to need to start explaining right fucking now. Is this some scorned lover you never warned me about?"

Ezra's tone is patient. "Naveen's a friend. Someone I've trusted for a long time. I told him if he wanted to cash in on his story, I'd be fine with it. I encouraged it, even. I'm glad he did. He'll be able to buy that summer cottage he wanted."

"Ez," I say, at a loss. "Why?"

My friend's expression softens, the change visible regardless of the fact that I can't see his eyes. "Because if people know I was with him, they'll be less likely to assume we've been fucking around all these years."

I shake my head, my chest in a vise. "It puts the spotlight on you. They'll dig into your past, try to find other men you've been with."

He shrugs. "Good. I was ready to come out. I have been for a long time. But I won't have them rake you over the coals. You don't deserve it, and you didn't ask for it."

"But I accepted it."

"For me. Which is why I'm doing what I can to mitigate the damage."

I swallow harshly. "For me."

His lips hitch up at the corner.

Shawn's voice is dry when he cuts back in. "If you two are done, I need to know what else you've orchestrated without telling me."

Ezra groans. "*Jesus Christ.* One day. Give us one fucking day to enjoy some peace and quiet. We'll be home tomorrow, and we can discuss it then. I'll even let you set me up for a talk show appearance if it'll make you happy."

"Ezra."

"One day, Shawn. This is important."

Our agent relents with a sigh. "I'll be here when you get back."

"Joy." Ezra ends the call, plunking my phone down on the counter beside the telescope box before pulling off his sunglasses to rub his eyes. He looks tired. Worn down.

"Hey," I say lightly, wanting to pull him away from the storm that awaits us. "Remember the first time I showed up at your place, your old place, when Naveen was over?"

He snorts. "Oh, God. He freaked."

"He tried to tell me he was your plumber. As if he'd have needed to be in his briefs to look under your sink."

Ezra's smile splits wide. "He didn't know you knew about him. About *me*. Then he about fell on his ass once he recognized you. He was starstruck."

"You were far more famous than me, even then," I point out.

Ezra waves a hand dismissively. "You were famous enough. Naveen has never seen me that way. It's hard to view a friend you once saw eat a worm on a dare as a celebrity, even if they are one."

My smile is soft. "How is he?"

"Good. Dating again."

I nod. It's been years since I last saw Naveen. Same as Ezra. "Are you really going to do an interview?"

Ezra nods slowly. "Yeah. One of us will have to be the first. And you know how I love a good crowd."

My friend's smirk doesn't fool me one bit. Sure, Ezra has always been comfortable in crowds. He's never had a problem being the center of attention and knows exactly how to play up his fame.

But he's not doing this for himself. He's doing it for me. Because he'd rather it be him than me taking that first bullet.

"What time's the show tonight?" I ask, collapsing the telescope and putting it back in the box.

Ezra feigns confusion. "The show? I have no clue what you could possibly be talking about. But, theoretically, we should get there by seven-thirty."

I huff a laugh, and Ezra grins, replacing his sunglasses on his nose.

"Ready to go? You're getting that telescope."

"I am," I agree, eyeing the fur still draped around his shoulders. "Are you buying that coat?"

"Absolutely yes."

Ezra heads toward the front of the store with a swagger in his step. I follow. Of course I do.

The employee at the register looks from Ezra to me as we approach. If he caught any of our conversation on the phone, he doesn't mention it. Then again, I doubt he'd have heard a word if he was in this spot the entire time.

"What've you got?" he asks, squinting at the tag Ezra plucks off his coat. He writes the numbers on a pad of paper as I set the telescope on the counter. "Together or separate?"

Ezra pulls out his wallet. "Together, please."

"You know, you look like an actor my niece likes," the man says, squinting at Ezra.

My friend beams. "Is that so? Should we take a picture so you can show her?"

The man chuckles, slipping the telescope into a plastic bag. "Suppose so. She'd probably get a hoot out of that."

Oh Lord.

Ezra pulls off his sunglasses as the man finds his phone beneath the counter. I don't even object as I'm tugged into the shot. Ezra snaps a selfie of the three of us before handing the phone back, and then he proceeds to chat the stranger up as if they're long-lost friends.

Everywhere we go.

"Have a good day now," the man says a good ten minutes later.

The door jingles as we pass through, and Ezra gives me a grin. "His niece is going to be in for a shock."

Understatement.

"Hey, Ez?"

"Yeah?"

He stops beside the driver's side door of his vehicle, his sunglasses sitting atop his ballcap now and his new fur coat far too warm for the temperatures. There's a smile on his face, his brown eyes crinkled against the sun, and I feel a swell of immense gratitude looking at him.

Where *would* I be without Ezra Gold in my life? If I'd taken another path. If we'd never met.

Would I be nearly as happy as I am now, not knowing half of my heart was elsewhere, waiting for me to come home?

"No matter what," I finally say, "I love you, too. That will never change."

The look in his eye is one I know all too well. Fierce, aching devotion.

CHAPTER 24

Ezra

The planetarium parking lot is surprisingly full when we arrive. There are loads of families walking toward the doors, parents bringing their children to marvel at the stars.

Grayson looks just as excited as the kids, although he's hiding it well behind a mask of calm. The truth is in his eyes. They glimmer as he looks over at me, the freckles along the bridge of his nose a constellation all his own.

He tries to sound shocked but fails miserably. "Why, a planetarium, Ez? I never would've guessed."

I snort. "You know, for being an actor, you're terrible at lying. Shall we?"

He finally cracks a smile. "Let's do it."

Ballcaps in place, we approach the front door. There's a banner just inside with this month's theme.

Grayson raises an eyebrow. "Mythology of the constellations?"

"Guess so. Do you know this stuff?"

He shrugs, the two of us heading toward the line leading into the large theatre. "Maybe a bit? Not sure how much I remember, though. I learned it in high school, which was, what, thirty years ago?"

I gasp. "Keep your voice down, sir. No one needs to know our age."

The woman in front of us looks back, chuckling to herself. She does a double take when she sees my face, so I give her a wink.

"Jig's up," I whisper to Grayson, the two of us nearly to the theatre entrance now. "We've been spotted."

"You know, for being an actor, you're absolute shit at remaining inconspicuous."

"I can't help it if my charisma betrays me," I say, mock-affronted. "Would you have me tone myself down?"

Despite my clear teasing, Grayson's expression softens. "No. Never that."

Well, shit.

I wipe a fake tear from below my eye, and Grayson rolls his.

After showing our tickets on my phone, Grayson and I are let into the theatre. I nearly stumble. The entire room is circular, the ceiling domed and displaying a dazzling, lit night sky. The stars twinkle overhead as we search for our seats, the rows of chairs leading steadily downward.

There were pictures online, but seeing it in person is entirely different.

"This is gorgeous," I whisper.

Grayson doesn't answer me with words, but he nods his agreement, his gaze on the stars above. Conversation buzzes steadily around us as Grayson and I settle into our seats. I imagine they'll turn the lights even dimmer once they start the show.

"Do you recognize anything?" I ask, trying to pick out constellations. The projection of the sky on the ceiling is breathtaking, and I wonder if it's real imagery or digitally rendered.

Grayson points. "Orion's Belt."

"The hunter."

He nods, hand moving over slightly. "The Big Dipper."

"Naturally bigger than the Little Dipper."

"Naturally," Grayson agrees, a hint of a smile on his face. He points in another direction. "Cassiopeia."

"Wait, which one is that?"

Grayson takes my hand, leaning against my shoulder as he draws my finger through the air in front of us. "Right there. Looks a bit like a skewed W?"

"Ah. I see it. And...the sword."

Grayson pauses before moving my hand over. He draws the shape of the sword, up the blade, over the hilt, and then down again. "The sword in the sky."

I'm about to ask if he likes that one best considering the fondness in his voice, but the lights in the room flicker. Grayson lets my hand go, and the theatre falls silent. A soft spotlight comes on as the ambient light dims, leaving only the stars above and the small platform at the center of the room. The woman there turns on her mic, a smile on her face I can barely make out from where we are.

"Welcome, everyone," she says, her voice gentle and almost hushed, as if in deference to the stars themselves. "Thank you for coming tonight. We have a wonderful presentation lined up for you that focuses on the mythology behind the constellations most known to us. Now, you'll see at the top of the seat in front of you is a small panel. This will provide a speech-to-text translation of tonight's show. It's also where you'll vote on our featured constellation. So if you would, please take a moment to silence your cell phones and decide which constellation you'd like to examine most in depth. The choice, ultimately, is yours."

Grayson and I remove our ballcaps as the presenter gives a brief overview of the planetarium, turning in place as she talks so that no one is looking at her back for long. I eye Grayson's panel, curious about which constellation he'll choose. Seeing him pick the sword, I quickly do the same.

He shakes his head, but there's a smile curving his lips.

"All right, final votes please. We're closing the poll in three, two, one. Ah. You've picked the Sword of Leandros. My personal favorite."

The dome overhead shifts, the sky rearranging and the constellation of the sword coming into sharper focus. It feels as if we're traveling toward it at an alarming speed, the sword getting bigger and bigger until it's filling the entire ceiling, each of its stars brightly lit and connected by lines drawn to enhance its shape.

"As you can see," the woman says, "the Sword of Leandros is made up of twelve stars, forming a near-symmetrical visual representation of a sword. It sits in the northern sky and can be seen year-round where we live. One of the most easily recognizable constellations, you likely spot it often, but you might not know the tale behind how the sword came to be in the sky."

The projection shifts again, a warrior outlined by stars, the sword in his hand. My skin prickles, goose bumps spreading over my arms.

"The myth of Leandros originates in Greek storytelling, but it's been found in similar variations throughout the world. The tale tells of a warrior, Leandros, known to be the fiercest swordsman of his time. He was rumored to be unbeatable. And because of this, he was a prized part of the king's army."

The image reforms, the warrior now standing in front of a battalion, his sword raised high, a helmet on his head. The stars making up the picture seem to glimmer, as if dancing.

"Leandros's age isn't precisely known, but best estimates put him to be in his late thirties at the time he fell. Because yes, like many myths and legends, this one does not have a pretty end. What we do know from his documented tales is that Leandros survived many battles, both large and small, against beasts and man."

The projection shows a charging boar, the animal bursting into tiny stars as it meets Leandros's blade. The entire image changes then, the rest of the warriors disappearing, the multitude of stars coalescing into the shape of a woman.

"One seemingly uneventful day, Leandros returned to his private home outside the king's walls to find a woman waiting for him in robes of white. A goddess, worshiped and feared in equal measure for the blessings—or curses—she would lay upon the town. Her beauty was unmatched, and she demanded Leandros come with her. For he was the best warrior, and she wanted him for her own."

The woman above holds out her hand, beckoning Leandros closer. He turns away.

"Leandros denied her. For days and weeks on end, she returned only to be turned away. When she sent a rampaging bull with shoulders taller than a horse's head, Leandros struck it down."

The image shifts, showing the scene, Leandros's sword once again felling the creature with ease.

"When snakes appeared suddenly within the town's walls, Leandros, with the help of the royal army, eradicated every single one."

This, too, is shown above, countless snakes bursting into tiny stars that reform as the tale goes on.

"He was not to be deterred by the goddess's wrath. Nor her beauty, which she offered him freely. Her gifts of gold and the finest weapons were also denied, left outside his doorstep. There was not a single thing she could do to sway Leandros away."

The stars disappear then, all of them. For a moment, there's endless black. Until Leandros reappears, a man beside him.

"The reason why is quite simple." The two men reach for one another across an expanse of deep blue space. "Leandros was in love."

I pull in a breath as their hands touch, tiny stars, like sparks, lighting between their fingertips.

"We don't know the name of Leandros's lover. None of the stories give him one, which suggests he wasn't notable himself. A merchant, perhaps. Or a peasant. But it didn't take the goddess long to learn of his existence."

My stomach sinks as the image of the men morphs, becoming more indistinct. The goddess walks into view, and I want nothing more than to strike her down before she can reach the pair. The feeling is so strong, so visceral, my hands shake with it.

"She found them one day," the presenter says, her voice quiet. "In the wheat fields behind Leandros's house. She was enraged, a fury like no other, for no one denied her as Leandros had."

The image shows the goddess becoming larger, the stars making up her outline turning to red.

"Seeing the sword lying on the ground, she picked it up and spoke a curse against its blade. Leandros tried to stop her. Of course he did. But even he was no match for a furious goddess. She drove the sword through his lover's heart, the cursed blade promising repeated death as punishment for Leandros's refusal."

The projection shows the goddess piercing the starlit man through his heart, brilliant white stars falling like pigmentless blood around his body. My inhale is sharp, my own chest feeling so tight it's as if I'm being pierced, too.

"That, perhaps, should have been the end of this tragedy. Without his lover, the goddess would be free to take Leandros for herself, his grief too strong for him to fight."

I swallow heavily as the Leandros above cradles his dead lover in his arms.

"But what the goddess didn't consider..." our presenter says, pausing only briefly. "Was love."

The image shifts again, Leandros picking up his sword. The goddess reaches for him, but she doesn't make it in time.

"Leandros took up his fallen sword, and without a single second of hesitation, he pierced himself through the chest, choosing an eternity of death with his beloved over the offer of immortality with a goddess."

Grayson's hand lands on my own, his grip tightening to the point of pain. His gaze is trained upwards, but there's a single tear rolling down his cheek, the sight of it reminding me so clearly of the day he found his star-boy. He had the same expression on his face then. The same anguish.

My own breath shudders as the woman speaks on, the projection above shifting once more. Leandros disappears. His lover, too. And the goddess. All that's left is the sword, blinking in the sky, the point aimed downward.

"Some say the stars themselves wept at the loss of such pure devotion, placing the sword in the sky so that the young lovers could be guided together in the next life. Others say it was the Fates. Either way, the constellation we now know as the Sword of Leandros sits bright above, a beacon for many who draw strength or courage from its celestial blade."

Sadness echoes in my chest, and I turn my hand up to meet Grayson's, winding our fingers together.

"Now, it's impossible to say how much of this legend is based in fact and how much is fiction. But we do know the Sword of Leandros didn't appear in literature until around 800 BCE. Compared to the earliest depictions of Orion's Belt found carved on a mammoth tusk some 32,000 years old, this makes the sword in the sky one of the most recent constellations to come into being. Dating of the stars has confirmed them to be just over 3,000 years old, which puts them in their relative infancy. Stars, as you know, can live to be millions, *billions* of years old."

The woman continues to spin in a slow circle as she speaks to the filled theatre, the sword shimmering above.

"What's stranger yet is that each star mapped in the outline of the sword is the same precise age. They came into existence at exactly the same time. Multiple star systems are certainly not unheard of. But twelve stars born at once and gravitationally bound in a stable array? It's impressive, to say the least. I don't think we'll ever know if myths like Leandros's were true. But I'd like to think if the star-crossed lovers are out there still that they're together."

My breath puffs out of me as Grayson's hand squeezes my own tight.

The show continues with a shorter breakdown of other famous constellations. But try as I might, I can't get Leandros and the sword out of my mind. I'd never heard the myth before, and I don't know why it's hitting me so hard, but the idea of Leandros and his lover dying because of a vengeful goddess?

Fuck.

Eternal death. Dying again and again and again...

"Hey."

Grayson's quiet voice pulls me from my thoughts. The lights are on in the theatre now, and I blink rapidly, trying to orient myself. A quick glance upwards shows the night sky projected against the inside of the dome, the stars twinkling gently once more.

Grayson is watching me with concern. "You okay?"

I nod, but I don't know if it's true.

We make it out of the planetarium without being stopped, although I do notice one teen snapping a picture of us in the lobby. The stars are visible outside, not quite as brilliant as they were in the theatre, but beautiful all the same. They're easier to see here, so far from any cities.

Would Grayson ever want to move out to the middle of nowhere where he could better see the stars? Maybe I could find something small to buy, a place we could retreat to when the rest of the world is too demanding and we need to escape.

It could be our own. No paparazzi. No well-meaning agents or fans vying for our attention. Nothing but him and me and peaceful quiet beneath a blanket of unending stars.

We climb inside my Escalade, but I don't immediately start the vehicle. I can feel Grayson watching me.

"Ez." His voice comes out choked, his blue eyes stormy when I meet his gaze. "I know them. In here, I do."

He taps his chest, and I nod in a stilted jerk, not needing to ask *who.*

"Did you feel it?"

There's a desperation in Grayson's tone, as if he needs to know he's not alone in this. My friend has always been intuitive. It's uncanny, really, the way he can make split-second decisions about a person he's never met before, and his gut instincts about them are always correct. It's as if he operates on a wavelength others can't see or understand, myself included.

But this...

The memory of Leandros holding his lover comes to mind. The way I ached with it. Still do. The feel of my own chest being torn in two, as if my heart was dying right alongside the fearsome warrior who was staring his absolute worst nightmare in the face.

"Yeah, Gray," I answer, my voice a hoarse whisper. "I felt it."

CHAPTER 25

Grayson

Ezra is quiet for most of our return trip home.

We spent our final night doing our absolute best not to think about the real world and what was waiting for us. The two of us snuck into the gated pool at the hotel late after hours and watched the stars until well past midnight. And then we lay side-by-side in our king-sized bed, talking about the trips we could take. The places we could see and where Madison might like to visit.

But with every hour that passed in our blissful bubble, the morning loomed closer.

I'm not used to Ezra being so withdrawn, but I leave him to his silence as miles of highway pass. For all I know, he's plotting the next ten steps in his plan to guide the media's response to our supposed romance. I know Shawn thinks Ezra is too laissez-faire about his image, especially now with everything that's happening. But Ezra is always one step ahead. He's simply quiet about his maneuvering.

The man would make an excellent chess player if he ever got the inclination. Or even a war general.

Ezra's shoulders get tense as we drive the side streets toward home. I reach over, squeezing his arm, and he shoots me a tiny smile. Always a brave face. Always brave, period.

The reporters appear once we turn onto our drive. They race toward the vehicle, cameras flashing, questions shouted our way that we ignore.

Ezra's smile is rueful. "Ready to face the music?"

"The symphony has already begun," I murmur.

The gates open slowly in front of us, Ezra maneuvering forward through the crowd. No one dares step inside, but they continue shouting as the metal clangs shut behind us. Shawn's vehicle is waiting in front of the garage, and Ezra lets out a mighty sigh.

"It's not too late to run," I tease. "We could dye our hair. Live on some remote island where no one knows our faces."

He snorts. "Don't tempt me. Maybe one day, though. Me. You. Goddamn meringue. I swear to God, I'm going to learn."

I huff a small laugh. "Sounds like a perfect, simple life."

A wistful smile breaks out across Ezra's face before he squares his shoulders, ready to go off to battle.

Shawn is waiting for us in the kitchen, a glass of sparkling water on the table in front of him. His laptop is out, as well as his phone and a tablet, all open to various articles that have popped up in the past few days we've been gone. I'm surprised there's no whiteboard with ominous red string connecting the lot.

Without preamble, Shawn begins. "Here's where we're at. There are photos of Grayson coming here with increasing frequency over the past couple weeks, ever since he moved in. There are pictures of you two from over the years, questioning how much of your bromance was a lie. There are articles about Grayson and Camilla, detailing the recent divorce. And there's a shit-ton of buzz about what this means for Hollywood, two of its prominent stars being queer."

Ezra offers our agent a beer he grabbed from the fridge. "Shawn. Book me an interview."

Shawn looks from the beer to Ezra's face.

Ezra waves the bottle enticingly. "Low-calorie."

With a *humph*, Shawn grabs it, twisting off the top. "You're serious?"

"Deadly." Ezra sprawls out on the couch. I take my own seat in the living room, Shawn joining us and sitting delicately on a wingback chair Ezra and I found years ago that he had reupholstered. "Set me up with one of the talk show hosts we like, and I promise you won't have to do a thing. I'll set the record straight."

"The record." Shawn's eyes ping slowly between us. "Being that you two are just friends and there's nothing whatsoever else happening here?"

Ezra heaves a sigh, but there's a smile on his face when his head lolls my way. "The record being... The two of us are wildly, irrevocably, and madly in love."

Shawn takes a big gulp from his beer. "Well, shit."

Ezra's lips turn up at the corner, his eyes full of mischief as he sends me a wink.

Shit, indeed.

"Wine?" Harper asks, a bottle and two glasses in her hand as she joins me on the couch. She pours without waiting for an answer.

My attention is locked on the TV.

I offered to go with Ezra to his interview, but he politely declined, telling me it'd only stress me out more to be there in the wings doing nothing. He wasn't wrong.

But I'm still stressed. Not about what Ezra will say or how this will impact us. I'm nervous for *him*. That he's doing this on his own. But he was adamant about that, too, knowing my preference for such things.

Sometimes, the force of Ezra's love nearly knocks me on my ass. I know people in our life don't get it. Madison. Camilla. Shawn. Even Harper, who merely winked and nodded when I told her the truth of Ezra and me. No one believes us, that we could possibly want to spend our lives together—share years and create memories—without a sexual or romantic component.

But why can't we? Ezra is my person. And I'm his. I've never questioned it, not once in the last twenty years. I found him, and I knew.

I love that man more than I'll ever love anybody, my own daughter withstanding. Why can't love, in any form, be enough? People want to shape us into something we're not because they can't see the beauty there. They don't understand it, and I ache with that knowledge.

Because don't they realize?

Love is boundless. It's immeasurable and immense. Beauty on its own. It's the reason a person's eyes soften. It's why we go to great lengths just to make someone smile.

Romance, sex, friendship, even, are all secondary to what love is at its core. It's the very makeup of our being. It's our essence, reaching out to another and finding our reflection in kind.

Love is who we are. What we have to give.

And having that returned to us? It's an affirmation of our very being. That we're understood. Accepted. That we're real.

Why try to place limits on that? All love is to be treasured.

And Ezra's love is a treasure I won't ever part with willingly.

Harper nudges my arm, passing over the wine I didn't ask for but am grateful to have. "Are you freaking out?"

I shake my head, setting my prior thoughts loose as I accept the glass. "No. I'm fine."

"No offense, but you don't exactly look it."

That has me laughing softly. "Really, I'm okay. This is Ezra's show. I'm just here to watch."

Harper hums, glancing at the TV that's streaming the talk show Ezra will be appearing on soon. The host is making his introductory speech to the audience, hyping everyone up, joking about a few topical current events.

"It's not exactly a surprise, you know. You two."

"Yeah?" I ask.

Harper sets her own wine glass down on the coffee table, scooting her legs up onto the couch. Her sweater nearly swamps her entire body, as large as it is. It's one of the fashionable kind that hangs off her slim shoulder. "I mean, you guys have always had this *thing*. It's magnetic. And everyone can see it, but being on set with you two?" She whistles. "I could feel it. You guys are so in sync, like you're tied together, moving as one."

My lips pull into a smile because it's always felt like that to me, too.

"I know I haven't really known you guys long," she goes on. "But I'm happy for you. I kinda wanted to hate you, I'm not gonna lie. I mean, Ezra Gold? Shit, the man is fine."

My laugh this time comes from deep within my belly. So I've heard, time and time again. I understand on a fundamental level, of course. I can see Ezra's good looks. But to me, he's never been his outward appearance. He's just...my Ezra.

"But I couldn't be mad at either of you," Harper says around a sigh. "You guys are too *nice*. It's tragic, really. Guys like you aren't supposed to be nice."

"That's a shame. I think niceness should be expected, not the exception."

She raises an eyebrow. "It's like trying to argue with a ray of sunshine."

I huff a laugh, but words from the TV catch my attention. The host, Jeffrey Maxim, is talking about his guest now, a secretive grin on his face.

"Shit," I mutter, my nerves returning, even though I know this has already happened. With the delay, Ezra is likely on his way home by now.

Harper rubs my shoulder. "It'll be okay. Whatever happens, I'm sure of it."

"Thanks," I say, despite the heavy beat of my pulse. "I appreciate you being here for this."

Shawn spent the interview at the studio with Ezra. I would have invited Madison, but she has an important final tomorrow, and I didn't want to pull her away from studying. Harper, on the other hand, was all too willing to come keep me company.

"Are you kidding?" she says, a cheeky smile on her face. "I wouldn't miss this for the world. Ooh, here we go."

Harper grabs her wine, resettling on the couch as Ezra is called onstage. The audience cheers and hollers, the sound ridiculously loud. Ezra plays it up, giving them a wicked grin as he walks Jeffrey's way. The two shake hands, Jeffrey saying something quietly off-mic, and then they take their seats, Jeffrey behind his desk, Ezra on the small couch beside it.

"Ezra Gold," Jeffrey says. "It's an absolute pleasure having you here. When's the last time I saw you? Five years ago?"

Ezra clutches his chest. "Four, Jeffrey. Honestly, I'm hurt that you don't remember."

The crowd laughs, and Ezra sends them a wink.

Jeffrey for his part, looks repentant, in an amused way. "My apologies. *Four* years. Either way, it's been a while. What have you been up to? You just finished filming *A Worthy Deception*, isn't that right?"

"Sure is." Ezra fixes his jacket as he settles more fully into his seat, ankle crossed over his knee. "But we both know I'm not here to talk about my newest movie."

The crowd *oohs* at that, and Jeffrey shakes his head. "To the point. All right, I can admire that." He leans toward Ezra, elbows on his desk, as if their conversation could somehow be private. "Is it true Grayson Fox is living with you?"

Ezra's lips twitch ever so slightly, something most people probably wouldn't even notice. "Yes. That's true."

There's an immediate reaction, murmuring from the audience and even Jeffrey's eyebrow flying up. "Okay, explain to me what's going on there. Your whole bromance... Was that a lie?"

"No. Grayson is my best friend. That was never a lie."

"But now?" Jeffrey asks. "C'mon, Gold, don't leave us in suspense here. What's the deal with you two?"

My heart thumps in time to Ezra's soft smile. *God*. Even across space and time, I can feel him.

"Grayson Fox." Ezra's tone is almost lazy, as if the name is one he's maybe heard before. "Yeah. That man is the love of my life."

Jeffrey sits back dramatically, and Ezra winks at the camera, the audience outright screaming now. My phone starts to ping, but I ignore it. If it's Madison and important, she'll call. Everything else can wait.

"Well, good grief," Jeffrey says.

Harper fans her face beside me. "Good *fucking* grief is more like it."

Ezra waits out everyone's reactions, looking as if he has all the time in the world. Harper takes a sip of her wine. That wink of his, I'm more than certain, was for me.

Finally, Jeffrey rallies. "Excuse me if I seem a little shocked, but I'm not sure any of us saw this coming."

"Because being queer is so unheard of?"

"No," Jeffrey says easily. "Because you've always been touted as quite the ladies' man in the media."

I can see Ezra refraining from rolling his eyes. He's never dated. Not exactly. But his public meetups with women, even friends, have been well publicized over the years. It's part of the gig for someone as well-known as Ezra.

"Was all of that a cover?" Jeffrey asks, quite the bold question.

Ezra never loses his composure. "No. I've always been equal opportunity."

Jeffrey holds a hand Ezra's way. "So that makes you..."

"Bisexual. All my life. It's not new. Not to me, at least."

"Yet you've never been seen out with men."

Ezra hums. "It's not something I made public."

"Until now," Jeffrey points out. "And what about Naveen Arya? Is he an ex?"

"Of sorts." Ezra's smile makes it clear what he means by that. I can all too easily imagine Shawn in the wings having a coronary at that precise moment.

Jeffrey simply chuckles. "All right. Has Naveen been the only one?"

"My, my, Jeffrey. Quite the personal question, is it not?"

Jeffrey shrugs.

Ezra only makes him sweat for half a second before saying, "No, he wasn't the only one. I fooled around a bit when I was younger. You know how it goes. But Naveen...he's the only man I've been with since then."

"Except for Grayson."

Ezra smirks, which seems, to the audience, to answer the question. Even though he didn't answer it at all.

"Speaking of Grayson," Jeffrey goes on. "What's his story? He was married before."

"Yes, he was."

Jeffrey waits, clearly expecting more, possibly about my own sexuality, but Ezra doesn't give him anything. I snort, taking a sip of my wine.

"Is marriage something the two of you are interested in?" Jeffrey asks, pivoting.

Ezra shakes his head. "Nah. I never saw myself getting married, and Grayson doesn't want that again. It's not something either of us needs."

"But you two *are* serious?"

"If you're asking if there's anyone else for me, the answer is no."

The audience *awws*, and Jeffrey leans forward again. "Is this a new development? You two have been friends for quite some time. Ever since you first filmed alongside one another twenty years ago, isn't that right?"

"I see where you're going with this, Jeffrey, and the answer is no." Ezra's voice is hard, his expression sterner than before. "Grayson was never unfaithful to his wife. And if he were here now, he'd tell you himself that it was me who all but pounced the moment his divorce papers were signed."

"Didn't waste a minute, did you?"

Ezra's expression eases, and he chuckles. "No, I did not."

There's not a doubt in my mind Ezra told Jeffrey to guide the interview specifically in that direction, if only to have the chance to defend me and Camilla publicly. None of this is by mistake. Ezra is making a statement. An unequivocal one.

"If Grayson were here now," Jeffrey says, picking up on Ezra's thread, "what would you say to him? I think we're all dying to know."

Ezra lets out the softest exhale, his chest drawing down with it. He aims his gaze directly at the camera, the look in his eye stealing my very breath.

"I would say I'd have loved you in whatever form you came to me. In whatever time. I would defend you with my dying breath, and I would follow you wherever it is you go. The pieces of us were made to fit, Gray. To be drawn together and shared. You told me once bound stars are destined to go out together. And I'm glad for it. Because I can't imagine a life, now or ever, without you in it."

The audience once again rumbles in a chorus of *awws*, but I only have eyes and ears for Ezra.

"You're quite the romantic, aren't you?" Jeffrey asks.

A slight smile graces Ezra's face. "Some would even call me a poet."

"Well, there we have it. Poet Ezra Gold, everyone."

The audience erupts in cheers and clapping, and a pair of warm, familiar arms slip around my shoulders. Harper jolts, letting out a curse before realizing it's Ezra. He simply chuckles, the sound like quiet thunder near my ear.

"What do you think? Pretty good, right?"

"You're an absolute ham," I tell him, my throat tight.

"Well, I like ham, so I'll take that as a compliment." He smacks a purposely messy kiss against my cheek before standing upright. "Harper. Good to see you."

"For what's it worth," our costar says, setting her empty wine glass down, "the people who have a problem with you two? Fuck 'em. You guys have already made it. You're stars, babies. And no one, not even the harshest critic, will dull your brilliant fucking shine."

Ezra's gaze meets mine, a small smile on his face. "You know what, Harper? I think you're absolutely right."

CHAPTER 26

Ezra

It's late when Harper leaves, Grayson and I promising we'll catch up with her in a few weeks at the premiere. With the house quiet, we naturally drift outside. The air is cool tonight but not unpleasantly so, the surface of the pool calm, like glass.

Grayson leans his arms on the back of a chair, glancing at me. "Was Shawn happy with the interview?"

"As happy as he ever is. Appeased, I think. Now he has a narrative he can stand behind."

Grayson nods.

"Camilla?" I ask.

"Haven't heard from her since the interview, but I asked Shawn to keep her updated from now on. I'm done trying to justify myself to her, and every time we talk, it's all I do."

"You shouldn't have to," I tell him seriously. He's done enough of it. "I'm proud of you for recognizing that."

The smile he gives me is warm. "Coming from anyone else, that would sound condescending. But...thanks. I'm ready to move on."

With me.

I don't say it, but the thought warms me from the inside out.

Grayson lets out a sigh as he looks up at the barely visible stars. "Do you know why I became an actor?"

That has me turning fully his way, intrigued. "I don't. But I've often wondered."

"It wasn't something I ever had aspirations for. I don't care about the fame. I wasn't even sure if I'd be any good at it. But I had to try... Because of you."

"Wait, what?" I ask, my heart beating fast.

Grayson's gaze meets mine, unflinching. "I saw one of your movies at the theater. It was your big break, as they like to call it, but I didn't know that at the time. You were young. Twenty-two, I think. I saw you up on that screen, and I had to know you."

"Gray..."

"It doesn't make any sense. I know that. I just...I felt you. In here." He taps his chest, and I draw in a shaky breath, my eyes burning. "So I came and found you."

"Jesus Christ, Grayson. In all the years we've known each other, you never told me that."

"Because it would sound a little nuts, don't you think?"

"And now?" I ask, my voice hoarse, even as a soft smile spreads across my face.

He shrugs. "Now I know you'd understand."

I blow out a breath, blinking back tears. "You've turned me into a sap, Fox."

"You've always been a sap for me."

I bark a laugh, and Grayson grins, going on.

"It's true. You've always treated me as the most important person in your life. Me and Madison."

"Because she's family."

"See? Most people wouldn't feel that way." He lets out a gentle huff. "But you're not most people, are you?"

"Careful," I tease. "You'll give me a big head."

"I'm positive there's no way it could get bigger."

"Hey," I faux-grouse, making a grab for him. He deftly evades me, skirting around the pool as I follow. "Grayson."

"Ezra," he parrots, continuing to back away.

"Get over here."

"So you can put me in a headlock? Pass."

"You don't have your phone on you, do you?"

"No... Why?"

I lunge, grabbing Grayson around the middle and pulling him with me into the pool. The water rushes over us, sound cut off for mere seconds before Grayson kicks upwards and we break the surface.

He laughs. "You dick."

"It's heated," I defend.

"As if that's the point. You're a menace."

"And you're stuck with me."

Grayson shakes his head, but there's a smile on his face as we wade in the water, the surface rippling around us. The soft glow of the lights makes him look almost ethereal.

Maybe we could visit the sea during our next trip.

Grayson's voice floats my way gently. "Do you think it's possible?"

"What's that?"

"Reincarnation... An eternity of death."

His words hit me like a blunt force to the stomach. I swim to the edge of the pool, holding on to the side as my pulse steadies. Grayson joins me, close enough I can make out the smattering of freckles across his nose.

"I don't know," I finally manage. "But considering human consciousness is still one of the great mysteries, I don't see why not? Who's to say what it is that sparks us being...*us.*"

He doesn't respond for the longest time, and I watch him as he watches the stars. "I want to believe it."

"Yeah?"

He nods, his chin on his crossed arms. "I have to, Ez. Leandros? The warrior?"

My breath catches as Grayson goes on.

"I have to believe he found his lost lover again. The thought of him being alone..." His words choke out, but pain flares bright in my chest, the memory of the starry warrior holding his love all too fresh in my mind.

"It's probably just a story," I say, the words ringing hollow even to my ears.

The look Grayson gives me tells me he doesn't believe it. Not that it's only a story. Not that I believe it, either. "I want it to be true. Because the thought of ever having to say goodbye to you..." He inhales a ragged breath. "It's near crippling."

The stark emotion in Grayson's voice has me closing the distance between us in an instant, clasping the side of his neck with my palm. His skin is cool, the tips of his hair damp against my fingers. "Gray... You won't ever have to say goodbye to me."

"You can't know that."

"I can, actually. Goodbye is for parting. You and I? We're bound, remember? You told me yourself. Never say goodbye to me, Grayson Fox. Only...see you soon."

He swallows harshly, his lips together in a tight press. I can see the waver in his expression, the break in the shield he's trying so desperately to hold up. But Grayson has never been a warrior. He's far too good. Too pure for it. His heart is tender, a quality I've always admired about my friend.

I don't mind being his shield. I'd shield him from everything given the chance. Even death.

Grayson allows himself to crack when I pull him close, pressing a soft kiss to his temple. His arms come around me tight, both of us soaked in our clothes, his inhales shuddering past my ear.

Maybe we can't live forever. But I know down to my marrow—wherever his soul goes, mine will follow.

I hold Grayson for long minutes, losing track of time beneath the darkened sky. Neither of us moves. Neither of us wants to. It's not until he starts shivering that I force myself to let go.

"Why don't we get out of the water," I suggest. "Before you freeze."

"It's heated. Remember?"

I snort. Such a smartass.

Grayson climbs up the ladder first, and I follow, both of us leaving wet footprints on the way to the shed. There are pool towels inside, and we each grab one, drying the best we can before heading into the house.

When I get out of the shower, washed and dressed, I look for Grayson. I find him standing just outside the slider door, sweatpants and a t-shirt on.

I crack the door open. "All right?"

He nods, his arms held high. I realize, after a second, he's looking through the collapsible telescope he found at the antiques store.

"Can you see better with it?" I ask, stepping out beside him.

One of his eyes is closed, the other looking through the lens. "Only a little. The stars are mostly obscured. Just...larger blurs than before."

"Which can you see?"

"The tip of the sword. It's brighter than the rest."

"Does that mean it's bigger?" I ask.

"In this case, yes. Want to see?"

Grayson holds the telescope out, and I accept it. It takes my eyes a second to adjust, and Grayson explains where to look. At the corner of the fence and then straight upwards. There, amidst the fuzziness of what I presume to be clouds, is a star.

"How do you know it's the tip of the sword?" I ask him. I can't see any of the rest of it.

"Just do."

I raise an eyebrow. "All right, Mr. Astronomer."

He huffs. "Hardly."

"You could've been," I point out, handing the telescope back.

He simply shrugs. "Maybe in another life. Come on. There's something I want to do before bed."

I nod before glancing up at the sky one more time. The tip of the sword is barely visible with the naked eye, but I swear it winks amongst the dark.

Back inside, Grayson makes his way into the kitchen. He pulls a carton of eggs out of the fridge, his hair still wet from his shower. The brass telescope sits on the counter nearby.

"It's two in the morning," I say curiously, watching him move about. "A little early for breakfast, don't you think?"

"This isn't breakfast."

Grayson starts cracking eggs, separating the egg whites from the yolks. The whites go into a large mixing bowl. The yolks, he dumps in a storage container.

It finally dawns on me. "Gray... Are we making meringue?"

"Well, right now, *I'm* making meringue. You coming or what?"

Smile wide, I join Grayson at the counter. He nudges the carton of eggs toward me, and after washing my hands, I crack a few myself, separating them the same as he did. We let the egg whites warm as the oven heats, Grayson telling me about the drama club Madison joined at her college. She doesn't want to be an actress, but she's always loved being behind the scenes. She even joined us for filming on occasion when she was young.

Once the oven is ready, we beat the egg whites until they're frothy. We add cream of tartar, vanilla, and salt, and beat again. Lastly is the sugar. I'm fairly convinced we've fucked it up, considering the white doesn't look anything like the picture on Grayson's tablet, but then, slowly, it starts to change.

Grayson nudges my arm with his elbow. "See? Just have to be patient."

"Not my strong suit," I admit.

He snorts.

Finally, we spread the egg mixture onto a sheet pan, making it as circular as possible.

Grayson places the pan near the top of the oven and closes the door. "Ten minutes. After that, we find out our fate."

"Ominous," I mutter.

Grayson starts cleaning up, and I grab the tablet to check the news. There are already articles popping up after my interview, the headlines making me shake my head.

"What is it?" Grayson asks, even though I didn't say a thing.

I read one of the titles aloud for him. "'Ezra Gold confirms he and boyfriend Grayson Fox are more than onscreen partners.'"

Grayson hums. "That's not so bad."

"I never called you my boyfriend."

He laughs lightly. "Ez. You said I'm the love of your life. What are people supposed to think?"

I huff, but he's not wrong. We knew this is how it would go. I set the tablet down, not in the mood to think about the media and their assumptions. The timer dinging has me jumping to my feet.

Grayson watches on in amusement as I pull the meringue from the oven. It looks…

"Holy shit," I say excitedly. "I think we did it."

"Congrats, chef."

"This was ninety percent you," I point out. "Mine have always turned out flat."

The meringue is absolutely perfect, the top ever so slightly golden, the baked egg whites holding their shape. I use a spatula to slip it carefully onto a plate.

Grayson lets out a curious sound. "Why meringue?"

"Remember that time in Chicago? When we filmed there, oh…too many years ago to count. It was shortly after we met."

He's silent for only a second, thinking. "The restaurant we visited before we left. They had honey meringue."

"Yep," I say, setting the empty sheet pan aside. "It was *so* fucking good. Do you remember it?"

"I do now."

Grayson opens the cupboard next to the fridge and grabs a jar of honey from inside. My chest feels tight as he drizzles the honey over the top of the meringue. The one at the restaurant looked far fancier, but this is perfect. More than.

"That was the night you told me you thought you were ace," I say gently, grabbing two forks from the drawer. "It was like a dam had burst, and you couldn't stop talking about it. I remember sitting with you in our hotel room and just feeling…"

Grayson's voice is quiet. "Feeling what?"

"So much love. God, I loved you even then."

He smiles softly. "What did I say? Such a sap."

I can't refute it.

Grayson joins me on the stools in front of the counter. "Go on. Try it."

Exhaling, I press my fork against the meringue. It breaks apart just as it should. I bring a piece to my mouth, chewing slowly, the honey warmed from the freshly baked meringue.

"Fuck," I mumble.

With a chuckle, Grayson cuts off his own piece. We eat the entire meringue in silence, the texture perfectly airy and crisp. The honey adds just the right amount of sweetness.

I hum happily once we're done. "That's one item checked off my bucket list. The perfect meringue."

Grayson sets the empty plate and our forks in the sink for later, and we head toward the hall. "What else is on your list?"

"Not sure yet," I admit. "But I have time to figure it out. Isn't that what you told me?"

We stop outside Grayson's bedroom, his clear blue eyes holding my own. "Yeah, Ez. We have plenty of time."

I can't quite resist tugging him close to kiss his temple. "Night, Gray."

I've only taken two steps toward my room when Grayson's voice halts me. "Ez? Would you stay tonight?"

"Of course," I answer, quickly retracing my steps.

Grayson doesn't bother flicking on his light. I follow him into his darkened room as he stops in front of his dresser. There's a soft clunk. The brass telescope being set in its place. I hop into Grayson's bed before tugging off my shirt and tossing it aside. Grayson sighs as it hits the floor, but he doesn't pick it up. He rolls into bed next to me, his heavy exhale resonating inside my own chest.

"All right?" I check.

"Yeah. It's just nice to have you close sometimes."

Understanding that fully, I take Grayson's hand in my own. His skin is warm when I press a kiss to his knuckles. "Anytime, Gray."

He nods once, his head rolling gently on the pillow. I let our hands fall between us, still clasped tight.

When Grayson speaks, his voice is as soft as a whisper. "If it is real, I'll find you in the next life."

I inhale a shuddering breath, looking at his outline in the dark. I don't need light to know the man beside me. I know him as I know the beat of my heart. And if, as he says, there is a next life? I have no doubt he'll find me there.

I lift Grayson's hand again, my lips brushing his skin. "I'll be waiting."

CHAPTER 27

Grayson

I find Ezra inside the in-home gym and stop in my tracks.

He's wielding a wooden sword, grunting as it hits the hanging bag he's using as target practice. His motions are fluid. Precise.

"Ez?"

He flashes me a quick grin before slashing the bag again. "Got the role."

"The period piece?"

"Mhm." Another strike.

"That's great. I know how much you wanted it. I thought, maybe..."

I don't need to say it aloud for Ezra to understand. "Guess me being queer wasn't a deal-breaker."

"It shouldn't ever be."

His smile is rueful. "No, but you know we're not there yet. Maybe someday."

"I hope so," I tell him truthfully. "You remember we have a premiere to get ready for, right?"

Ezra curses, whipping around to look at the clock on the wall. "Lost track of time. Shit."

I laugh as Ezra all but tosses the wooden sword aside and runs past me. A door upstairs slams shut a minute later, and the shower comes on.

I head back to my room, pulling my suit out of my closet. It's simple and black, but I prefer that to trying to stay up-to-date with the latest fashion trends. I dress as Ezra showers, picking a white t-shirt to go under the suit jacket, knowing Ezra would choose it for me given the chance. This is a movie premiere, after all, not an office event.

Suit on, I head to my dresser for socks. I pause as my gaze lands on the brass telescope sitting beside the old photograph of my star-boy, as Ezra would call him. There's a pang in my chest as the man looks back at me, a sort of ferocity in his gaze I admire. Not for the first time, I take in the star tattoos mapped across his chest. I heavily suspect they're covering top surgery scars, although I have no proof. Just a gut feeling.

Whoever he is, he looks confident showing off the lean line of his torso. I slip the button on my suit jacket so it lies open, wanting to share in that confidence. To bring him with me tonight. Even if no one else knows it, I'll know.

The water down the hall shuts off, and I run my finger along the edge of the frame.

"Whoever you are, you're stunning."

Ezra is in the living room when I emerge. He's still shrugging into his clothes, his own jacket a deep navy that fits him to a T. The man makes the fabric look like priceless art.

"You're wearing a tie?" I ask, surprised.

He adjusts it with a grin, the slim fabric gold, like his name-sake. "Thought I'd be fancy. And don't you *dare* go change. You look great."

"I look underdressed compared to you."

He scoffs, tugging his jacket sleeves straight. "Please. You look phenomenal. Grab one of those for me?"

I look where he's pointing and spot a bouquet of deep red roses sitting atop our table. "Where'd these come from?"

Ezra sounds smug. "Me. Picked them up earlier. Happy premiere, Gray."

I shake my head. The flowers are beautiful. A good three dozen of them if not more. "Such a sap," I say to myself, reaching for the vase. Careful of the thorns, I pluck a single rose free from the rest and bring it over to Ezra.

He grabs the kitchen shears and snips off the end of the stem, leaving only a couple inches of green below the starkly red flower. Hand on my lapel, he tucks the rose into my front pocket. "Perfect."

I clear my throat. "You know, for being a fellow aromantic, you're quite the romantic."

Ezra barks a laugh, winking at me as he pats my chest. "Call it romance. Call it what you will. All I know is you're the only person I've ever bought flowers for."

"That can't be true."

"It is. Would you like to see my credit card receipts?"

"Not necessary," I assure him, knowing full well he'd show me his purchases from the last twenty-plus years if I asked. My phone dings, and I pull it free, pressing the button for the gate to open. "Our car is here."

Ezra smooths down his jacket as we walk toward the door. "Are you ready to watch yourself off me in cold blood up on the big screen, Fox?"

"Excuse me," I say, indignant. "You drew your gun first."

"I didn't aim it at you!"

"Semantics. You were the bad guy."

"Bad is so subjective." Says one of the most golden-hearted people I know. Ezra's expression sobers quickly, turning thoughtful. "This is the first time people will see us together since we announced..."

"Being together?"

"Together adjacent."

I snort a laugh. "For all intents and purposes, you're my damn boyfriend now, Ezra Gold."

His eyes go soft. "How about...partner?"

I mull that over, liking the sound of it. "Partner. Yeah. That fits, doesn't it?"

He nods, checking his pockets one last time before grabbing the doorknob. With a smirk I'd recognize anywhere, he twists his wrist and opens the door.

Flashes go off from just outside the fence, paparazzi and reporters alike stationed outside our home as they have been for weeks. We've given the media very little to splash across the tabloids, not for lack of trying on their part. The frenzy will die down eventually, but for now, eating at home and going out as little as possible has helped us avoid the sharks.

As Ezra said, this will be the first time we're appearing together in public.

Ezra reaches for the back door of our ride, but before either of us can get in the vehicle, one of the members of the crowd rushes forward. I'm absolutely shocked, considering I've never seen a single person try to breach the walls surrounding Ezra's home before. Ezra himself goes still in an instant, snapping to attention as the woman's camera flashes inches from my face.

"Grayson," she says in a rush. "What do you have to say about the end of your relationship with Camilla? Was Ezra the reason for your split?"

"Hey." Ezra's voice is harsh, and he moves to stand between us.

The woman doesn't get the hint, her camera clicking away as she tries to edge around Ezra. The heavy device clips my shoulder in her haste, and I internally groan.

Ezra is the nicest person there is. Until you piss him off.

In a lightning-fast move, Ezra snatches the camera from the woman's grip.

She reaches for it. "Hey, you can't—"

"You are on my property." His tone is clipped. "Threatening the man I love with a blunt object, no less. I most certainly can." Ezra chucks the camera into the bushes at the front of our house, whipping out his phone in the process and pointing toward the gate. "Get the fuck out before I call the police."

She wavers, taking a step toward the bushes, but Ezra starts dialing. With a curse, she dashes out of the gate, the reporters trained on her now.

"Jesus, Ez," I say, keeping my voice quiet. "That'll be in the news."

He looks unrepentant, opening the car door wide and waving me in. "She fucked up."

I can see him firing off a text to Shawn as I slide into the vehicle, likely to have the camera taken care of before the woman tries to get it back.

"Everything okay?" our driver asks.

Ezra gets in beside me and closes the door. "Peachy. We're ready to go."

Cameras continue to flash as we drive out through the gate. It closes behind us, and I gaze at Ezra's scowl as he taps angrily away on his phone.

"It's a good thing you didn't have your sword," I mutter.

Ezra's grin tells me how very much he would have enjoyed that.

As our driver brings us toward the premiere, something Ezra said a while back niggles at my memory. "What did you mean? When you asked if I'd want to move?"

Ezra sets down his phone, blinking a few times as the anger melts off his face. "I thought, well, maybe you'd enjoy living somewhere quieter. It wouldn't have to be all the time, or even right away, but... I could see it. Couldn't you? Somewhere private out of the city, where you'd actually be able to see the stars and I could go grocery shopping without being mobbed?"

I huff a laugh, and Ezra smiles in response.

"What about our house?" I ask him.

He shrugs. "We'd keep it. Like I said, it wouldn't have to be all the time."

"Where would we go?"

His face brightens immediately. "Anywhere we want. That's the point. It'd be ours and ours alone, Gray."

I consider it, the notion more and more appealing the longer I think it over. We're often away when filming anyway, separately or together. Having a second base to come home to? Somewhere off the beaten path without paparazzi at our doorstep?

Ezra must be able to read it from my expression because he pounces. "You like the idea."

"I don't not like it."

"A glowing review, everybody." He throws his arms out theatrically, going so far as to bow in his seat. "However will I cope with such accolades?"

I shake my head as Ezra wipes a fake tear from below his eye. "It's a good thing I know how to tolerate you."

He clutches his chest as if betrayed. "Tolerate. Ouch. The pain, Grayson. You wound me."

I give his cheek a pat, and Ezra snorts. "I like it," I finally say. "The idea of having another place."

"We'll tell Madison but no one else."

"Not even Shawn?"

"Doesn't need to know."

Our car slows, pulling up behind a procession of vehicles. It's mayhem up ahead, a red carpet rolled out and countless reporters vying for a snippet from the many movie stars heading inside.

I can't help but sigh just a little.

"I'm sorry." Ezra's softly spoken words startle me.

"What for?"

He waves a hand toward the chaos. "For this. I didn't know you did this for me. And now that I do…"

"Hey. Don't start thinking like that. I don't hate this gig."

"You don't love it."

"I enjoy a lot of it," I tell him seriously. "Especially when I get to act with you. It's all the rest I could do without."

He eyes me as if to make sure I'm telling the truth. "We could quit."

It's not the first time he's said it. It warms me. It really does. But I shake my head.

"No, Ez. Not yet. I'm not done. And neither are you. I think we have a good few more movies to make together, don't you?"

"You sure?"

"Positive."

He nods slowly, and our car inches forward. There are still a few vehicles in front of us, and we wait our turn.

"When you're ready, tell me." Ezra's tone is serious. "We'll quit together."

"Planning on going out with a bang?" I joke.

He winks in that devastating way of his. "It's almost like you know me."

I chuckle, and the vehicle moves again.

Ezra rubs his hands together. "Here we go. Our moment, Gray. Ready to go supernova?"

"This isn't our end," I point out.

He scoffs. "Of course not. After all, dying stars birth new ones. Isn't that what you said? This is just...our next step."

I suppose it is.

Ezra offers his hand as our vehicle stops in front of the red carpet. Our driver steps out, but Ezra doesn't once look away from me. "I love you, Grayson Fox. With everything I am and everything I will be. Don't ever forget that."

I swallow down the swell of emotions threatening to overwhelm me. I've never doubted Ezra's love. Not for a single second.

I accept his outstretched hand, bringing it to my lips and placing a kiss on his knuckles, as he so often does to me. "More than all the stars," I tell him, my own love so vast I ache with it.

His smile is blinding, and it's all too easy to see why the world fell for Ezra Gold as I did. There's only one difference.

They don't know him the way I do. And they never, ever will.

"Supernova, huh?" I mutter, earning another wicked smirk from my friend. "I guess it's time."

Ezra knocks on the window, and our driver opens the door.

Cataclysmic. Ruinous and miraculous.

Ezra and I step out to a brilliant flash of stars.

PART IV

Caspian and Lee

CHAPTER 28

Caspian

"Abraham?"

"Yes, my love."

I turn my head toward his voice, the dirt unforgiving beneath my shoulder blades, the threadbare blanket providing only the slimmest amount of comfort. Abraham's gaze is aimed upwards, his chest bare, although it's hard to see him clearly in the dark. The walls around us block much of the light, even as the stars overhead shimmer.

"Tell me again," I request of him. "Tell me about our home?"

Abraham turns his face to look at me, a smile both painful and bright appearing. "It will be small." His voice is soft, his hand finding mine and pulling it atop his chest, fingers toying with my own. "A hearth so we may cook and keep warm. Plenty of land surrounding us and a few animals to keep us company."

"Or keep us fed."

He chuckles lightly. "That, as well. We will have everything we need, my heart. And nothing we won't."

I understand what he's saying. We'll be safe in our home made for two. No one to condemn us. No one to stop us from living the life we want. Together.

"*I cannot wait for it,*" *I tell him truthfully, my chest so tight pulling in a breath is difficult.* "*I cannot wait to see our life.*"

Abraham swallows roughly, rolling toward me on the cold, hard ground. His mouth covers mine, soft and sweet. There's an apology in it I don't want.

I want to believe in our future. That it could exist.

I want to believe.

I want.

I open my eyes with a start, my heart racing, the room around me bright. With a groan, I assess my situation. I remember my alarm going off and getting out of bed. But now... I'm on the floor. My knee is aching, most likely a new bruise forming there. Nothing else hurts as far as I can tell.

I take my time pushing upright. First sitting, and then when I'm sure my head isn't about to swim again, I stand. Sunlight is flooding through the window, brightening the bedroom. A few boxes sit in the corner by the dresser, possessions I haven't had the time yet to unpack.

The sun...

Oh no.

I'll be late.

I scramble to get dressed, barely taking the time to brush my teeth and wash my face before I'm out the door. My heart pounds as I swing my leg over the seat of my mechanical bike, the band around my wrist shifting as I grab the handlebars. I blink a few times, clearing the memory of darkened, starry skies and warm lips from my mind, and then I pedal.

Miles of nothing pass as I head toward the hiking trails nearby. Well, not *nothing*. There are houses, their solar roofs reflecting the light, acres and acres of varying farmland, and even businesses along the road near the center of town. The school. A few local restaurants. A car-charging station with a couple old gas pumps. But compared to the city I grew up in, I might as well be in another world.

I take the turn toward the state park I've been visiting every morning since I arrived two weeks ago. The sun is nearly in position, and I curse aloud, skidding around the curve into the parking lot. For once, a vehicle is occupying the otherwise-vacant space, and my pulse jumps.

I brake quickly and hop to the ground, my backpack bouncing. There's not much in it. A satellite phone, in case I lose reception. Water. The portable defibrillator. I tighten the straps so it sits snug on my back, stow my bike near a tree, and jog toward the start of the trails.

Sweat lines my brow as I make my way toward the cliffside a good four miles from the parking lot. I'm running late, which means I'm moving faster than normal. I nearly trip over a tree root on the path but right myself at the last second, cursing once again as my knee aches, still sore from my fall this morning.

Calm down, Caspian.

There's no telling if today is even the day. He hasn't shown up before.

But there's a truck in the parking lot. It could be him.

Or it could be anybody.

I shake off my thoughts and focus on the trails, the path familiar to me now. It's a nice day, the temperature in the mid-sixties, the trees around me letting in dappled light and the area quiet, save the occasional small animal I hear but don't see. Finally, after nearly forty minutes, I reach the incline that leads to the top of the cliff.

It took me an entire day to find it the first time, not having a concrete idea of where to look. All I had were clues. An image of tan rock underfoot. A view of a river and trees along both sides. Scattered branches on the ground and leaves that helped me identify the tree species in the area.

And the man. Of course, the man.

I had the general location narrowed down over a year ago, but it was the trail marker I finally saw that led me here to this town. To these trails specifically. And to this cliff.

I look out over the river now, the foliage green and lush below. The sun cuts through the area where I'm standing, bathing half of the rock shelf in light. It's nearly time. I set down my backpack and take in a breath before turning.

He hasn't shown yet. It's only been two weeks, but each day, I've stood here and waited. And nothing. The sun moves on, and no man.

It has to be soon. Before the leaves change color. It has to be…

A crack has me stilling, my heart feathering so quickly I can feel it in my chest. Another soft crack, like a twig breaking. Footsteps, maybe.

I hold my breath, every hair on my arms standing on end. There's a flash of muted color that appears from around a bend of trees. Dark hair and a broad body. Eyes rising to mine and surprise flashing before his footsteps falter.

I stare at him, not sure if this is even real. Is it real this time? Is it happening?

"Hi," I breathe.

He blinks once, a good couple dozen feet away from me. "Um, hi." His voice is deep. It rolls over me, so much different in person. So much more alive. "I didn't expect to find anyone here."

He offers a small smile, his eyes flicking to my backpack on the ground. It must reassure him to see me with hiking gear because he continues walking up the path toward the clifftop.

I can't stop staring.

"Nice day." He tugs his water free, gulping down a few mouthfuls before looking over at me.

I haven't said another word.

"What's your name?" I ask hoarsely, dying to know the answer. I've been wondering for so very long.

He caps his water. "Lee. Nice to meet you…?"

The end of his sentence hangs as he holds out his hand, a clear question there. I accept his palm, so warm and solid and real.

His answer catches up to me, and I huff a disbelieving laugh. "Your name is Lee?"

"Um. Yes?"

Our hands part, and he watches me curiously before prompting me again.

"And you are?"

I pull in a shaky breath, smiling as genuinely as I can. "It's nice to meet you, Lee. I'm Caspian."

He nods once, looking out over the valley below us. The sun glitters off the surface of the river, the scene idyllic.

I can't believe he's here.

The silence stretches, and he glances at me again, his eyes skipping from me to my bag to my wrist before making a return trip to my face. "You all right?"

I nod, although I can't blame him for asking. I probably look like I'm in shock.

"It's just… I've been waiting such a long time," I tell him.

His brow furrows. "For?"

My breath puffs out, another small laugh. "You."

He stills, a hint of wariness entering his expression. "Pardon?"

"Do you believe in fate, Lee?"

He turns to face me fully now, on guard. I don't worry about it. I know he won't run. His voice is calm and steady, despite his visible caution. "What do you mean?"

"Fate," I say again. "I knew you'd be here."

"Right... And, uh, who are you again? I haven't seen you around."

"I'm Caspian. I just moved here."

His hand flicks momentarily toward his pocket. Where his phone is, maybe? His eyes never leave mine, even as I stay perfectly still. "Are you a threat to me, Caspian?"

I bark a laugh. "No. Never that."

"How'd you know I'd be here?"

My smile is weak. Strained. "I just did. You don't have to be scared of me."

"Yeah, well, you're not making a whole lot of sense."

I know. I've been hearing that my entire life.

He shifts subtly, keeping a respectable distance between us. "You knew I hiked here? Yet you didn't know my name?"

I shake my head slowly. "No, I didn't."

"But you were waiting. For me." He glances toward the diverging trails that lead away from here, most likely deciding his safest course of exit. "Why?"

I let out a slow breath. "You have a pacemaker, isn't that right?"

He goes still, his entire body tense. "What?"

"There's a pacemaker nestled against your heart."

"How do you know that?" His words are spoken ever so slowly. Carefully. There's a flicker of fear on his face now, but still, I know he won't run. And I need him to understand. To not be afraid.

Of me.

Of this.

I clear my throat. "In two minutes, your pacemaker will fail, Lee."

He blinks at me, his chest rising and falling. "What are you talking about?"

"It'll fail."

"No. It's in perfect working order. I just had a check a couple weeks ago."

I shake my head, licking my lips and wishing I had my own water bottle in hand to wet my throat, but I don't dare grab it now and risk startling him. "I'm sorry, but it'll fail."

"Look... I don't know who the fuck you are or how you know private information about me you shouldn't, but stay away from me, all right? I'm going to go, and—"

"You won't," I tell him, sure of it. I know it in my bones. I'd bet my very life on it. "You'll stay right here with me, and you'll go into cardiac arrest in just over a minute. But I promise you it'll be okay. I wish I could explain, but I don't have the time. I'll tell you everything when I can, but for now, I need you to stay calm, and I think it would be wise if you sat down."

I know he won't, but I try anyway.

He shakes his head again, taking a step back. One of his boots is in the light slanted across the rocky cliff, the other in shadow. My chest constricts, but I push away my fear. I know it'll be okay. I know it.

"Listen." His voice is low, as if speaking to a spooked animal. "I don't know you, and I don't know how you possibly know me. But you're freaking me out."

"I know," I tell him sadly. "Just please...remember I'm here to help, okay? I mean, look at me." I open my arms wide. "You could easily overpower me, right? I'm no danger."

He takes another step back toward the trails, both boots in shadow now.

Twenty seconds.

"For what it's worth," I tell him, "I'm so glad to finally meet you. It feels as if I've been waiting for this all my life. I just wish... I wish it didn't have to be like this."

He stares at me blankly, and I see the first flicker in his eyes that something's wrong. "I don't... Why are you here?"

He takes another stumbling step backward, his water bottle falling from his fingers as he blinks several times.

My smile is both sad and resigned. "I'm here to save your life."

Lee swallows heavily, his eyes losing focus. He looks as if he wants to say something, but then he's dipping toward the ground. He catches himself on one knee, as I've seen him do dozens of times before. Hundreds, maybe. Brown eyes meet mine, genuine terror there.

"It'll be okay," I promise him, voice cracking.

Lee's heart stops as I watch, the man pitching onto the rocky ground. With my own chest in a vise, I grab my backpack and do exactly what I came here to. What I'm meant to.

I bring Lee back to life.

CHAPTER 29

Lee

There's a soft beeping when I wake, the sound coming from far away. An uncomfortable surface beneath me. And...the unmistakable antiseptic smell of a hospital.

I blink open my eyes, my heart rate spiking. A blanket is pulled up under my arms, an IV leading from me to an automatic fluids station. The lights in the room are set low, a small mercy. But I'd recognize this place even in the pitch black, being a frequent flyer as I am.

I press the call button at the side of my bed and try to remain calm as I wait for a nurse to arrive. I remember hiking. I remember...a man. With short dark hair and wide, sad eyes. He told me...

My hand flies to my chest, and I register the ache there. As well as the bandage beneath my thin hospital gown.

"Ah, someone is awake," the nurse says, bustling through the door with a smile on her face.

"What, uh..." I clear my throat, the dry and scratchy feel of it unwelcome but not unexpected. "What happened?"

"Well," she says calmly, reading the machines next to my bed, "you went into cardiac arrest."

A beat of silence passes. "I died."

"For only a minute or so. Not long at all, all things considered." She offers me another smile, tapping something on her touch screen. "You were incredibly fortunate you had someone with you."

Caspian.

His name comes to me in a burst, blue eyes, tumultuous and bright, entering my mind.

"My pacemaker?" I ask roughly.

The nurse winces some, her eyes flicking to mine as she comes over to the bed. She checks the IV line and straightens out my blanket. "It malfunctioned. They're still investigating why, but you've been given a new one. Just a little ahead of schedule, hm?"

Right. I rub my chest lightly, the bandage small, covering an incision I know from experience will be less than an inch wide.

"I'll have the doctor in shortly to talk to you," she says, stepping back to her screen. "In the meantime, how's the pain?"

"Oh, uh..." I take a second to think it over. "Not bad."

"Good. You're due for another dose of pain meds in about a half hour, but let me know if it gets worse before then. Would you like some juice? Grape? Apple?"

"Grape, please," I say, feeling a little numb.

She nods, giving me another soft smile. "I'll be right back then."

As she exits the room, I catch part of a conversation happening in the hall. I recognize one of the voices, even though I only heard it for a few minutes. Caspian sounds as if he's recounting what happened at the park. Talking to the police, perhaps? The door hits the jamb and stops short of shutting fully, allowing me to hear the exchange.

"And you had the defibrillator in your bag?" the unknown person asks.

Caspian's gentle voice follows. "I did."

"Why? Seems like an odd item to carry while hiking."

"Well…" There's a pause before Caspian says, "I know Lee has a heart condition. So I wanted to be prepared."

Said heart beats like a drum.

The other person makes a short sound of acknowledgement. "And how do you know Lee Donovan?"

Another brief pause. "We're friends."

He lied. Why did he lie?

"Can you tell me what happened after you used the defibrillator?"

Caspian goes on to explain that as soon as I had a pulse, he called emergency services. He talks about staying with me in the time it took for the paramedics to arrive at our spot four miles up the trails. He mentions walking back with them as I was carried away on a stretcher. I wasn't awake for any of it.

The nurse walks back through the door as Caspian recounts the ambulance ride. The door shuts fully this time, blocking any more of his story from my ears.

"Your juice," the nurse says, setting a cup on the table beside my bed. "Is there anything else I can do while you're waiting for the doctor?"

"No," I tell her, my voice sounding as if it's being dragged along sandpaper. "Thank you."

She nods before leaving the room, the soft beeps I heard earlier still echoing through the walls from somewhere unseen. I take a sip of the grape juice, the cold soothing on my throat and the sugar a welcome hit that has my eyes slipping shut.

My pacemaker failed. It malfunctioned when it shouldn't have.

How did he know?

A soft knock precedes the door opening again. Caspian peeks his head inside, an almost shy smile on his face. "Hi. Can I come in?"

I find myself nodding, and he steps fully into the room, fidgeting with the band around his wrist. I noticed it before. Back in the woods. Was that earlier today? Yesterday? The wristband looks like some sort of medical alert bracelet. I can just make out the word "seizures" on the side now that I'm looking.

Caspian seems unable to tear his eyes off me as he stops near the bed, even as he looks guilty for staring. He opens his mouth once and then twice. "Feeling okay?"

I clear my throat. "I feel like I got hit in the chest by a truck."

He nods, wincing some. "Right. Uh..."

"I would have died," I cut in. Caspian's eyes snap back to mine. "I did die. I would have...stayed dead. If you weren't there."

He licks his lips once, nodding slowly. He appears nervous, his gaze skittering around now, even though it never leaves me entirely.

"You said you'd explain."

He pulls in a short breath before looking off to the side of the room. Heading that way, he grabs a chair and returns, setting it close. He sits on his knees atop it, keeping him level with the height of my bed. He's a slight man, but he must be at least mid-twenties.

"I'm sorry I was so blunt." He seems far more chagrined than when he was telling me my pacemaker would fail. "It's just... I knew we didn't have much time, and I didn't want you to be afraid."

"Yeah, well... You telling me I was about to go into cardiac arrest wasn't exactly comforting."

His face pinches. "I know. And I'm sorry. It just...it had to happen that way. I don't think I could have changed it even if I tried."

My pulse beats heavily. Caspian seems to notice my unease because he sighs before opening his mouth again.

"I saw it happen, okay? I've seen it countless times over the past however many years. Not all of it. I never caught your name. Some of it was blurry, or I'd get bits and pieces at a time. But I knew your heart would fail because I saw it happen. Again and again and again."

I reach for my juice. The liquid goes down in a lump, and I cough around it, working to clear my throat. Caspian reaches for me like he wants to help, but I hold up a hand.

"You saw it," I repeat. "As in...you had, what, a vision?"

After a moment, Caspian shrugs.

"Jesus," I mutter.

"I wouldn't blame you if you don't believe me." He sounds so very small when he adds, "No one ever does."

I let out a slow breath, setting my juice aside and closing my eyes for a minute so I can think. "You had a defibrillator with you. I heard you say that to someone outside."

"Yes."

"Because you knew I'd need it?"

A slight pause. "Yes."

"Because you knew my pacemaker would fail and my heart would stop."

"Yes."

"Because you saw it happen. In a vision."

A longer pause this time. "Yes."

I crack open my eyes, finding Caspian watching me with a wary blue gaze. "I don't...*not* believe you."

He looks close to laughing, but there's definite relief on his face. "Well that's leaps and bounds ahead of everyone else in my life."

His words cause a pang in my chest, something akin to sympathy flaring. But I don't know this man. I'm not sure I can even trust him.

And yet... He's single-handedly responsible for saving my life, isn't he?

How couldn't I believe what he's saying, at least in part? No other explanation makes sense. Him being there wasn't a coincidence. He was waiting for me. Waiting to save my life.

I swallow around the lump in my throat. "I, uh, guess I should thank you?"

His smile is almost sad, but that relief remains. "You don't have to thank me, Lee. You've saved my life so many times. The least I could do was repay the favor."

His words have me stilling, but before I can say anything more, the door opens. Caspian and I turn as one.

"Well," my doctor says, breezing into the room, "I was hoping I wouldn't see you back here so soon, Lee. I hear we ran into some trouble while hiking?"

Caspian slides out of the way as the doctor checks me over, taking my vitals and explaining briefly the surgery he did to replace my pacemaker. It's not the first time, considering my congenital heart defect.

"Do you have someone who can help you get home?" he asks, finishing his examination. "I'm clearing you to leave, but you'll want to take it easy for a few days. Especially considering the extra stress you were put under."

The stress, I assume, being my temporary death.

"I can help." Caspian's offer is soft but hopeful.

The doctor raises an eyebrow my way, and I nod slowly. "That's fine," I tell him.

With that settled, Caspian and I are left alone once more with the promise that a nurse will be in shortly to assist with my discharge. Caspian stands near the window, fidgeting with his wristband again.

"You have seizures?" I ask.

His head whips my way, hand dropping from the band, as if he hadn't realized he'd been touching it. "Um. So they say."

"So they say... Who?"

"My doctors. Do you live alone?"

"I have a cat," I answer slowly.

He nods, giving me the ghost of a smile.

It isn't long before my nurse returns, and Caspian and I are heading out of the hospital. When he opens the back door of an ordered ride, I raise an eyebrow.

He shrugs. "I can't drive."

Well, then. I ease inside without too much difficulty. My chest is still sore, but the pain isn't terrible. Once I have a nice meal in me, I'm sure I'll feel good as new.

Maybe I should put more consideration into allowing this stranger I barely know into my life and home. But... If Caspian was any danger to me, he wouldn't be here, would he? He would have simply...let me die.

I brush the thought away, my mortality not something I want to examine too closely right now. Closing my eyes, I wait for the driver to bring us...*me* home.

It's a relief to step inside my house, as if I've been gone weeks and not a mere day. Shelly yowls from somewhere upstairs, her tiny paws padding heavily down the stairs before she's streaking my way. Caspian makes a sound of surprise as my cat vaults herself up my chest and onto my shoulder. I cough a breath, wincing at the dig over my incision, but Shelly's purr quickly drowns out everything else, my cat rubbing herself on my cheeks and head like a feline possessed.

Caspian watches us curiously. "Is that...normal?"

"Pretty normal," I assure him, dropping the hospital bag with my possessions near the couch. Caspian sets his own backpack down before following me into the kitchen, standing just inside the doorway as I open the fridge. "Hungry?"

"You're planning on feeding me?"

By Caspian's amused tone, I'm fairly sure he recognizes the absolute ridiculousness of this situation. For whatever odd reason, it helps to settle me.

"I'm planning on feeding myself. And, since you're here, it would be rude of me not to offer."

His lips twist into a smile. "I can help."

"Or you can sit," I say, grabbing eggs and bacon before heading to the pantry for a loaf of bread. "And you can explain."

"Thought I already did."

Shelly hops down as I grab her food. She weaves through my legs several times, waiting for her half-full bowl to be full-full before digging in. I set the container back in the pantry and eye Caspian. "Explain more."

He huffs a small laugh. "What's her name?"

"Shelly," I tell him, gingerly reaching for a pan from the rack before turning on the stovetop.

"Because she's a tortoiseshell?"

"I never said I was inventive."

"I never said you weren't."

I raise an eyebrow, but Caspian simply smiles. "Explain," I repeat. "Who you are. Where you came from. More about...how the fuck you knew about me. And...hold up. You don't drive. Is that because of the seizures?"

Caspian lets out a slow breath as I grab a ripe tomato for the breakfast sandwiches I'm planning. "I don't even know where to start."

"The beginning."

His eyes hold mine, serious and calm. "That was a very long time ago."

"Start *somewhere*," I urge.

He nods, placing his hands on the table. "My name is Caspian Wilder. I'm twenty-five. Yes, I don't drive because of the seizures. I bike instead. A mechanical bike, not electric. I used to live pretty far away from here but came because I had to. And I know you because I saw you."

"Many times," I say slowly.

He nods again.

A thought occurs to me. "More than the heart failure?"

He doesn't answer right away.

"Caspian..."

"I'm trying to ease you into this."

"Ease me into *what?*" I ask, our meal all but forgotten.

He blows out a breath. "Who I am to you."

My bruised heart thumps, and Caspian's eyes meet mine again, holding.

"Do you believe in fate, Lee?"

CHAPTER 30

Caspian

Lee stares at me, the pan on the stove starting to smoke.

"Your eggs," I tell him.

He curses, spinning to deal with the eggs before flipping the couple strips of bacon he added. The smell of grease cuts through the room, making my stomach rumble. I barely ate a thing these past twenty-four hours.

Lee is quiet as he pulls out slices of bread, but I know his mind is working overtime. I feel like I'm messing this up, but I don't know the right way to go about this. I'm practically vibrating out of my skin with the need to be closer, but I can't *do* that yet. To Lee, I'm a veritable stranger. He doesn't know me like I know him, even though I barely know him at all.

Once the sandwiches are made, Lee sets a plate down in front of me and takes a seat. We eat in silence, Shelly the tortoiseshell cat grooming herself in a sun patch now that she's eaten her own meal. She's cute, her green eyes assessing me before she goes back to licking her ass.

Lee waits until I've finished my final bite to lean back in his chair, arms crossed in front of himself. He winces slightly, shrugging one shoulder as if needing to resituate. I wonder if his incision site is sore. Or perhaps it's his heart.

He opens his mouth to speak, but I cut in, already knowing what he's going to say. "Explain. I know. I'm trying."

His lips twitch.

I huff out a breath, pushing my plate aside before leaning my weight on the table. I'm tired, even as the prospect of sleep doesn't sound the least bit appealing. Not now. Not that I'm finally here.

"Does the name Penelope mean anything to you?" I ask.

Lee stills, his chest rising and falling in a big breath. "It was my mother's name."

Ah, God.

I rub over my chest, offering a small smile. "I'm sorry for your loss."

"How did you know that?"

"I didn't. Know about your mother, I mean."

"Then..."

"I know about your daughter."

He inhales sharply, and soft, brown eyes float into my mind.

"Papa?"

"Yes, Penelope dear."

"When can we go back to the zoo?"

"We haven't even left yet." The man looks amused, the little girl clinging to his hand batting brown eyes his way. He smiles down at her, his gaze adoring. "Soon, I'm sure."

"Promise?" she asks.

Lee's eyes rise to mine, piercing and familiar all at once. "We promise. Isn't that right, my love?"

I pull in a breath, my rib cage aching with the force of it.

Lee is watching me with concern. "What was that? Did you have a...vision?"

"No," I say, clearing my throat. "Just a memory of one."

He blinks several times, his eyes searching mine. "Of me and...my daughter."

I offer a shaky smile. "You're taking this better than I expected."

He scrubs a hand roughly over his jaw, rasping against dark stubble. "Yeah, well, you showing up five minutes before my heart was going to stop kind of makes it impossible not to believe you. I have a daughter. Really?"

"You will."

He drops his face into his palms. "Jesus. This is...a lot."

"But you believe me?" I ask, unable to keep the wobble from my voice.

Lee lets his hands fall, that warm brown gaze I've seen in so many different faces meeting mine. "It's kind of hard not to."

The relief I feel is staggering.

Lee must see it on my face because he holds his hand out across the table. A lifeline freely offered. "Hey. It's all right."

I accept his palm, his skin warm if not a little dry. It feels so normal, so *right*, and I grip him for all I'm worth.

No one has ever believed me before. My parents. My friends. And why would they, when the things I've seen are never about them? I couldn't prove it. Even my doctors thought I was lying or in need of psychiatric care, at least the scant few I tried to explain it to before locking myself down tight. They labeled it as seizures. And maybe they are.

But they're so much more than that.

Visions. Past. Future. Fate. Call them what you will. I know the truth.

Lee lets out a trembling exhale, and I realize he must be exhausted. Of course he is.

"I'm sorry," I say quickly, his hand still in mine. "Do you need to rest?"

"Not a bad idea." He glances around as if looking for something. Answers, perhaps. "I can't believe I'm going to ask this, but...would you stay?"

"Yeah," I breathe out. "Of course."

"Yeah, okay. Living room?"

I nod, and Lee lets go of my hand to grab our plates. He all but dumps them into the sink before waving for me to follow. His living room has two couches, one long and one short, and a lone chair. He flops unceremoniously onto the larger of the couches, and Shelly races over, hopping up beside him. She waits until Lee is comfortable, one arm behind his head, his other placed over his heart, before draping herself across his chest and purring loudly.

Lee's eyes stay on me as I settle on the couch facing him. "Are you going to rob me?"

I snort. "No."

"Where's your bike?"

"At the trails still. I'll get it later."

He hums, his blinks slowing, although it seems as if he's doing his best to stay awake. Shelly is making biscuits on his shoulder now, looking so comfortable I find myself more than a little jealous. Of a cat.

"Who are you to me?" Lee's voice is solemn, his question causing my breath to stutter. "In these visions you see, are you my...husband? My lover? My friend?"

I swallow heavily, a smile tugging at my lips, even as I ache fiercely inside. "All of those," I tell him. "More."

His brow furrows, but he doesn't ask anything else. He continues to blink until, finally, his eyes don't open again. The midday sun shines through the window beside us, the house around me cozy and warm. I watch Lee breathe. Watch the steady beat of his pulse at the crook of his neck.

For as far as we've come with medical advancements in the last century, Lee still needs a machine to keep his heart pumping. And he always will.

I slide down until I'm lying flat on the couch opposite him. With the man I've spent so many years looking for right in front of me, so close I could touch, I let my own eyes close.

We've got time.

When I wake, Lee is sitting upright, staring at me. I startle, rubbing my eyes as I try to orient myself. The sun is lower in the sky now, early evening.

"Everything okay?" I ask.

He nods once.

I push myself up, glancing around. "I, uh…"

"Bathroom's down the hall. And there's a glass of water on the table beside you."

"Thanks," I mutter, choosing the bathroom first. When I get back, I drink most of the water while Lee continues to stare.

I don't realize I'm toying with my bracelet until he nods his head toward it slightly. "How often does it happen?"

I assume he's asking about the seizures.

"Most days," I tell him truthfully.

He leans his elbows onto his knees, his hands clasped at his chin. "I'm thirty-two."

"Oh. Okay?"

"I have a sister, but she's living over in Europe right now."

I open my mouth, but Lee goes on.

"I teach math at the local high school. And co-coach the football team. I have a painfully normal life. A cat. No partner. No kids...yet. I read before bed, bound books, not on my tablet, because holding something that's equated with being old these days makes me feel connected to the past. And I have no clue why that's important to me. I was born with a heart defect. I recycle, compost, and keep my solar tiles clean. I have a fondness for old movies. Again, the whole *past* thing. I consider myself painfully pragmatic, yet here you are, sitting in front of me, and suddenly I'm wondering if magic is real. Who the fuck are you, Caspian Wilder?"

I press my lips tightly together, battling the tears I can feel threatening to fall. I don't even know why they're there. Maybe because I'm finally getting pieces of this man I've never glimpsed before? Because of why he's sharing them with me in the first place? Maybe because...because I think he's going to believe me.

I lick my lips before answering him. "I'm yours."

Lee barely blinks. "You realize how that sounds, don't you?"

"It's the truth."

He exhales, leaning back, the broad lines of him taking up a substantial portion of the cushion he's on. "I can't decide if it's brave or foolish, how transparent you are."

"I don't have a choice."

"Don't you?"

I shake my head slightly. "Not with you."

Lee shuts his eyes, pinching the bridge of his nose. "I need to get my truck. And you need your bike."

"Sure. Shall I call us a carriage?"

He opens his eyes slowly, peering at me.

I shrug. "You said you like feeling old."

Lee huffs a short breath, shaking his head as I grab my phone to order a ride. I swear there's a smile on his face hiding not far below the surface. It's nearly dark when we get to the park, and Lee helps me load my bike into the bed of his electric truck.

He hesitates once we're inside the vehicle, his hands flexing on the wheel. "Where am I taking you?"

"That depends, I guess."

"On?"

I hold his gaze. "Whether or not you want me gone."

He groans, looking pained. "Jesus. One day. I've known you *one day*."

"I've known you a lot longer."

He blinks several times, gaze aimed up at the roof, his hand rubbing over his mouth and stubbled chin. "God. Fine. But you're sleeping in the guest room."

"If you want."

He doesn't say a word to that, only pulls out of the now-closed park. We stop at my rental first so I can grab a bag of essentials. Most of my things are still boxed up. Unpacking hasn't been a priority.

Back at Lee's, he cooks us dinner while I take a shower. I thought I would feel more...frantic than I do now that I'm finally here. I've been racing toward this point for so long, after all. Searching for this man for *so* long.

But all I feel is...eerily calm. Settled.

I never expected Lee to believe me. At least not this quickly. To maybe even *accept* me.

I probably should have known better.

Lee is in the kitchen when I get downstairs. He spares me a glance as I join him at the table, Shelly licking her paw not far off. He's a great cook. The pasta dish is full of flavor, chicken and cherry tomatoes giving it a healthy edge. I wolf down a good portion before coming up for air.

"I can help with groceries," I offer, knowing my cooking skills are not at the same level as his.

He raises an eyebrow. "Planning on staying long?"

At my non-answer, Lee huffs a breath.

"When do you go back to school?" I ask, grabbing his plate to clean up before he has a chance.

I can feel him watching me at the sink. "Monday. Do you have a job here?"

"Not yet. I only got to town a couple weeks ago, and I've been...busy with other things."

"Tracking me down."

Water runs over my hands as I still. I watch it cascade from me to the plate to the bottom of the bright stainless steel basin, my head going hazy in a way I recognize. I set down the dish and lower myself to the floor before I can drop. I hear Lee's voice, asking if I'm all right, but it's already too far away. He's a blur, and the water is running, but...

But I'm...

I...

"Over here."

I follow the voice into the cavernous overhang, water running down the rocks to either side of me. The air is humid here, salt in my lungs as I breathe in deeply. He's up ahead, the net in his hand holding a rather small treasure. The grin on his face has me smiling in response.

"Have you become a fisherman?" I tease, the tiny crawfish in the net trying to free itself.

He scoffs, but I can tell he's pleased to have caught it. "I am a man of many talents. Come, my love. Let me show you."

I take a step back, and his expression flickers. Amusement. Excitement.

He steps toward me. "Do you plan to run?"

"Do you fancy yourself a hunter, as well? First a fisherman. Now this?"

"If you run, I will catch you."

I hum, taking another step back, my pulse pounding as the water falls like rain beside my ears. "Do your worst."

I've barely turned when his arms come around me, hefting me into the air. The heat of him at my back, the familiar scent of him, have my muscles going lax in an instant. The net falls to the water as he turns my chin in his grip, his lips a feather pressed to my cheek, his voice a low rumble.

"Kiss me, my love. I have caught you. And I shall have my prize."

I arch my neck back, finding his eyes with my own, honey-brown and the scorching promise of a forever just like this. I offer him my lips, my own promise spoken in return.

"I am yours, my warrior."

My eyes whip open, my inhale sharp.

Lee's wide, frantic gaze is on me. "Caspian."

"Fine," I croak, wiping away the tears that are running down my cheeks. I heave myself into a sitting position, the cupboard below the sink at my back.

Lee's hands are outstretched, not quite touching me. "Was that..."

His question hangs, but I nod, pulling in a few breaths, one after another, to steady myself.

"Was it bad?" He finally settles a hand on my arm, helping me to stand. Shelly weaves around my feet, meowing loudly and looking up at me with green eyes as concerned as her owner's.

"No," I manage, my smile an aching, trembling thing. "No, it wasn't bad at all."

"What was it?"

How do I even explain it to him?

I wipe away the remainder of my tears, my chest pulled tight, as if still in the past, tethered to a point long since gone.

"It was...the very start."

Lee's eyes trace over my face, as if trying to read me. To understand. "The start of what?"

My answer for him is simple, although it's not simple at all.

"The first time I fell in love."

CHAPTER 31

Lee

I watch Caspian as he sleeps, his hands tucked under the pillow at his cheek. I said he'd use the guest room, but when bedtime came, I couldn't seem to let him go, not even so far as a few doors down the hall.

He didn't question why I led him to my own room instead. Merely slipped under the covers and closed his eyes.

Is this a dream? Some fantasy I conjured inside my head? Am I lying unconscious on the forest floor? Dead?

I don't think so. Moonlight bathes Caspian's face in light, the flicker of it as clouds pass convincing me this must be real. He's here, whoever he is.

"I'm yours."

I rub my chest, not sure whether the ache there is real or imagined.

I don't remember falling asleep, but I wake to an empty bed. I'm up in an instant, my heart pounding as I race out into the hall. Empty, as is the bathroom. I head down the stairs, not sure what I'd do if Caspian is gone.

But he's not gone. He's sitting in my living room, eyes wide as I come to a halting stop at the foot of the stairs. Shelly is lying in his lap, purring loudly as she kneads his thigh.

I try to calm my breathing. Try to remember it's *fine* if Caspian goes. He lives close by, and it's not as if he could stay here forever. What am I even expecting? Do I *want* him to stay? Maybe I just want answers.

Worry lines Caspian's face. "Are you okay?"

"Fine."

He raises an eyebrow. "Want to try again?"

I stare at this man who barged into my life, upending all I thought I knew. The man who's apparently seen my future or his own or who-the-fuck-knows-what. He's sitting on my couch, the tiniest smile on his face like he understands what I'm feeling. How can he possibly? I'm spinning in a void, no direction up, my sense of what's real distorted beyond what I can rationally comprehend.

"Tell me another one," I say, raking my fingers through my hair as I step into the room. His eyebrow remains lifted until I clarify, "Something else you've seen."

He hums, watching me as I take a seat nearby, a single cushion between us. He continues petting Shelly, my cat eating up the attention, her paws flexing in bliss. "There's no way for you to know if it's true. It hasn't happened yet."

"Tell me anyway."

Caspian closes his eyes, as if recalling whatever it is he's seen. My pulse hammers as I wait, the beat of it loud in my ears. "It's dark. And you're outside. It's cold, but you're wearing a warm coat and don't seem to mind it. The stars are out."

"Are you there?"

Caspian's eyes open, blue meeting mine. "I have to be. That's how it works."

"Go on."

He inhales a soft breath. He doesn't close his eyes this time, but his gaze is distant. "The stars are out, and you're looking up at them. You say, 'They're so bright tonight.' And then you look at me."

"Is that it?"

"No."

"But you don't want to tell me?"

He shakes his head slowly. "I can't."

"Why?"

Caspian seems to weigh his words before speaking. "Because I want to know it's real when it happens. That I didn't put words in your mouth."

There goes my pulse again. "Did you forget you already named my unborn child?"

He huffs a laugh, a smile on his face as he looks down at Shelly. His cheeks are pink, and the sight of it—him, my cat, that blush—has me feeling fondly protective in a way I can't easily dismiss.

He didn't say it outright, but we're together in that future he sees. Aren't we? He's there, at the very least. He's still in my life. Far from now.

His lips twist ruefully as he meets my gaze. "You likely would have picked the name anyway. Because of your mom."

That's true. Penelope would be my first choice for a daughter.

I heave out a breath, rubbing the tops of my thighs and realizing I'm still in my sleepwear. "I'll...be right back."

When I get back downstairs, dressed for the day, Caspian is in the kitchen, looking through my fridge. "What do you normally eat for breakfast?"

"Let's go out."

His head whips my way. "Out?"

"You're new here. And from what you've said, I take it you haven't had a chance to see town?"

"Not much of it."

"Then let's go out. There's a nice diner five minutes from here. Unless you'd rather stay?"

He frowns a little, closing the fridge. "No, that's fine. It's just... Is that okay? Your doctor said to rest."

I offer a wan smile. "I'm feeling well enough for a short trip. Believe me. It's not the first time I've had my chest sliced open."

Caspian's face pales, a sharp breath sucked through his lips. The reaction surprises me, and I step forward, offering my hand to keep him steady.

"Hey, you all right?"

"Can we not...talk about your chest being open? I can't... I don't..." He shakes his head quickly, and I tug him in without thought, my arms wrapping around him, my hand rubbing soothing circles over his back.

"I'm sorry. I wasn't thinking."

"It's fine," he murmurs, but clearly I hit a nerve.

"It was a quick outpatient procedure," I remind him. "Hardly invasive, not like it used to be. I'm fine to drive, and I can even start exercising again in a week or so. I promise it's no big deal."

Caspian eases back, the stern expression on his face nearly making me laugh. That is, until he speaks. "You died, Lee. Forgive me for not wanting the reminder."

"I'll always have the scars," I point out.

My pulse picks up when Caspian places his palm on my chest. The bandage is still there beneath my shirt, freshly changed this morning. The surgical glue looked pristine when

I checked, only a thin pink line proof of the new pacemaker beneath my skin.

Caspian traces his finger over the spot as if he can feel it, when I know he can't. The new generation of devices are so slim, they don't even leave a bump. Not like my first one did when I was a child.

His voice is near a whisper. "I've seen you die so many times. I don't think you understand, Lee."

No, I don't think I do, either.

My pulse feathers beneath Caspian's fingertips, his eyes filled with more sorrow than someone his age should hold. I wrap my hand over his, stilling his nervous motions, and those eyes ping to mine.

"Sorry." He steps quickly back, his hand slipping away. "Breakfast sounds great."

I watch Caspian walk from the room, my inhale shaky.

I don't think anything is going to be the same after this.

The drive to the diner is quiet but short. Caspian watches out the passenger window the entire time, the hum of the engine barely there amidst the roll of tires on pavement. The parking lot is decently full, considering it's the weekend. I find a spot, and Caspian hops out, looking around curiously.

"Preferences on seating?" I ask as we walk toward the door. "I'm guessing your lap is out?"

I stutter a step at the barely there words, and Caspian laughs lightly.

Jesus.

As if he hadn't offered that suggestion, he says, "Booth would be fine."

We're seated at a booth minutes later, a waitress taking our drink orders before we're left with menus to peruse. Caspian seems intrigued by the people in the restaurant. I suppose, if he considers this his new home, getting to know the locals might be a priority of his.

His focus shifts to me before long. "You said you co-coach the high school football team?"

"I do," I answer, setting my menu down. "It's good fun. Barely any injuries anymore with all the new rules and regulations in place, which is great for the kids."

"Not like the good ol' days, huh?"

I huff. "You say that like you lived it."

Caspian simply hums, looking away, missing my narrowed gaze. "What's your mascot or...team name or whatever?"

"We're the Warriors."

His head whips back my way so fast, he nearly knocks his drink over with his elbow. He steadies the glass, eyes wide.

"What?" I ask, alarmed.

"You're... You..." Caspian starts to laugh, and I'm officially at a loss. He wipes a tear from below his eye, voice choked. "It's nothing. Nothing at all."

"Right... Does this maybe have to do with the stuff you shouldn't know but do?"

He seems amused by the vague wording of my question. "Something like that."

"Mhm." I set my arms on the table, putting us closer as Caspian works to compose himself. "And are you ever going to tell me all these...somethings?"

He lets out a quiet breath, his elbows on the table mirroring mine. "In time."

"Because you're trying to ease me into...all this?"

"Yes."

"You know, I've never really been the type of person to rely on faith," I tell him.

"No, that's certainly not you."

My head rocks back at the casually confident statement, and Caspian gives me an almost apologetic smile. I don't bother asking how he seems so sure of it. So sure of *me*.

He goes on in a softer tone. "I'm not asking you to blindly trust me, Lee. I'm asking you to get to know me. To form your own conclusions."

"Conclusions about..."

He shrugs a little, his hands folded on the table, so near to mine. "Me."

The unspoken *us* hangs in the air. Because learning who Caspian is ensures there's an us in some capacity, doesn't it? Whether we become friends or...*more*, as Caspian put it.

I shake my head. "I didn't expect you, Caspian Wilder. But I also didn't expect to die at thirty-two, so there's that."

He winces, and I cover his hand with my own, squeezing gently.

"I'm sorry. It's just...it's been an interesting few days. I'm fine. I promise."

Caspian looks as if he wants to say something, but our waitress returns to take our order. When she goes, we're back to staring at one another, the silence between us heavy. Caspian fidgets with the band on his wrist, the word "seizures" glaringly obvious now that I know what to look for.

"Do you have that for if you're in public?" I ask. "So people know to leave you be?"

He nods, stopping his fidgeting.

"Is it dangerous to you? Having such frequent...episodes?"

Caspian shakes his head. "Apart from the occasional bump or bruise, no. They don't cause any lasting damage."

I nod, swallowing. The one he had in my kitchen wasn't what I expected. He wasn't seizing or convulsing. He barely moved at all. It was like he passed out, except his eyes never fully shut.

"Suppose we make a fine pair, huh?" I joke. "Me with my heart defect. You with your...condition."

He smiles, and it's so soft and, fuck, *knowing* that I have to glance away. My pulse is racing again, and I can't tell if this is a Caspian effect or something else altogether. It's almost a relief when our food arrives, offering me a distraction.

I unroll my silverware. "So what is it you want to do? Job-wise. Do you have a particular field of study you're specialized in?"

Caspian hums, cutting into his pancakes. "I'm an astrophysicist."

I drop my fork onto my plate, the clatter loud even amongst the din of the restaurant. Caspian watches me in amusement as I get my wits about me. "Fucking what?"

He laughs outright, looking incredibly smug at having caused such a reaction. "You heard me."

"Jesus Christ. How?"

He answers before I've finished doing the math in my head. "I started college at seventeen and finished my graduate program a year early. Since then, I've been...busy."

Looking for me.

I clear my throat. "So, uh...what do you plan to do here? As you might've noticed, we're a fairly small town."

His lips twitch. He's enjoying this far too much. "I noticed. I'll likely work remotely. I have an offer to participate in one of the global space initiatives."

When I don't say anything, Caspian looks up from his food.

"I'm sorry," I say slowly before taking a full, deep breath. "Are you talking about colonization?"

He shrugs. *Shrugs.* As if it's no big deal.

"Jesus Christ," I repeat, scrubbing my face.

"I can't go up myself." Caspian sounds dismayed by that fact. "The seizures preclude me from eligibility. As would your heart defect."

I nod, although I certainly never had aspirations of going up into freaking space.

Caspian lets out a soft sigh, clearly not of the same mind as me. "But the first civilian mission is scheduled for ten years from now. And...I'd like to be a part of it. To help make it happen."

"You're going to help the first shuttle of humans settle in space?"

His smile is one I'm starting to recognize. It's him knowing more than he should. It's a secret. One he's more than confident in. "Yes. I am."

Caspian goes back to eating his pancakes. And I realize...

Finding out who this man is isn't even an option, is it? It's inevitable. A course I couldn't correct even if I tried. He's here, the gravitational pull of our lives now intertwined, one and the same.

No. Nothing is going to be as it was before.

And I think I'm absolutely okay with that.

CHAPTER 32

Caspian

"It's starting."

The call has me abandoning our drinks and hastening out onto the deck. Ezra is lying flat on his back, a blanket spread out under him. He chuckles when I nearly trip in my hurry to join him.

His hand brushes mine once I settle, a grin on his face I see briefly before looking up at the sky. It's dark out, the navy above looking nearly black. Stars glimmer, so big and bright I could map hundreds, maybe thousands if I wanted. The moon is only a sliver, a curve of sunlight reflecting off its surface.

But it's not the stars or the moon I'm looking for now.

Ezra points. "There."

A streak of light flickers through the dark, followed quickly by another. We watch in silence for long minutes, the meteor shower its own kind of show. A spectacular one. There are no horns blaring here. No busy city noise or light pollution hindering our view. The air around us is quiet, this place our own little slice of secluded paradise.

Ezra's voice is hushed. "It's beautiful."

I can only nod.

He lets out the softest of sighs, his words sounding the same. "'For what is more beautiful than heaven?'"

I glance at Ezra in the dark, my eyes acclimated enough now that I can see his features. "Practicing your poetry, Copernicus?"

"My astronomy." He grins in that way he does. Ezra has more wrinkles on his face than he once did. Some gray in his hair he's done his absolute best to hide under a pristine dye job. He refuses to admit he's aging. That we're aging.

I, on the other hand, don't much mind it. Not when I'm aging with him.

Yet despite the years that have passed, my friend hasn't once lost the spark of what makes him...him. To his fans, he remains infamous. The great Ezra Gold.

To me, he's still just...my Ezra.

Ezra's expression is soft as his eyes drift over my face in turn.

"What is it?" I ask.

"Just that...sometimes I think heaven is here with you."

My heart kicks, my chest warm and aching and tight.

He reaches out, his finger tapping a few points on my cheeks and nose. "You carry the stars with you, Gray. Your own constellation I can look at any time I want."

"My freckles?" I ask hoarsely.

He nods, his brown eyes dark beneath the stars above. His fingers wrap around my own, and he brings my hand up to his mouth, pressing a kiss there. "Love you."

He says it simply.

It's not simple at all.

Our hands rest between us as the last of the meteors streak across the sky. My eyes never leave Ezra's. "More than all the stars."

"Caspian."

The voice startles me. Fingers drift across my cheek, one brown-eyed gaze exchanged for another as light assaults my eyes, the twinkling of stars overtaken by the sun high in the sky. It's such an abrupt shock, I roll over, blinking down at the ground as I find my bearings.

Lee checks in again. "Caspian?"

"Fine," I tell him, the grass beneath me soft. Far softer than the deck boards. I clear my throat, the lump there left over from before. "Was I out long?"

"A few minutes. Longer than the other times."

I nod, sitting up, a dried leaf crunching beneath my palm. Lee's rake is lying on the grass now, the wheelbarrow I'd been using to haul away the first of fall's dead leaves resting on its side nearby. "Sorry if I scared you."

A small smile graces his lips, even as concern lingers in his gaze. "I'm used to it. Snack break?"

I nod again, and Lee helps me to stand. Shelly greets us when we walk inside, scaling my chest to wrap around behind my head, her whiskered cheek butting against my own. Lee chuckles, even as I rub the small scratch left behind from Shelly's climb.

He pours me a glass of juice first, passing it over as I take a seat at the table. Then he sets to work making us a bite. "Want to tell me about it?"

I hum, considering how much to say. "There was...a meteor shower. It was gorgeous."

Lee raises an eyebrow. "Why do I get the feeling you're leaving a lot out?"

"I am."

"Why?"

"Because I'm not sure you're ready to hear it."

He walks over, setting a plate of crackers and grapes in front of me. I appreciatively eat some of both.

"Let's recap, shall we?" Lee holds up his hand to tick off his fingers, and my lips twitch. "In the past month, I've learned I have a daughter on the way. Congratulations to me. I've found out you're a freaking genius who also happens to have visions of the future. I've spent nearly every day apart from my working hours with you because apparently I can't stand it when you go back to your place. And my cat now loves you more than she loves me. I'm fairly certain at this point, nothing you say could shock me."

I lick my finger clean, holding Lee's gaze. "It's not only the future I see."

His mouth falls open. "The fuck, Caspian."

"Told you," I mutter, downing the last of my juice. Lee follows me when I stand, his hand on my arm halting me in the hall outside the kitchen.

"Explain."

I bark a laugh, and Shelly goes scrambling off my shoulders. I wince at the tiny claw massage over my back.

Lee isn't smiling, and I deflate with a heavy breath.

"I see the past, too," I confirm.

He never lets my arm go, although his grip isn't remotely tight. "But... You said you have to be there. That's how it works."

I nod once.

I can see his gears turning, and I wait, the clock in the hall-way ticking quietly. "When you say the past...are you talking about your childhood?"

"No."

"Okay... You're talking about before you were alive?"

"In a way."

"Oh, fuck."

Lee sits down right in the narrow hallway. I join him, my back against the opposite wall, our feet side by side. Sunlight drifts in from the back door, lighting the floorboards near my foot.

"Do you see now why I've been trying to ease you into it?" I ask.

"How is that possible?"

"How is any of this?"

He blows out a breath. "What have you seen?"

"A lot," I admit. "Ancient Greece. Migrations across untamed lands. Vikings who sailed the high seas. I've seen the Black Death. Colonial America. The beginning of this century."

He inhales a shuddering breath. "And the future. Do you see farther than this life?"

A beat passes. "Yes."

"Oh my God." Lee braces his elbows on his knees, staring at the floor between his feet. I give him time, my heart racing. Finally, he says, "I think I need a minute."

"I'll go," I say, making to stand.

Lee grabs my ankle before I can, his eyes meeting mine. "Stay. Please. I just... I need a minute."

I nod, settling back down, Lee's hand around my ankle holding tight. He leans against the wall behind him, his eyes shutting as his head rests back on the wainscoting.

I wonder if he can feel my pulse beneath his thumb. If he knows the beat of it as I know his. If, somewhere deep down, he recognizes my heart. If he feels the pull of it as I've felt him all these many years.

It's torture not to close the gap between us, tenuous as it is. Not to demand he open his eyes and *see* me. Not to tell him everything, every detail big and small, so he can understand. So he can believe it.

But I can't tell him all of it. Not yet. There are some things a person needs to feel in their own time. In their own way.

So I sit. And I wait. As I've been doing now for weeks.

Lee opens his eyes after what feels like a lifetime. "Someday, you're going to tell me everything."

"Yes," I agree.

"But today isn't that day, is it?"

I shake my head slowly.

With an exhale, Lee pushes to his feet and holds out his hand. I clasp his palm, and he tugs me upright. His eyes hold mine for a long moment, seeking, searching. Perhaps he can't see the past or the future as I can. But he can see now. He can see how I feel, surely.

Sometimes I wonder if I can see the same.

Lee heads past me out the door. I follow, making sure Shelly doesn't escape after us.

He picks up his fallen rake, glancing my way as I right the wheelbarrow. "You really don't have to help with this, Caspian."

It's not the first time he's said it, but I didn't listen then, either.

"If I'm living here, doing yardwork and chores isn't really helping," I point out. "It's my responsibility, too."

He pauses in raking up the last of the leaves. "Are you living here now?"

"You set up the office for me to use."

He leans his arm on his rake.

"We sleep a foot apart," I add.

His lips twitch.

"Lee, you rarely let me leave. You said it yourself. Don't pretend like you don't want me here."

He shakes his head but goes back to raking, amusement lacing his tone. "You're cheeky."

"And you're stubborn. You could admit you kinda like me, you know."

Lee appears to mull that over, as if it's something he has to actually consider. "I kinda like you. I guess."

"A ringing endorsement," I mutter, smiling when Lee chuckles.

We finish raking the leaves from his yard, the rooftop solar tiles glinting in the waning sun. It's hard to believe so much of our energy used to come from fossil fuels and processes that were destroying our planet. And before that, we relied on candles and oil lamps to see.

So much has changed.

And so very much is exactly the same.

Lee cooks dinner as he does most every night. He likes it, I've found. The process is soothing to him, and I suspect he enjoys it even more now that he has someone other than himself to cook for. I have no problem complimenting his food. And he has no problem whatsoever preening under the praise.

As Lee goes to shower before bed, I take a few minutes to answer my work email. I'll be officially starting my job next week, working from home most of the time on the endless specifics that still need to be hammered out in order to send engineers, scientists, bioengineers, doctors, agriculturalists, countless other specialized astronauts, and eventually civilians up into space. There will be times I'll need to fly to Command Center. Possibly even elsewhere if I'm needed somewhere on site.

I don't mind. Not so long as I can come back here. Back home.

When I find Lee, he's sitting up in bed, reading a bound book. He gives me a hint of a smile as I join him, flipping a page. So much of what I've seen of Lee has been inside my own head. Glimpses of him older, of this house years from now and the child running through its halls. Pieces of conversation or soft smiles that make my heart ache. Him in the woods, dropping shakily to one knee as I stand there, helpless to stop what I know is coming.

Watching his heart cease to beat. Feeling his pulse kick back to life under my fingertips.

I've known this man in a dream that's not a dream at all. But now he's here in front of me, full of life and warm blood and a mischievousness as he raises an eyebrow that tells me I've been caught staring. I don't care. I can't stop. The snapshots I have of him aren't enough. I need every moment I can gather. A lifetime of them.

Lee closes his book and sets it aside. His lamp is on, bathing the room in a gentle glow. "Something on your mind?"

"A lot."

He hums, turning to face me more fully. For as cautious as he's been, there's no hiding the way Lee is attuned to me. I move, and he follows. The opposite is also true.

"Tell me one thing on your mind."

It's a request, not a demand, but I speak all the same. "So much of my life has been spent elsewhere. And now, I'm *here*. In this time and this place, living a present I don't know. I know how it ends. How it began. But I don't know...this."

Lee watches me closely, the lack of judgement on his face so unlike what I've experienced in my life that I nearly sag with it. "Do you want to know?"

"No," I admit. "Because then what would be the point in living it? This is my adventure to live. To learn and love and grow. People debate destiny and the linearity of time. They debate free will. But regardless of all that's set to be, we're here now. No matter what end waits over the horizon, every one of our choices matters because we're living them. We're not powerless unless we believe ourselves to be."

I can see on his face that Lee doesn't understand what I'm trying to say. My inhale is shuddery, my heartbeat quick. How do I put it into simple words?

"I'm ecstatic," I tell him. "Because I'm living *now*. And I really like where I am."

He swallows heavily, his eyes roaming over me. "I like that you're here, too."

"I know you do."

"But it scares me."

"Because of how we met?" I guess.

He nods slowly.

"And if I were anyone else?" I ask, my pulse firing. "Someone you met at a bar or went on a date with?"

He takes his time to answer, the heat in his gaze not of my imagination. "I would want to kiss you."

My voice comes out at a whisper. "So do that."

Lee's eyes hold mine for so long, I expect him to turn away. He doesn't. His hand comes up to run slowly over my jaw, a brush downward before his fingers trail up again. Goose bumps erupt over my skin as he hooks me, holds me, his thumb near my ear.

The first press of his lips to mine is so soft I barely feel it. I don't breathe, waiting for it to come again. It does. Lee meets my mouth with a soft grunt I can feel in the pit of my stomach. He sucks in a breath, and I do the same, oxygen invading my lungs, the atoms of my body straining with the singular goal of getting closer to this man. The one I've waited for time and time again.

It's one thing to know. And completely another to *live*.

Lee draws back from the kiss on a gasping breath, his forehead pressing to mine. My hand is tangled in his shirt, his still on the side of my head. His voice is hoarse, rough, when he speaks. "Do you believe in fate, Caspian?"

I smile at the question returned to me. He must know the answer, but I give it still. "Yes. Do you?"

"I'm starting to."

CHAPTER 33

Lee

I watch Caspian charm my coworkers, fellow teachers and administrative staff alike falling under his spell. We're at the high school luncheon, the school closed to all but staff today as we learn the updates to our online grading system. Caspian joined us when we broke for food.

He's not the youngest one here, but it's close. The seven-year gap in our age feels large in number, and yet, there's no denying Caspian is wise beyond his years. There's an ancient sort of knowledge in his eyes, and I understand that now.

All he's seen. All he's lived through, even vicariously.

There's a question I've yet to ask him, unsure if I'm prepared for the answer. He said he's there in every vision. It's him, somehow, even if it's not.

It boggles my mind to even try to comprehend the why or how of it. But that's not what I can't bring myself to ask.

What did he say that one time? I assumed he was talking about my cardiac arrest, but now...

"I've seen you die so many times."

I swallow down the boulder trying to lodge in my throat, offering a quick smile when Caspian looks my way. He says something to the group he's talking to and heads in my direction, most everyone done with lunch now. Dessert is waiting nearby. Small pieces of chocolate cake and some rather concerningly pea-green gelatin.

"Hey." Caspian's voice is soft as he stops in front of me, not quite touching. I can tell he wants to. He's been restraining himself ever since our kiss. Since before then, too.

I hold out my hand, and Caspian lights up. Our fingers tangle, my heart pounding so heavily I wonder if my device will record the anomaly.

"Hi," I finally manage. "Are you utterly bored yet?"

"Not at all. Your colleagues are great. Did you know Emmeline taught physics at a collegiate level before moving here to be closer to her wife's family? We exchanged numbers. She has some interesting insights on superfluid space-time that—what? Why are you smiling like that?"

I bring Caspian's hand up, kissing the back of it, and he inhales a sharp breath. That hitch, the way his eyes flare and hold my own, has me repeating the motion—a soft press of lips to skin—before I let our hands drop. "I like learning who you are, is all."

"And what are you learning?"

The breathlessness in his voice has me fighting a grin. "A few things actually. One: that you're an absolute geek when it comes to space. And, apparently, I really like that. I like hearing you mumble about your work when you think I'm not paying attention. I like the way you get excited every time it comes up."

He nods weakly, a gesture for me to go on.

"Two: you're quite fearless. I don't know why that surprises me considering the way we met, but I find myself charmed all the same every time I see your bravery in action."

He repeats the word quietly. "Charmed."

"And three," I continue, steeling myself. "I would be a fool to ignore all that simply because I felt...blindsided by your arrival in my life. To ignore how brave you've been with me. How your excitement makes me happy in turn. How I'm fairly certain I more than like you, and I don't know what that means or where we go from here, but I know I don't want you gone. That's the last thing I want."

Caspian's smile grows slowly, a flower in the summer sun. "That third one was something about yourself, not me."

I hold back my laugh. "Yes, well... It has to do with you."

"It does." He glances at the dessert table as a few of my fellow teachers stop there to grab plates. I can feel eyes on us, but I don't look away from Caspian. His focus returns to me, and he seems...hopeful, perhaps, at the simple fact that I never once let go of his hand. "I don't have all the answers, Lee."

Somehow, I highly doubt that. "But you know what you want."

"Yes."

"And you're waiting for me to catch up."

His lips tip into a smile. "We have time."

I blink up at the cafeteria ceiling, a few banners hung for the snowflake dance that'll be here in less than two months. "I think we should go on a date."

When I bring my gaze back to Caspian, that hope is bright in his eyes. "A date."

"Yeah, you know... That thing people do when they kinda like one another?"

His eyebrow pops up. "I thought you more than liked me."

"God," I groan, Caspian's smirk all but convincing me I'm in over my head when it comes to this man. Although I knew that from the moment we met, didn't I? "I don't know if I can handle you being this cheeky. I have a heart condition, you know."

Caspian pats my chest. "You'll manage."

He sounds so sure.

I clear my throat. "Guess I don't have a choice, huh?"

Caspian's eyes ping between my own, his tone turning serious. "You do. You always have a choice, Lee."

"Doesn't that kind of counteract the whole fate thing?"

I notice my coworkers starting to regroup and realize our lunchtime is nearly over. Caspian's hand on my chin brings my attention squarely back to him.

"You're only powerless if you believe yourself to be." The words are spoken firmly, the same ones he gave me before. "We always have choices in life. *We* weave fate, Lee Donovan. Not the other way around."

I don't have a chance to decipher his meaning before the principal calls us back to task. I give Caspian's hand a squeeze. "You okay to bike home?"

His lips spread into a smile, and it takes me a second to realize why. *Home.* "Yeah. I'm good. See you tonight. For our...date?"

I groan again. "No pressure."

"None."

Caspian lets me go and waves a goodbye to Emmeline as he heads out of the cafeteria. I watch him until he's out of sight.

Emmeline catches my eye as I return to our table. "Your boyfriend is lovely, Lee. Where did you manage to find him?"

I huff a small laugh, not bothering to counteract the *boyfriend* assumption. "Would you believe me if I said he fell from the sky?"

She grins at that, her catlike eyeglasses giving the physics teacher a playful yet sharp vibe I've always found suited her. "Well, you know what they say about shooting stars."

"What's that?"

"When you see one, you have to make a wish."

I hum, our school's tech gal launching back into the online grading system as my mind whirs.

Make a wish, huh?

What would I wish for when it comes to Caspian?

His voice floats into my mind. *"I'm yours."*

I blow out a slow breath as I realize I have my answer.

That. I want precisely that.

When I get home, Caspian is in the office upstairs, talking on the phone. I'm grateful for his preoccupation, even as Shelly announces my arrival with several loud meows. I swoop her off the hallway table she's perched on, shushing her gently and obeying her demand for head scratches as I bring my haul, cat included, into the kitchen.

Shelly, sensing dinner is imminent, jumps down and pads toward her food bowl. I fill it up, and then I set to work.

By the time Caspian comes down the stairs, everything is ready. I set the final touches and wait, my heart thudding.

Caspian freezes when he reaches the entrance to the kitchen, his eyes flicking first to the makeshift picnic I set up on the floor where the table used to be and then to me. "Lee, what..."

"It's too windy outside for the candles," I explain, watching him take everything in. The blanket spread out under plates of food and a platter of small desserts. The candles lit on the windowsill and along the countertops, creating a soft glow as the sky turns slowly dark. The table, even, pushed to the edge of the room, out of the way. "I thought about taking you out, but I realized all our best conversations happen right here. At home. And I thought...well, that's its own kind of magic, isn't it?"

Caspian lets out a soft breath that might be astonishment. "Do you plan to woo me, Lee?"

"If you're open to it."

In answer, he steps into the room, sitting on one of the pillows I set out. I quickly join him, legs crossed in front of me. Caspian looks at the candles beside us, reflections flickering in the windowpane, each a dual flame. There's a sort of wistfulness in his expression that has me wondering what he's seen that reminds him of this. The candlelight. Maybe even the darkened sky.

He hums lightly. "I used to live in the city."

"Yeah?"

With a nod, his eyes return to me. "I like it here, though. Where you can see the stars. Where it's quiet and peaceful and...kind. People are so kind these days. Not all that long ago, it would have been illegal. You and me."

My heart nearly cracks down the middle. "It shouldn't have ever been like that."

"No. It shouldn't have." He's quiet for a moment, his fingers toying with the edge of his plate. "I know some people think it's fear or necessity that's pushed us as a society. Why we've advanced. Why we're launching into space, creating a safety net for human life to flourish. I don't think that's it."

"No?" I ask, unable to look away from the gentle planes of Caspian's face. His eyes glimmer in the candlelight, fire amongst sky. "What do you think the reason is?"

His smile is soft. Pained, almost. "Love."

That takes me by surprise. "Not biology? Our drive to procreate? To survive?"

He shakes his head, a slow movement. "It's all intertwined in a way, but no. We're not leaving simply to survive. We don't explore the vastness of space because we're scared of what's out there. Or scared of what will happen if we stay on a dying planet. A person doesn't fear the end. They fear losing what they've gained. They fear loss. And the greatest loss, the thing we hold most dear and what drives our passion, our thirst for knowledge, the bonds we forge along the way...is love. It's the universal language. It transcends space and time and every barrier put in front of it. Even light gets swallowed by the gravity of a black hole. But love? Love is the reason we seek to see beyond it."

My swallow is more than a little rough, the ache in my chest familiar now where this man is concerned. "What do they call that? There's a name for it, is there not?"

"The event horizon."

I nod, trying to find my breath. "I won't claim to understand what it could mean, seeing beyond that point. But..."

Caspian looks concerned by whatever he hears in my voice or sees on my face. "But what?"

My smile for him is meant to reassure, but it feels brittle at the edges. Not because I don't mean it. But simply because I'm trying to find my footing again after having what feels like my entire world tugged out from under me.

"But if that's how you feel about love," I finally manage, "then I count myself lucky to be the person you were searching for."

Understanding lights in his eyes, and he draws in a breath, moisture pooling that he rapidly blinks away.

"I told you I believe you," I remind him.

He nods.

"So however it is you love me, I'll do my absolute best to love you back just the same."

He doesn't say anything to that, but a small sound leaves his throat. I scoot my pillow around the blanket until it's beside his. His leg is warm pressed against mine, his breathing soft as I hand him a plate. We eat in relative silence as I block Shelly's attempts to steal our desserts. I don't know if Caspian feels as overwhelmed by all of this as I do, having had years to acclimate—his whole life really—versus my months. But I strongly suspect I'm not the only one feeling the loss of gravity beneath my feet. The shifting of reality. Of all I thought I knew.

When our dinner plates are empty, I bring the desserts closer. "I assume you still have room? It's no pea-green gelatin, but I did my best."

He huffs a small laugh. "You didn't eat that, did you?"

"Oh, hell no. That stuff had stomach troubles written all over it."

He chuckles, plucking a small lemon tart from the tray.

"Full disclosure," I say before he can take a bite. "I didn't make these myself. You can thank the bakery in town for that."

"It's the thought that's perfect."

Caspian hums as a piece of the tart disappears between his lips. I try not to stare, but it's near impossible not to. The dim light of the room and the candles casting light across Caspian's face makes me feel as if I'm in a dream.

Is this how he feels every time he has a vision? Like every second is too important to miss? I don't dare blink, scarcely breathe. But then Caspian is handing me a dessert off the tray, and I look down at the offering.

A piece of crispy baklava.

"My favorite," I murmur, accepting the treat. The combination of pistachio and honey is divine, and I nearly moan at the first hit of it against my tongue.

Caspian looks amused. "I know."

I cock my head, wondering if I should even ask how he guessed as much. But Shelly takes that moment to get past my defenses, her tiny paws perilously close to the remainder of our desserts. Caspian scoops her up quickly and efficiently, cradling my cat as if she's a child. Shelly melts, allowing him to scratch her stomach, a feat not many men have attempted and lived to tell the tale.

"You've bewitched us all," I mutter.

Caspian's gaze swings to me. "Have I?"

He looks pleasantly startled when I run a hand through the short hair at the side of his head. He leans into the touch, much as my cat would, his eyes fluttering closed. If I weren't already under his spell, that would do it. Seeing his trust. His longing so close to the surface. The way he's offering himself. Freely and without barriers of his own.

I don't know what the future holds. But right this instant, I know with a certainty I feel in my bones, in my very makeup, that I could fall in love with this man if I let myself.

I bring my mouth to his slowly, his lips tart from the lemon but sweet as well. He doesn't shy away. He's in my kitchen, in my life, waiting for me to come to conclusions he already knows. My kiss is a question, asking him if this is it. If he feels it, too. His answer is in the way he opens to me, my poor cat abandoned in favor of Caspian's hands holding me tight, telling me I'm on the right track.

We kiss until the sky is fully dark, the candles half-burnt, leaving wax trails on my countertops. And even then, we don't go upstairs. Not right away. We lay our heads on the pillows, lying side by side as we battle sleep, talking about the stars and the future and the now.

I think Caspian was right. Our choices matter. Every one of them.

And I've already made my choice.

CHAPTER 34

Caspian

Lee is in the shower when I wake, the soft patter of water tempting me to join him. It's a struggle to abstain, heading for the bathroom in the hall instead. But I'm trying my best to let Lee set the pace between us. To not push too far too fast.

A smile settles on my face as I brush my teeth and get ready for my day. It's the weekend, which means I have Lee all to myself.

I beat him back to the bedroom, the water shutting off as I'm standing in front of the dresser, contemplating clothing options. The door to the en suite opens a minute later, and Lee steps through, wrapped in a towel, his steps faltering when he sees me standing in only my briefs and a t-shirt.

My pulse skitters, my eyes drifting down his torso and the light smattering of hair that trails even lower. The subtle scars on his chest. The broad shoulders and tapered, yet soft, waist. He doesn't move, and neither do I, rooted to the floor when, in days past, I would have pulled on my pants and left him to his privacy.

I can't move away from him now. Don't want to.

Lee must see the desperate invitation in my eyes because he steps closer. The heat from his shower practically rolls off his skin, flushing my own.

"Morning." His voice is gruff and sleep-hoarse. Tinged, maybe, with something else.

"Morning."

His gaze rakes over me, possibilities I recognize swirling in his eyes, and *stars above*, if he keeps looking at me like that, my willpower will be gone.

"Lee..."

"In this future you see. In the past... What is it that calls you?"

My breathing, already short, hitches. Because we're dangerously close to a truth I can't unspeak.

But Lee draws me in, his palm warm on my neck as he angles my head to the side, kissing just below my ear and then further down toward my shoulder. My resolve wavers, his lips pressing cracks into my already trembling façade.

"Caspian." His voice is a murmur, his skin warm beneath my palms. Warm and real. "I haven't run yet."

No, he hasn't. And he won't.

"You," I tell him. "Every time, always, I see you."

His breath catches, but his lips never leave my skin. They travel up my neck, even as they tremble. Those lips journey to my mouth, asking permission freely given, parting and greeting and feeling as if they never want to say goodbye. His tongue flicks against my lip, and I answer in kind, every piece of me ready and joyously shouting for whatever it is he wants. Because it will always be what I want, too.

I would be his friend, his confidant, his loyal supporter. I would wait for him, bleed for him as I know he would do for me. I would love him with every one of my last breaths.

There is not a world, not a lifetime, in which I am not his. Utterly and singularly.

Lee pants out a breath as the kiss deepens, his exhalation mixed with a groan I haven't yet heard from the man. His towel is close to falling, and I grab the ends, using my grip on it to tug him with me toward the bed. He falls overtop of me, damp hair dripping onto my cheek, his mouth fused with mine and feverish in a way I've been aching for.

Fingers slip under my shirt, my name a question. "Caspian?"

"Please," I tell him, begging, demanding.

His mouth drops to my neck again, kisses laid across my skin as he inches my shirt higher, his towel slipping onto my leg. I grab him by the hair, tugging his head to the side so I can see his body that's now bared to me. The swell of his ass cheeks. His dick hanging low, hard and swaying with his movements. Lee huffs a laugh but doesn't begrudge my appraisal, instead using the opportunity to kiss down to my stomach. His ass rises with the move, and I groan, my own cock tenting my briefs with the need to be closer. Any way. Every way.

I help Lee get my shirt over my head, his mouth on my chest, tongue swirling over my nipple, his cock brushing against my thigh. His lips find mine again, and we're moving. Lee pushes down my briefs. I hook my heels behind his ass. His cock slides against my own, and his mouth, *stars*, his mouth and mine dance as if we've been doing this our whole lives.

I want to weep. Want to cry and laugh and scream at the sky that I've found him. I've found him, and he's mine, and he will *always* be mine.

Lee cradles my face, his other hand gripping my hip as we rock together. There are images in my mind. First times and nervous joy on a blanket inside a broken-down hovel of a house with only stars for a ceiling above. A warm body under me, my hips moving to the sound of my lover whispering *my love, my dear, my heart*. There are lips against my temple, soft and sweet, both in friendship and passion, then and now. There's a devotion in my heart I know won't ever abate. Not for an eternity.

I roll Lee to his back, following his momentum and wrapping our cocks in my fist. His eyes are wild, pleasure spiking as I jerk us together, a shower of sparks from him to me and back again. His hand on my cheek keeps me close, our breaths mingling, a near-frantic edge to his gaze I understand.

"We have time," I assure him, recognizing the fear on his face for what it is. The thought of losing all he's now gained.

Lee stutters out a broken cry as he comes undone, tugging me to him, taking from my mouth as he would his next breath. A tear slips down my cheek as I follow him over the edge. I can practically taste the salt of it. The sea on the air. Hear the waves, the wind through the wheat, the clink of metal. The sweetness of honey on my tongue.

Lee swallows down my sob, tucking it safely away like light curving over the horizon. He kisses me again and again, not stopping, his body rolling over mine as he cocoons me away from the rest of the world. There's only him. His arms. The scent of him. The familiarity. The resolve in his touch. The reverence in each kiss.

If this were my end, I could accept it. I could accept it knowing next time I'll have him the same.

A yowl outside the door is what has Lee reluctantly pulling back. His eyes hold mine for long minutes, a furrow appearing and disappearing in his brow as his fingers card through my hair. His lips are red, kiss-swollen, and I have no doubt I wear a burn from his stubble on my skin.

Shelly yowls again, making her displeasure at being ignored clear, and Lee's lips twitch into a resigned smile. "Give me a moment?"

I nod, and he scoots backwards down my body. He stops briefly, one knee still on the bed, his eyes raking over me, fire there and a promise that heats my veins. With a groan, he keeps on, ignoring the cum on his stomach and walking out the door without so much as a stitch of clothing.

I almost jog out into the hall just to watch him.

Shelly meows as Lee's footsteps pad down the stairs. He fills her bowl, which was certainly still half-full, the murmur of his voice sounding as if he's scolding the feline for her impatience, his ire halfhearted at best. I take the reprieve to clean up in the bathroom, grabbing a cloth for when Lee returns. It doesn't take long. He steps back through the door not a minute later, his hair a beautiful mess, his eyebrow winging up when I toss the cloth his way. It slaps against his chest before he catches it, the sound causing me to chuckle.

He wipes himself clean with an appreciative hum. "It's even warm."

"Modern marvels never cease."

Lee drops the cloth off in the bathroom before coming back my way, his cock soft now but the man no less enticing. With a deep groan, he stretches out beside me on the bed, seeming in no hurry to be anywhere else. It's early still. Only nine in the morning, the sun doing its best to warm us before the winter descends.

Lee's fingers trail a pattern on my thigh, his head in his hand and a pensive frown on his face. I give him time to think, sensing he simply needs a minute. It's no surprise when he finally speaks up. "Why do you have the visions?"

I pull in a slow breath, having wondered that many times throughout my life. Why now? Why never before? Why, as far as I can tell, never again?

"I don't know," I admit. "Why were you born with a heart defect?"

His eyes meet mine, gentle amusement there. "Are you saying we're a broken set?"

"No," I answer around a chuckle. "I just think...some things aren't meant to be known."

He hums, his amusement slipping away, seriousness taking its place. "Every time... Every time, it's me?"

I nod.

"How do you know?"

"I just do," I tell him. "I'd know you anywhere."

He inhales a stuttered breath, his fingers rolling together before he goes back to tracing shapes on my thigh. "Why is this happening?"

A glint of metal. A sunny day.

I unglue my tongue from the roof of my mouth. "A curse," I answer. "A gift."

I can see the questions in his eyes, but I don't know what to tell him. How do you tell someone they sacrificed everything for you?

"Will you share it with me?"

"Someday," I promise.

He nods, accepting that, his forefinger writing what I think is my name. One of many I've been given. *C-A-S-P-I-A-N.*

He writes his own next, each letter drawn slowly and methodically against my skin. *L-E-E.*

He has no clue who he is. I can't decide if that, too, is a gift or a curse.

We stay in bed for most of the morning, until our stomachs start to protest. Our afternoon is spent largely outside, enjoying the last of the fall weather before it's gone. I look for the constellation I know sits high to the north.

But like every day, it's hidden in a sky full of blinding light.

Twigs and leaves crunch underfoot as I follow Lee up the path toward the cliff where we met. He knows these trails far better than me, having been walking them for most of his life.

He wasn't particularly happy when I packed the portable defibrillator just in case. But considering what happened last time we were here, he didn't fight me on the decision.

My backpack bumps against me lightly, my jacket tied around my hips. The trees are a multitude of colors now, no longer only green. We take our time hiking, reaching the cliff after an hour or so.

Lee stops there, pulling out his water and sitting on the rocky ground. I do the same, the river below glinting.

"I talked to my sister yesterday."

"Oh?" I ask, glancing at Lee's profile. The sun lights the side of his face, making him shine golden. "Did you finally tell her about the cardiac arrest?"

He groans. "Yes. And about you."

My pulse stutters.

Lee looks over at me, a crooked smile on his face as he squints against the sun. "She's excited for me. It's been a long time since I've dated. And...I've never lived with a partner before."

It takes me a second to find my voice. "So you admit we're living together?"

Lee barks a laugh. "Caspian, you moved all your shit in the first week. We're obviously living together."

I can't stop my smile, and Lee looks amused.

He shakes his head a little, reaching for my hand, his palm warm. "Sometimes I worry because it feels like it shouldn't be so easy. But then I think about you going or...or something happening to you. I think about this changing, and it's hard to breathe. And I realize...it's not easy at all. It's complex. And immense. And I don't understand half of it. But I feel safe every time you're near. I trust that. I just wish..."

He doesn't finish his sentence, so I prompt him. "You wish?"

"I wish I could remember."

I don't need to ask him what. I roll his hand in mine, looking at the lines etched into his skin. His life, this one, a small piece of who he is.

"I want to show you something," I tell him. "When we get home."

He looks curious but nods, and I know this is the right choice. It's time.

Lee and I finish our hike, him showing me a few of his favorite spots. I see the trail marker that led me here. The one I glimpsed earlier this year inside my head. The memory I'd yet to live.

When we get home, it's midafternoon. Shelly greets us at the door, the little mountain climber leaping atop Lee's shoulder. I give her chin a scratch, understanding her immensely. I feel the urge to climb this man often.

The two of us eat a quick snack before showering. Lee's hands on my body have my blood pooling hot in an instant. Him dropping to his knees, brown eyes gazing up at me adoringly, has my heart falling a little deeper down that unending well.

Boneless and sated, we get dressed, and I tell Lee to wait in the living room while I grab what I need. It's been a while, years, since I last looked at the letter. Not that it matters. I have the words memorized.

The paper is thick between my fingertips, a replica print of the original. My heart aches at the sight of it. Maybe it won't help Lee remember. But I have to try.

He's waiting on the couch when I get downstairs, one arm up on the couch back, his leg bent on the cushion and Shelly contentedly curled in the bend. He sees the paper in my hand and sits up a little taller.

"I found this by accident," I tell him, sitting beside the pair. "Or...maybe I was led to it. I don't know. Either way, I was in high school. We went on a trip to a museum, and they had a display on queer oppression throughout history. There was a plaque in front of this letter, explaining where it came from. It was donated by a woman whose mother found it in the house they'd lived in, tucked away under a loose floorboard. There was a whole bundle of them. The letters were personal, so the donor kept most of them private. But this one...this one she shared so others could read it. I knew the moment I first saw it. I knew exactly what it was."

Lee's voice comes out ragged. "What is it?"

I pass the memento from the museum's gift shop over, the scrawl on its surface slanted but neat. Letting out a breath, I say, "It's a piece of your past."

CHAPTER 35

Lee

My hand trembles as I take the letter from Caspian, his blue eyes almost sad. I have no idea what this is, but I start to read as Caspian's hand settles on my ankle, a soft offer of support. The top of the letter is dated July 16, 1791.

To my J,

Do you ever think of the night you had to leave, my heart? I think of it often, even as I try not to. I remember your voice telling me to turn. The haunted look in your eyes. The sound of your footsteps walking away from me. And the words you last spoke.

I spent years wondering why Catherine would not tell me where you had gone. I thought, surely, she mustn't know. For why else would she keep it from me? I understand now. You were so close. So close the entire time, and if I had known, I may not have been able to resist the urge to go to you. And then what of my mother?

You left to keep us safe. I know you did. Our love would not be accepted, no matter how right we knew it to be in our hearts.

You left to keep us alive. But I died a little more every day you were gone.

Nine years, my star.

My mother passed away in the wintertime. The ground was cold and hard when we laid her to rest. I remember looking up at the stars and wishing with everything I had that you were with me. I wondered if you still loved me so. I should not have doubted it, for I knew, if you were looking at the stars, you would be feeling the same.

Nine years.

Do you remember the day you returned to me? I thought it must be a dream. You looked different than my memories of you. Older. There were tears in your eyes, and I thought for certain I must be dead, too. For what else could explain you appearing before me?

Catherine knew where you were. She wrote to you when it was safe, and you came for me. You came, and together, we ran.

It's been thirty-two years since that day, my love. Thirty-two years tucked away in this home all our own. I can see you now through the window, tending to our gardens, the bees flitting around your head. A smile sits on your face, and I ache with it. I love you more than I have ever loved another. I love you as only I can.

Wholly. Absolute.

I suspect we have many years yet left, my heart. We have not much, but we do not need it. Our roof, our hearth, our bed. It is enough. I would not change a single facet of this life we've shared.

I cannot claim to know what waits for us when we leave this world. But I beg of you to make the same promise you gave me that night so very long ago. No matter where, no matter when, be it swiftly that you return to me.

From now until the last star blinks its final breath,
Your beloved Abraham.

My vision blurs as the letter drops to my thigh. I can barely breathe, my lungs refusing to cooperate, my heart held in a vise. Caspian sets the letter aside as he crawls swiftly onto my lap, Shelly scrambling. He settles his weight on me, his hands on the sides of my neck. His eyes are wide, fathomless blue.

"Breathe. Lee, *breathe.*"

I pull in a shuddering gasp, the pain of it sharp in my chest.

Caspian lets out a breath, his thumbs running soothing circles over my pulse. "Again."

I follow his instruction, forcing my lungs to inhale. A tear slips down my cheek, and he kisses it away, tucking himself against me. I wrap my arms around him tight, my entire body shaking.

"I know." Caspian's voice is quiet. "I know, Lee."

"Was that..." God, how do I even say it? "Was that...me? It felt like..."

It felt so familiar. Like a recollection of a dream. My rational mind is telling me there's no way. It's impossible. But my heart...

Caspian lets out the softest of sounds, a laugh almost, but not remotely cruel. It's *relief.* "Yes."

"That was you and me? I..." *Christ.* "Who were they?"

"Jasper and Abraham."

"Were they the same? I mean, are we always the same?"

Caspian leans back, his thumbs rubbing the moisture off my cheeks. "No, not exactly. Think of it like...nature versus nurture. Every person is shaped by their experiences. We're no different."

I shake my head slowly, the ache in my chest sharp. "They had a sad story."

Caspian's gaze holds mine. "Only in part."

I imagine they're not the only ones who went through heartache, but I can't bring myself to ask. Not right now.

"They're memories, aren't they?" I realize, voicing my thought aloud. "All you've seen. All you will see. The…visions. They're memories of the lives you've lived?"

Caspian's expression is near anguished, even as he smiles. "Yes, they are."

"And the future? *Jesus*. Actually, no. I'm not sure I can handle trying to wrap my head around non-linear time right now, so maybe don't answer that just yet."

He chuckles lightly, his fingers threading through my hair. It's a soothing touch, as grounding for me as I suspect it may be for him.

"Do you always remember?"

His face falls slightly at the question, a frown pulling at his lips before he flashes a small, brave smile. "No."

Ah, God.

"So next time…you won't remember this?"

He shakes his head. "No. But it's okay. I know I'll be with you. That's all that matters."

The tears in my eyes spill free once more. He called it a gift. And a curse. To know all he remembers will be lost…

"Don't." Caspian's tone is gentle. He kisses my cheek, one and then the other. "Don't you see, Lee? I have nothing to fear because I know exactly what's waiting for me."

"Because fate decided it?"

"No." The one word is vehement. Sure. "Because I chose it. Chose *you*. And you chose me. No matter what comes between us or what tries to tear us apart, I will always find you. And I will always choose you again. Fate did not make me fall in love, Lee Donovan. You did that."

I blink back the sting in my eyes, drawing Caspian down to fit our lips together, inhaling a shuddering breath as I try to untangle all I'm feeling.

"I'm sorry," I rasp against his mouth. "I'm sorry I don't remember."

"How could you possibly? But you feel it."

It's not a question, yet I nod all the same. "I don't want to forget again."

There's a hitch in his breath before he kisses me, harder than before. His eyes are shining when he leans back. "Remember me now, my warrior heart. It's all you can do."

With a lump deep in my throat, I stand, walking with Caspian in my arms toward the stairs. His legs stay around me tight, his hands tangled in my hair and his lips on mine as I feel my way toward our bedroom.

"I don't want to lose you," I admit, clearing the doorway.

He kisses my cheek, my nose, my lips. "You won't. Not ever."

"Tell me?" I beg, laying Caspian on our bed, my body draped over his. "Tell me what's next?"

He looks up at me for a long moment, blue eyes coming to a decision. "You're seven. You'll meet a boy with a birthmark on his face. You'll tell him it reminds you of a star."

Ah, God.

"And then?"

"You'll be best of friends. You'll follow him everywhere he goes. You won't understand until later what it means."

"And you?" I ask, tugging Caspian's shirt over his head.

"I'll know before you do."

My laugh is hoarse. "Of course you will."

He unbuttons my pants, his eyes holding mine, serious and solemn. "It will be a good life, Lee. I promise."

I don't doubt it. How could it be anything but perfect if I have him?

My shirt clears my head, Caspian tossing it aside as my hands trail down his chest and stomach, fingers looping around his belly button, a tiny galaxy all its own. I slip back to remove his pants, his breaths visible in the rise and fall of his chest.

"Can I have you tonight?" I ask him, slipping my fingers beneath the band of his briefs and tugging. His cock bobs, and I trail my fingers along the length of it before seeking out Caspian's gaze.

There's a gentle smile on his face that nearly knocks me off my feet, his answer in the way he rolls to his stomach, one leg hitched up as he looks back at me. "You have me, Lee."

I steady my breaths as I kick off my pants, underwear following. Grabbing lube, I make my way back to Caspian. He watches me with a keen gaze, not shy in the least, his eyes raking over me as mine do the same to him. Bare skin. Flushed cheeks. Eyes that seem to pierce to the very heart of me.

I wet my fingers before draping myself back over his body, my lips pressing kisses up his spine, my fingers rubbing slow circles against him. He pushes back to meet my hand, his own on his cock, his thumb rolling over the head as I press a single digit into his body. Tightness. Heat. The stranglehold of a muscle not yet ready to give way.

"You're gorgeous," I tell him, not sure if I've spoken the words aloud yet. "You make me desperate. In every way I could be."

He reaches back to circle my cock, giving me a slow stroke that has my body up in flames. "I've been desperate for you since the moment we met."

I groan, nestling my nose against the warm skin at the back of his neck, pumping my finger inside of him as he lets my cock go, getting a grip on my hair instead.

He tugs gently. "Come here."

I oblige, meeting Caspian's lips, warm and urging, his body yielding enough for me to slip a second finger in alongside the first. He moans against my mouth, and I ache to be closer. Every piece of me closer.

"Lee." He's panting now, so soft and silky against my fingers, his body shaking as I aim to drive him as wild as I can before filling him with my cock. "Now. I need you inside of me now."

"You hold my strings, don't you?" I murmur, removing my fingers as soon as a third fits easily inside. He doesn't deny it, stroking his cock as I shift my hips into place, the heat of him lining my front and his hair tickling my nose, smelling almost of roses. I press a kiss to his cheek, my cockhead resting against his ass, my hand holding myself steady. "Caspian?"

His voice is a breath. "Yeah?"

"Will you fuck me sometime? Do you like that?"

The pained moan he lets out has a grin lighting my face. "Anything you want, Lee. We can take turns. Flip. I'll fuck you so hard you can't walk for a week. But right now, you need to *move*. Before I take matters into my own hands."

My chuckle is raspy, but it dies off the moment I press forward, my cock slipping inside the heat of Caspian's ass. He turns his face against the bedsheets, groaning, arching up in a silent plea for more. I press kisses to his cheek, his neck, the freckles along his shoulder, everywhere I can reach as I work inside his body. Three smooth strokes. Three strokes, and I'm seated fully.

We breathe out in tandem, and I reach for his hand, threading my fingers through his. Caspian turns his face, bright red lips parted, so much trust and bliss in his expression I'm floored by it. The first glide of my cock inside his body has a groan leaving us both. It feels divine—of course it does—but it's Caspian's whispered, "More," that has me rolling my hips again and again. His eyes flutter closed, his face resting so peacefully against the sheets that my protective instincts flare.

There's no giving this man up. No getting over him, not that I'd want to. We were always supposed to find our way here. I believe him in that.

There's a word for it. One we've both been dancing around.

Soulmates.

Maybe this isn't the first time I've fallen in love with Caspian Wilder. But it's a first for me.

Caspian holds tight to my hand as I sink into him with languid strokes. There's no hurry. No rush now that we're tied as one. We breathe together. Move together. Bodies dancing and rutting and slick with sweat. Caspian is murmuring words that sound like praise, like a prayer, a constant litany I let wash over me. I catch *safe* and *found you* and *no one can take it away*. I whisper my own promises. Telling him I'm not going anywhere, that neither is he, that I'll fight for this, for him, because there's no other option.

Minutes pass in an endless stretch, feeling like days, like a lifetime. I'm barely hanging on, afraid for this moment to shatter but moving forward nonetheless.

"Caspian," I croak. "Tell me again. Tell me who you are to me."

His fingers dig against mine, blue eyes flashing. "I'm yours. Forever, Lee. I'm yours."

With a stutter inside my chest, I wrap my hand around Caspian's cock and watch him fall apart. It's beautiful, the tortured ecstasy that has him breaking to pieces all around me. I fall with him, because for all the choices I'll face, there's no choice in this. I'm pulled under, awash in a sea of stars, suspended in time, in space, in nothing and everything at once.

I can't bear to let him go, not even for an instant, but Caspian doesn't ask me to. We roll to our sides, my cock slipping from his body, Caspian turning in the cage of my arms. I tuck my face to his hair and breathe, his arms wrapped around me tight, his voice soothing me, telling me it's okay, that it'll all be okay.

My voice is hoarse when I speak. "Will you answer something for me?"

Caspian pulls back to see my face, a small frown on his. "If I can."

"When do we have our daughter?"

His lips press tightly together, a shimmer in his eyes he quickly blinks away. "Not for a while yet. I don't know exactly when, but..." His fingers card through my hair, right near my temple. "You'll have some gray."

I let out a rough laugh. "And after that? Do we have time? Will we...will we have a long time?"

Caspian's gaze holds mine, the softest of smiles on his face, even as a tear slips from the corner of his eye. "Yeah, Lee. We'll have plenty of time."

I nod, pulling him to me, Caspian's cheek resting over the heart that beats because of him.

"Okay," I breathe, my pulse mellowing, my eyes slipping shut to images of this man in my arms. I think I can see it. Our life. If I try, I think I can. "Yeah. Okay."

CHAPTER 36

Caspian

The first snow falls on a Tuesday.

They're fat flakes, dropping slowly from the sky. I watch them from the window as Lee tells me about his senior-year student that tried the age-old excuse of *my dog ate my homework.*

"If his dog ate that tablet, you bet your ass the vet in town would have known about it. And considering Emmeline's wife hasn't heard a peep, I'm guessing the kid simply forgot. Come to think of it, I'm not even sure he has a dog. Caspian? What're you doing?"

"Watching the snow," I tell him, looking back as Lee walks across the kitchen, the dishes from our dinner cleaned up.

He wraps his arms around my stomach, chin over my shoulder as he peers outside. "The snowflake dance is this Saturday. Are you coming with me to chaperone? You can be my date."

I feign a sigh. "If I must."

He snorts, knowing I'm happy to join him. "What do you think, movie before bed?"

"Sure. Let's do it."

We settle on the couch in the living room, Shelly joining us before long. Lee looks offended when she chooses my lap over his, but he pets her all the same. He flips through a selection of old, outdated movies, stopping on one and raising an eyebrow in question.

I can't stifle my laughter.

"What?" Lee looks genuinely confused. "*A Worthy Deception* is a great movie. Ezra Gold? Iconic actor. And Grayson Fox? Hot. They're brilliant in this, too. Did you know they announced their relationship right before the premiere? Surely you've seen it? It's a classic, old or not."

"Oh, I've seen it. And *lived* it."

Lee looks from me to the movie and then back again. "*No*. No fucking way."

"Yes."

His mouth drops open. "For fuck's sake, tell me I wasn't Grayson Fox. I can *not* be attracted to myself."

Lee looks horribly concerned for the entire half minute I can't stop laughing. He groans, slumping on the couch. Finally, I'm able to put him out of his misery. "You were Ezra."

"Oh, thank fuck." He scrubs a hand over his face. "Gold and Fox. Holy fucking shit."

"Still want to watch it?"

"Are you kidding? I need to watch their entire catalogue again. My *God*, Ezra Gold was such a ham. I'm kind of embarrassed for myself."

Lee shakes his head but starts the movie, peppering with me a million questions as the opening credits roll. My smile is wide, my eyes, more often than not, on Lee instead of the show.

He's still muttering to himself two hours later when we get up off the couch, the hour late. Lee starts turning off lights, but I pause in the back hallway, looking out the glass-paned door. The snow has stopped, a fine dusting on the deck and over the top of the trees. The stars are glittering tonight, so vibrant I can feel their pull.

"Hey, Lee? I think I'm gonna..."

I mean to say *step outside*, but my voice doesn't come.

Lee calls my name, sounding very far away. "Caspian? Am I losing you?"

Arms come around me as I sink to the floor, the stars swirling, swirling, like water down a drain. I blink, everything hazy and then sharp, and—

"Knock, knock."

I still the motion of my hand, the water in the tub continuing to swirl. "Come in."

The door opens, and Arthur peeks his head into the room. "There you are. I thought, for a moment, I might have lost you."

"Never that," I assure him.

His smile is fond as he steps fully into the bath, closing the door behind him. It's dark out, the candle on the sill the only light by which I can see him and him me. He watches as I set the water swirling again.

"What are you seeing, my dear?"

"Gravity," I try to explain, stars traveling in the vortex of water. Planets, too, caught in the spin. Forces so grand, so vast, I'm unsure if we'll ever fully understand them.

Arthur lowers himself beside the tub, his fingers combing the knots from my hair. It doesn't take long, short as the strands are. "Perhaps it's time."

"Time for what?" I ask curiously.

His lips quirk, the secrets there as vast and familiar as the universe. "186,000 miles."

My heart leaps as it does any time those words are spoken. I pull the stopper hastily from the tub, and Arthur chuckles, stepping back to grab me a towel.

Once dressed, we climb the spiraling staircase to the third floor. The observatory is cool tonight, the first of the year's snow melting against the glass. I come to this room often, but my favorite are the times I come here with Arthur.

Arthur takes a moment to light candles around the periphery of the room, creating a soft glow that feels romantic in the dark with only the stars to watch us. He spreads a blanket on the floor once done, but before I can lie down, he grabs hold of my hand and spins me into his arms.

I let out a soft laugh, Arthur's smile warming me through. "What are we doing?"

"A dance."

"Is that so?"

"Mm."

I wait as we stand perfectly still. "Arthur... Should we not be moving?"

His eyes shine bright, that mischievous glint I love so dearly present. "Whenever you are ready, my love."

My breath stutters as I realize Arthur is waiting for me to lead. Slowly, I shift my hand from his shoulder to his lower back. He follows me as I take a step and then another. We move in a slow waltz in the center of the observatory, flames flickering around us in a symphony all their own.

Not for the first time, I'm hit with the overwhelming, bone-deep knowledge that this man sees me for all I am. Somehow, some way, he sees me. And accepts me. Encourages me. Loves me.

I'm beyond fortunate to have found my husband in this life. To have a man like Arthur Kane to call my own.

When our dance comes to a close, Arthur bows low before walking me over to the blanket. We lie down side by side, the stars glittering overhead through the glass, their light coming from so very long ago.

"Arthur?"

"Yes, Charlie dear?"

"Will you make me a promise?"

He turns his head, a furrow in his brow. He's so handsome I ache with it. "Of course. What is it?"

I wrap my hand around his, holding tight. "Even when we're old and gray, bring me here? Bring me to the stars?"

Arthur lifts our joined hands to brush a kiss against my knuckles, his lips familiar and so very warm. His voice, when he speaks, is full of a devotion I can feel in every beat of my heart. "My husband. My love. One day, you and I will dance amongst them. Just you wait and see."

I blink my eyes open, the stars in my vision clearing, dark night giving way to a dimly lit hall and a familiar, concerned face staring down at me. Lee brushes my hair back, my head resting in his lap, my chest so tight it feels as if I'm bound.

"Okay?"

I offer him a shaky smile. "Yeah," I answer, clearing my throat. "Would you come with me to look at the stars?"

Lee watches me for a long moment before nodding. We get up off the floor, Lee's grip sturdy as he helps me to stand. He grabs our winter coats, and the two of us step outside.

It's cold, a breeze nipping at my cheeks as we walk across the deck, our boots leaving imprints in the thin layer of fallen snow. I pull up my hood before using my hand to dust away some of the flakes. When I lie down, Lee joins me, his breath whitening the air in my periphery as we look up at the sky.

So many stars. Endless. But all I see are twelve. Twelve flickering points of light making up a sword, the tip of the constellation's blade shining the brightest.

Lee hums quietly. "Good night for stargazing, isn't it?"

My heart pounds, and I turn my head to look at him, at the gentle smile on his face and the glimmer of moonlight in his eyes. My voice is only a whisper. "Yeah, it is."

"They're so bright tonight."

The words are spoken casually, but Lee freezes the moment they leave his mouth. His head whips my way, his eyes wide and searching mine as he realizes this is the moment I told him about so long ago.

My smile wobbles. "Did you know when you look at the stars, you're looking back in time?"

He shakes his head, a slow roll against the decking.

"By the time the light reaches us, years have passed. Decades, even. You're seeing something from another life-time."

"Caspian..."

"When I look at the stars, Lee, all I see is you. My past. My present. My future. Every future on every star yet to shine. Always, it's you."

Lee reaches for my hand, his fingers wrapping around mine as the snow starts to fall once more. There are flashes in my mind. Cameras shuttering and a booming laugh, a finger tapping the freckles on my nose, and my friend smiling at me as if I'm his whole entire world. A room encased in glass, snow falling gently outside the panes and candles all around as my husband asks me to guide him in a dance. A flickering oil lamp and heat-slick skin moving together, pleasure rising sharp and sweet, the roofless hideaway failing to keep out the cold but warm words pressed to my skin speaking of love and a forever I desperately wish to see. There's a time so long ago much of its history is lost, where water lapped at the shore and a warrior appeared, everything I didn't know I needed.

There's another time, not far from now, a woman named Penelope having grown and a familiar face beside me, wrinkled and handsome, his lips pressing a kiss to my knuckles as he tells me how lovely it's been, a life spent with me.

There's pain, and there's joy, and there's love.

Love.

Love.

My vision blurs as Lee squeezes my hand tight, his own eyes wet with tears. "You already know what I'm going to say?"

"Yes," I admit. "But I'd like to hear it all the same."

He brings our clasped hands to his mouth, his kiss on my skin proof he knows exactly who he is, who I am, even if he can't remember.

"I won't pretend to understand what it is that brought you to me, Caspian. I can't see it as you do. But I know my own heart. And I know you've told me nothing but the truth."

I swallow roughly as Lee smiles, his breath warm on my skin.

"This is where you ask me the question, Caspian."

My laugh comes out as a croak, my voice much the same. "Do you believe in fate, Lee?"

His eyes hold my own, brown and gold mixing in a hue I'd recognize anywhere. Any time. "I believe in *you*, my love. Which is why I can say with absolute certainty... I love you. In this and every life."

I inhale a shuddering breath, snowflakes drifting down around us like stars.

I remember the moment I first fell in love.

It wasn't when I saw him for the first time. It wasn't even the first time we kissed. It was simpler than all of that and infinitely more complex. It was moments we gathered between us. It was intention and a little bit of chance. It was a choice where I stood with my feet in the water and knew I could accept what was being offered or I could step away.

I wanted to be caught. Caught and kept close. I wanted to be loved, and I was. For millennia. Time and time again.

And I'll be loved still, for an eternity to come.

I roll over Lee's body, a snowflake suspended on his eyelash, his cheeks red from the cold. He doesn't seem bothered by it, nor my chilled palm as I cradle his face in my hand.

"This and every life," I repeat. My own promise. My own vow. The absolute and utter truth. "I am yours, my warrior. And I will love you until everything goes dark."

EPILOGUE

A bell is rung as a vessel docks at the harbor, tradesmen loud as they hawk their wares. Nets are brought ashore, the smell of spoiled fish strong here.

I continue toward the center of town, the walls surrounding the stalls and households far off, my own private home farther still. My sword sits at my left, the metal never far from my grasp if I can help it.

Children run in the space between merchants, minders attempting to corral them. A few mutter apologies my way, but I simply nod and continue on. It's no bother to me.

I'm nearly to the shoemaker when I see a new stall set up, a man I've never met before standing behind a table. His hair is golden, shining in the sun, his skin tanned and his muscle lean. I move his way.

He spots me approaching, his eyes running quickly from my face to my sword. I'm not in full armor, but he recognizes me for what I am.

"Greetings," I say, stopping before his stall. There are small cakes set out, dainty morsels I daresay I'd finish in two bites.

"Welcome."

"Are you selling these?"

He makes a short sound. "You do not want those."

"Do I not?"

"No." He lifts a lid from beside him, pulling a slim rectangle of bright yellow out. "Here."

"Will it cost?"

His lips quirk. "Of course."

Taking his wrist in my hand, I bring the offering close. The merchant's eyes widen when I snag the food from between his fingertips, my lips brushing his skin. My own eyes widen as I register the taste on my tongue.

He clears his throat, reclaiming his hand. "Honeycomb."

"It is delicious. You have a hive?"

"Yes."

"And the cakes?"

"Baked myself."

I hum, licking honey from my bottom lip, a move he follows with his gaze. "Do you have more for me?"

His lips press into a smile, even as he busies himself with straightening his stall. "Perhaps tomorrow."

"And what if I do not wish to leave as of yet?"

His eyes meet mine, startlingly blue, far more beautiful than the waters off our shore. "I hardly believe I could force you."

He pointedly eyes my sword, and I huff a laugh.

"I think you doubt your power," I tell him. "Where are you from?"

"Not far."

"But you are staying?"

"I am."

"Good," I mutter, nodding to myself. "What is your name?"

He raises an eyebrow. "That will cost you, as well."

"Will it? How much?"

He seems to weigh this. "For the honeycomb, you come back tomorrow."

"For another treat? That hardly seems like payment."

"And for my name..." He pauses, eyes running over my face for a moment, seeming to come to some conclusion. "For that, a proper meal."

"Is that so?"

"It is."

I hold out my hand. "I accept your terms. Although I must warn you, they weigh heavily in my favor."

"Then it seems our goals are aligned." His palm clasps mine, his eyes seeming to twinkle in the sunlight. I feel it like a blow to my sternum. Not even glancing, no. Piercing and beautifully sharp.

"I am Leandros," I offer, not yet letting go. "Your name?"

He nods his head shortly. "Aster, my good warrior."

"Aster? Your parents named you for the stars?"

His shrug is slight.

"Fitting," I say, bringing his hand up. "You have stars in your eyes with the way they shine."

He pulls in a soft breath when I bow my head, my lips brushing his skin.

"It is my absolute honor, Aster, to have met you in this life."

He watches me closely as I release him, my palm cold without his to warm it. "You will return tomorrow?"

I place my hand over my heart. "It is my solemn vow. After all, I am in your debt."

"Then I shall see you again."

"Quite swiftly. Perhaps another for the road?"

Lips in a smile, Aster retrieves a second piece of honeycomb. He snaps his hand back when I reach for him, instead waving me forward. I lean his way and open my mouth, and he sets the delicacy on my tongue.

I savor every bite as the honey drips down my throat.

"Soon, my star."

Aster purses his lips at such familiarity, but his eyes tell me he's pleased to hear it. He nods his head once more. "My warrior."

There's a grin on my face as I walk through the merchants' stalls. When I glance back, Aster's face is set in much the same. The sun glitters overhead, the clank of the shoemaker's tools drawing my gaze forward once more. If I listen hard enough, I can hear the water still lapping at the shore. An inhale draws salt-tinged air into my lungs.

Tomorrow.

Tomorrow is a new day.

I cannot say for certain what it will hold, but I feel in the deepest parts of me that from now forward my life has branched on a new path, one of many possible outcomes. My tomorrow is not the same as it might have otherwise been had I missed Aster. A single encounter, and hope sits in my heart.

Whatever the next day brings, and the one after that, my future has certainly been changed.

Irrevocably.

Miraculously.

Forevermore.

The End

ABOUT THE AUTHOR

Information about Emmy Sanders and her complete list of works can be found on her website. Subscribe to her newsletter, join her Facebook reader group, Emmy's Enclave, and connect via email or social media:

www.emmysanders.com

Find online:
www.facebook.com/emmysandersmm
www.instagram.com/emmysandersmm